13

Night Patrol and Other Sto

NIGHT PATROL AND OTHER STORIES

Mikhail Kuraev

Translated from the Russian by

Margareta O. Thompson

DUKE UNIVERSITY PRESS   *Durham and London 1994*

"Captain Dikshtein" was first published in
English translation in *GLASNOST: An Anthology of
Russian Literature under Gorbachev*, ed. Helen Goscilo and
Byron Lindsey (Ann Arbor: Ardis, 1990).
© 1994 Duke University Press   All rights reserved
Printed in the United States of America on acid-free paper ∞
Typeset in Cheltenham by Keystone Typesetting, Inc.
Library of Congress Cataloging-in-Publication Data
appear on the last printed page of this book.

Contents

Acknowledgments This book would not have been published without the initiative of Thomas Lahusen, head of the Department of Russian at Duke University. Mikhail Kuraev's letters and conversations were naturally essential resources. I also want to thank the following persons: my colleague Elena Krasnostchekova at the University of Georgia for helping with many colloquial expressions; Byron Lindsey of the University of New Mexico for lending me his interview with Kuraev; Ralph Kirschner for helping with naval terminology; Marlene Pratto, at the Academic Computer Center, University of North Carolina, Greensboro, for letting me use the center; James Thompson and Donna Farina for reading the manuscript; and Betty Stowe, Administrative Assistant in the Department of Germanic and Slavic Languages at the University of Georgia, for helping me in many ways. Also thanks to Ardis for permission to republish "Captain Dikshtein" from the anthology *GLASNOST.* Any errors, of course, are those of the translator.

Translator's Note An adaptation of the Library of Congress style has been followed for transliterating Russian names. Certain changes were made in an attempt to approximate common American usage. So, for example, it is Yaroslavl, not IAroslavl', Trotsky, not Trotskiĭ, VOKHR, not VOKhR, and Samoyed, not Samoed. Explanatory notes are given for many people, places, and unfamiliar terms.

Introduction

Russian Literature under Glasnost

The political changes and increased intellectual freedom following Mikhail Gorbachev's accession to power in 1984 and his policy of glasnost have had significant results in the field of literature. In the late 1980s, several types of writing found their way into print: "held-back" works, one of the best known being Boris Pasternak's *Dr. Zhivago*; accusatory works detailing illegal arrests, repressions, and other horrors during and after Stalin's rule—for example, Anatoly Rybakov's *Children of the Arbat*; and new fiction by writers who refer to themselves as "people in their thirties and forties."

Although the policy of glasnost has ensured an increasing amount of intellectual freedom in the Soviet Union during the last several years, the expected plunge into experimental prose of all kinds has not occurred. So far, there have been very few, if any, writers who have tried to continue any of the many literary movements of the early twentieth century, such as Symbolism, Acmeism, and Futurism. Hardly anyone has explored the European "nouveau roman" of the 1950s or later Western styles. Consequently, glasnost literature does not look radically different from pre-glasnost Soviet literature and is usually not very far removed from the so-called progressive literature that began in the Khrushchev era, reflected in the works of Iury Nagibin, Vasily Shukshin, and others. Thus, at the moment, Russian literature is generally not innovative. For example, the main publishing event of 1989 was, in the opinion of the critic Natalia Ivanova, not a new work of fiction but Solzhenitsyn's *Gulag Archipelago*. In spite of the plethora of new, independent publishing houses, young writers have almost as many difficulties getting into print as in the days of strict control, because of the backlog of "held-back" works. Their chief problem is no longer censorship but the perennial paper shortage.

Among the handful of widely acknowledged leaders among the new Soviet writers are Tatiana Tolstaya, Evgeny Popov, Viacheslav Pyetsukh, and Mikhail Kuraev. These writers have a few features in common, including the fact that they write short fiction rather than full-length novels and that their protagonists usually do not come from the upper classes or the intelligentsia. Compared with the others, Kuraev is much more fascinated with history—primarily the history of his own country, from the earliest times to the recent past—and he has a special interest in the times of Stalin. All his works are steeped in history. Although his protagonists usually live in the 1950s or 1960s, their lives unfold against the historical background of the locale in which they reside.

With the exception of the screenplay "Seven Monologues on the Open Sea" ["Sem monologov v otkrytom more"], written in 1990, Kuraev has so far shown no inclination to tackle contemporary problems in his fiction. His literary style is far from clear and simple, and it is hardly intended to educate readers in the spirit of socialism. In these respects he joins the ranks of the many writers and critics who have broken with the original socialist realist requirements. However, he has one thing in common with the writers of socialist realist literature in that he does write for a purpose: to save from oblivion the remarkable and often crippled fates of some of the humble and unknown citizens of his suffering motherland. He writes about the little man, caught up in the events of his time, like "a grain of sand in the historical arena. . . . He tries to stand up, to endure as best he can."

Kuraev's Biography

Among glasnost writers, Mikhail Kuraev is unique. All the other writers who have come to the fore since 1985 carry "baggage" in the form of works published when censorship still reigned, when they had to make compromises in order to get their works published. In contrast, Kuraev's first story, the novella "Captain Dikshtein" ["Kapitan Dikshtein"], was published in 1987, two years after the beginning of glasnost. Kuraev was not, however, a complete newcomer to writing, since for some years prior to 1988, he had been a scriptwriter for Lenfilm Studios in Leningrad.

Knowing something about Kuraev's biography adds to our appreciation of his works, since their every detail—no matter how strange—is based on his own personal experiences and observations. In one of his letters he remarks, "We live in a fantastic reality; life itself, the turns of history, people's fates are unlikely, amazing, and fantastic." Even though he uses real events, he spins them together in a uniquely creative and artistic way.

Looking back at his life, Kuraev considers himself fortunate in that he was spared some of the worst tragedies that befell the Soviet people. He comments in a letter:

> It is even embarrassing for me to tell about my fortunate biography. I was born in Leningrad in 1939 into a family of engineers. . . . The war found me and my two brothers in Leningrad while father was working at a construction project near Murmansk. Many of my relatives died during the siege in 1941, including my baby brother. My mother, my older brother, and I were taken across the Ladoga ice* in 1942.

The history and architecture of his native city figure prominently in most of his works, and the locale of the story "Petya on His Way to the Heavenly Kingdom" ["Petia po doroge v tsarstvie nebesnoe"] is the construction site of the hydroelectric dam in the Murmansk district where his father worked.

Kuraev attended a school in Leningrad that was marked as target No. 465 on German artillery maps, a detail that he used in his screenplay "Seven Monologues." After graduating, Kuraev attended the Leningrad Theater School and simultaneously enrolled as a correspondence student at the Institute of Philosophy in Moscow. Instead of passively reading the dramas of others, however, he decided to write his own, and he worked as a scriptwriter for the Lenfilm Studios from 1961 to 1988. Kuraev received prizes for some of the many scripts that he completed, but only six films were actually produced, and he is not satisfied with a single one of them. After twenty years as a scriptwriter, during which he often saw his ideas twisted or destroyed during film production, Kuraev was more than ready to turn his talents to a genre that allowed him full control over the finished product.

Kuraev's Fiction

Though he had no intention of publishing anything, Kuraev jotted down various incidents that interested him while working at the film stu-

---

*Kuraev is referring to the highway over the ice, which was used during the blockade to bring in supplies and evacuate as many civilians as possible.

dio. He did not consider himself a novelist, and therefore he did not feel restricted but wrote whatever occurred to him. Eventually he combined some of his notes into a long work, "Captain Dikshtein." His friends encouraged him to submit it for publication, but no editor showed any interest until the manuscript reached the prestigious journal *Novyi mir*. Much to Kuraev's surprise, none of his editors suggested that he shorten the novella or write in a simpler style, in spite of its great length and complexity. It appeared in *Novyi mir* in September 1987.

The novella traces the story of an unnamed sailor with curly hair who assumed the identity of Igor Ivanovich Dikshtein in the early 1920s. At the beginning and end of the narrative, set in 1965, Igor Ivanovich is an old man. He puts on his coat, goes out to return some empty glass bottles, buys beer, and dies. Half of the story is about the 1921 Kronstadt rebellion. There are long and meandering asides about many seemingly irrelevant details, but each of them does in fact have a definite purpose; it may characterize a person or the times, or it may represent a traditional literary metaphor or symbol. Often Kuraev tells the entire life of a protagonist through one of these asides.

The reader may indeed get the impression that Kuraev tried to cram all of his ideas into this single huge novella. Because of its complexity, "Captain Dikshtein" may be both Kuraev's best and worst work so far. Notwithstanding the lack of appreciation by some reviewers, this work was quickly chosen for translation into several foreign languages; an English translation appeared in 1990 in *Glasnost, An Anthology* (Ardis Publishers, 1990).

In view of the fact that "Dikshtein" is such an intense and rich work, one might have doubted whether Kuraev would be able to repeat his first success. Luckily for Russian literature, however, Kuraev published three more works within two years—the novellas "Night Patrol" ["Nochnoy dozor"], "A Small Family Secret" ["Malenkaya semeinaya taina"], and the screenplay "Seven Monologues on the Open Sea" ["Sem' monologov v otkrytom more"]. Yet another story, "Petya on His Way to the Heavenly Kingdom" ["Petya po doroge v Tsarstvie Nebesnoe, povest'"] came out in *Znamya* in February 1991. In 1992 three additional works appeared: "The Tender Emotion of Friendship, Notes of a Man From the Provinces" ["Druzhby nezhnoe volnenie, zapiski provintsiala"], in *Novyi mir* 8 (1992); "About Rembrandt and Myself, A Self-Portrait" ["O Rembrandte i o sebe, avtoportret"], in *Druzhba narodov* 8 (1992); and "The Bells Are Ringing, A Metaphysical Reading" ["Kuranty biut, metafizicheskoe chtenie"], in *Znamya* 12 (1992). A long novella, "Montachka's Mirror" ["Zerkalo Montachki"], was published in *Novyi mir* 5–6 (1993).

Kuraev's second work, the novella "Night Patrol," is much more unified than "Dikshtein." It contains all the best features typical of Kuraev's writing so far. History forms an integral part of the action, especially the history of Leningrad (now St. Petersburg again) during Stalin's time. Readers of "Night Patrol" will not be able to walk through St. Petersburg without looking for some of the many places that Kuraev describes so vividly—for example, the embankment where the hero could smell soup cooking as he went to make his first arrest. Kuraev is very knowledgeable about local lore, but he makes no effort to incorporate it smoothly and conventionally in this text, which is composed of two distinct narrative voices—the guardsman and the author.

This story makes a strong emotional impact because Kuraev shows how people willingly supported the long reign of terror. He relies on the literary device of estrangement in presenting the main narrator, Polubolotov, as a person hateful to both author and reader. Though Polubolotov proudly claims to be more humane than his fellow guardsmen, it is quite clear that he lacks any feelings of justice or human kindness. The author brilliantly succeeds in showing how rule by terror destroys the human personality.

As a result of the appearance of "Night Patrol," Kuraev has, without question, become a significant presence in Soviet literature.

So far, the absence of a strong plot and of the element of suspense has been a trademark of Kuraev's writing; he usually reveals the denouement near the beginning of a story and then offers us the choice of reading or not reading the rest. If we choose to read it, it must be because the text itself is interesting. Accordingly, in his later story, "Petya on His Way to the Heavenly Kingdom," Kuraev announces on the first page what will happen to various characters, but the significance of this information is not clear to the reader, who does not yet know who they are.

"Petya" is the first of Kuraev's stories that is not set in Leningrad; the action takes place in a small town on the Kola Peninsula. There is no chronological sequence whatsoever in this work; we are introduced to Petya and the other protagonists at a few important moments of Petya's life. It seems that we are reading Petya's biography, but in fact we just observe him on certain occasions. It is the hero's personality that constitutes the most interesting aspect of this work. Petya is a retarded youth who is humored by everybody in town, following the Russian tradition of honoring "holy fools."

The conventional expectation is that a "holy fool" should speak out against deception when others are silent. Petya should, according to this model, denounce the many injustices in this town that is essentially a penal colony. But Petya does not do the expected; on the contrary, he consistently displays his admiration of authority as personified by Stalin. Since he is a simpleton, we can forgive him, but how about all the sane and educated people in the town who feel as he does? Is Petya perhaps a reduction to the absurd of the typical Soviet citizen who has sold his soul simply to survive? Is the degraded life described in "Petya" worth the price of one's soul?

The convicts in the labor camp are also not what might be expected; they are neither noble intellectuals nor dangerous criminals. They are for the most part inoffensive petty crooks, brought here to be worked to death on a questionable construction project. There are paradoxes on every page, including the ultimate example in the postscript, in which we learn how Stalin, the Father and Teacher, was relegated to virtual official oblivion shortly after his death.

Kuraev's Literary Style

Gloomy themes and unheroic protagonists typify much, if not most, of current Russian writing. These features are typical also of the so-called "alternative prose" that is often characterized by a sense of irony and a lack of commitment by the author. Kuraev's work does not fully fit this definition. Even though he does use irony and the above-mentioned gloomy themes and unheroic protagonists, his commitment to his own ideals sets him aside from the writers of "alternative prose." Another salient feature of his style is its indebtedness to his literary predecessors. As he remarks in an interview:

> I have been asked about my attitude to Dostoevsky and Gogol. . . . The existing literature is so vast that a new writer necessarily follows in somebody's footsteps. I don't consider any particular older or contemporary writer to be my teacher. . . . It would be ridiculous to deny my debt to Gogol; to be compared to him is flattering to any Russian writer. . . . Gogol's genius has such a high energy level that one can't help being radiated by it. I can never distinguish what is from Kuraev and what is from my favorite authors, or from those I despise.

Kuraev is right when he mentions Gogol; the reader is struck by the obvious connection between Gogol's and Kuraev's prose. Not only does Kuraev use epigraphs from Gogol's works for "Dikshtein" and "Night Patrol," but also the texts themselves contain many instances of Gogol's influence, especially his use of digressions, and even direct quotes from his works.

In addition to digressions, Kuraev also uses many other traditional literary conventions, such as symbols, similes, a mixture of narrative voices, estrangement, and inverted chronology. "Dikshtein" is bursting with symbols; so is "Night Patrol," with its pervasive bird symbolism featuring the nightingale and seagull. Kuraev's preference for inverted chronology leads to his disdain of suspense, as when he starts with the denouement, a technique which requires that he inform the reader of the outcome of the plot. It is noteworthy that after many years in the film industry, Kuraev should have largely abandoned the elements of plot and suspense in his fiction. His goal is not, however, to keep the reader in suspense but to chronicle, and thus preserve, the lives of some of his humble contemporaries, who would otherwise be forgotten. He says in an interview: "I believe that not even these commonplace people should be lost. Their lives are worth something, too, and they should be remembered because their lives held no less pain, suffering, hope, love, and courage than the lives of those we consider heroes."

Captain Dikshtein

A Fantastic Narrative

From the SEVASTOPOL *they're firing,*
Too short and too wide!
And cadets keep on diving
Beneath the ice, beneath the ice.—Popular song, 1921

But then, what a backwoods and what a nook!
—N.V. Gogol, DEAD SOULS II

On January 27, 196–, in the town of Gatchina, in the house on the corner of Chkalov and Socialist streets, on the second floor, in apartment number eight, in a corner room already filled with grayish morning mist, the dream was leaving Igor Ivanovich Dikshtein.

He hadn't awakened yet, but the objects and figures that had filled the fragile haze of his dream began to assume weight, settling in a place where you could no longer make things out or bring them nearer. The morning pushed into his dream with its unconditional concreteness.

Even before he opened his eyes, Igor Ivanovich realized that he was waking up. His first thought was how not to start thinking about anything, otherwise it would all be over—he'd wake up. Dreams attracted Igor Ivanovich with their special insubstantial construction of a world.

Igor Ivanovich himself could hardly have explained clearly this forceful attraction of dreams, where life was no less queer than it was for him when he was awake, but where all the fateful intricacies of people and events, in contrast to those in life, had only one happy ending—awakening. His inability to explain this came not from his secretive character or from being tongue-tied but rather because he wasn't in the habit that you and I share, perhaps, of not dwelling on the question "why?" when you are successful or when luck and happiness just seem to come effortlessly. Endless questions usually arise in precisely the opposite situation. But in contrast to most people, even when fate dealt him a blow, Igor Ivanovich never asked the banal question "why?" directed at some unknown being. He knew exactly why.

One can only suppose that without being aware of it, Igor Ivanovich was attracted to dreams because of his secret power over the unpredictable world hidden in the most remote and tiny cranny of his watchful consciousness; and this power changed falling into flying, the horror of a dreamed execution was dissolved, upon waking, into the happiest feeling of resurrection, if not immortality. Even love wasn't miserable, but easy—and shame, pain, grief—all these were subordinate to the merciful will of the vigilant guardian angel who stood watch at the boundary line.

So now, too, he stood at the very edge of the precipice and tried to lean forward, realizing through the most remote cranny of his waking consciousness that nothing terrible and irreparable would happen anyway. He wanted to have a good look, to see the bottom, but he was thwarted by slender living things, bare twigs or perhaps roots growing out of the impenetrable depths. His feet were still touching firm ground, but someone was pulling him down harder and harder; he felt that he was hanging above the abyss. He felt suffocated by fear. Suddenly his chest felt spacious and cold, the precipice opening beneath him penetrated him, pierced him, and his heart sank, but the emptiness became solid, and his inhalation, familiar as an old trick, made him weightless, and soon he was hovering above the abyss and falling slowly, tense with expectation.

As he fell, pierced by this endless fall, he didn't think about the fact that there was a bottom to the abyss, but tried to get a look at a large bird falling alongside him, tumbling headfirst, then turning sideways, twisting in a most surprising fashion, and because of this Igor Ivanovich couldn't examine or identify it, although the whole time it seemed to him that he knew this bird. And the question didn't arise as to why the bird didn't spread its wings and why these wings didn't hold it up, although once in a while they'd flap around like wide rustling curtains, but would immediately give way, making the bird turn over so strangely.

. . . The pine was motionless, it stood at the edge of the precipice that wasn't really a precipice but simply the edge of a pond, and this pond looked familiar.

Igor Ivanovich didn't notice that his right eyelid had opened a fraction by itself, and he started to peer hazily through his eyelashes at the picture hanging by the foot of the bed. As soon as Igor Ivanovich realized this, he immediately squeezed his eyes shut, but this overly energetic movement caused the dream to disappear.

He stayed still in order to slip back to where the bird was, to restore everything to its former state, but the abyss was settling quietly in his chest, and even his closed eyes couldn't keep back the day that was invading Igor Ivanovich's body from all sides.

Well then, so be it.

He didn't need to open his eyes to see and sense the bright morning silence in the room that had gotten cold during the night, to see the double-shelved veneered sideboard of classic prewar design with a mirror in the central recess, something like a rectangular grotto in which there stood a cup from the court service of Emperor Paul's reign with the imperial monogram and a painted plaster sailor with an accordion, also the cupboard, the table, six unmatched chairs, including two sturdy Viennese ones, and the doormat woven of colored rags, the burned-out Moskvich radio with two channels in the place of honor by the window, the flower in a rectangular container beside the radio, its wide shiny leaves hiding the icon of Saint Nicholas the Sailor in the corner.

Everything was still and quiet, as at a parade a moment before the starting signal: "Attention!"

It was quiet in the kitchen—so Nastya must be peeling potatoes or gone to get kerosene.

Igor Ivanovich sank into contemplation of the sideboard without opening his eyes.

This was really something. Quite something. He'd gotten it from his elder daughter, Valentina, who was on the verge of throwing it out at a time when you could easily get thirty rubles for it, or twenty-five at the worst. If you stood there a little longer, persistently, you could easily get thirty. That's too much? Well, okay. That's with delivery! Even to Kolpany. I'll borrow Pavel's cart and it'll be no problem. Why, it's as light as a feather. And with the cart it's a breeze. There! You want it, you give me three tenners and it's all yours. Will that hurt? You can't afford it? Oh, you like it, don't you? See, it's got this mirror . . .

Igor Ivanovich was already asleep again and was selling the sideboard at the bazaar in freezing weather.

To those who didn't know Igor Ivanovich personally and to those who to this day have never heard of him, these daydreams about thirty rubles for such a piece of junk—with two legs missing, with dark cracks on the veneered sides and on the little doors that had resulted from earlier efforts to give the sideboard the look of mahogany by using manganese on it, not to speak of the cracked back, but who cares about the back if it can't be seen anyway—so then, these greedy dreams could really portray Igor Ivanovich as a fantastic hero, but only in the most ordinary and least flattering sense.

How remote all these hasty suppositions are from the real—the truly real—Igor Ivanovich.

So as not to confuse the reader who's giving over a small part of his life—also unfortunately not eternal—to me and Igor Ivanovich, it should be pointed out that Igor Ivanovich at this moment is that inhabitant of the town of Gatchina who's been bald since age thirty-five (just like King Henry III of England, a fact Igor Ivanovich did not even suspect), who's sprawled in a relaxed position under a red quilt in a white duvet, in an oversized metal bed built at the very beginning of the century in a well-known Petersburg factory that subsequently was converted to the production of airplanes. Here he is, in a state of undress, known to almost the entire Chkalov Street, completely unadorned, unless you count as adornments the neat little bows of tape, holding together his underwear at the ankles, which indicate his love of order rather than his former inclination to stylishness.

The clear-cut thought that there had been no point, after all, in Valentina's throwing away such a thing brought Igor Ivanovich back to reality; he still hadn't opened his eyes and hadn't noticed the transition from the dream.

The thought that he had carried over from his dream absorbed him completely. Selling the sideboard, going to Valentina's, and just like that, without taking off his coat—bang!—slapping thirty rubles down on the table. Here, take it and don't throw things like that around. So they don't need a sideboard. And do they need this polished piece of junk! Even if it was made at the Gatchina factory, so what? Who cares about the polish if it doesn't even have a mirror? But this one's got one. You can shave if you want, or comb your hair, straighten your collar, your tie . . . It's true that it's not very convenient to look at yourself, the mirror's recessed and it's a bit dark, but so what! What kind of ass would think of shaving in front of a sideboard?

Only man can know that state of exalted bliss which comes from dispensing nonchalant generosity and casual charity, which elevate the soul and mind to heights of true freedom and divine wisdom.

Yes, you could also give back the thirty rubles just to feel, in the fullest sense, like a father who has experienced life and understands something about it, and knows how to live!

In the kitchen a knife clanked as it fell into the sink, and the faucet grunted.

Igor Ivanovich grew tense. Was the water going to run? When there was a strong frost the water pipes froze, but there didn't seem to be any frost yet. . . . The hissing changed to a belly grumble. All the pipes in the house began to rumble. They shook as if wanting to throw off the confining shell of the dwelling that stuck to them. The tension mounted. The pipes shook hollowly, choking on something or fighting against a superior will. In his mind's eye Igor Ivanovich could see the three-inch basement vent oozing with grease and he knew what to do if it happened again. . . . But after sputtering three times, the faucet grunted, spat once or twice and then began to hiss reassuringly.

The water came pouring out in an even stream as if nothing was the matter.

Igor Ivanovich opened his eyes quickly and easily.

He immediately saw the wall clock beside the picture. Actually he didn't see the clock itself, but the hands showing thirteen minutes to three. "Hey." Igor Ivanovich grinned at the smirking face of the clock and shifted from examining the hands to observing the pendulum. A regular pace, a businesslike sound, nothing unnecessary, just as it should be. The clock was running . . .

Igor Ivanovich didn't use this clock to tell time, although he spared no effort to maintain its faltering movement.

Five years earlier the clock began to stop and it took quite a bit of effort to restart it. The clock worked only in one position, not vertical at all but leaning slightly to the left. Then when it was wound up, a weekly procedure, the clock would get nudged just enough from its ideal position so that it wouldn't run any more. And then enormous patience and great respect for Paul Bourré were required, as well as the conviction that the clock would perhaps still serve for several generations, so that one wouldn't regret the time and effort needed over a day or two—or three—to push the stopped pendulum and to help the clock find that single convenient position which allowed the clock to continue its work.

That time, five years earlier, Igor Ivanovich took the clock to the repair shop. The repairman turned out to be serious, attentive, and unhurried. After examining it carefully he refused payment. "There's nothing here to fix," said the repairman. "This was a good clock. But nothing lasts forever and this one is finished." If he had spoken differently, with too much sympathy, or condescendingly or carelessly, Igor Ivanovich would definitely have started arguing or, if worse came to worst, he would have taken the clock to Leningrad. While the repairman was talking he touched the clock with one hand and looked past Igor Ivanovich as though talking about himself.

The repairman was old, Igor Ivanovich wasn't young, and the clock had grown old too.

After returning from the repair shop Igor Ivanovich hung the clock in its old place, mostly to hide the spot on the faded wallpaper, but it started ticking and ran superbly for two or three months, cheering Igor Ivanovich with its immortality. Then it began stopping again, but Igor Ivanovich was implacable; he wouldn't allow it to die and it kept on running, telling some kind of special time of its own. And it wasn't important if it told the correct time or not, the important thing was that it ran at all.

But let's be completely frank. Igor Ivanovich simply couldn't go to sleep when the clock stopped, he would eventually fall asleep, of course, but it was distressing and sad to be immersed in this motionless, soundless darkness. A few times he woke up when the clock had stopped in the night and right then and there tried to start it up again. "Don't be crazy," said Nastya and dropped back to sleep.

Inside Igor Ivanovich there had imperceptibly formed not exactly a thought or conviction but almost a foreboding that death is when time stops, and perhaps this is why he took such care of the clock.

For two months now the clock had been running perfectly. Gone was even the light jingling of the spring that used to inspire a certain anxiety in Igor Ivanovich. The pendulum filled the room with a soft clicking sound, as though a horse were stepping on the cobblestones outside the window, going on its endless way, calm and dignified. Tick tock, tick tock.

Since he had stopped telling time by this clock, Igor Ivanovich moved it to where it was less prominent and where it would be easier to get to in the night; and really, why gawk at the clock if it was obvious anyway that it was now half past nine at the latest.

"Nastya, I'm getting up," shouted Igor Ivanovich, rolling over on his side and starting to tuck in his blanket for warmth.

"Kolya's supposed to come today," shouted Nastya from the kitchen.

"Do you think I forgot?" shouted Igor Ivanovich, who had actually forgotten that Nikolai was coming and threw off his blanket.

For a second his long body in underpants and shirt lay motionless on the bed, getting used to the cold, but after a minute he started waving his arms, changing this into a motion distantly related to gymnastics. In all this tumult of quick body movements one could distinguish only two flappings of the arms, once to the side, once together, and then he smartly pulled on his pants.

I suppose that each person who knew Igor Ivanovich Dikshtein personally has a *moral obligation* to preserve from oblivion the features of this man who factually didn't exist; this would actually constitute an attractive fantastic element in any narration about him. And this observation isn't intended as a reproach to the literary and artistic authorities of those days for their remarkable blindness in not preserving a single sketch from life of Igor Ivanovich. And it is, of course, not a reproach to the dogma of a canonical type of hero who provides the bulk of our literature and painting. Igor Ivanovich doesn't intend to push anyone out or to assume anyone's place. Having only once in his life assumed someone else's place, so to speak, he never again pushed anyone out, never made any claims and, strictly speaking, didn't occupy any space at all.

Actually, why should a man who, it might turn out, didn't even exist suddenly claim anyone's attention? Or aren't there any heroes around? Or is the author completely . . .

No, Igor Ivanovich wasn't just anybody, no, not just anybody . . .

Judge for yourself: except for a single secret that he himself had almost forgotten toward the end of his life, he was remarkably open in his fervor, sincerity, and integrity.

So what if his emotions occupied, frankly, a very small space, and his sincerity concerned things that didn't excite anyone else's interest, and no one ever tried to bribe him? So what? Do sincerity, fervor, and integrity really lose their value because of this, or does it make it easier for us to find a man in whom these three qualities were joined together so successfully? I wouldn't be acting against my conscience if I added to this honesty, goodness, frankness, and an acute sense of justice. Perhaps this is still not enough to attract us to a hero who isn't of the canonical type?

But most of all it's the memory of the *quiet chroniclers* that moves me to this labor—those who stay silent and wait, and later, when they are convinced that unconcerned forgetfulness reigns, they begin to compose the fate of the dead man, report suspicious rumors and information about him, or, worst of all, erase him altogether from history.

"Nastya, I think that we should slaughter a rabbit today, the one with the funny ear," uttered Igor Ivanovich with remarkable ease, behind which one could barely discern considerable mental stress, as he looked around the kitchen nonchalantly. It's well known that Igor Ivanovich had six rabbits, not ten.

While Nastya is getting ready to answer, we might note that Igor Ivanovich knew the whole rabbit business quite well and only lack of space prevented him from expanding the business: his animals were hardly ever ill, and they bred well. He could also skin them and process the hide better than most. Only one moment in rabbit breeding, indicated by the little word "slaughter," was beyond his ability. We may recall the very first time when Nastya said, "You should slaughter the old gray one." Igor Ivanovich froze for a second and then answered Nastya distinctly, looking sternly at her: "That isn't in my nature." "That gray one" and all the others—both gray and white ones—were killed by the neighbor Yermolay Pavlovich Efimov or someone else.

Nastya looked attentively at Igor Ivanovich standing there with his hands in his pants pockets, and she attributed this sudden suggestion to his uneven character.

If all eyes looked like Anastasia* Petrovna's, there would be much more human kindness and truth in our life!

Everybody remembers how in 1942 five extra people were taking shelter in her twenty square meters of living space in Cherepovets. Then her cousin, miraculously evacuated from Leningrad—who already had one foot in the grave—descended on her with her two children. For almost two years the guests occupied not only the entire bed but also three places at the table. Then the young and eternally hungry Valentina and Evgenia rebelled. Then there sounded forth the historic words, spoken simply and uncompromisingly by Anastasia Petrovna: "If anyone doesn't like it in my house, I won't keep him here."

Her own children didn't like it, and she didn't keep them.

"Maybe he's not going to have dinner with us."

"Why not?" Igor Ivanovich gave a start. "He has to be in court at one. How long will that last? Until dinner, then he'll come. I'm surprised at you . . ."

Nastya was used to Igor Ivanovich's asserting his worldly wisdom with either surprise or resentment, depending on his mood.

"I'll make mushroom soup. He loves it. We'll open a can of stew for the main course. He's skinny, let him have some fun still," added Nastya, without transition now referring to the rabbit with the funny ear.

Igor Ivanovich hadn't counted on stew, so he decided to reply as generously.

"Do we have any empty bottles to turn in? I'd like some beer for dinner, especially with the stew. That would be nice."

"You know yourself that there aren't any," said Nastya calmly, pouring water into a saucepan. "Wash out the oil and turn them in."

*Nastya's full name.

"I'm telling you that they won't take them," Igor Ivanovich said, continuing a long-standing argument.

"Don't talk nonsense, they're normal half-liter bottles like port wine, why shouldn't they take them? Tear off the labels, that's all."

"Do we have kerosene?"

"Yes, I got some."

"So why didn't you wake me up?"

"You were sleeping so well. And since I woke up at seven, and couldn't go back to sleep. . . . Your color isn't good."

"I must stop staying up late at night," said Igor Ivanovich, snorting over the sink. "Let's make it a rule: at ten—taps. Otherwise the morning is lost. The best time of the day."

Nastya was used to these fits of imposing order and she just sighed. Igor Ivanovich was drying himself with a waffle-weave towel, so he didn't hear the sigh.

Five dusty bottles were standing under the sink.

The sink was of the antediluvian kind installed in homely Petersburg kitchens, not with the very earliest water pipes but perhaps with the second-oldest ones, when all artists everywhere were enchanted by lilies, sedgegrass, seaweed, swamp and lake vegetation, and emaciated naked women with flowing hair. Now it's hard to know what used to be the name for the washtub underneath the faucet before the appearance of these iron basins cast in a corrugated pattern, wide above and narrow below. Most likely it was those basins that gave the generic name "scallop" to all subsequent objects with an analogous purpose. This scalloped basin looked like a large crater and wasn't very convenient, but it didn't seem possible to replace it since it was located near the door, and to put in its place a modern rectangular, enameled little trough (Nastya's dream) would mean blocking the already narrow entrance to the small, triangular kitchen which had somehow resulted from one of the numerous and extensive renovations of this rather uncomfortable house.

The reader, of course, has absolutely no interest in watching Igor Ivanovich deliberating how best to remove the dried-up oil from those opaque and sticky bottles. The reader does, on the other hand, expect a speedy explanation of how Nastya, the elder daughter in her family—who, as everybody knows, used to live with her sister and parents in a fine apartment on Old Peterhof Canal near Obvodny Canal, a stone's throw from the Triangle factory and very near the famous Narva Gate—how Nastya had ended up in this awkward little apartment in Gatchina with three smallish rooms shaped like lopsided triangles. Actually there were two triangles: the entrance with the toilet, and the kitchen, while the living room was more like a distorted trapezoid.

The one in the best position to tell about this move is the head of militia station No. 13 in the former Kolomenskaya District, Grishka* Bushuev. But he died just about the first day of the war, which caused the sharp-tongued younger daughter, Evgenia, to say straight out to Lyuska Bushuev, when she visited her childhood apartment after the war: "That was God's punishment!" "Zhenya,** please, I really wouldn't know. Only don't speak ill of the dead." Which was all that Lyuska Bushuev, a widow with three children, could think of to say.

After he had become head of station No. 13, Grishka continued to live poorly somewhere near the Moscow Terminal on Ligovka, or maybe on Kursk Street. But he remembered the apartment at Old Peterhof from the time when he was still a police operative and went on requisitions, and when by 1935 he had settled in with the new order and enjoyed an authority which opened up great possibilities, he remained faithful to his dream and easily exposed the exploiter who had made his nest right by the Narva Gate.

An amazing male Irish setter moved in along with Grishka. Grishka called him Nero, clearly arguing with someone. The dog was strikingly handsome and no doubt purebred. It even seemed that he himself knew the high quality and value of his genealogy, and so when Grishka took him out in the yard to do his business and gave commands (apparently to impress the residents) like "Nero, fetch," then Nero just smiled with his carefree, cheerful face and didn't fetch. These outings with the dog, calculated to have on any spectators a strong psychological effect with a certain political overtone, were sometimes undercut by Lyuska, who was right nearby, leaning out the window of the roomy kitchen on the third floor and announcing to the entire courtyard: "Grisha, hey, come and eat your potatoes with linseed oil!"

Grishka would get furious and obscenely curse his wife and Nero, too.

In all probability his aesthetic sense indicated to Grisha a certain disharmony: Nero's tamer shouldn't be tempted by potatoes with linseed oil. How many times had he told Lyuska: "Keep your lack of culture to yourself. Look how people are laughing at you. It's the class enemy that's laughing at you."

*Grishka and Grisha are both familiar forms of Gregory.
**A familiar form of Evgenia.

The capitalists and landowners, swept out of Petrograd-Leningrad, would be pretty surprised if they could see within their ranks on the garbage dump of history Pyotr Pavlovich and his wife, their two grown daughters, their son-in-law Igor Ivanovich and three grandchildren.

The concept of Yezhovshchina* has, one would think, been sufficiently illuminated and exhaustively described in the relevant literature; this concept sheds light on numerous subjects lying beside the road of history, and if anything needs additional research, then it would be only "Bushuevshchina," that is "Yezhovshchina" within the boundaries of one separate militia district.

So, Nastya's father, Pyotr Pavlovich, who was well-respected in the Kolomenskaya District, walked around until 1935 in a derby hat, had a mustache with amazing points, loved tight-fitting coats, and considered himself a manufacturer, inasmuch as he referred to his establishment by the harsh name of "louse-scratching factory," either because of some inexplicable pride, or in order to suit his democratic clientele. The barbershop of Obvodny Canal remained in good standing and was left to Pyotr Pavlovich in a sort of sublet from the Health Inspection Department, where he continued to work for two years immediately after Soviet power was established.

Pyotr Pavlovich suffered because of his work force. And that work force was, as we know, Petka Kudryavkin, nephew of the nurse Tatyana Yakovlevna, also named Kudryavkin. He had been taken on as an "errand boy," not from the village Zaluchie, where Tatyana Yakovlevna came from, but from the little-known village of Leshchin. He had been hired long before.

But in 1934, when Pyotr Pavlovich tossed the snow-white cape over the shoulders of his client in the barbershop on Obvodny Canal and shouted out his habitual, "Boy, get the water," it was not Petka who brought the water any longer. At that time an old woman was working as the "boy." . . . In view of our chosen genre, this fact is completely natural, and what's more, if such a fact couldn't be found anywhere in history, then we would have to invent it in the interests of the genre—in order to achieve a more entertaining and fantastic result.

So, in the guise of an errand "boy" Pyotr Pavlovich's middle-aged wife

*Nikolai Yezhov, nicknamed "the bloodthirsty dwarf." He headed the NKVD (secret police) from September 1936 to January 1939. During this period, known as "the Yezhovshchina," over three million people were killed and many more arrested by the NKVD.

enters onto the stage of history. She was already a grandmother at this time, and her entrance would have been a total success if she hadn't confused her boss, by continuously using Pyotr's nickname, and saying, "I'm coming, dear Petenka,* I'm coming," to the great dissatisfaction of Pyotr Pavlovich, who had a name to maintain.

Petka Kudryavkin, who was by this time working as a master barber, was disinclined to call the "boy" and, telling the client something amusing, flew into the back room where the hardworking Olya bore all the rearguard maintenance of the barbershop on her gaunt but still strong shoulders.

And this is when Bushuev brought down and dispossessed Pyotr Pavlovich and put in Petka Kudryavkin.

. . . And how could one explain to the Cheka troika** in the few minutes provided that, for Pyotr Pavlovich, Petka Kudryavkin was compensation for the son God hadn't given him, that Petka was Pyotr Pavlovich's pet and dandy, that to Petka much was allowed, forgiven, and forgotten, that Pyotr Pavlovich, who had during his long life trained quite a few high-class master barbers, was proud of Petka.

No, at that turbulent period the Cheka troika had neither the power nor the time to listen to all these petty bourgeois tales about class peace between a bunch of exploiters and the exploited masses. Bushuev's punitive hand liberated from hostile elements Petya, the barbershop on Obvodny Canal and the apartment above the barbershop.

So is this how Nastya and Igor Ivanovich ended up in Gatchina?

Oh no, such a hasty assumption can arise only once on the rectilinear paths of historical consciousness, or perhaps twice—if imagination is lacking.

We won't speed up history, it has already happened and it can never become different no matter how many times it is rewritten. We will not hurry, if only out of respect for those who did not have and will not have any other life than the one they were given.

However, if you are in a hurry, take a look at the end and we can say good-bye.

But even unhurried histories sometimes acquire an amazing tempo.

In twenty-four hours, actually rather hurriedly, and actually without having time to collect himself, Pyotr got rid of the Singer sewing machine

*Petenka and Petka are both diminutives for Pyotr.
**Cheka was the name of the secret police immediately after the Revolution. Troika here means a group of three persons.

on which the handy Olga Alexeevna used to do all the sewing for her family, barely having time to sell everything he could as fast as he could and for a song, and after numerous quarrels and mutual accusations the dumbfounded Pyotr Pavlovich and his family managed to load their things and set off to their destination, the town of Cherepovets. Only after the war could the decimated family minus Pyotr Pavlovich and Olga Alexeevna make their way to Gatchina, following the older sister Valentina, who worked through the war near Cherepovets in a rear unit involved in repairing army weapons. At the end of the war this unit was apparently relocated closer to Leningrad, and Valentina, a labor-union organizer and shockworker,* was the first to gain a foothold in Gatchina and later brought the other family members there.

But what about Igor Ivanovich?

Why haven't we seen his face or heard his raspy voice during these stormy events that shook the family?

Igor Ivanovich behaved extremely sensibly and circumspectly, not often the case with him, but here he wasn't thinking of himself, since he knew that if Bushuev should try to get at Pyotr Pavlovich not through Petka but through his son-in-law, that is, himself, then the family might be sent off considerably farther than Cherepovets.

It is possible that Igor Ivanovich will disappear a few more times from the pages of this fantastic narrative, drop out of sight during even more important events, but this is not because these events do not concern him: quite the contrary—he will disappear or drop out of sight only to assume the place assigned to him in world history.

The bottles were washed unhurriedly and carefully. The entire procedure, no matter how Igor Ivanovich tried to prolong it, was over quickly, in half an hour or so. It wasn't just that Nastya thought that the bottles would be accepted and had conveyed this to Igor Ivanovich, although it must be said that he came to believe this profoundly and fully, but that while scraping, shaking, washing, sniffing, and examining the glass against the light, he was seized by the wonderful idea that he was making money, not much, but still money, and this gave him a sense of being involved in something serious and worthwhile even when fussing around with kerosene and greasy dishwater. Igor Ivanovich was a good worker: he could sew a pretty good rabbit-fur cap, he could line slippers and build a shed, he was a roofer, and to some extent, a porter, he led a mandolin class at the

*A shockworker produced more than the assigned quota.

Raznoprom Union, where he also did other jobs, he repaired shoes, but didn't like to, he could saw wood and even liked chopping it, but whenever the uncertainty of his pay gnawed at his heart, which was unhealthy anyway, it took away some of the pleasure of the work. Perhaps it was for just this reason that he was always glad to take on any job with fixed pay: what was important here wasn't the profit but the mental harmony and peace derived from the clear understanding of his future. So, even while fussing with the bottles, he wasn't thinking about the concrete twelve kopecks but rather about money in general, and about the beer which he would drink with pleasure, but mostly he was thinking about the beer which would embellish his dinner. In his mind Igor Ivanovich all but delivered a pretty decent lecture on the benefits of beer in general—and with dinner in particular—but he stopped himself in time and directed his imagination in another direction.

Maybe he should get a bucket of beer? He'd get more than in bottles . . .

But this treacherous thought was immediately brushed aside with all the ruthlessness of a man who knows the price of timidity. And it wasn't a problem of finding and washing a bucket to carry it in, but just that the whole idea of a good dinner somehow got undermined, perverted, and distorted. To deprive himself of the pleasure of easily picking off the cap with its dented edge, of seeing the foamy head in the glass, of enjoying the lively taste of the light beverage that made your head spin just like the springtime air when it smells of ice and snow . . . And as for the dinner table, it is one thing to have three bottles, or maybe only two, but altogether another to have a bucket . . .

Perhaps one might at this point suspect Igor Ivanovich of innocent cunning. Perhaps he had on purpose gotten this silly, preposterous idea about a bucket of draft beer only so he could crush it once and for all— and then with all kinds of details affirm the only correct and—above all— utterly beautiful idea of bottled beer for dinner.

After Igor Ivanovich had quickly drunk his tea, eaten his roll, and put on his coat, he discovered that his shopping bag was missing, the bag he usually took back bottles in, the little yellow net bag.

"So take this bag," Nastya said, and pulled out a bag sewn like so many things in their home—the cloth on the round table, the curtain over the door into the room, the cover on the chest—from an old worn-out plush curtain that Igor Ivanovich had obtained at the Raznoprom Union Club.

"What? You want me to look like a bumpkin? Look, where's the yellow net bag?"

"God knows, I haven't seen it for a long time, just take this one."

"Great! This is something new. I'm supposed to take the bottles in a potato bag?! Nothing's in its place here. Is it really that hard? When you bring home the bag, unpack the things and hang it up. Look, here's a nail just for it. Is it really that hard?"

It's easy to imagine how moralists of various orientations will pounce on Igor Ivanovich to expose the moral vulnerability of his attempts to locate precisely the yellow net bag. Let him look, let him look! Only blind pride could prevent one from seeing in his searching a search for and affirmation of order, this highest good, the highest master of the world to which formerly even the gods were subordinated. And since I know that the net bag is lying in the pocket of the kerosene jacket (he himself put it there) I'm not going to interrupt his search, for the philosophical and ontological meaning of his action is much higher than its everyday meaning.

"A tidy cook is better than a chef," said Igor Ivanovich, softening his sharp pronouncement with a smile while looking in the nooks and crannies of the kitchen.

Nastya calmly moved from the primus stove to the sink and from the sink to the kitchen table.

Igor Ivanovich pressed on: "Tidiness isn't only putting things in order. For May Day and Easter we have it orderly too. Tidiness is not just cleaning up but maintaining order, it is when it's always neat, that's what . . ."

Igor Ivanovich Dikshtein himself could have put his signature to these aphorisms with both hands, not the Dikshtein we have been discussing so far but the one whose acquaintance we will make in the near future. But Anastasia Petrovna had heard all these variations on the theme of neatness and order a hundred times and therefore turned a deaf ear for the hundred and first time.

"I'm afraid I won't manage on the primus. You might carry in a couple of little logs. I'll have to light the stove."

"Hey, here I'm leaving, and now it's take off your coat, put on the padded jacket, and out to the shed you go. . . . Where were you earlier? Did I refuse? You keep changing your mind. Now it's something new again, now it's go to the shed . . ."

It was actually quite easy for Igor Ivanovich to change his coat and bring in the firewood, and the realization that Nastya would herself bring in two logs at a time even crept into his breast and made him feel ashamed; he could even see how her heavy body swayed as she climbed up to the second floor on these stupid stairs, but to agree was still harder, even impossible. Today firewood, yesterday kerosene, tomorrow something else, the day after something else again. . . . There ought to be some kind of order finally. Igor Ivanovich didn't admit even to himself that he was rejecting the pleasure of changing his coat.

An outsider wouldn't understand the profound meaning of this changing of clothes but would interpret it rather superficially, and Igor Ivanovich himself hadn't even once reflected on the pleasure he experienced when changing his coat for the padded jacket or the kerosene jacket. It wasn't that he liked the padded jacket more than the coat, but the very ability to change his clothes in spite of his never having acquired a single new item of outer clothing since he got married and not having had any made for himself—the very ability to change coats was like a step in the direction of a kind of life where a person is surrounded by lots of necessary objects that have been invented and made just for his convenience. The energy provided by nature for the transmission of positive emotions in connection with the acquisition of new things or the making of new clothes in Igor Ivanovich found an outlet in the quest for and recognition of merit in every separate item of his diverse clothing.

The padded jacket, the regular jacket, and the coat—each item accentuated in its own way the strict proportions of his lean figure and in a way directed it toward specific accomplishments and actions. Each of Igor Ivanovich's three articles of outdoor clothing was distinctive not only by its style and material but primarily by the degree of wornness, and only secondarily by its different accompanying details. The padded jacket, for instance, which was of better quality than the jacket or coat—apart from the tiny hole which had appeared the devil knows how beside the left outside pocket—had an inside pocket, a neatly sewed-on piece of dark blue satin. Igor Ivanovich had never had occasion to use this pocket, but when he wore the padded coat he was aware of the presence of the pocket and knew that a pocket was always useful, it could suddenly come in very handy. And another story from long ago bound Igor Ivanovich to this padded coat with tender sympathy. Once he put it on to go outside to help Vasily Dmitrievich build a proper dovecote; Nastya saw his thin face with deep vertical wrinkles in his sunken cheeks, his high forehead extending into an extensive bald area, his concentrated inward look, and the stern crease of his narrow lips, she saw all this and said, "You really are my professor of sour cabbage soup."

He understood that she was trying to cover the fact that his appearance impressed her greatly with this joke, and almost every time he put on the padded jacket he hoped to hear that "professor" again. And although Nastya didn't say anything like that again, he would wager his head that he had heard it more than once, praise the Lord.

The regular jacket had other qualities. In addition to the fact that it had been remodeled from a black navy coat and carried many memories, it was also a work of skill and intense imagination. This jacket was also an answer to those two of little faith, Nastya and Valentina, who insisted that it was impossible to make something useful out of that old coat that didn't really have a patch of good cloth left on it. The jacket now had a strict purpose: it was worn to go for kerosene and in the autumn to work in the garden plot, since the plot was next to the highway and you had to look decent in public.

Two years earlier Igor Ivanovich had been struck by the fact that the coat, which had in its turn been altered for him many years ago from the spring coat belonging to Vladimir Orefievich, Nastya's brother-in-law, looked so worn-out and impossible. After that, he wouldn't put it on for half a year; at that time, by the way, the jacket hadn't been appointed to kerosene jacket yet. But after the toppled primus stove gave the final name to the jacket and he had nothing to wear for good, Igor Ivanovich again put on the coat and was amazed because it no longer gave that discouraging impression of being totally impossible, as it had before. "What a stupid whim, why haven't I been wearing it?" Igor Ivanovich kept wondering.

So now this happy situation had come about, which made it possible for him to change his clothes and which provided him the complete satisfaction of having to make a choice before each new circumstance.

It will probably never be possible to explain satisfactorily why, when he put on that particular coat, Igor Ivanovich also put on a certain facial expression which you could only call a readiness to ward off insults. Something in his face made him look almost proud and even slightly defiant, and observant people might notice that when wearing this particular coat Igor Ivanovich was especially sparing with words.

But before following Igor Ivanovich down Chkalov Street and then at once left on Gorky Street, watching him greeting acquaintances reservedly and slightly more ceremoniously than usual, we must return to his exit from the apartment, otherwise neither his progress to the container return center nor his purchase of the beer will be fully understood.

While Igor Ivanovich was looking for the yellow net bag it seemed to him that if only he found it, he could show Nastya how you really could make a minor but very useful improvement in the housekeeping routine without extra words or fuss. Yes, yes, turning in the bottles and going to the store, all this would be very simple, not at all difficult if you didn't turn it into a major event. And no need for extra talk. You'd take the net from the place where it belonged, put on a coat, and after fifteen or twenty minutes you'd be home again. That's all. But no . . .

In the end, Igor Ivanovich discovered the net in the pocket of the kerosene jacket. Ten minutes before he stuck his hand into this pocket, bunched up the net in his fist and quickly transferred it to his coat pocket, he was already suspecting that it might turn out to be there, but he drove this thought out of his mind as well as he could and looked for the net even in the dish cabinet in their room, grumbling that because of such a trifle you had to rummage through the whole apartment.

Once his coat was on, it turned out that he wouldn't be able to go out independently and efficiently. He had to ask Nastya for money. For this reason he started to shine his shoes after he had his coat on and was chased out by Nastya to the landing outside the front door. Then Igor Ivanovich took his thick winter cap, decided to brush it off too, but went out on the landing on his own.

Nastya's lack of understanding might seem to an outside observer like craftiness, even refined craftiness, but only to an outside observer and not at all to Igor Ivanovich. He knew that in the morning especially Nastya had to make the most careful calculations about all the circumstances of the coming day, and as she was stirring in the saucepan or regulating the flame on the primus, she was barely paying attention to her movements but was tensely and with concentration calculating the combinations of their life, ordering them in a temporal sequence, attributing to each action a degree of importance and an amount of effort needed to overcome the complicating circumstances. Igor Ivanovich joked that this mental work was "political economics," but in his mind he respected it; he often grumbled because of her proposed decisions, but inasmuch as he himself could never suggest anything worthwhile, in the end he accepted Nastya's program both for the coming hours and for the following years. Nastya was the elder of the sisters and Pyotr Pavlovich used to lovingly call her "little elephant" because of her good sense and calm disposition. If Igor Ivanovich ever remembered this nickname, it was just during these moments of "political economics" when she didn't notice that she was being stared at, and she didn't sense how much he enjoyed looking at her at that moment. Her gray hair, with its steely shine, was firmly held down by a comb but didn't stay slicked flat—a look Igor Ivanovich didn't like—but retained its whimsical and irrepressible curl, and her still thick, luxuriant helmet of hair reminded Igor Ivanovich of a plowed field lightly covered by the first pure snow. Her large features were motionless, as though preserving the peace necessary for the internal concentration on her difficult mental work. Igor Ivanovich knew that Nastya could even answer questions in this state or ask about some minor thing without breaking the thread of her main reflections.

"Will you give me something?" asked Igor Ivanovich, examining himself in the large crooked mirror fragment above the sink.

Nastya wiped off her hands and took out her handbag, counted through all her cash and handed over fifty-seven kopecks.

Igor Ivanovich gave Nastya a peck on the cheek that earned him a smile, a light poke in the chest, and a "drunkard," after which he started toward the door for the third time this morning.

"Why did you stick the bottles in your pockets?" asked Nastya.

"Well, never mind, it isn't far," said Igor Ivanovich lightly and shut the door carefully.

The landing on the second floor in front of the entrance to the two apartments was the same size as the command bridge of some kind of smelly torpedo boat. Enclosed by a railing, it enabled one to overlook a very wide area which apparently had at one time been utilized more rationally. The down staircase clung to the wall like a ladder for three flights of stairs, occupying very little space, since it was rather narrow. Above the street door there were two windows at the level of the second floor, on an empty wall. Apparently at one time there had been a room there, but how it had been propped up without any support under it was incomprehensible. Why, in a house with cramped little rooms cut up over and over again dozens of times and, finally, to the great joy of the tenants, joined into separate little apartments with similar conveniences, why did there remain so much extra space? Was it possible that a humanity-loving architect proposed to build in the near future not just one but two elevators in this house—one for passengers and one for deliveries—since there was room enough for both? They had failed to widen the stairs for reasons unknown to Igor Ivanovich. When a visitor came in from the street for the first time and saw the landing up above with the entrances to the two apartments, he didn't even notice the stairs leading to this landing but experienced a momentary bewilderment, since the railing on the stairs and the surrounding walls were both painted bright green and blended together to the untrained eye.

Then the guest's eyes would fasten upon the two vertical beams directed upwards to where the upper landing opened up, looking like a balcony, and the perplexed traveler would begin to wonder about the purpose of this balcony and at this point it would involuntarily occur to him that, although not very wide, the three flights of stairs running along the wall provided the only actual access to the upper living quarters. But the perplexity of the curious stranger didn't cease at this point. The space opening before him was so very considerable that the question involuntarily arose as to where the living area was located, because the two-story house, covered with boards, standing with its corner at the intersection of two streets, didn't give the impression of a building with such a spacious vestibule. And the fact that there wasn't any of the usual household junk in this entry hall only strengthened the impression that no one lived there.

As he went out onto the landing, Igor Ivanovich flattened with a mechanical movement the sharp lapels of his coat, which hung like fangs above two rows of almost identical big black buttons. At one time, in the style of the forties, the sharp triangular lapels proudly stuck up like the ears of a young rabbit. In all probability the tailor made some kind of engineering miscalculation—the flowers of fashion fade quickly—and the sharp tusks of the lapels at first stuck out from the chest, then slowly started to turn down. At that point the coat was transferred from Vladimir Orefievich to Igor Ivanovich. Essentially, the small movement, intended to give the lapels a vertical position, was useless, since after three minutes the tusks again resumed their aggressive appearance, but Igor Ivanovich had made it a rule not to pay any attention to his appearance once he'd finished dressing, and permitted what little negligence might appear subsequently. It doesn't at all become a man to be too smooth and, as they say, have all his buttons buttoned.

Igor Ivanovich himself didn't notice that his lack of stiffness had turned into a rule, a habit, and sometimes even led to minor misunderstandings. Once in a while Nastya even had to indicate to Igor Ivanovich the need to pay attention to those buttons which needed to be taken notice of even in the most informal dress.

After Igor Ivanovich had already gone out onto the porch, the door upstairs opened and Nastya shouted after him: "Gosha,* get some cigarettes!"

Igor Ivanovich didn't turn around and didn't acknowledge that he had heard, since he might not have.

On the street Igor Ivanovich was concentrated and restrained, businesslike and sparing with words, collected and purposeful, emphatically laconic in his answers to questions about his own health and that of Anastasia Petrovna.

Having forgotten to put the bottles into the net while on the stairs, he

*Diminutive for Igor.

decided not to bother with it at all, seeing that the walk was only five minutes long.

Yermolay Pavlovich's wife, who didn't miss a single historic event, lived in Number Five on the first floor and came out in front of Igor Ivanovich just as he stepped out into the yard. As soon as she saw three bottles in his hands and two sticking out of his pockets, Yermolay Pavlovich's wife, who knew Igor Ivanovich to be an exceptionally tidy man, was ready to bombard him with questions, but she knew, or rather felt, something in Igor Ivanovich which didn't permit her to treat him like she did everybody else. In connection with this last observation there is a certain need to linger a little over Yermolay Pavlovich's wife, who, incidentally, didn't give a brass farthing for her fourth husband.

There needs to be at least some kind of justification for the introduction into this fantastic narrative of Yermolay Pavlovich's wife, who, if she served as a model, would be suitable only for monumental sculpture or at least for monumental painting. Let us say straight out that if Yermolay Pavlovich's wife could explain the feelings that governed her few aspirations in life, we would receive the most interesting evidence of the power over people which Igor Ivanovich possessed without even guessing it.

Yermolay Pavlovich's wife was a bulky and simple woman who, as everybody knows, deeply despised all her husbands, and Yermolay Pavlovich was no lucky exception. When she listened to his discourses, which were as a rule not devoid of common sense and simplicity of expression, she would invariably grunt, shrug her shoulders, make some kind of farewell gesture with her hand and, turning away her rather large face, she would say à part, "Lie some more!" However, it was noticeable that during Yermolay Pavlovich's conversations with Igor Ivanovich about things that weren't accessible to her mind, blinded as it was by pride, she didn't butt in or hush up her husband—on the contrary, it was as though she received what her husband said into her consciousness, nodding in agreement. And there was no other power in the world that could overwhelm Yermolay Pavlovich's wife with her exclamations, her waving arms, her drawn-out screeching, so unexpected in such a large person, and the way she narrowed her eyes and squeezed her thin lips together into various shapes. The shattering power of her sighs, groans, whimpers, and ability to despise people in the most diverse ways was felt even by the Germans billeted in her house on Volodarskaya Street during the occupation; not only did they not permit themselves any excesses but when they left they warned her that they would burn the house down and suggested that she get ready to put out the fire; to appease their conscience before Germany the great, they felt obliged to sprinkle kerosene on a corner and touch it with a torch for formality's sake, and without looking back they slunk off to the houses across the street, where there is now a new marketplace, and indeed they skillfully burned them down without noticing that the future wife of Yermolay Pavlovich used an old doormat to beat down the flames before they had time to spread. And here is a strange thing: only in the presence of Igor Ivanovich did this woman, who recognized no limits, listen more than speak, restrain herself from gestures and sighs, and in order not to seem like a fool during an intelligent conversation, manage to slip in a couple of words, smiling sweetly and addressing Igor Ivanovich exclusively: "Who are you and what can I eat you with?"*

This silly saying, which she delivered regularly only because she didn't know anything more appropriate, always made a strong impression on Igor Ivanovich: he instantly became tense, he tossed his head, and distinct deep vertical lines appeared on his hollow cheeks, which made a hidden strength discernible in his face; he waited for more, but Yermolay Pavlovich's wife was satisfied with the effect she had achieved and just smiled, playfully threatening him with her little finger. Yermolay Pavlovich shook his head accusingly and immediately tried to steer the conversation onto rabbits, which, after years of friendship with Igor Ivanovich, he had become very skilled at slaughtering. Yermolay Pavlovich's last name was Efimov.

"I put Yermolay in line for cabbage," said Yermolay Pavlovich's wife instead of "Hello. You need any?"

"Thank you. Nikolai is coming. I can't." There was a note of sympathy in Igor Ivanovich's voice, as though he had been asked for help, instead of offered a favor.

"Then we could get you some," his monumental neighbor shouted after him.

"Ask Nastya, I'm in a hurry," shouted back Igor Ivanovich, half turning around.

Now, it really was a five- or ten-minute walk. We must use this short time for two things: to give the reader the minimal information about Igor Ivanovich's fantastic fate, and, naturally, to examine through the prism of history the city of Gatchina, where the hero is presently domiciled.

Igor Ivanovich's place of birth was Zagorsk, which from approximately the middle of the fourteenth century until the current, twentieth cen-

*A rhyme in Russian.

tury was called Sergiev Posad after its founder, until 1919, when the city was known as Sergiev; in 1930 it was renamed for Vladimir Mikhailovich Zagorsky, the well-known revolutionary and secretary of the Moscow Party Committee, whose life was cut short at the hands of the counter-revolution in the stormy year of 1919. When Igor Ivanovich heard that Sergiev was to be renamed Zagorsk he approved of it, as he also, incidentally, approved of changing the name of Trotsk to Krasnogvardeisk in 1929, although he didn't imagine that he would have to live out his remaining days and years in Krasnogvardeisk, which in fact changed its name once more to the original name of Gatchina. For the sake of completeness we must note that even if Igor Ivanovich had known that V. M. Zagorsky's real name was actually Lubotsky, he would have accepted even this circumstance with approval.

Igor Ivanovich's childhood in the family of a railroad employee who had advanced along the difficult path from switchman on the station Novy Vileisk on the Libavo-Romen Railroad to luggage checker at the Sergiev station on the Moscow-Yaroslavl Railroad abounded in extremely ordinary events. From his mother, a kind and illiterate woman, Igor Ivanovich inherited an ear for music, and with help from the psalm reader's bow, which was used to beat him if he made mistakes when singing alto in the church choir, he achieved a fine understanding of various musical elements, which enabled him to learn to play the mandolin without difficulty.

Igor Ivanovich's father also had an ear for music, and considering himself to be a Muscovite rather than a resident of Sergiev, on major holidays—in contrast to those Muscovites who sought grace in Sergiev—he thought it was absolutely necessary to hear the service in one of the distinguished cathedrals of Moscow. Once on Maundy Thursday during Holy Week he had squeezed in under the tall vaults of the Christ the Savior Church on Volkhonka, and the baggage checker, who had properly fasted, heard the famous trio of Chaliapin, Sobinov, and Nezhdanova all together. One might say that all of Moscow had come out and gathered together to hear "The Good Thief." After communion, anytime he felt his heart moved, and without regard to the church calendar, he would intone: "The good thi-i-ief . . ." "At the first hour . . ." his mother, who loved to sing, would chime in at once and with a glance invite her son to join in. "Glo-o-ory to Go-o-od" the adolescent alto voice found itself a spot in the harmony, and the whole family together grieved in their hearts over someone else's suffering, forgetting their own, and for a short moment the family was carried from their own house, which in size hardly exceeded the smallest Russian bathhouses, to the base of three crosses where a cruel and partly unjust execution was in progress.

Close observance of the vanity of church life had deprived Igor Ivanovich of any poetic feeling for ancient legends, and the presence in Sergiev
during almost the entire year of a large multitude of cripples and beggars
fruitlessly hoping for a miracle deprived Igor Ivanovich also of pragmatic
religious belief; the only thing that connected him with the world of the
unknown and the beautiful, like dreams and hope, was music. The memory of the family singing about the repentant thief seemed to him many
years later like a warm ray shining from a receding and generally cold
distance.

A guardian of conservative traditions, Igor Ivanovich's father saw
science and education chiefly as a means of getting away from heavy and
dirty work. Life offered numerous examples confirming the truth of his
point of view at the dawn of our century, but even more at its end, as a
result of the flourishing of scientific institutions, general literacy, and the
entry onto the historical arena of a great number of amazing personalities
of doubtful education but who nevertheless possessed one important
and invaluable asset—the power to direct the destiny of a large number of
people. It is true that Igor Ivanovich's father didn't have to look far—there
were some examples in the immediate vicinity—and the first and best
example was his younger brother, Vasily, who realized all his dreams and,
in addition, obtained the post of stationmaster at Koshary. In a predomi-
nantly peasant country where progress in easing the heaviest farm labor
and in the production of food lags behind science, which progresses by
giant steps, the position of Igor Ivanovich's father, considered by many
smart alecks to be rather stupid, should be recognized as deserving attention, if only to explain the short progress along the road to enlightenment
made by Igor Ivanovich himself.

In his childhood Igor Ivanovich once did something—it was a minor
incident, but it remains completely unsolved to this day. Although all the
participants of this event died before Igor Ivanovich, he related this incident once in a while without making corrections or adding any details, as
though he might be caught incriminating someone.

His sister Vera was three or four months old at the time. His mother
went out somewhere with the girl in her arms and gave the boy a silver
half-ruble so that he wouldn't get bored. The boy played with the coin in
the small front room, but spent more time looking out the window than
playing. On the floor there was a basin with slops for the piglet. The boy
kept tossing the coin in the air and catching it until the ill-fated toy fell into
the basin. Igor Ivanovich distinctly remembered his fright. His mother
came back and asked where the coin was.

"I don't know, it fell."

And so he kept saying, "I don't know," both before and after his father came home.

His father, who got a salary of twelve rubles and ten kopecks, took the loss of the fifty kopecks very much to heart.

Igor Ivanovich watched his parents look all over the floor and move everything that could be moved away from the walls, but naturally they didn't find anything.

The basin was taken out to the pig.

Just before going to sleep, when his mother came to make the sign of the cross over him for the night, he confessed.

They went out to the pigsty but the slop basin was already sitting there clean.

Igor Ivanovich told this episode from his childhood more often than any other, but nobody ever thought of wondering about the reason for this particular attachment. You might even notice that Igor Ivanovich remembered this event not only when people were talking about various losses and disappearances or about how people reject money because of some higher idea, but that this incident floated to the surface mainly when people started talking about that inexplicable and mysterious something that surrounds man and even exists inside man himself. In all likelihood Igor Ivanovich was sometimes forced to remind himself that fate itself had, so to speak, prepared him to be a man capable of inexplicable deeds.

. . . The crunching sound accompanying Igor Ivanovich as his shiny boots stepped on the trampled snow imparted a categorical decisiveness not only to this movement but also to his feelings. In this crunching there was the clarity and exactitude of the flute whistling from Emperor Paul's regiment, which started and guided the soldiers marching on the palace parade ground. In Igor Ivanovich's quick pace there was the openness of a person who clearly realizes his goals and abilities, a person who can't imagine a life different from how it appears to him in its everyday concreteness. Those who have read Tacitus and have watched Igor Ivanovich's stride may recall that haste has the appearance of fear, while moderate slowness looks like confidence. I venture to affirm decisively that not only—yes, fear, which had in fact once nested in Igor Ivanovich's heart—well, not only had fear evaporated and flown away never to return but not even the nest remained, nor the place where in earlier times the nest itself took up a rather large space, as they say, from head to toe. So his rapid walk, looking like haste, should be explained only by the quality of his footgear, which wasn't intended for freezing weather.

The snow crunched distinctly and monotonously beneath Igor Ivanovich's light boots.

It was the stride of a real man.

And the crunching of the snow was proper and decisive; a woman would throw herself at a man who could walk like that, forgetting and abandoning everything else in the world. Igor Ivanovich had in mind a beautiful woman with sorrowful eyes, expressing mute vulnerability and hope. It is as clear as two times two is four that the beautiful woman, tired out by offers of all kinds of emotions and love, believes only what she herself can find, and she is searching, searching, searching, looking everywhere with hope in her eyes. She needs an independent and decisive man. And what could express the worth of a man better than his stride? Nothing. A glance of blue lightning flashed from under a lilac-colored little cap in the direction of Igor Ivanovich and a tender murmur of gratitude rumbled in his chest; in his state of concentration Igor Ivanovich didn't notice that it was only the neighbor's daughter greeting him, Marseillaise Nikonovna's older daughter, whom we won't meet, but Marseillaise Nikonovna will come up further on. Thus, singed by lilac lightning, Igor Ivanovich chuckled silently—why aren't I twenty-five years old?—forgetting that it was just at the age of twenty-five that he was cast into the abyss of trouble which had the most fantastic consequences for the rest of his life.

Igor Ivanovich walked past the one-story little houses on low stone foundations. The windows looked out onto the street and were placed at chest level of someone of average height, and therefore, the despairing residents had hung up homemade signs on the walls requesting passersby not to stop in front of the windows or look inside. It is possible that not all the authors of these plaintive and sometimes stern posters suspected that in Gatchina there is a long tradition of *looking in people's windows*, as opposed to Kishinev, where it is done exclusively for the purpose of philandering.

The little town of Gatchina is located on a sort of island that rises up in the middle of a damp swampy lowland. The slightly elevated higher part is occupied by the imperial palace and the cavalry barracks attached to it, while the vast northeastern part, gradually turning into swamp, was set aside for the townspeople to build on.

High society and the aristocracy from the capital spontaneously shunned this place as though some kind of evil omen hung over it; which is perhaps why Gatchina, in contrast to Tsarskoe Selo, Pavlovsk, and Peterhof, had the gloomy appearance of a minor provincial town.

None of the buildings in Gatchina go together, in which fact the esteemed historiographers see not so much the richness of imagination on the part of the builders and house owners as the diversity of poverty. There was a much stronger similarity among the interiors of the citizens' dwellings, where the furniture, dishes, and decor—consisting of homemade rugs, embroidery, and houseplants—served as an indication of domestic comfort and civil well-being.

His Majesty Nicholas I received Gatchina as his property from his dear departed mother and loved to stay here every autumn in true patriarchal style. But his summer visits seemed more like warlike raids when the sovereign, filled with martial ardor after successful maneuvers at Krasnoe Selo, came out to Gatchina at the head of the cuirassiers, covered with dust and glory. He held a review on the parade ground in front of the palace and arranged for the housing of the family members who came with him, but himself galloped off to Kolpino, where his tent was put up near the little church, where he ate supper all alone and cooled down after his martial exercises. And even in the absence of the emperor, the Head Table, set after the maneuvers, and the Family Table, and especially the Gentlemen's Table, could feel sharply the inflexible spirit, decisiveness, and will of the new master of the palace.

In the fall, in contrast, His Majesty was at peace and filled with good will: he bothered no one and he even liked the local inhabitants to treat him with that trust and love that characterizes relations between children and their father.

The simplicity of their relations went so far that the inhabitants weren't prohibited from looking in through the windows of the palace when the imperial family was sitting down to dinner or tea or were spending the time in conversations and entertainments in the style of *European luxury.*

In his concern for the proper organization and external attractiveness of the town, His Majesty dispatched to Gatchina a notebook with drawings representing facades to be used for the residential structures and instructions to build on foundations no lower than three-and-a-half feet. One concludes that before these instructions the windows of the residences were even closer to the ground. Not only didn't the prescribed height prevent the residents of the structures from surveying the street and the passersby but the passers-by were in their turn able to observe the interiors of the residences, satisfying the need nowadays referred to as information hunger.

Although Gatchina served as Emperor Nicholas I's residence for very short intervals of time, the circumstances of the imperial visits were such that the town always had to be ready to receive the august guests, and these circumstances imparted life and energy to the city.

However, as the chronicles testify, the graces which the tsar from time to time showered on the town did little to enable the town to move along the paths of progressive development.

By the time of the events described here, the town had long forgotten about the tension produced by the possibility of imperial inspections. Those restless times had receded into the distant and not-so-distant past, and the *Kammerfurier*'s* journals and the other journals with articles entitled "Kerensky in Gatchina" were turning into dust in the archives. The People's Theater in the Palace of Culture hadn't opened yet and hardly anyone could remember the performances and divertissements by French theatrical companies or the plays performed at court by highly placed personages and members of the imperial family with the participation of the sovereigns themselves. By the way, the chiming bells of the palace towers were lost during the war and the twice-renamed town— which was Trotsk for a short time, then for slightly longer Krasnogvardeisk—then again received its original name, and, thanks to the advantages of living in a quiet province, the town consoled itself with the idea that life there was "no worse than elsewhere."

The highway from the Smolensk Gate in the south to the Ingeburg Gate in the north divided Gatchina into two unequal parts, and if the area to the left of the road leading to the capital could correctly be called historic, where all the significant buildings and events are noted and described by historians and the minor events were punctually noted in the *Kammerfurier*'s journal, then the area to the right of the road, occupied by the town itself, can equally correctly be seen as on the side roads of history, where for the most part there reigns a passive and contemplative attitude to historical reality, not described by anyone.

The very highway dividing the town bears the marks of historical movement; first it was called the Kiev Road, then it became the Great Prospect, after that the Prospect of Emperor Paul I, and in the last segment of history it finally became the October 25th Prospect. To the left all was unique and inimitable: the palace, from the outside reminiscent of a military fortress, whose stern exterior appearance contrasted with

*A court official of the sixth rank who kept a journal recording court ceremonies and events.

the refined luxury of the interior accoutrements; the vast park which, with its ponds, lakes, bridges, footbridges, terraces, the Sylvia Grove, the Menagerie, and its own fleet and artillery, had no equals; the round threshing-barn with a crenellated tower; the *Connetable*'s* quarters; even the barracks, ordinary cuirassiers' barracks, shone with the names of the architects Bazhenov, Brenna, and Starov. At the same time the structures, events, and names in the right-hand part of the town, vast and gloomy, forcibly reminded one of that classical Russian city in which you can ride for three years without ever reaching the border. So can we consider the changing of the Constable Department with a watchtower to the Department of the Interior a worthy historical event, and the changing of Constable Street to Revolution Alley? Few people nowadays know the name of Kuzmin, the architect who built the Peter and Paul Cathedral at the intersection of Malogatchinskaya and Boulevard streets, since the most memorable page of his biography was probably his ten-day stay in prison by order of the sovereign for exceeding the estimate approved for making icons and wall paintings in the cathedral. The city's inhabitants are proud of the house of the famous artist, ethnographer, and caricaturist Shcherbov in the whimsical architecture of which hardly anyone would recognize the hand of the architect Krichinsky, who was at that time engaged in the construction of the Principal Mosque in Petersburg . . .

We can further scrape together a rather short list of composers and writers who in their search for peace and solitude fled to this backwater so near the capital. But what Russian city that had stood and endured on this unstable ground for a couple of centuries would not have acquired its own Kuzmin, or taken pride in its own Shcherbov, or mentioned with respect five or six celebrities who, on their way to immortality, had once or twice rested under its dusty linden trees?

And yet, Gatchina is incomparable! Where else could you find a place where side by side, close to each other but on opposite sides of the narrow highway, clocks ran differently, showing different time! On the left the bells of history struck with a measured imperial pace, while to the right the fine sands of destiny kept right on pouring through the silent clocks of eternity . . .

But did Gatchina really have a history?! Its own history, and not the history of the whims of its innumerable proprietors? What did he want to convey, that first man lost in the abyss of time—yes, there really was a first

*The high constable, a military title.

man!—who for some reason named the lake Khotchino?* Did he give it some thought? Or did he toss it off as a joke as he was freezing or languishing from heat, or feeling sentimental or furious. Was he old or young? God knows! He has rotted and left us the puzzling word as a reproach to our pride, to our ability to understand and explain everything. What did the Novgorod scribe think, or did he think at all as he diligently entered into the cadastres for the Votskaya section of the Novgorod lands in the final year of the fifteenth century, the village of Khotchino by the Khotchino lake among the other grand ducal volosts, villages and settlements in the Dyatlinsky churchyard? The little village also seems to have belonged to Novgorod, but then Emperor Peter I deeded "the poor Finnish farmstead" Gatchina to his sister as a gift. From that time on Gatchina was passed from hand to hand along with all its male and female souls of the adjoining twenty villages, with all the lands, fields, fallow lands, meadows, woods, moss-covered bogs, and common pastures. And among the many who thought of Gatchina as their very own there were distinguished men, for instance, Kurakin, privy councillor, and Prince Boris Alexandrovich; there was the fortunate stepson of Baltic Germans, Archduke Blumentrost, adopted by a fatherland that had no special liking for its own sons; this ownerless land then went as a reward to a court steward, then reverted to the treasury for debts, only to become a gift to the thirty-five-year-old general-ensign and cavalier, Grigory Orlov, a great hunting enthusiast. The Empress Catherine II often donned the uniform of the Infantry Guards and, drawn by a feeling of friendship, she desired to absent herself from Tsarskoe Selo and go to the Gatchina farmstead to visit the "Gatchina landowner," accompanied by a small suite. Exhausted from the journey, the empress would partake of dinner with her gracious host and after the meal she was pleased to stroll a little around the lake, amuse herself at cards with the courtiers in the gallery, not forgetting to have supper at the usual hour with the personages in her accompanying suite. Gatchina was also offered as a gift to that great champion of kindness and justice, Jean-Jacques Rousseau. It is hard to say what turned the French enlightener away from the temptation to become a landed proprietor and slave owner at Gatchina, but it couldn't have been the healthy air, the amazing water and the knolls surrounding the lakes, forming pleasant nooks for walks and daydreaming, as the generous empress-donor described it. Presumably the deciding factor was the truthful empress's

*The name *Khotchino* suggests the Russian words *khotet' chin*, meaning "to want a noble rank."

communication that the "local inhabitants understand neither English nor French, let alone Greek and Latin." As it happens, there has been no noticeable progress among the local population in this respect during the last two centuries. After the empress's favorite, Grigory Orlov, had gone to find his repose in the Lord, the forgetful little mother at once gave this castle and property, erected by the assassins of Peter III, to the victim's son, her ill-fated heir, Paul Petrovich. Being a practical man and always expecting the worst, the heir appreciated above all the distance of the castle from the little mother's eyes, the fastness of its walls, and the possibility of finally building on this fickle ground a firm and solid nest in the German style. The dexterous servants of the muses fashioned, as best they could, the historical foundations according to the whims of the current owner, managing to read the very word "Gatchina" as German and to affirm its discovery in the refined verses: ". . . and this is Gatchina's fair duty, outside and inside full of beauty."* In agreement with the wishes of the emperor, and thanks to the talents of the rather rough Brenna and the imitative Lvov, Gatchina came to look like a small German town. Rathaus, hospital, public school, post office, church, army orphanage, glass and porcelain factory, weaving factory, hatter, a fulling mill, and as if straight out of an illustration to a German fairy tale, the Priory Palace with a pointed spire on an octagonal tower—all this gave the village, raised to the rank of town, a new design and appearance; where the former appearance disappeared to and whether anyone grieved over its loss is not known. The decorations of the palace, capable of satisfying the most sensitive tastes of the true art lover, and the beautifully arranged and adorned park were combined in a most unexpected manner with a disregard for the everyday conveniences of life. Just take the staircase, for instance, narrow and steeply winding, connecting Paul's rooms in the palace with the interior chambers of Maria Fyodorovna. Historians are amazed to this day: "How could the empress and her daughters, the grand duchesses, and the ladies-in-waiting, all dressed in ceremonial Russian clothes," climb up this stairway on those days when for some reason the royal procession went from the lower floor to the upper, and then from the throne room to the formal chambers?

Gatchina's heyday with its civic improvement and military might came during the difficult thirteen years of an "exercise in patience" by its

---

*Author's note: An attempt to present "Gatchina" as a German derivative—*hat Schönes,* or "has beauty."

tempestuous owner, who was doomed to wear the mask of an obedient, appreciative son, for many years endlessly tormenting his soul with the thought of the crown his mother had stolen, and finding support for his hopes and an outlet for his passions in endless military exercises and games. The all-powerful and almighty master of the throne whose momentary caprice and passing fancy could determine the fate of numerous people was tortured by his inability to live his own life; he moved back and forth among *his own* three palaces at Pavlovsk, Gatchina, and Kamenny Island in Petersburg, but nowhere did he feel quite like himself, that is, like a benefactor, a peacemaker, an enlightened and just father to his peoples . . . Where, then, can the people be if even his own children had immediately been removed from their parent by Her Majesty—his mother—and placed under her guardianship and upbringing?

On the camp bed, beside his Wellington boots, he, too, has vanished, suffocated with the silent consent of his son, as though in his last palace— the strongest, most reliable, and richest one—he had just broken camp in his tireless and aimless wanderings.

So the remarkable castle remained in Gatchina, splendid scenery for a senseless show performed no one knows why or for whom.

Gatchina, Gatchina, whose misery are you? whose happiness?

Just like the steep, overhanging shores of the River Slavyanka which revealed the compressed history of the earth, you are lying there thrown open before all, like a forgotten book on the side of the road, "a city without a county" of the royal ministry, where the mayor is the emperor himself! Where better than here does the great empire reveal its secret essence? Where but here can you see the threads, invisible elsewhere, joining the highest point situated, maybe, on the top of the cross adorning the crown, with an indistinguishable point somewhere on the worn-out soles of the humblest subject of the empire? Where, better than here, were played out and maybe are being played out even today fantastically impossible stories capable of astounding those people who haven't yet unlearned or lost the ability of being amazed to the bottom of their hearts, regardless of their having long since become used to a life where every manifestation and detail is explained?

At the time of the events described here, the city was living through its possibly most favorable period as far as the diverse and versatile development of a network of bottle collection points is concerned. It is worth mentioning that at this time the phrase "salon for the collection of glass containers" couldn't have occurred even in the brains of our domestic Jules Vernes. On the contrary, the ban against receiving empty glass bottles in the same place where filled ones were sold forced the bottle collectors to seek shelter in the most unlikely buildings, parts of buildings, and buildings five minutes away from being ruins.

Omitted from Intourist's travel itinerary, the town had with a great effort extricated itself from the desperate misfortune, the bottomless pit into which it had been cast by the German invasion.

Incidentally, among the first buildings to be restored and opened to visitors was the Pavilion of Venus on the Island of Love in the Gatchina park. The occupiers who had slogged to Gatchina, risking their lives, in the early forties of this century, did not spare the works of their former fellow countryman Mettenleiter, who had become an academician in Russia in the art of "genre painting in the Flemish manner" and who painted an eighty-meter-long ceiling entitled *Triumph of Venus* in the pavilion of the same name. The court painter's countrymen used the frolicking cupids on the ceiling for target practice with their loud parabellum pistols; they hadn't had enough of the pleasures of bachelor life in the active army, so they riddled Juno, the patroness of marriage, with bullets; and since they hadn't quenched their desire to see Venus in all her nakedness, they shot the tender Horae, the goddess's servants, who were holding her veil, and then demonstrated their courage and fearlessness by slaughtering with well-aimed bullets a rabbit which, as everybody knows, is a symbol of timidity . . . They stole the mirrors in the embrasures between the enormous weightless windows, but were unable to steal the marble vases with fountains that were fixed to the floor, so they simply broke them, apparently with their rifle butts. . . . All these details became the property of history only because the Pavilion of Venus itself, built entirely of wood and covered with a light wicker trellis, capable of instantly going up in smoke from any cigarette butt carelessly crushed in a corner, remained standing—in contrast to a large number of stone palaces, tens of pavilions and residences, and hundreds of monuments and obelisks, all constructed from much stronger materials.

The destroyed buildings, which incidentally included the palace, were not so much rebuilt as adapted for public use, to house both people and institutions. The wounds, even though treated hurriedly with the strength and means available, remained wounds. The most characteristic element of the buildings, which were neither artistic nor historical treasures, became the additions attached alongside, on top and in front—an amazing symbiosis of stone-and-timber constructions, as a result of which a plank shed had been affixed to what was formerly a hotel built in an imitative Italian style, and it was hard at times to distinguish a dwelling from a warehouse and a warehouse from a dwelling.

The sad monuments to hastily knocked-together postwar life had become dilapidated by the mid-sixties and demanded decisive new efforts in order to maintain minimal living conditions, and since they presented a danger to the residents, they were accordingly vacated, and this offered a very rich and varied choice to the agents who ran glass collection points. We recall that some kind of collection point existed for two years even in a rather nasty movie theater, described in its day by Kuprin but which in our time is closed and destined for immediate demolition.

The house to which Igor Ivanovich was heading gave an unfinished impression. Its smooth two-story walls with windows like eye sockets without eyebrows still awaited, it seemed, some minor finishing strokes before it would acquire its face. But for some unfathomable reason there were no provisions for giving the house a face. Most likely because it had been moved from the street to a back lot, to an empty place surrounded by squat storehouses of well-laid bricks, two-story sheds of planks, and smaller sheds built of the most unexpected materials: doors and bodies of cars, small pieces of flatcars and metal sheeting, but mostly of bits of planks and tar paper.

The smooth wall with the two rows of windows that seemed carved out with a razor in grayish cardboard was broken by a small entrance with two steps leading to the third window from the right, which had from necessity been changed temporarily into a door. Straight from the street you came into a room through which you could go directly into the kitchen—between the kitchen and the room there used to be something like a vestibule, but to make it more convenient they had removed one wall completely and moved the other almost up to the street entrance. The walls retained traces of the detroyed dwelling in the form of spots from pictures and photographs on the faded wallpaper, a piece of cardboard from a loose-leaf calendar, a bedraggled round stove, and an ancient Empire armchair with a leg missing but nevertheless upholstered in tapestry, even though the fabric was all ripped up.

This drastic remodeling had created a small entrance hall that could accommodate five or six persons with their bottles, and an extensive area filled with wooden crates.

The house had been vacated two years earlier, but prematurely, as it turned out, because in the fall of last year permission was given to rent out a part of its premises for temporary use.

Igor Ivanovich walked up to the entrance where, at the most, ten people were shifting from foot to foot in the freezing cold. After reading the sign fastened to the door, he acknowledged the group with a nod of his head and an indistinct sound, something like "Good day." After hearing something equally indistinct in reply, he asked clearly, "Been gone long?"

"She left with Vitka," said some lady shrilly.

Igor Ivanovich calculated quickly: the assistants were named Shurka and Kostya, the shop manager was named Viktor Pavlovich, but he was never called Vitka, so therefore she must have left with her son. She might have gone either to the doctors' clinic or she might have been called to the school. Everybody knew Anka: she wouldn't be held up at either place, she wouldn't be long.

Igor Ivanovich took his place in line, patiently stamping his feet in the cold and huddling himself into his clothes to preserve his body heat better. "Did she leave long ago?" Igor Ivanovich asked, but the question dissolved in the freezing air, the silence broken only by the noise of snow being crunched, as the people returning bottles shifted from foot to foot.

"So young and drunk already," said a girl with three bottles, watching how two fellows were walking.

One was wearing an unbuttoned padded pea jacket of military cut with a sloppy bedraggled old scarf that didn't cover his bare red neck, and enormous felt boots so big that it seemed you could wear them even over normal boots. The fellow stopped and greeted the company with a happy smile.

The second one went directly to the notice on the door. In each hand he firmly held a pair of bottles by their thick necks with his fingers red from the cold and shining lustrously like ice-covered firebrands after a winter fire.

"A bust?" said the one in the pea jacket, still smiling, both asking a question and stating a fact. The unexpected obstacle had ruined his plans but hadn't yet spoiled his good mood.

The one reading the notice started to pull at the door. The fellow was sturdy and the door shook dangerously, threatening to fall outwards along with the door frame, and if it did, it occurred to Igor Ivanovich, Anka would be closed for at least a week.

"You guys, don't bother anything here. Just stand in line like you're supposed to, and there's no point in fooling around. There!" proclaimed Igor Ivanovich, not even looking at them but instead seeking support from the line.

"Gramps," said the happy fellow, convinced that it was possible to get along with anyone in the world since anyone could understand their situation, "See, we don't have enough to buy a bottle of 'Faust Patron,'" he said and shook the heavy bottles.

"And do you think we turn them in to buy bread, or what?" said a little guy, sticking his face out from his raised collar.

Everybody laughed, the fellows too; only Igor Ivanovich didn't laugh because he was preparing for serious business.

"Hey, Ma," said the happy one, "are you going to stand here?"

"Of course!"

"Turn in ours, too . . . It's all the same to you!"

"What am I—your collection point?" said the woman with three bottles in a net. "Everyone stands in line, you have to, too."

"We can't, people are waiting for us," the other one quickly came to his aid.

"Drunks just like yourselves are waiting for you, but I left my children at home," said the gregarious matron.

The happy one turned gloomy, searched along the line as though choosing someone he could talk to. Everyone looked somewhere past him.

"Peo-ple . . ." the fellow grinned maliciously, looked at the bottles, and swinging sharply, clanked first one, then the other against the wall.

"Now stop acting like hooligans!" said Igor Ivanovich threateningly.

"It's OK, gramps, hang on," the fellow said and placed the four large bottles beside his boots. "Alik, give me yours." And he added two more. "Here, pops, hand them in like you're supposed to, buy like you're supposed to. Don't freeze your nose off!"

The fellows strode off briskly.

With such boots and a padded pea jacket, thought Igor Ivanovich, you would be able to stand here half the day.

"Take the bottles, take them . . . look how they tossed them," said the gregarious woman.

"See, they get drunk, and then they get on their own nerves and others' too," said the woman with three bottles.

"Are you going to take the bottles?" Once again the little guy peeped out from his collar.

Snakes were writhing in Igor Ivanovich's mind.

"Six times seventeen . . . more than a ruble . . . I put them in their place, called them to order, but to pick up the bottles now . . . I probably should take them, but so as not to lower myself . . . I have to get the net out . . . More than a ruble, why that's three more beers. Three plus three, six bottles of beer, but why get so much beer, better to get something more substantial . . ."

If Igor Ivanovich had stood ten or fifteen minutes longer beside these ill-fated bottles, getting used to them, getting used to thinking about them, then he could have most likely moved these lawful trophies into his net with a natural-looking, unhurried motion, but at that moment the one in the collar peeked out again.

"Are you going to take them?" And he took one bottle in his hand as though he meant to look to see if the neck was chipped or if there was something in it. "No, it's a normal bottle." And he put it in his bag, which he had pulled out of his pocket specially for this. "This will come in handy."

Then he took a second bottle and for propriety's sake he started to examine it as well.

Igor Ivanovich kicked the bottle beside him and it spun around on the trampled snow.

"They set them up here!" Igor Ivanovich took a step to the side.

"They're just right for me," said the little guy, and no longer examining each one of them, he gathered up the rest and ran over for the one Igor Ivanovich kicked away.

"See what a smart aleck," said the woman with the three bottles. "Did they give them to you, huh?"

"I asked the comrade, he didn't want them, but they're just what I need . . . They're perfectly good bottles," he grunted and sank back into his raised collar.

There was nothing left for the women to do but to exchange condemning and ironic smiles about the pushy guy.

The street was cold and empty, a typical morning.

Not only was Igor Ivanovich afraid of the cold; he was even afraid someone might notice this fear.

"Nice frost," he said to everyone's surprise, addressing no one in particular, and then fell silent, energetically wiggling his toes inside his boots.

A famous polar explorer, probably Amundsen, contended that cold and frost are the only things that humans can't get used to, and if he could have stood right now beside Igor Ivanovich and could have understood

Russian, he would certainly have been highly interested in the announcement so unexpectedly coming from a man in a cap and light boots. In this connection it's necessary to digress once again in order to finally direct the narrative firmly into its fantastic channel.

Along with Zagorsk and Gatchina, the city of Kronstadt, located on the flat and low-lying island of Kotlin, must be recognized as a propitious place for the staging of a fantastic story. To be sure, no one is surprised when reading official accounts of the events that took place on this island that the facts seem enigmatic from an ordinary point of view.

It is reliably known that 3,000 sailors and 1,500 soldiers took part in the armed uprising of September 1905,* but when this spontaneous revolutionary uprising was suppressed, 4,000 sailors and 800 soldiers were arrested, of whom 10 were sent into exile and 67 were rewarded with prison terms.

Much more enigmatic and inexplicable from the point of view of the practical sciences are the traces left in official publications by the bloody mutiny of 1921. The military historians of the future will be more than a little surprised to find that among those who attacked a first-class naval fortress from the ice fields—open to the wind where you could find cover only behind the corpse of a comrade who had fallen before you—the losses were very modest: 527 men. Yet, among the defenders of the fortress, twice as many fell in the course of the assault. A sense of satisfaction is also aroused by the assertion that among the attackers only one in ten was wounded. From the point of view of mercy and the love of mankind, this information is very comforting; but completely unnecessary questions immediately arise. Namely, didn't Tyulenev's brigade lose exactly half of its complement during the first hours of the fighting? And a brigade consists of a minimum of three regiments. Does that mean that Reiter's brigade, which was the first to burst onto the Petrograd dock at Kronstadt, wasn't depleted by one-third during twenty minutes of battle? Does that mean that the Nevelskoy Regiment didn't fall at Italian Pond? Or that the cadets of the Brigade School, thrown in to cover the retreat of the drained and defeated Nevelskoy troops, weren't killed to the last man? Or that the commander of the bleeding Consolidated Division, digging in on the eastern edge of the island, didn't report that it wasn't humanly possi-

*There were two rebellions in Kronstadt during this period: one in September–October 1905; the second in July 1906.

ble to hold on but that by retreating they could avoid total annihilation? And why is it that only Petrograders remember that on March 8 the young commander of the Seventh Army threw 3,000 selfless Red Cadets into the attack on a fortress with a garrison of 30,000, and how on their way to the stronghold the cadets took ice-bound and inaccessible forts with bayonets and grenades, how they somehow came bursting into the town and in the town they fought and fell without thinking of glory or thinking of how historians, afraid of catching colds and trouble at work because of ideas of a higher order, would consider that their death and loss of blood hadn't taken place.

The Kronstadt Mutiny, unlike the July uprising in Kronstadt in 1906, is still patiently awaiting its historian.

The events of February and March 1921 were reflected strangely in the contradictory and surprising reports about them. It all started with everyone trying to forget these events. A five-volume history—in a substantial dark red binding, decorated with portraits and pictures lovingly covered with shrouds of lacy onionskin paper, and even including a Red Guard armband—illuminates at length the entire Civil War all the way until its end in 1922, but its vellum pages contain neither a narrative nor even a mention of the mutiny which, in Vladimir Ilich Lenin's opinion, represented a greater danger for the Soviet power "than Denikin, Yudenich, and Kolchak together."* Even the memoirs of the participants in the event, which have partially come down to us, came out sometimes missing a beginning, sometimes missing an end, and sometimes completely missing a middle. The memoirists, some of whom had never set eyes on each other, seem as though by agreement to have become mute and victims of amnesia as soon as the story touched on details excluded from the boundaries of history. Certain historical personages who were at the forefront during the Revolution and the Civil War and who also played some role in the Kronstadt events, suddenly disappear as though they had fallen through the ice along with the hundreds of nameless Red Guards and Cadets who attacked the impregnable naval fortress at night during a blizzard. The rounded-off count of victims on either side, where the numbers end in two or three zeros, arouses sadness about the disdain for those tens, not to speak of the hundreds or thousands; and it also exposes

*Generals of the White Army.

the historians and statisticians to rebuke for their haste to reach absolutely correct conclusions while omitting details and particulars . . .

So where are you to look for fantastic heroes and fantastic events if not in the black holes of history, which, one must assume, swallowed more than one careless, curious man who dared look over the edge! Exactly here, where life is compressed into super-dense matter, where cities freeze in the glow of fires, where the bowels of snow-covered battleships burn from desperation, where bandages and blood are indissolubly baked and caked together; where horses, unused to flight, hover over the ice, rearing on their hind legs in the sky from the explosions, becoming the last things seen by the fighter who has gone mad from the rumble and the roar, shielded from death by a mother's prayer and a white robe* given out before the attack. Where if not here among the panting steam engine and the arrogant armored cars sniffing the spring air with the blunt snouts of their machine guns—where if not here where we were born—should we not all gather, we who remember, who saw, who know . . . to toss a handful of earth and go our silent ways . . .

The results from the uprising of 1906 are clear at least: 1,417 persons convicted, 36 executed. However, it's significantly more complicated with the mutiny, though one thing can be asserted with authority: the mutiny of March 18 was crushed, and Igor Ivanovich Dikshtein was executed on March 21. The reader expects an immediate explanation and assurances that Igor Ivanovich's death was accidental, not at all necessary and, as it were, not quite death, and although there obviously is some small basis for such an opinion, one has to remember the mutiny, so furious and bloody, and the cruel and merciless fighting on both sides, in order not to be misled about death during war. One might call life during a war accidental, but death—not at all.

Between the events of July 1906 and February 1921 one cannot overlook the mutiny of the mobilized sailors in Petrograd on October 14, 1918, which was in a social and political sense the precursor of the Kronstadt Rebellion of 1921. On the one hand, the mobilized sailors couldn't yet free themselves from their peasant feelings and carried within them the dissatisfaction of the kulak** and middle-peasant masses with the politics of the dictatorship of the proletariat; but on the other hand, according to the

---

*White cloaks were distributed to infantrymen to be used as camouflage against the snow.
**Prosperous peasants who supposedly employed hired labor.

cogent remark of the commissar of the Baltic Fleet, "all the counterrevolutionary blackheads hadn't been squeezed out" yet from among the mass of sailors themselves. And the slogans then were the same as they were two and a half years later at Kronstadt: "Free Soviets," "Down With Commissarocracy," and the like. And the instigators were the same: leftist Social Revolutionaries, maximalists, anarchists. The experience in the spring with the liquidation of such attitudes in the mortar division of the fleet made it completely clear that it would probably be necessary to resort to revolutionary repression in order to remold the mobilized sailors.

But they managed without that. The constant misfortune of the left SRs was their inability to estimate their chances for victory and their desire to make a big splash as fast as possible.

The mutiny clanked its weapons, but on October 14 they went out to demonstrate, leaving their arms in the barracks, and they refused to go without an orchestra. As is well known, the crew of the Second Fleet was located next to the Mariinsky Theater, and that is where the sailors went to get an orchestra right in the middle of a performance of *The Barber of Seville* (the performances used to start early in the day). They apologized and politely explained to the audience and the conductor their purpose for mobilizing the orchestra and asked the musicians to go outside and line up with their instruments. The strings and the harp were told not to bother; they focused on the winds. But a snag developed with the percussion. The principal big drum, the pride and joy of any orchestra, turned out to be solidly anchored in the orchestra pit. First they tried to remove it nicely, then they started to apply force—and all this during the whistling and hooting of the politically backward public, the majority of whom were petty and middle bourgeoisie. It was especially insulting for the sailors to hear the shouts, including the epithets "Bolsheviks" and "Commissars," but it wasn't possible to explain to the audience that they were going to march with the drum precisely against the Bolsheviks and Commissars. In the end the percussionist of the orchestra, the man who had suffered most, promised to extract the same sound from the medium drum as he would have from the large one. They had to agree to this compromise since it turned out to be impossible to tear the big drum away from the theater without significant damage to both.

At the Nikolaevsky Bridge the demonstrating mutineers had already been frightened by an accidental salvo of rifles, and they became confused and started back toward the barracks.

Igor Ivanovich heard this story when the crew of the battleship *Sevas-*

topol was passing a resolution demanding of the Commissars of the Baltic Fleet "a strict investigation of these elements" and asked that they not stop "at anything, even if they had to remove several dozen men from the midst of the mobilized forces."

In 1921 it started almost the same way in Kronstadt, only it didn't continue or end the same way.

The row continued through February of that year; the sailors from the ice-locked vessels got bored with the inactivity and the meetings and had nothing else to do but calculate how complete or how short the rations were, to observe the slipshod work of the quartermaster in charge of supplies, and to carry on endless conversations about their villages, the land, free trade, the long drawn-out mobilization, and the antiprofiteer detachments assigned to catch anyone bringing food into the city to trade.

With dull faces they loafed around on the dirty, dingy ships and didn't even clear off the snow for weeks on end. Interest in politics and in literature was fading by the day despite the abundance of lecturers who gladly came to the ships for payment in food. They went unwillingly to lectures on political topics and, therefore, hardly any of that kind were held. The Political Section's program of lectures for soldiers and sailors included such subjects as "The Origin of Man," "Italian Painting," "Greek Sculpture," and "The Stone Age." For some reason there was much demand among the sailors for a lecture about a totally landlocked country—"Customs and Life in Austria." But as a rule, even if thirty or forty men got together in the messroom to listen to some lecturer or other, it all came around to the same endless questions about land, free trade, and the antiprofiteer detachments.

Refusal to obey orders became almost commonplace on the ships, and a slack attitude toward their duties also became noticeable among Party members. The issue of furloughs caused ferment among the crew, which was expressed in the independently convoked regimental meetings at which the crew refused the alloted five percent of furloughs; they demanded more. The sailors wanted to have it out in person with the fleet commander and his deputies and demanded the convocation of a brigade-wide conference.

Yes, this was no longer the same navy or the same *Sevastopol* that had unanimously passed a resolution against the dissatisfied new recruits and adroitly shelled the mutinous Krasnaya Gorka fort in the fall of 1919.

To replace the revolutionary sailors, scattered on all fronts from the

Ukraine to Siberia, came a raw mass of peasants who were tired of "war communism" and ready to explode from any spark. And at this time also, as the historians testify, the Judas Trotsky, "shipped to Kronstadt many of his people from the provinces where kulak uprisings were widespread."

By 1921 Kronstadt was like a badly guarded and maintained powder magazine.

On February 28, the senior clerk on the *Petropavlovsk* pushed through a resolution in favor of "Soviets Without Communists." Men went over to the other battleship, since both ships were standing along the sea wall in the harbor of Ust-Rogatka. On the *Sevastopol* a general meeting supported the resolution.

Delegates were sent to Petrograd to find out the cause of unrest in factories and plants, and at the same time to test the mood on the *Poltava* and the *Gangut*, which were docked at the Baltic Shipyards in the city, out of commission, but still formally a part of the First Brigade of battleships.

Many generally considered that the whole row originated on the battleships, and therefore they later went over the *Petropavlovsk* and the *Sevastopol* with a fine-tooth comb. As far as the *Gangut* and the *Poltava* were concerned, they can thank the twenty-six-year-old, non-Party member commander of the Communist detachment on the Petrograd naval base, Misha Kruchinsky, who, without his belt or gun, went up on deck of the battleship, which was frozen fast in the Neva's ice. On the ship the mood was one of terrible excitement, kept at boiling point just then by the success of the Kronstadt rebels who had easily repulsed the first assault. What he told the crew of the *Gangut*, who were shouting angrily and brandishing their weapons, and the delegates from the *Poltava*, no one can tell any more, but after a two-hour meeting both crews found it best to hand over their weapons and ammunition and to leave the ships. Cadets from Petrograd were posted as guards on the decks of the empty dreadnoughts. Evidently quite a few people must have prayed for Kruchinsky's health, since he went through two wars, joined the party in 1942, and lived to a ripe old age.

The news about the *Gangut* and the *Poltava* instantly reached everyone and knocked the breath out of the Kronstadt agitators, who had been asserting that sailors don't turn on each other and who had depended firmly on the twelve-inch guns of the battleships being held to the temples of the city.

. . . Everything in this history consisted, as it were, of two completely opposing halves, just like weather in the changeover from winter to spring—frost and thaw, puddles and snowstorms. Here is the brigade of battleships—split in half, there are two powers at Kronstadt—and the troops in both the Petrograd garrison and the fortress waver back and forth, even the Bolshevik party cell at Kronstadt broke in two—one for the mutineers and the other categorically against them. And there is nothing more to say about the *Sevastopol*. Evidently since its birth the ship had been predestined to have two fates: two names, two wars, two fleets, two hearts—one of coal and one of oil ... Only in her declining years, after the long life given her by a kindly fate—when the main battery was fired, the glass lampshades and light bulbs on the lower deck broke with a crash, paint and insulation rained down, and the rusty supports for the lockers that had served out their time fell out from the bulkheads—did the battleship once again regain her original name, changed back to the *Sevastopol* from the *Paris Commune*, before being decommissioned (now from the Black Sea Fleet) and scrapped for metal.

Still, it is much harder to investigate and describe the fate of a single man than the history of a state, a city, or a famous ship.

In spite of the obscurity concealing the origins of Igor Ivanovich and people like him, it is possible to establish something, but only with the greatest effort. However, in the information brought to light, for the most part certainly reliable, there may be one or two inaccuracies which simply can't be checked. In order to reduce the chance for error to a minimum, it is necessary to resort to the time-tested method of writing extensive biographies both of ancient and not-so-ancient heroes about whom nothing at all is known—or almost nothing. One collects grains of trustworthy details preserved by the grateful memory of mankind and generous chance, and one submerges oneself in an abundance of circumstantial information—about the times, weather, fashions, rumors, geological and sociological processes—drawn from earlier editions that have been checked, thanks to which the one or two invented details in the hero's biography begin to look more or less plausible.

... While still in Helsingfors on October 28, 1917, Igor Ivanovich had read the speech by Trotsky, the chairman of the Petrograd Soviet, in the newspaper *News of the Kronstadt Soviet of Workers' and Soldiers' Deputies** about the installation of the new power and the new victory of the lower classes over the upper, which had been unusually bloodless, unusually successful; aware now that the establishment of a dictatorship places

**Izvestiia Kronshtadtskogo Soveta rabochikh i soldatskikh deputatov.* Later referred to as *Izvestiya.*

the lower above the upper, he could clearly see his own place in this struggle—namely in the middle. He definitely had no use for the benefits brought by the overthrow of the provisional government. He didn't need land, he didn't care to own the factories and plants, the freedom which had begun on March 1, 1917, was more than enough for him (it could even be reduced a little); and as for the war, it wasn't particularly burdensome for the navy, and the idea of an immediate peace seemed to him so unrealistic that it appeared to be merely a tactical slogan of the Bolsheviks.

Igor Ivanovich Dikshtein was one of the "black marine-guards," those who had not finished their training, a short-statured noncommissioned officer from among the students who had ended up in the navy during the war. He had a sparse and, consequently, untidy-looking little beard, glasses with silver frames, and a quiet command: the hold of the No. 2 turret of the main battery. Having effortlessly learned all the rules of the maintenance, care, and storage of ammunition, he diligently "nursed" the ammunition with Germanic precision, often earning the approval of the senior artillerist of the *Sevastopol*, Gaitsuk, whose death will be described below. After the peace of Brest-Litovsk many officers and warrant officers of the old army and navy were cashiered, receiving tickets for furlough with the following text: ". . . Discharged until recall, to return to original status." Igor Ivanovich was in no hurry to return to his "original status"; in Petrograd there was hunger, and according to the information that was so widely discussed at endless meetings and discussions in the noncommissioned officers' wardroom, the coming year, 1921, didn't promise any relief. The substantial Red Navy ration deserves detailed description, since the workers in Petrograd didn't receive half as much: one-and-a-half to two pounds of bread, a quarter-pound of meat, a quarter-pound of fish, a quarter-pound of cereal, sixty to eighty grams of sugar—and all this per day. It's true that many had a desire to eat bread or something else even after just finishing a navy meal. The basic quantity was supplied regularly and without interruption according to wintertime norms, but the food allowance wasn't always of good quality. Instead of cereal they were often given frozen potatoes, and there wasn't enough fat and sugar . . .

His mother and younger brother had died of hunger in 1919 in the cramped apartment on the fifth floor of an old house on Petropavlovsk Street in Petrograd, which is why the problem of survival became Igor Ivanovich's single main aim. He could foresee, he could calculate, but more and more often some not unexpected chain of events already underway somehow destroyed his apparently well-calculated designs . . .

At first all went according to his calculations.

Anticipating mobilization, Igor Ivanovich went as a volunteer, which gave him perfectly obvious advantages, the right to choose a branch of the service and even a specialty. At the same time his joining the navy eased the situation of his family, which lived on his father's small pension. He chose the safest place on the ship—the shell magazine, and he was right, because even at a time when all duties on board had slackened and there was no order left, the ammunition keepers enjoyed undisputed authority. The duty details were allotted on a democratic basis, the watches were kept miserably, the snow lay uncleared on the decks, the ice wasn't hacked off, but the artillery watch—guarding the hold and responsible for the condition of the ammunition and the water supply system, for fire-fighting and flooding of the magazine—were given strict orders and they did their job conscientiously. Even the most dense country sailorboy soon understood what it meant when the cartridge chambers were defective and the powder magazines were in a mess.

Igor Ivanovich didn't intend to spend his whole life in the navy; he wanted to survive all these unpleasant things, finish his education, and live the solid and secure life of a Russian engineer. Therefore, he avoided any kind of political activity, called himself a sympathizer but didn't specify with whom, and in his heart he didn't condemn the crews of the *Aurora*, which had sworn allegiance to the provisional government on practically the day after the unsuccessful July rising, and then frightened that same government with a blank shot from behind Nikolaevsky Bridge during the night when the Winter Palace was taken by the Bolsheviks.

It would be absolutely untrue to assume that at the time when all of the people were supposedly ready to rally round a single great goal, when the thirst for freedom was on everybody's lips and their hearts were filled with a desire to forge ahead, it was only Igor Ivanovich Dikshtein in his central section below the turret where the shells were stored, among the shelves, caissons, and storage containers with whose help the shells were loaded on carts and moved to assembly tables—that only he didn't feel a thirst for freedom and a desire to forge ahead. Of course he felt this, but only for a very short time, and after certain events that followed one another, literally one day after the other, and both times right in front of his eyes, Igor Ivanovich became reserved and preferred not to speak aloud either of his thirst or of efforts to forge freedom.

In accordance with battle orders, in the winter of 1917 both fleets of battleships were anchored off Helsingfors.

On March 2, the day after they had received the news that the autocracy had fallen, Rear Admiral Nebolsin was killed. And on March 4, when Admiral Nepenin—who was arrested because he refused to resign the Supreme Command of the Baltic Fleet without an order from the provisional government—was taken away from the Helsingfors Harbor, they shot him right by the gate in full view of the crowd.

Both events were referred to in the newspapers as incidents, and no one had to answer for them, which is what struck Igor Ivanovich most of all.

Igor Ivanovich locked himself in below three armored decks and with even greater diligence looked after the Westinghouse-Leblanc air-conditioning system, which provided a temperature of 15–20 degrees centigrade in his automatically regulated magazine. With the utmost attention he took care of his three hundred wards, which were spun by brass driving bands and had all sorts of armor-piercing and ballistic points. Like a diligent first sergeant of ammunition he strictly inspected the hermetic seals on the cases containing the bagged charges of powdered nitroglycerin in magnificent combustible silk; checked that the ammunition carriers moved easily as they turned on a spherical strap, checked the functioning of the small hoists for the sixty-kilo charges, and fussed over the rubber rollers in the projectile cradles that protected the fuses and the driving band of the four hundred-kilo shells.

Finding himself in Petrograd in February 1921, Igor Ivanovich at once felt the striking similarity to the events four years earlier, although the number of people in the city had noticeably decreased.

. . . It wasn't even that it had decreased, but you might say that the city had been depopulated; from the 2.5 million inhabitants in 1916 there remained only one-third—fewer than 800,000. The working class, the support of the revolution, had been dispersed as well, you could barely find 90,000 of them—a fifth as many as in 1916. And it was no longer composed of the same people; now it was whoever might want to avoid being drafted into the army by working in the factories or just out to get a worker's ration card. The lack of manpower was replaced by Red Army conscript laborers—army units that received work orders instead of their long-awaited demobilization. Citizens were brought in from thirty-seven provinces as conscripted and mobilized labor, only no one could really count them, since they ran away if they could, just like the first builders of Petersburg. They also concealed their trades and, in general, after the victorious end of the war, they simply didn't wish to live far from home in barracks under semimilitary discipline. These conscripted workers worked like they lived—and they lived badly, as far as living conditions and food and clothing went.

At the Eighth All-Russian Congress of Soviets, Trotsky, who was responsible for transport, assured the country that the coming winter "doesn't threaten us with destruction, doesn't threaten us with the total paralysis that we might have expected by midwinter." It's hard to say what the optimism of the leader was based on, but the paralysis approached before winter reached its midpoint.

However, economic difficulties concealed the political crisis, which had already surfaced in the speeches of the peasants at that same Eighth Congress of Soviets. ". . . Everything is fine," said a cunning delegate with the usual peasant resignation, "it's only that the land's ours but the grain's yours; the water's ours but the fish's yours; the forest's ours but the wood's yours . . ." For this reason the peasants unwillingly participated both in timber cutting and in supplying the city with provisions. Having freed the poorest peasantry from forced requisitions, the authorities started to call not individual peasants but entire villages to account for delayed and inadequate fulfillment of the quotas for food and firewood imposed by the People's Committee for Supplies, and this provoked opposition from the backward masses.

In January Petrograd received a third as much fuel and firewood as planned, and in February only a quarter. The winter was a hard one, freezing cold and with big snowdrifts. The stony center of the city began to heat itself by using the wooden outskirts. One hundred and seventy-five buildings were razed and the 165 cords of wood obtained in this way were distributed equitably: two-thirds went to the population and one-third to heat institutions. In February, fifty more structures were condemned to be torn down. Understanding that this resource was, like all others, limited, the Petrograd Soviet published a decree explaining to the citizens that the *tearing down of buildings* could be undertaken only with the permission of the Council of National Economy.

Although the harvest in 1920 wasn't bad, the trains with provisions crawled toward the city at an average speed of eighty-nine kilometers per day, sometimes only thirty-four kilometers per day. Food spoiled on the way, eggs arrived rotten from Siberia and potatoes froze on the way and arrived inedible.

On February 15 not one train with provisions made it to the city. There was no grain reserve; that is, there was, but only for a day or two and only if it was distributed in half rations. And so it was during all of March.

In January the specially formed Commission for Supplying the Capitals, under the Council of Labor and Defense, had decreased the rations of bread by one-third for ten days, giving out two days' rations every three days. This decision applied not only to Moscow and Petrograd but also to the Ivanovo-Voznesensky region and Kronstadt. However, upon the expiration of the stipulated period, the Petrograd Soviet was forced to announce the reduction of bread norms for some citizens, and for others the special food rations were cancelled.

Without fuel, without food, without qualified workers interested in working, you can't produce much, and ninety-three enterprises had to be closed down and not just any, but ones like the Putilovets, Lessner, Treugolnik, Franco-Russian, Baranovsky, and Längenzippen plants. There were 27,000 people without work, one-third of the workers remaining in Petrograd, but during the emergency stoppage the government guaranteed for all the right to receive rations and average wages calculated on the basis of piecework plus bonuses. In order somehow to retain the workers' vanguard in Petrograd, orders were published for them to report to work every day for registration. The newspaper *Petrogradskaya Pravda* reported on the resourceful tobacco workers who, after the prohibition against using electric energy, had started up manual machines and in this way employed 125 men, while 200 men worked on finishing the articles and another 428 started to clear away the snow and bring in raw material. Attempts to use electricity even for a short period at the closed-down enterprises were cut short at the outset, because 150 plants continued working at full capacity, although it is true that "slowdowns" crippled the work. This word "slowdown" was on everyone's tongue and appeared quite often in print and in official documents, though it didn't make it into any dictionary and one can only guess that the new usage replaced the terms "labor unrest" and "strike," which had outlived their usefulness.

Anxiety and dissatisfaction reigned in the city. Exhaustion—terrible exhaustion, inhuman exhaustion—nourished the gloomy mood of the people who had beaten the White Guards, banished the interventionists, endured all deprivations and adversity, starved, frozen, and survived typhus and cholera, people who had waited three years for peace and had been hoping for an immediate improvement in their life.

First a shop at the Baltic plant would stop work; then the workers at laundry No. 1 would refuse to unload firewood . . . The workers who previously had spared no effort in the defense of Soviet power now began to present demands to it; their mood was being manifested mainly in their demand that the population should be satisfactorily supplied with food, but there were also demands of a different kind: the workers at the Dyumo plant demanded to be given soap and an authorization for public baths.

The Provincial Party Committee of Petrograd sensed all the tension of the moment, and at a meeting at the end of February these prophetic words were spoken: "We have come to the moment when demonstrations might occur."

Demonstrations began at the end of February.

In the editorial entitled "Hands Off!" *Petrogradskaya Pravda* openly admitted that counterrevolutionary agitators had "succeeded in causing slowdowns at the plants." They caused slowdowns at the arsenal and the Trubochny plants, at the Laferme tobacco factory, at the Baltic plant, at the First Nevsky thread factory—it isn't possible to list them all. The "slowdowners" demonstrated in the city with demands that those arrested be set free; they disarmed the guards, taking away not only their rifles but also their cartridges. Red Cadets dispersed the crowd without using their weapons, but some shots came from the crowd and injured one cadet.

Just as in February 1917, there was open agitation against the government and, just as then, the same problems, including the absence of fuel and food, were blamed on the government, which was now the Bolsheviks. Just as then, a motley crowd gathered in front of the barracks and army schools, testing the mood of those who had weapons; in the factories and plants spontaneous meetings were taking place; in the same way attempts flared up to disarm now this, now that guard. And if in February 1917 the Junkers were the pillars of support for the government, then this time the heroes of the day were the staunch and militant Red Cadets. Their appeals to the Petrograd workers were filled with threats of decisive action, and their statement that "yesterday we didn't fire a single shot, but tomorrow we may no longer distinguish the innocent from the guilty, the honest but misled toiler from the dishonest provocateur and scoundrel" resembled the appeasement efforts of a shaky government.

From word of mouth it was reliably reported that Zinoviev,* who headed the recently formed Committee for the Defense of Petrograd, had moved it into the Peter-and-Paul fortress. This measure corroborated reports that a revolt would break out in Petrograd any day now.

*Grigory Zinoviev, 1883–1936, Soviet politician.

The Committee for the Defense immediately released the appeal "Beware of spies! Death to spies!" The newspapers explained: "It is a well-known fact that England, France, Poland, and others have their spies in Petrograd . . . The Military Council proposes through the Commissions of Struggle against Counterrevolution to take immediate measures to uncover all espionage organizations and to arrest those who are spreading evil rumors and sowing panic and confusion."

The Bureau of the Petrograd Party Committee put on the day's agenda the specific question: "Measures to be taken tomorrow in connection with mutiny in the factories." The session was long and stormy and finished in total darkness, since the supply of electricity had run out. In accordance with the resolutions of the bureau, Cheka troikas were formed in local districts, special mission units were reestablished, and Party members were mobilized. A curfew was imposed for 11 P.M.; in any case walking in the street was unsafe since street lighting no longer existed. Theaters of an "unserious nature" were to be closed, and at "serious" theaters the start of performances was moved from seven to six in the evening.

The biggest icebreaker in the world, the *Ermak*, cut the city in two halves several times a day by breaking up the sled tracks across the Neva and the footpaths worn by citizens, mercilessly blowing smoke out through its two gigantic straight smokestacks in front of the few pedestrians roaming along the empty embankments. The bridges were raised for the entire night, which was normally never done in winter, and cadets in full fighting gear marched along the streets with songs and bands, inspiring courage and confidence in those who needed it and warning the enemy: "No tricks!" Wires from the field telephones snaked through the streets and gave the city the appearance of a battlefront.

Petrograd remained gloomy and empty, armored cars loomed *as though forgotten* at the crossings of the main streets. The faces of the populace bore the stamp of exhaustion and confusion.

The desperate appeals of the Petrograd Soviet and the Provincial Party Committee to the working class who had come out in the street— "Back to work! Back to work!"—drowned in the united chorus of Socialist Revolutionaries, Mensheviks, and mixed antigovernment people calling for the Bolsheviks to be removed from power and thrown out of the Soviets. The proclamations of the Anarchists urged people to "overthrow the autocracy of the Communists."

Handbills also turned up with reminders of the Constituent Assembly: "We know who is afraid of the Constituent Assembly. They will not be allowed to rob and will have to answer before the people's representatives for their deceit, robbery, and all their other crimes. Down with the hateful Communists! Down with Soviet power! Long live the Constituent Assembly!" Here it was difficult to figure out who had a hand in it—maybe the Socialist Revolutionaries, maybe the Constitutional Democrats. But the hand of the deacon of the Luga cathedral was visible in the homemade posters put up all over Luga: "Rejoice and celebrate—soon the White liberators will come!"—the district Revolutionary Troika recognized that without difficulty.

On the whole it was comparatively peaceful in the outlying Petrograd areas. The population was even getting used to the wandering bands of twenty to thirty deserters; the peasants established a roster for housing them—for the responsibility of receiving and then sending these armed and hungry gangs on their way. In the Rozhdestvensky and Gatchina precincts posters appeared: "Long live the Constituent Assembly!" But there were no notable peasant outbursts, unless you count the misunderstanding over the hay in the Smerdovsky precinct.

On February 24, martial law was imposed on the city, and a few days later a state of siege was declared. The Petrograd Soviet passed a resolution to demobilize the army labor detachments, and all citizens were brought to the city as conscript labor; they all received two weeks' wages and a free ticket home. In this way part of the most dissatisfied and, therefore, the most explosive elements were removed from the city.

Unstable and unreliable troops, who were beginning to ferment, especially the navy units, were immediately sent out of Petrograd on three troop trains to the Caucasus and the Black Sea.

Cadets faithful to the Bolsheviks and special units stood guard at the buildings of the local Soviets and protected the Party committees, telephone stations, railroad stations, bridges, and major thoroughfares of the city. Patrols of cadets caught counterrevolutionaries and their accomplices and sent them to be dealt with by the merciless revolutionary troikas.

Holding meetings and the presence of outsiders were banned on the ships and in the institutions of the Baltic Fleet; those who were observed carrying out agitation were subject to arrest, and in case of resistance force was ordered.

The Petrograd Party organization was maximally mobilized to drive back the mutineers and to uphold order.

In Oranienbaum a requirement that the populace provide transport was imposed and carried out calmly and in an orderly fashion as more and more troops, equipment, and ammunition were brought to the shore.

The railroad workers' behavior was beyond praise; however, they may have been afraid of mobilization.

It was typical that the "spontaneous" assemblies and meetings were attended exclusively by non-Party elements; it was precisely the non-Party people who claimed that the Communists were to be blamed for all the current difficulties, although at that point it was already easy to understand "for whose mill these wolves in sheep's clothing were bringing grist," as a historian would so cogently say later.

And again a thirst for "freedom" appeared on many lips.

When Igor Ivanovich first embarked on the *Sevastopol*, in the beginning of the summer of 1916, he hesitated to tread on her, to take his first step on her top deck, swabbed to the color of yellow amber, as smooth as a table top from bow to stern.

The sun, shining brightly, was blindingly reflected in the brass, chrome, and bronze parts of various machinery, handrails, gangways, speaking tubes, and portholes; all this metallic grandeur seemed to be newly cast and forged and the metal, shining like fire, seemed to be still hot.

Later on Igor Ivanovich began to notice that the closer freedom came, the more the bronze and chrome tarnished and the more the deck somehow gradually developed the dismal appearance of a provincial town's sidewalk. Igor Ivanovich was convinced that this dirt came to the ship not from the visiting delegations and agitators, not from the commissions and delegates who were constantly testing and shaping the mood of the battleship's crew, but that it crept out directly from the depths of the ship itself. This was inevitable, just as inevitable as the messy appearance of any broken or negligently maintained mechanism in which some pipe inevitably drips, dirty black lubricating oil oozes out of a broken packing, and a flange that's not turned all the way causes a leak.

Uncertainty and forced inactivity depressed and demoralized the men.

The strongest response caused by the unrest was felt by the crew in the hold and the stokers who were stationed at the battleship's twenty-five boilers; the least heard, the least noticed, they now crawled upwards to forge freedom—noisy, implacable, harsh, vociferous. Looking at them, Igor Ivanovich thought that freedom or not, someone had to stay in the dank hold all the same, someone had to be roasted by the fire-breathing furnace and drink the tepid water from the teakettle suspended on a string.

A fellow with a scalp lock came to his mind, one of the "specters," painted and drawn all over with tattoos just like a gazebo in a city park; he was sitting surrounded by his mates from the No. 3 boiler in the sun by the stern funnel and singing softly, accompanying himself on a mandolin:

> In the midst of a rye field I was born
> to the slave of tyrant masters.
> Great woe lay in store
> for the child's innocent heart.

Igor Ivanovich noticed the long clever face of the stoker, his strapping figure and rather good ear, and his appearance somehow didn't go with the accusing-orphan words of the popular song. Igor Ivanovich's observation, although fleeting, was correct, but how could he have known that the singer wasn't really born in a field of rye but in a normal railroad worker's family and that he had inherited his fine ear for music from his mother, an illiterate woman who remembered many songs and refrains? On the other hand, Igor Ivanovich knew for certain that one square meter of the furnace-bar in the Yarrow boilers used on the battleship consumed two hundred kilos of coal per hour, and consequently he always looked upon the stokers with sympathy.

As if overhearing Igor Ivanovich's thoughts about the orphan's song, the scalp lock interrupted it in midword and started to play something piercingly tender, apparently improvising as he went along. The thin vibrating sound of the mandolin, like a titmouse that had accidentally flown in under a shipyard roof, dashed above the deck between the structures towering in the sky, among the gun turrets and the enormous smokestacks, supported on the outside by ribs.

The stoker, who was pursing his lips importantly, would nod his head without noticing anyone near him, and then bend his ear down as though he couldn't hear the strings, which sounded trusting and open under his fist, corroded by coal. And the thin, vulnerable sound filled one's heart with self-pity and longing for one's woman and child, for the forest, the field, for solid land where it befits a man to live instead of huddled together shut up in the stifling belly of a floating fortress.

On March 1, on Anchor Square—by then renamed Revolution Square—Igor Ivanovich and this man from the No. 3 boiler happened to stand next to each other.

March 1 turned out to be the noisiest day in the history of Kronstadt. On the square in front of the cathedral people were walking around alone and in groups—there were workers from the steamship wharf, the electrical plant, and the shops, women and teenagers—almost ten thousand people had gathered, half the city and garrison.

In contrast to the majority of the units, both the officers and the crews of the *Petropavlovsk* and the *Sevastopol* came to the meeting organized in ranks with music but, true, without flags. The motley crowd near the rostrum yielded before the neat columns of sailors from the battleships. It was their precision and the perfect position they held that helped turn the meeting in the intended direction.

Company columns of the *Sevastopol*'s crew reformed, and the artillery and the stokers ended up side by side. Igor Ivanovich cast a glance at the scalp lock and tried to place his face, but without the mandolin, without the tattoos covering his body, even his back, he couldn't recognize him and didn't especially try, having gotten used to the fact that the crew he met offship all seemed quite familiar, but who they were and where they were from was hard, sometimes even impossible, to remember.

Comrade Kalinin, chairman of the All-Russian Central Executive Committee, mounted the rostrum. He had come to the square on a light sled over the ice of the gulf. He came without security guards and guides, straight from the door of the political division of the 187th Detached Rifle Brigade at Oranienbaum.

He had come to speak with the sailors and was greeted with applause. They were waiting to see which way he would turn, but when he started the same old Bolshevik song, they wouldn't let him talk. Petrichenko,* his coat unbuttoned, waved his sailor's hat and interrupted Kalinin, saying let's hear instead the delegates who went to Petrograd to find out the reasons for the unrest in the factories and plants. He gave the podium to the anarchist Shustov, a sailor on the *Petropavlovsk*. According to him, people in Petrograd were just waiting for an uprising at Kronstadt and had put all their hopes on it.

Using this, Petrichenko came up with a resolution: freedom for the leftist socialist parties and free elections of "new Soviets," and went as far as setting free those arrested for counterrevolutionary activities and removing the antiprofiteering detachments that combatted speculation and profiteering.

The battleship had the decisive word here, too.

Then Kalinin could stand it no longer and gave a sharp speech, warn-

*A senior clerk on the battleship *Petropavlovsk*, who became a leading member of Kronstadt's Provisional Revolutionary Committee.

ing that history wouldn't forget or forgive this shameful action, and that future generations would curse the sailors of Kronstadt. Further, he said that starting that very day the Petrograd Council of Labor and Defense would withdraw the antiprofiteer detachments from the entire province and would allow free deliveries of provisions to the city . . . But it was too late, they didn't believe him anymore.

The scalp lock for some reason wiped his fingers on his pea jacket and unhurriedly, paying no attention to the fact that the crowd was roaring, stuck four fingers in his mouth, rolled his eyes as he got his fingers in place and gave out a sound as sharp as the whistle of a whip.

. . . The sturdy health that came from his mother and the staunch prejudices concerning education that came from his father had led the tall fellow with the scalp lock to enlist in the navy and become a stoker at the No. 3 boiler of the battleship *Sevastopol.* This fellow from Sergiev Posad, near Moscow, which had only become a city in 1919, had imagined himself immediately chewing the ribbon of his sailor's cap and strolling through the streets and avenues of Petrograd as "the pride and beauty of the Revolution," in the firm hope that during the coming hungry years he could put the burden of his food and military clothing on the shoulders of the Commissary. He'd been charmed by the tales about the Baltic Fleet and the romantic image of sailors in bell-bottoms who, with a slightly rolling and threatening walk, ply the fairways of world history. How could he have expected to find himself surrounded by boorish peasants dressed in shabby, secondhand navy uniforms? The endless conversations—in the stoker room, on the crew deck, and wherever crowds gathered—about land, forced requisitions, and the harsh new regime in no way corresponded with what the new recruit had expected to see and hear on the ships of the revolutionary Baltic Fleet. Therefore, when the unrest broke out, with endless meetings, resolutions, and protests, the sailor with a scalp lock seemed to wake up. He didn't miss a single noisy meeting and whistled amazingly loudly with four fingers.

On the orders of the battleship brigade staff, one hundred men were sent daily to Petrograd to unload firewood and to clear the snow off the tracks near the Nikolaevsky railroad station. No volunteers could be found and the brigade HQ warned all commanders and commissars that if the order wasn't carried out, they would be "put to justice before a revolutionary tribunal," but the scalp lock was not against going to town one more time and was even eager to do so. The colder the boilers on the

Sevastopol grew and the worse the winter cold became, the brighter the flame of love for a barber's elder daughter grew in the stoker's heart.

After finishing his work at the railroad station he didn't hurry back to Oranienbaum with his mates, but after changing into a new uniform jacket, and decorating himself with a well-pressed ship's ensign, he set off to his fiancée's, looking slightly mysterious and excited. He always grabbed an armload of wood for them, and his pockets were usually bulging pleasantly with a pound or two of millet, consequently he felt confident in the house of his future father-in-law. He let drop a few words to suggest that he personally didn't wish to accept this life but would pretty soon take some decisive steps. To seem more important he asked the papa whether the battleships *Poltava* and *Gangut* from his brigade were still anchored in the Neva. The barber got confused and just twitched the bars of his mustache, but his clever wife, who always believed in the best, consoled her future son-in-law: "Where could they go before spring? They'll stay there, of course." And the fiancée laughed so that the sailor's heart raced, as it did when he saw her for the first time behind the enormous crystal-clear window of the barber's establishment. Stressing the fact that one-half of the battleships were anchored off the city and the other half were under steam in Kronstadt, the future son-in-law let it be understood that this distribution of forces corresponded to some important design of his—the son-in-law's—own. Silence ensued.

The conversation got noticeably livelier when they started talking about the new life, how the city's population had dwindled, and how the conscripted workers only ate up the bread and started slowdowns.

With the impassiveness of a society person reporting news from the other hemisphere, Olga Alexeevna mentioned that a pound of bread cost only 370 rubles in September, but now was already at 1,515. And, actually, the subject was abstract, since the family was completely unable to pay that kind of money for bread. In March they were asking 2,625 rubles a pound, but this price, also, could feed only curiosity. The scalp lock pointed out the significance of wages, but Pyotr Pavlovich, who knew how to count kopecks, made a few simple calculations, converting the pay rate of the proletarians in 1920, amounting to many thousands, to the value current in 1913, and then the current monthly wages seemed quite humble, somewhere between sixteen and twenty-one kopecks a month.

Then the sailor declared that money was a holdover from the past, that it had already irretrievably lost its significance, and emphasized the cost-free distributions, and here it was impossible for Pyotr Pavlovich to come back with anything. Since 1920 food had been given out free for coupons, at the end of 1920 city transport, communal services and baths had also become free, and now they had even stopped charging rent. It might be "war communism," but it was still Communism.

Pyotr Pavlovich agreed and remarked reasonably that it was both correct and wise to assign the population to public dining rooms, in view of the habits of our fellow countrymen, because if they handed out the miserly rations all at once, then the comrades would eat it up all at once and might not go to work anyway, but this way, according to the Petrograd Commune, 600,000 people, almost the entire population of the city, were fed more or less regularly.

Nastya related that for the purpose of economizing on fuel, the holidays would be extended, and since January 19 and 22 were red-letter days on the calendar, a resolution would be passed proclaiming from January 19 to 22—the whole work week—a holiday.

As an active participant in the political activists' collective at the Sanitation and Hygiene Department, Nastya knew the holiday program planned for all five days. At this point she recalled that Comrade Agulyansky, secretary of the committee organizing the celebrations of the third anniversary of the February Revolution, was going to receive from the Council of Trade Unions one pair of shoes, four pairs of socks, and twelve buttons, the buttons being in place of the coat and hat he had requested. Laughing, Nastya told how many signatures—and from whom!—Comrade Agulyansky had to collect and how at every point, in every office, the coat and hat underwent a miraculous transformation, at first combining into a winter overcoat, then dividing into a three-piece suit; the suit then shrank to a waistcoat, the waistcoat turned into a set of underwear, but the underwear wasn't available, and he had to accept twelve buttons.

The sailor was gazing admiringly at Nastya and could hear only her laughter and see her even white teeth and the curl which was bouncing and dancing by her ear. The future in-laws treated the scalp lock attentively and seriously, having already seen how people who were earlier considered ignorant and insignificant had suddenly become part of "the vanguard." What could be said about this? Nothing. He was awfully impatient, the enamored stoker, and amused his fiancée with his earnestness: he wanted as quickly as possible to take the path toward Socialism outlined on many banners. Since he was a "nobody," he had lately been living with the exciting presentiment that he would become "a real somebody." The Bolsheviks were a pretty good example. They had been "nobodies" and just look, one, two, three, and they were kings. They had given the orders, commissared the country, and enough, now let somebody else have a chance . . .

And now his soul was hovering above the seething crowd, intoxicated either with its own power or from a sense of impunity.

The Commissar of the Baltic fleet, Kuzmin, who had sensed the tense mood a day earlier, couldn't believe that it was going to turn into an uprising, and he tried to cough out a speech about the military traditions of Kronstadt, but he wasn't allowed to speak. "Have you forgotten how they shot every tenth man on the northern front?!" they shouted from the crowd. It was subsequently proven that Kuzmin hadn't participated in the "decimations," but he defended himself from this reproach in a peculiar way, screaming to the accusers that he had shot traitors to the cause of the working class and would do so again, and in his place another man would have shot every fifth man instead of every tenth.

Without thinking the scalp lock screamed, "Down with him," and to make it more convincing he stuck his fingers, formed in a circle, in his mouth and produced a whistle as piercing as a needle. Igor Ivanovich, on the other hand, started thinking. He always felt ill at ease when people bragged about killing out of conviction. He saw how the tall thin Kuzmin in a long cavalry overcoat scorched the crowd with the gloomy stare of his deep-set eyes, how he sucked in his hollow cheeks, how he opened and closed his straight mouth, which seemed never to have known a smile, how he waved his sleeve with a very wide cuff. He saw all this but couldn't hear or understand a single word.

"Remember," shouted the fearless Kuzmin to the crowd of many thousands, "remember that you can talk about your needs, about what needs to be reformed, but reform doesn't mean starting an uprising! Remember that Kronstadt, with all its ships and artillery, no matter how formidable, is only a dot on the map of Soviet Russia!"

"You shot a lot of people—that's enough!" "Don't you threaten us, we've seen your kind!" "Away with him." "Down with him!"

All kinds of scum like the prison commandant were already shoving toward the rostrum with hysterical speeches against the Communists.

Igor Ivanovich was paying absolutely no attention to the scalp lock from the No. 3 boiler who covered his frozen ears with his hands, grinned, shouted something, and whistled so that it rang in the ears of those standing near him. The place was swarming with people who were grinning, whistling and screaming . . .

Yes, here they should have gotten used to each other, or perhaps have become better acquainted before they were caught up in a common diaster, while their hearts were open—the scalp lock's heart was wide open and Igor Ivanovich's open a crack, more open than at other moments in his short life; if they had only stepped on each other's feet, pushed each other, even inadvertently, looked each other in the eye and remembered . . . But there's nothing more stupid than to suggest various paths along which history could have developed in the distant past, especially at a time when its current path isn't influenced in any way even by a great many people who not only read but also write.

This is the time to point out that although the scalp lock, as opposed to Igor Ivanovich, was both stately and tall, and his mustache, unlike the scanty beard of the ammunition custodian, was thick, there was nevertheless more similarity between them than might appear at first glance.

The similarity lay in the fact that the one with the mandolin didn't understand anything, although he thought that he understood everything and was filled to bursting with enthusiasm. And Igor Ivanovich simply didn't understand anything period, although he sensed with his semi-technical mind that behind the visible part of the events there was some mechanism hidden from him, the function of which he could neither calculate nor compute, and therefore he was, as always, far removed from stormy emotions.

Generally speaking, in the No. 3 boiler room complete clarity reigned as far as the future path of history under the leadership of the recently formed Kronstadt Revolutionary Committee, the "Revkom," which had chosen the *Sevastopol* as its base of operations because of its safety. Such nearness to power relieved the conscience of doubt and the heart of hesitation.

Kronstadt was curious about the situation on the *Gangut* and the *Poltava*, which were wintering in Petrograd, but on the battleships they were curious about Kronstadt. On March 1 two delegates left the *Poltava* for Kotlin; one didn't return, vanishing God knows where, and the other didn't notice the events that were rocking the island on that day because he was nursing a grudge in his heart: "Let their meetings be damned; they didn't even offer me a meal, the devils!"

The news that they were unable to learn from the offended delegate became known from the political agitators who had gone to Petrograd. Actually, there weren't all that many who went, maybe two hundred, so the fortress preserved its strength, especially since none of the agitators returned. Special patrol units caught the sailors attempting to take thousands of handbills to Petrograd with the "resolution" of the mutinous fortress. The mutineers themselves demonstrated their democracy, their lack of fear of the ideologically defeated enemy, and their total faith in the justice of their cause by publishing without comment in their own *Izvestiya* the text of the twenty thousand handbills dropped onto the island from airplanes, guaranteeing life and amnesty to the rebels only on the condition of immediate and unconditional surrender.

Petrograd got ready in earnest for decisive events.

A circular from the Political Department required that all more or less "major misunderstandings occurring among the crew" should be reported to the security section of the Political Department.

For the most part the dispatches reported a lukewarm attitude toward Soviet power and a bad one toward the Bolshevik party. From the *Pobeditel* it was reported that: "Among the crew there is ferment because of the events, but it is not spilling over in either direction." So that the uncertain mood of the sailors would not swing to the other side, they took control of the guns on the ships wintering in Petrograd, furlough and shore leave were cancelled for the Communists, the Communists were given arms, and on many ships martial law was declared. These decisions were received with nervousness on the vessel *Samoyed* and the destroyer *Kapitan Izylmetev.* On the destroyer *Ussuriets*, the minesweepers of the First Division, and the icebreaker *Avans*, these events were correctly interpreted. It was also quiet on the harbor ship *Vodoley II*, where the conversations, judging from the dispatches, mostly concerned the predominance of Jews in government institutions. An interesting slogan was devised on the dispatch boat *Krechet*: "Long live only the power of the Soviets!" Everyone could understand that behind that short little word "only" stood the removal of the dictatorship of the proletariat and the leading role of the Communists, that is, the main points of the Kronstadt program.

The sailor Tan-Fabian, a participant in the famous meeting at Kronstadt on March 1, was especially active in the icebreaker-rescue detachment stationed in Petrograd. On icebreakers of the same type, the *Truvor* and the *Ogon*, he succeeded in having the "resolution" passed with the overwhelming support of the Communists even though on the *Ogon* three Communists voted against and four non-Party members abstained. As Ten-Fabian later admitted under interrogation, in order to put an end to any vacillation, on March 10 the *Sevastopol* and *Petropavlovsk* would pound the Smolny with their main guns. The crews of the icebreaker *Avans* and the rescue ship *Erey* weren't impressed by this and they refused even to put the "resolution" to a vote.

It later came out that of the numerous crews on the Petrograd naval base, only the two icebreakers and one auxiliary ship accepted the Kronstadt Resolution. It is true that, after the successful repulsion of the first attack, the Kronstadt mutineers were almost able to bring the crew of the *Yermak* over to their side in the hopes of breaking up the ice around the island and making the fortress inaccessible to infantry. The crew of the *Yermak* was removed, the boilers were extinguished, and a guard consisting of trusted Party members and sailors was posted on board.

On that same day, immediately after the victorious meeting, the war commissars were removed from command on the battleships.

The arrests began.

On the night of March 2 the telephone operator at the Kronstadt area communications center, a member of the mutinous Revolutionary Committee—called "comrade chairman," in the old way, and a deputy of Petrichenko—dispatched a telegram to all units and institutions: "Copy to all Kronstadt sentries: In Kronstadt at the present time the Communist Party has been removed from power and a provisional Revolutionary Committee is in charge. Non-Party comrades! We ask you to take the government in your hands for the time being and watch the Communists and their activities closely, and check all conversations so that there are no conspiracies anywhere . . . Elected representative of the Kronstadt area command, Yakovenko." Subsequently Yakovenko became the commissar of the Revolutionary Committee attached to the Defense Staff of Kronstadt, where he supervised cooperation between the engineers and officers.

But the numerous attempts of the Revolutionary Committee to control the anarchists and criminals were not successful; the latter even offered armed resistance, and disorder kept breaking out in the fortress. All sorts of scum, waving slogans about freedom, more and more openly embarked upon the road of self-government and total anarchy.

The power that had been grasped with such ease only a few days earlier now started drop by drop to seep through the fingers of the Revolutionary Committee.

A note with the ironic title "On Communist Foundations" in the *Izvestiya* of the Kronstadt Revolutionary Committee reported: "Since the temporarily arrested Communists do not need footwear now, these have been removed from them in the number of 280 pairs and sent to be distributed to the detachments of troops defending the approaches to Kronstadt. The Communists have instead been issued peasants' bast sandals. This is how it should be."

Actually, in place of their removed boots, the prisoners were promised torn-up greatcoats so that they could sew bast sandals for themselves from the coats, but in fact they didn't get any coats. It was a good thing that one of them had galoshes so that they could take turns moving over the stone floors of the prison in them.

Of the 26,687 men of the noncommissioned and political personnel on the Kronstadt base there were 1,650 members and candidate members of the Party, plus 600 more persons in the civilian Party organization of Kronstadt. These are, of course, large figures, but only a handful had been members before 1917 and more than half were a mass of peasants who had joined the Party in September of 1920, during the "Party week," before which, during that same month, 27.6 percent had been purged from the military Party organization in Kronstadt. The new Party rank-and-file began to talk with resentment about the "higher-ups" and "lower-downs" in the Party. In order to stop the talking, POBALT* issued an order on December 11, 1920, to all the heads of political departments to immediately carry out simultaneous replacement of 25 percent of the commissars, moving them "down" and replacing them with people from among the Party collectives. This was called a "shake-up" of the command structure.

The day before these events, the head of the Navy Political Section, Batis, telegraphed to the center: "Especial dissatisfaction within the navy does not exist. The influence of Right Social Revolutionaries and Mensheviks is negligible."

In the meantime, resignations from the Party and the decline of Party discipline reached their highest level in January and February. Instances were observed in which sailors refused to speak to the political instructors and had the same answer for all questions: "What business is it of yours?" and that was it for the conversation. The Party membership cards of the sailors who were leaving the Party were brought to the political department not by the responsible secretaries but by rank-and-file Party members in bundles; no one was summoned to the Party Commission, and the political department didn't even ask questions about the situation in the Party cells. The head of statistics barely had time to give daily summaries to POBALT. And what was altogether amazing was that on all applications to leave the Party had the same reason was given: "Because of religious convictions." Either grace had descended upon the naval base or the second coming of John of Kronstadt was directly observable from the battleships.

From the point of view of the contemporary development of progress and science, such an argument may appear as merely a naive trick that

*The Political Department of the Baltic Fleet.

could easily be seen through, but one need only look at the situation from a historical point of view for the picture to appear somewhat different.

The invented stories about the miracles performed by Father John Sergiev were so numerous and convincing that not only ignorant folk but also zealots of the faith were forced to recognize divine characteristics in the illustrious pastor, and Porfiriya Ivanovna Kiseleva, who had devoted herself body and soul to the glory of John and his followers, was exalted and honored as the Holy Mother of God. Despite the fact that after the death of John of Kronstadt in 1908 the Synod proclaimed that the teaching of John's followers was heresy and blasphemy, just remember how, even many years after both wars, members of his sect came to prostrate themselves at the basement window of the Scientific Land Improvement Institute, which was housed in the former John Sursky Convent, on Karpovka across from Textileworkers Street, formerly Charity Street; this is where a vault was built to hold the coffin of the Kronstadt miracle worker who had been especially revered by the family of Emperor Alexander III.

At first the meeting hit the Bolsheviks, and terror and repression began. Active participants and accomplices in the mutiny seized the members of the Special Section* and the Revolutionary tribunal.

One hundred and fifty men were thrown into the hold of the *Petropavlovsk*, sixty on the *Sevastopol*, and three hundred Party members were sent to the Kronstadt prison for interrogation.

The post-mutiny reregistration rolls of the Kronstadt organization of the Bolshevik Party showed that 135 persons had become involved in illegal activities and had carried out underground work. They were not able to break even those under interrogation. In one of the common cells the prisoners organized a prison newspaper which energetically explained the meaning of the events at Kronstadt. Despite the cruel threats and repressions, the Communists risked their lives to communicate with the deluded sailors, and later, already at the time of the assault, there were efforts to set up communications with the Party organization in the Seventh Army, which was advancing toward Kronstadt.

In response to the arrest of Communists in Kronstadt on March 5, the national newspaper *Izvestiya* reported the taking of hostages in Petrograd: adult family members of the generals and officers who had actively participated in the rebellion and other suspicious persons already under arrest.

On March 2, under cover of night, many active Party workers, led by

*A forerunner of the KGB in military units.

the commissar of the Kronstadt fortress, Comrade Gromov, as well as the entire Party School, consisting of one hundred men with rifles, machine guns, and ammunition, decided to leave the fortress. They left in an orderly manner, prepared to fight. Near the Second Artillery Division they saw drivers harnessing horses to drive off somewhere. A decision was made immediately: the machine guns and ammunition were loaded, and all 165 men left through the Citadel Gate and headed for Oranienbaum across the ice.

Incidentally, the mass shootings in Oranienbaum that the rebels would have liked and that they reported in their paper *Izvestiya* didn't take place. For example, in the First Navy Air Division, which had voted in favor of the Kronstadt Resolution, only 115 men were arrested—about half of the personnel; but only five of them, with the division commander Kolesov at their head, were executed in strict adherence to the sentence of the Revolutionary Tribunal, and 110 men soon returned to their unit and later even fought well in the Seventh Army, pounding the mutineers from the air.

The faltering Communists who remained in the fortress formed a "Provisional Bureau of the Kronstadt Communist Party Organization," which issued a declaration supporting the mutineers' Revolutionary Committee and all its measures.

The last to be thrown into prison for interrogation were the sailors from the tug *Tosno*, which was breaking the ice around the battleships. Both dreadnoughts were docked together, getting in each other's way when firing, and the sea wall in turn got in their way. But the vessels couldn't be pulled out onto the open roadstead; the tug broke the ice, but the ice broke its propellers, and when the main shaft of its engine broke, the Revolutionary Committee deemed this entire demonstration to be pure sabotage, and threw the sailors in prison. But the battleships remained idle.

In order not to lose face in the eyes of the country, and hoping for support, the mutineers explained by radio to the proletarians of all countries that they weren't commanded by White officers and that they weren't in communication with foreign powers. But after just a few days the "proletarians of all countries" could see how General Kozlovsky* was gaining more and more power, and the lack of reserve provisions in the

---

*General A. N. Kozlovsky was a former Tsarist general who was the military specialist in charge of artillery at the Kronstadt fortress. He would play a major role in the rebellion and, as the only former White general at Kronstadt, was useful for Bolshevik propaganda.

fortress compelled them to start negotiations with the Americans about possible deliveries. The American Red Cross depots in Finland had 3.6 million pounds of flour, tens of thousands of pounds of dried milk, fat, sugar, dried vegetables, and more than five thousand pounds of powdered eggs. Only Finland, treasuring her independence, refused major involvement, and about fourteen thousand pounds of food arrived on the island. Two days before the suppression of the mutiny the Kronstadt soldiers, sailors, and workers with top priorities received a quarter-pound of bread or a half-pound of rusks each, and one can of meat per every four men; instead of bread and rusks, the rest of the population received one pound of oats per day.

On March 7, after the last warning of the government had been rejected, the fort Krasnaya Gorka, just recently pacified by the guns of the *Petropavlovsk*, *Andrey Pervozvanny*, and the cruiser *Oleg*, opened fire on the mutineers.

The artillery barrage of Kronstadt was practically without consequences, since the firing was rather "general" in the absence of maps of the city and the forts, although such maps were available at the army headquarters.

The *Sevastopol* fired in reply.

As to who should open fire, this was decided more or less by itself; the exemplary state of the artillery magazine in the No. 2 turret of the First Artillery Division—that is, the main battery—was well known. The deafening reports broke windows in the buildings near the harbor, upsetting the residents and persuading them of the rightfulness of the cause and the invincibility of the fortress.

Igor Ivanovich was convinced that the opening of fire, the main work of a battleship, always began precisely in his section in the lower shell magazine. Therefore, after the announcement of battle alarm when everybody was running to battle stations to test the mechanisms, shouting in turn "Ready to fire" to the turret commander, Igor Ivanovich was always the last to give his report, not allowing even a second's pause that could cause a reproach for delay in reporting.

Those who have served in the army know the value of those details that seem negligible from the civilian point of view—like bell-bottoms that are just a little too tight or too wide, a pea jacket that is a little short or maybe longish, or the razor-sharp edge of a sailor's hat. In these expressions of one's personal will, initiative, and taste, strictly limited by regulations and the commander's eye, flickers the personality thirsting for its separate, special fate, unlike that of any other, after having become a number in a military unit, reduced to the common denominator through oath, regulation, and uniform. But what are mere pea jackets and sailors' hats? There are people who have won for themselves the right to have their own voice in military reports and who in time have become legendary in the regiments, batteries, and ships. Igor Ivanovich was already on his way to becoming a legend; he was almost permitted an intonation that wasn't quite according to regulation but was his own when giving his report on the state of the battle readiness of the ammunition store. From the azimuth gunlayer to the No. 1 gun crew (on ships the turret gun crew, on land the emplacement gun crew) they reported: "Ready to fire." Only Igor Ivanovich invariably reported—either over the communications system and heard by the whole turret, or on the telephone directly to the commander: "The shell magazines are ready *to open fire*." After firing or practice, the turret commander as a rule remarked to Dikshtein in a friendly way, in public, "You, Dikshtein, like to hold long conversations when reporting. What is that again—'to open fi-i-re.' That's a whole speech, you know." Igor Ivanovich smiled slightly and said smartly, "No excuse, sir." But if the next time he were to dare to report according to regulations "Ready to fire," he would certainly distress both his commander and the entire turret; these long speeches from the magazine were sort of the specialty of the No. 2 turret, its distinctive coloration, its signature, and even its talisman. Once while firing during an inspection by representatives from fleet headquarters, Igor Ivanovich reported the regulation way so as not to let down his superiors. And on that day the No. 2 turret performed worse than the rest; they misfired three times in a row, the galvanic circuit failed, the galvanic primers had to be replaced by percussion primers—in a word, it couldn't have been worse. And every last man in the turret was convinced that all this was because Igor Ivanovich's nonregulation rooster's crow hadn't been heard before the firing and for this reason no one gave the galvanizers and gun crew any trouble, or scolded or cursed at them; instead they were all cold to Igor Ivanovich for a week because they thought that he'd simply lost his nerve.

In reality, Igor Ivanovich's duty consisted of making sure that not a single shell under his supervision, either outwardly or in fact, differed from the ideal one which existed in the instructions and in the imagination of the ordnance authorities, and which had no distinctive marks and peculiarities such as nicks, scratches, or specks, either in the metal or in the paint. But nevertheless Igor Ivanovich could, as part of his job, not only separate and distinguish among shells of the same type but he even gave names to some of them, which, it's true, weren't notable for their variety: Piglet, Little Boar, Baby Hog, Porky, and so forth, a fact that he never admitted to anyone.

The path of the shell that Igor Ivanovich could see was short: grasped by a ratchet-wheel mechanism, it rocked for an instant in a metal claw, the hulking, half-ton thing—almost as big as a man—was placed on a cart to be brought by the feeder to the ammunition wagons, which were situated at the conveyor tube. Igor Ivanovich could not see the ammunition wagon, but he mentally followed the shell to the loading section and from there directly to the turret on the loading chute in front of the yawning breech of the gun.

When they were firing single salvos with only one gun and there was little work down below, as he heard the roar Igor Ivanovich allowed himself to be carried along the given angle of elevation with the shell toward its approximate, or precise, goal. With a full charge a shell of the main battery would remain in flight up to eighty seconds—that is, more than a minute—and during these long moments Igor Ivanovich could see in his mind's eye both the tiny scratches known only to him on the heated body of the projectile; and simultaneously, from the height of two hundred or three hundred meters (depending on the angle of elevation), he could survey the sea, shore, clouds, ground, all that the shell itself would see if it had eyes and the ability to admire its flight.

Now that the No. 2 turret was firing from all three guns, because it was impossible to fire from the No. 3 and No. 4 turrets, Igor Ivanovich didn't even have a second to make his aerial excursions, even though the way to Krasnaya Gorka was both short and familiar. Instead of soaring above the bay in his imagination, he was drenched in sweat in the lower artillery hold.

When darkness set in, both sides ceased firing.

On the night of the eighth, during a snowstorm, the forces of the Red Cadets attempted to attack the fortress from across the ice. Two battalions of the special forces regiment were even able to get into the city, chiefly thanks to stealth and surprise, but they were swept out by the insurgents, and the destructive canister fire from the forts prevented the reserves from approaching. Many cadets lay dead on the ice, and under the ice, and in the city.

Many attribute the failure of the first attempt to take the fortress by storm to insufficient political preparation of the attack, as if the cadets, with their rifles ready and carrying Lemon fragmentation grenades, were going to a political debate. The "debate" was preceded by two days of artillery preparation.

Trotsky, who had arrived in Petrograd at the beginning of the mutiny, impatiently demanded that they attack, convinced that the mutineers would "show the white flag" as soon as fire was opened on the fortress. On March 7 the Northern group of troops fired 2,435 shells on the fortress and forts, but even the additional 2,724 shells fired on March 8 failed to convince anyone. There were just a few six-inch shells—only 85—the rest were all three-inch ones . . . Aerial reconnaissance showed that the shells had landed short and it wasn't possible to see any destruction, either in the city or on the ships.

The artillery worked quite ineffectively in conditions of bad visibility, and merely disclosed the intentions of the command and in effect warned the mutineers of possible attack.

Of course, the political work couldn't be considered ideal, but why count on the morale and political constancy of the troops when the re-inforcements, which arrived the day before to that same 501st Rogozhsky Regiment, were completely untrained, and when immediately before the attack they had to be taught basic handling of the rifles and how to fire?

The command had a rather dim concept of the strength and weak-ness of the opposing side, and, for that matter, of their own army; in fact, besides the battalions of Red Cadets, ready to fight selflessly and to the death, there were unreliable regiments: for instance, the 561st of the 187th Brigade, consisting, almost to a man, of demoralized elements, captured Denikin* troops, and former Makhno** men. The tribunal of the Petro-grad military district had warned beforehand about the weak fighting ability of the regiment. And so it happened that at the beginning of the operation the Second Battalion refused to enter the attack. The Commu-nist element tried, of course, to convince the fighters, and somehow they succeeded in making them go out onto the ice of the Finnish Gulf. A wide sector of the attack was assigned to the regiment: the numbered batteries in the south, Fort Milyutin, and the strike on Kronstadt from the south. But communication between the battalions was practically nonexistent, so that the Third Battalion went in the direction of the No. 1 and No. 2 Southern batteries by itself. To ensure better control of the unreliable mass of soldiers, the battalion was led over the ice in a column, and only when they were shot at from the forts did they spread out in a chain. They

---

*General Denikin was a leader of the White Army during the Civil War.
**Nestor Makhno was a Ukrainian rebel leader who professed anarchy.

waited for the Second Company, lagging far behind, then they went to the left of the batteries to Fort Milyutin, where red flags waved to them. Forty paces from the fort they saw the machine guns the mutineers had put out, and heard the proposal to surrender. Everyone surrendered except the commissar of the battalion and four Red Army soldiers who decided to turn back, and on their way they forced back the Seventh Company, which was also on its way to surrender.

There were instances of refusing to enter the attack from among the cadet units as well.

In his account of the situation in the Northern battle sector, Commissar Uglanov reported the mood of disaster and hopelessness to the Petrograd District Committee as well as the fact that vacillation continued even on the morning of March 8—the day of the attack. Consequently, at first only the Communists and the more courageous of the non-Party comrades entered the attack.

The personal leadership and encouragement of the attackers by high-ranking Party workers and the most prominent military officers helped persuade the cadets to attack.

They occupied the No. 7 fort, the one nearest Lisy Nos, but were soon forced to leave it because of the loss of morale resulting from the concentration of twelve-inch artillery fire on the No. 7 fort from the other forts and the ships. The No. 7 fort was by this time disarmed, and there was no way to return the fire.

Uglanov reported honestly to Trotsky, Lashevich, and Avrov that it wasn't "feasible to rally the troops and attack the forts a second time."

If there was no order in the regiment of special forces, where two hours were wasted in composing inspired appeals—causing them to break the schedule for going out on the ice instead of efficiently carrying out the battle orders—then what could be expected from that Third United Battalion of the Twelfth Rifle Reserve Regiment, which had refused outright to attack on the night of March 7? Instead of carrying out the order amicably, the Red Army soldiers started to chant: "Give us food, bread, and overcoats!" It turned out that they hadn't gotten dinner on March 6 and had remained hungry the whole next day. Then the regimental commissar's assistant gave a firm promise to deliver some food by the morning of March 8. Exactly one-half of the soldiers had no overcoats. In the end, after prolonged discussion and much persuasion, the battalion went on the attack.

Food didn't arrive until March 9.

In Martyshkino the brigade school of the Junior Commanding Staff

(Ninety-third Rifle Brigades, Eleventh Division) didn't follow orders. When these cadets arrived at the battle zone of the Ninety-fifth Regiment and the commander appeared, the Red Army soldiers started to shout: "Why were we forced to come here?" The command "Attention!" did not pacify them. It was necessary to resort to punitive measures and to remove the most conspicuously disobedient Red Army men. Only after these measures and extensive Party educational work among the masses was the cadet school brought to order. And as early as the second offensive against Kronstadt, many Red soldiers fought heroically and received battle decorations.

The work of the Revolutionary Military Tribunals had a great educational influence on the Red Army soldiers. The tribunals reacted energetically to all unhealthy phenomena. They gave the malicious troublemakers and provocateurs what they deserved. The sentences quickly became known to the masses of the Red Army soldiers. The most important sentences were printed as leaflets. The political workers would gather the Red Army soldiers, read the sentences aloud, and analyze them on the spot, explaining that the tribunals divided the offenders into the malicious, the misled, and the just plain stupid. The Red Army soldiers usually approved of the punishments imposed by the tribunal.

When the women found out that wounded Red Army soldiers had been left on the ice after the first attack, they implored the Revolutionary Troika to give them a chance to remove the wounded from near the walls of Kronstadt. The continuous artillery fire didn't stop them . . .

The only "trophy" of the first assault was Vershinin, who was captured on the ice; he was a member of the Kronstadt Revolutionary Committee and a *Sevastopol* sailor from the draft of 1916.

The tragic fighting on March 8 was reported neither in the central press nor in the Petrograd newspapers; only on March 9 did the presidium of the Tenth Congress of the Russian Communist Party (Bolsheviks) consider it appropriate and necessary to give relevant explanations to the members of the congress. They learned of the real situation only from Trotsky, who arrived in Moscow on March 10.

"The partridges are biting back," joked the Kronstadt defenders, drunk with their own success. They had in mind Zinoviev's appeal as chairman of the Petrograd Committee for Defense, in which he promised to shoot all the Kronstadt rebels "like partridges."

Tired from his hard work Igor Ivanovich was in no hurry to rejoice and even avoided the gratitude of the Revolutionary Committee. He remembered well that at the end of 1919, when it seemed even to him that

Lenin had no chance of holding out, events suddenly reversed themselves completely. And now Igor Ivanovich adjusted his thoughts about the future of the incomprehensible, inexplicable, but completely real power of the Bolsheviks, which seemed to come from nowhere. But even though the Geisler fire control system of the guns can take into account the movement of the target during the trajectory of the projectile, the movement of the hull in the sea, the wind, and temperature, and therefore, also the density of the air at different elevations, and allows the exact prediction of the result, this adjustment for the inexplicable deprived Igor Ivanovich of any confidence whatsoever in the final results of his own remote calculations.

When the former battleship commander Vilken arrived on the *Sevastopol* from Finland (historians have proven that he was an English spy) and started to reward the lower ranks with silver rubles, like Suvorov after Izmail,* Igor Ivanovich didn't emerge from his hole under the turret, pleading the need to perform pressing tasks after the recent firing. He sent all the sailors up to the deck and stayed there alone, and, putting away the ammunition and arms supply journals, did nothing.

The personnel was lined up. Vilken walked around the formation and, at the tactful suggestions of the senior artillery officer and the company commanders, he shook hands with those who were to be rewarded and handed them a ruble. The scalp lock from the No. 3 boiler hadn't been proposed for a reward by anyone, since the power of the battleship had at that time been supplied only by the No. 1 and No. 4 boilers. But the scalp lock's dashing and bold look appealed to Vilken and he placed a heavy silver coin in the stoker's grimy hand.

To complete the picture let us note that at this very time Vasya Shaldo, recruited from the Petrograd Criminal Investigation Department, was hanging around the military harbor, after leaving the horse thieves of Petrograd to the mercy of fate, and was busy pinpointing the exact mooring places of the battleships. The *Sevastopol* was held fast by the stern to the pier at Ust-Rogatka, but the hull of the *Petropavlovsk* had been moved forward. Vasya estimated possible angles of bombardment.

Igor Ivanovich sat staring at the rivets, round as the caps of young mushrooms, supporting the storage racks; his internal gaze didn't encompass the events which had shaken Kotlin Island and the forts nearby, nor did it extend to Petrograd, but even within the confines of his own ship there were enough reasons for doubt and uncertainty.

---

*Aleksandr Suvorov (1729/30–1800) was a Russian military commander. In 1790 he stormed Izmail, a fort on the lower Danube.

The nature of these doubts could be explained by the fact that Igor Ivanovich constantly found similarities between the methods and means employed by the opposing sides. It was precisely in this spirit that events continued to develop up until the very last day.

The Bolsheviks and Communists remaining on the battleship after March 3 hadn't yet been completely deprived of their freedom of movement, unlike the arrested commissar of the ship, Comrade Turka, and they immediately decided to blow up the battleship. Through channels known only to himself, Igor Ivanovich had found out that the hold specialists Arkady Maidanov, Pavel Yanochkin, Ivan Osokin, and Andrei Turo were busily making preparations for this. They wanted to place blasting charges in his area of command as well, because they had reasonably decided that it would be easiest to destroy the battleship through the magazine of the main battery. Igor Ivanovich began to convince the comrades that it would really be better to scuttle the battleship by opening the Kingston valves after moving it out to deeper water, because if it exploded by the sea wall, then an enormous number of people would certainly suffer, and as an example he told them about the explosion of the battleship *Empress Maria* on the roadways outside Sevastopol. For example, it was practically impossible to calculate where the turret would fly and on whom it would fall, but it was certain that it would indeed fly a long distance. These arguments seemed suspicious to Maidanov—in fact Igor Ivanovich himself, with his obstinate lack of political feeling, seemed suspicious—and so the specialists from the hold set off in search of more trustworthy allies for their cause.

On the 17th, in the daytime, when the fortress was thundering, repulsing the second assault, the idea of blowing up the *Sevastopol* surfaced once again, but this time to prevent the Bolsheviks from getting it. Now the officers took charge of it. The mine officer Bylin-Kolosovsky also decided to place blasting charges in the model magazine of the No. 2 turret for the additional reason that, while the battleship was shaking from its firing on the attackers, many mechanical failures in the No. 2 turret suddenly cropped up: first the galvanic circuit went out, and as soon as it was repaired the rotating mechanism of the turret got stuck, then the thirty-horsepower motor of the azimuth layer burned out and it was necessary to use the combined strength of ten men to turn the turret at the speed of a tortoise, then something got stuck in the hoist—in a word, the shells were not brought up and hardly anything was fired.

The trouble in the artillery area on the day of the second attack was worse than ever. In the fifth, seventh, and ninth anti-mine platoons, one gun after the next went out of commission, naturally not without help from the gunner of the Tenth Regiment, Stepan Alexeev. During the second attack the crew in the hold was ordered to list seven degrees to be able to fire more effectively on Trotsky, who was approaching across the ice, but for some reason the seven degrees, already entered in the automatic control system, couldn't be achieved precisely; instead they got either more or less.

The senior artillery commander, Gaitsuk himself, together with the senior mechanic, Kozlov, dashed up to check the listing.

Everyone remembers that Gaitsuk came to a bad end.

After setting up his seven degrees and with his last words cursing at the hold specialists, he flew up to the bridge of the conning tower to his six-meter range finder to direct the fire. Which is where someone from the navy picked him off with a rifle (the bridge with the range-finder was open on all sides). The first shot hit him in the leg, which was like a warning, but in spite of his wound Gaitsuk didn't leave the bridge but continued to command, convinced that both his fate and that of Russia were being decided precisely where the *Sevastopol*'s shells were bursting. Nevertheless he was then killed by a second shot. The bullet hit him in the mouth.

Artillerist Mazurov took over the command. Hiding in the armored cocoon of the conning tower, leaving only the range finder operator and galvanizers on the bridge, he kept firing until evening, until 6 P.M., that is, until the fortress command became convinced that it wasn't possible to combat the attack with artillery alone but that they must arm the crews with rifles and lead the sailors out onto the ice.

Igor Ivanovich saw and heard, but mainly felt, that almost every command, almost every order and disposition, either wasn't carried out at all or was carried out somewhat ambiguously. Then there was the arrest of the battleship commissar, Turka. But what kind of arrest was it if no sooner than Commander Karpinsky had given the order to go ashore than Comrade Turka, who was under arrest, ran up to the top deck and explained to the command what to do and where to go, and along with the other agitators, detained the sailors on the ship and created a split among the crew? And by 10 P.M. Comrade Turka himself had already organized two detachments to defeat the rebels, occupy the city, and establish order.

The action of the second detachment under the command of Comrade Petrov was particularly successful. Turka, who remained on the ship, regularly received reports: they had been shot at by someone on the sea wall, they had managed to reach Lenin Prospect, they were under machine-gun fire near Engineers' Bridge, they had occupied the People's

House, where the Revolutionary Committee was located, and disarmed the guards consisting of workers and militia posted by the Revolutionary Committee. At 11:30 P.M. provisional power had already been established and a proclamation to this effect was issued.

To complete the description of the events it is necessary to go back in time to three and a half hours earlier on board the *Sevastopol*, where, for unknown reasons, a fire had broken out in the third furnace hold. The commissar, Comrade Turka, at once undertook decisive measures, the first of which was to set free the arrested senior mechanic, Kozlov, to direct the men in extinguishing the fire. The crewmen in the hold distinguished themselves by their energetic work and put out the fire, which didn't last more than half an hour.

Igor Ivanovich's education enabled him to discern the striking similarity between the events of the 9th of Thermidor, 1794, in Paris and the events of early March in Kronstadt. In the conspiracy against the Jacobins, as Igor Ivanovich recalled more or less clearly, both the right and the left joined forces. He forgot Collot d'Herbois but remembered Billaud-Varenne, both of whom, as we know, represented the Jacobins on the left; Danton's supporters from the right, the Girondists, Chaumette's supporters, and the Hébertists united with them, and it is worth noting that this whole motley coalition was supported by those without party affiliation— that is the *Marais*, the swamp. In the same way the Socialist Revolutionaries and the Mensheviks (right), the Constitutional Democrats (Kadets) and Maximalists (left), the Monarchists (extreme right), and the anarchists (extreme left) appeared in the role of non-affiliated participants in the Kronstadt events. The former had united in order to overturn the dictatorship of the Jacobins, and the latter in order to overthrow the dictatorship of the Communists.

On the day following the 9th of Thermidor, those to the right took the upper hand and started to liquidate the Revolution. Something similar also began at Kronstadt when it became clear that the Revolutionary Committee (left) would play the role of screen for and appendage to the Defense Headquarters (right).

However, there is no point in regretting that Igor Ivanovich didn't think of comparing these two events; the Thermidoreans were, after all, completely successful in suppressing the Jacobins, and their coalition turned out to be indestructible. And even an illusory faith in a victory by the mutineers might have taken Igor Ivanovich far, far away, first to Finland, and then even further.

The scalp-locked sailor from the No. 3 boiler room, who had twice listened to lectures by starving historians in the noncommissioned officers' ward room, might, in principle, have been able to draw a parallel if he had remembered the names of the parties or even their political orientation. But during both the first and the second lectures on the history of the Great French Revolution he was thinking more about the elegant simplicity of the guillotine. Being basically not a malicious man, he thought of how lucky Nicholas II and his family had been, since they were, after all, shot and not decapitated. He was amazed at the barbarity of the French when he heard that the invention of the tender-hearted Dr. Guillotin was even to this day performing medieval executions.

These brief details from the history of the staggering events during the French Revolution aren't offered here so that the reading public should recognize the author as an attentive reader of old journals. These digressions are necessary in order to explain why the battleship *Petropavlovsk* was renamed *Marat* after the March events. The renaming of the *Sevastopol* to the *Paris Commune* doesn't require any explanation, since the storming of the mutinous fortress took place, as everybody knows, during the fiftieth anniversary of the Paris Commune. According to the newspaper, the Kronstadt Revolutionary Committee refused to commemorate this bicentennial anniversary. The suppression of the mutiny occurred on March 18 precisely, and therefore it was reasonable and edifying to name the subjugated battleship the *Paris Commune* and nothing else.

But in reality, historical analogies illuminate little in the life around us; rather, they serve for the most part to entertain *beautiful young ladies thirsting for enlightenment* and bear witness not so much to the education of the historian as to his ability to look impressive. For simple mortals historical analogies are nothing more than a consolation, as if to say, well, we're not the first it's happened to . . . In order not to assume the entire responsibility for what has been said, I would like to quote that most objective idealist, Georg Wilhelm Friedrich Hegel, who could find something reasonable in literally everything. So, even he, after having studied all of history to the end, sadly turned the last page and wrote: "Experience and history teach us that peoples and governments have never learned anything from history and have not acted in accordance with the precepts which might have been derived from history." And this disturbing situation can be explained by the fact that if one so desires, one can always without difficulty find some kind of reason or circumstance which supposedly prevents people in present-day conditions from benefiting from an intelligent example or a good lesson from history.

Since the time when Joshua son of Nun stormed the proud towers of Jericho, which had stood immovable for ages beside the entrance to Canaan, it has been well known that only those weak in spirit rely on the strength of walls.

Since those biblical times it has been understood that an irregular army going into battle under the command of twelve sheiks from different tribes is just an unstable mass, subject to anarchistic moods, and does not represent a real military force in any way.

Both three thousand years ago and today only a regular army under the command of a single leader has a chance of victory; one can find countless examples in history of how the authority of an army leader became the source of strength uniting a nation.

Among those who were entrenched at Kronstadt there wasn't and couldn't have been a leader able to halt the sun in the sky, and darkness was the only armor capable of protecting the soldiers ready to walk across the unstable ice fields to attack the forts, to attack the inaccessible fortress.

However, an unprecedented attack on the naval fortress by infantry from the ice had also been undertaken by the Swedish general, Maidel, in January of 1705. They launched the attack in a freezing cold snowstorm but lost their way in the storm and weren't able to find their Rychert, Rissert, Retusari, or as it was called on German maps, Ketlingen; otherwise who knows how much more blood would have fertilized the ground on the uninhabited gloomy island named Kotlin.

The first admiral in the history of Russia, Fyodor Matveevich Apraksin, launched an attack from the ice with much greater success. For six days, also in the middle of March, he led a siege corps of thirteen thousand men across the ice from Kronstadt to Vyborg covering 130 kilometers, blockaded and took the fortress (magnificent for those times), thereby adding "with God's help" this strip to the marshy Izhorsk lands "of our forefathers and fathers," given away at one time by the feeble Mikhail Romanov* "in my name and that of my descendants," a very important border area . . .

But what sense is there in picking the bones of history if you can't

*Young Mikhail Romanov was named tsar in 1613. His descendants ruled until 1917.

find the answer to the simplest question there: why is it that a fantastic fate is given to certain people or, for example, certain towns, and not to others?

. . . March 16 and 17 were decisive for the fate of the mutineers.

The morning of the 16th was clear and sunny. The snow on the ground was getting soggy and was dissolving in the calm and sunny weather. The air had a spring fragrance, it was light, saturated with ozone, and it seemed that if you were to breathe deeply and hold your breath you could rise off the ground and almost hover without touching the snow with your feet.

In such weather it's impossible to believe that the boundless sky enveloping the earth is empty and dead, and to a religious man it seems quite possible that if your eyes were sharper and if you only knew where to look, you'd see the gates to the heavenly kingdom, the angels, and the apostle with the keys.

At the very edge of the sparkling white plain, hatched with the even lines of the forts set into the ice, Kotlin stood out, ghostly and unreal, with the steep domes of the Naval Cathedral, the factory smokestacks, the harbor cranes, the barracks, and the ships' masts.

Both the sky and the vast snow fields surrounding the forts and the fortress were clean and deserted.

The attack started from the sky.

The airplanes, clumsy and rattling, which had until now been harm-lessly dumping leaflets on Kotlin, started bombing the ships and the harbor on March 16.

The bombing raids on the fortress and the ships were mostly of a demonstrative character inasmuch as a bomb weighing less than a ton couldn't inflict noticeable harm on the besieged.

From overhead the nearest railroad stations, packed with troop trains, were clearly visible.

Oranienbaum, Old Peterhof, New Peterhof, Ligovo, and Martyshkino were filled with constantly arriving forces, equipment, and artillery.

Five armored trains and mobile armored detachments were waiting under cover, and they had already assumed their battle positions with the muzzles of their weapons pointing to the sea.

Regiments and battalions were occupying their starting positions. The narrow streets of Oranienbaum were crowded with columns of sol-diers moving in different directions; people were cursing at each other not at all as if they would have to go shoulder to shoulder toward death in a few hours.

They were readying and delivering the assault gear to the shore—to those places selected for the entrance of the troops onto the ice; they collected poles, boards, and wooden ladders for crossing cracks and open water.

There was no more room for the newly arriving troops to squeeze onto the narrow strip of shore; the Eighty-first Brigade arriving at Gatchina was prevented from disembarking and was soon turned back altogether and dispatched to the Lower Volga to put down mutinous bands there.

Just as the airplanes constantly circling above the ships and the island couldn't see the Lower Volga, they also couldn't see the faces of the soldiers, exhausted from chronic lack of food, nor could they see their tattered uniforms, nor their ruined, completely useless footwear. Also not visible from above was the fact that the soldiers, unable to remember the time when they had last received their full food rations, to their own surprise received two pounds of bread each with a hot meal and fat, and as a result of the confusion and commotion in moving from one station to the next, they contrived to receive their daily ration two or three times.

Twenty-five airplanes, defying the unorganized shooting, which splattered the smooth whitish-blue sky with buds of explosions, sprayed the ships and piers with their machine guns and dropped three hundred bombs. One fell right on the deck of the *Petropavlovsk*.

At two o'clock in the afternoon the artillery started roaring at the mutineers as though intoning a prayer for the dead.

Kronstadt struck back fiercely. It seemed that the entire island shook from each salvo of the battleships.

Toward evening it got warmer and the hollow, double rumble of three hundred gun barrels, which all day had shaken both sky and earth, gradually started to quiet down as though drowning in the fog that came floating in over the ice.

The ice was steaming and light whitish puffs of smoke were rising to the cool bright sky.

The fog was lying low and, from the command point on the south shore, the tops of the forts and the helmet-shaped dome of the Kronstadt Naval Cathedral could be seen, sticking out like islands in the unstable, sleepily swirling shroud.

The spacious premises prepared for receiving the wounded in the largest buildings on both shores of the gulf were still standing empty.

Institutions for children in the zone where the front was had been evacuated and the hospital at Razliv Station had been moved to underground premises.

The commander of the Western front, a man of firm character who had celebrated his twenty-eighth birthday exactly two months earlier, squinted with his left eye and examined through his brass spyglass the forts, the fortress, and the fires burning where shells had hit their targets. The spyglass had been given to him in 1919 after the capture of Omsk, as a gift from the Bolshevik astronomer Pavel Karlovich Shternberg, who had taught a course in astronomy at Moscow University. Now personally commanding the newly reformed Seventh Army and with all the armed forces in the Petrograd district and the Baltic Fleet under his command "in all respects," the commander of the Western front held in his hands all the strings of military action against the mutineers.

The army commander was indignant: they were shooting badly, the effectiveness of the firing was lower than all expectations, although the entire artillery was gathered into one concentrated force on the narrow strip of land between Martyshkino and Malaya Izhora. For six hours running, five heavy divisions and the sections E, S, and M from the special-purpose heavy artillery divisions of the main reserve, supported by one hundred medium-caliber guns, had fruitlessly hammered Kronstadt, spending half of the ammunition reserves available in the batteries (and the ammunition reserves were enormous). The fortress replied forcefully and accurately.

In Petrograd windows rattled.

Toward night the sky became overcast with high, fast-moving clouds, which in spite of the absence of wind, were flying in from somewhere beyond the edge of the sky, either in order to provide majestic but simple decorations or to conceal from the tender spring stars the bloody tragedy which was getting ready to be played out.

At midnight the infantry regiments began to descend on the ice which was eroding and groaning beneath their feet.

The rescue station was blazing like a luxurious bonfire. It had been lit by the well-aimed fire of the mutineers. The places indicated with markers where the 237th Minsk Regiment and the 235th Nevel Regiment of the famous Twenty-seventh Omsk Division were to go onto the ice were brightly lit by the high flames of the dry wood burning in a hot, crackling fire . . . Changing the decamouflaged zone was now impossible due to the congestion of troops and the just-completed redistribution of the Eightieth Brigade. Exactly at 4:15, fifteen minutes later than the time specified in the battle order, both regiments started to descend onto the ice.

The living, fluttering bristle of bayonets over the backs of the soldiers reflected the red flashes of the station burning down and seemed to be already stained with blood.

The ice exuded a tomblike cold and it was horrible to step on it with the water squishing under the snow, but there was no way of postponing it: on the twelfth, the day of St. Vasily "the Dripper," a spring storm had blown through, sprinkling the ice with the first light rain, and ahead was the day of St. Alexei "the Warm," when the ice would already be melting away.

They went onto the ice in columns, taking a risk both in regard to the enemy and in regard to the unreliable state of the ice. But since the command was uncertain of the mood of the soldiers, they had figured that a fighting man feels calmer in a column than in a line, and it is also easier to direct and maneuver a column than a line.

In the *Red Chronicles* it is written that "never in all the years of the Civil War was the Red Army soldier as well outfitted and as well fed as at the battle of Kronstadt." This is correct as far as food and clothing are concerned, but they weren't really successful in solving the problem of footgear. Some of the Red soldiers were marching on the wet ice and snow in swollen felt boots; there were even fighting men in bast shoes. On the other hand, each Red soldier had 100 to 150 rounds of ammunition this time, as opposed to the three or four clips of cartridges and a few fragmentation grenades they each had had at the time of the first attack.

One third of the delegates to the Tenth Congress of the Bolshevik Party, meeting in Moscow during these same days, left the session for Petrograd to take part in putting down the mutiny.

The wavering elements in the Kronstadt mutiny carried within their motley mass little certainty, clarity, or structure.

They were opposed by a comparatively small but monolithic and invincible organization. The staunchest and most inflexible fighters, the flower of the Party, its vanguard and leaders, secretaries of the Central Committee and the Central Control Committee, members of the Revolutionary War Committee, secretaries of the district committees, chairmen of the executive committees, commanders and commissars of divisions and regiments, journalists and writers all went down onto the ice on the Finnish Gulf as rank and file soldiers, having become the bearers of a united and inflexible will.

This extreme, unbelievable, and desperate measure could be understood by only those who realized the full danger of a petty bourgeois counterrevolution in a country where the proletariat constituted a minority.

The fate of the Revolution was being decided on the soft melting ice surrounding the smallish, low-lying island blocking the entrance to the shallow gulf.

Swallowed up in the darkness of night the columns went farther and farther out from the shore. The three hundred delegates to the Party Congress walked along with the ranks of the fighters, indistinguishable from them, inspiring decisiveness and firmness in the advancing army by their example of personal bravery and the spirit of self-sacrifice.

The bluish-white spokes of light passing through the high clouds by searchlights on the ships and in the fortress came down and searched over the icy surface of the gulf like the hands of a blind person, seeking victims for their as yet silent cannons and machine guns.

In the hushed fortress they were expecting an attack.

Behind the clouds the blindingly icy eye of the moon was sliding, moving against the wind; the thick impenetrable sky in the confusion of flying clouds was impassive and silent.

The leading ranks of the columns were crunching on the new ice formed on top of melted snow, and behind them the only noise was the chomping sound of hundreds of feet in the liquid, mushy snow.

Behind each column stretched telephone cables, not a single one of which would survive, nor would the telephone operators who were sent to locate the breaks and to reestablish contact.

The infantry fell on the ice, cut down by the dull beam of the searchlight, but it had hardly moved to the side before the fighters got up without a command and walked on in their soaked, white camouflage cloaks, which stuck to their legs, dissolving into the fog at a distance of six hundred paces.

It would have been possible to avoid falling in the wet snow, it would have been possible to avoid falling in the water that had oozed through to the top of the ice, if they had only known that the searchlights couldn't illuminate anything further away than two hundred to three hundred paces from the defenders of the fortress, because the blinding beam, shining blue like the steel of a good blade, struck the fog as if it were a solid wall.

It was only on the morning of the attack that the forces in fort No. 6 to the north and No. 2 to the south discovered the attackers practically beneath their walls.

Surviving witnesses would tell of the *profound impression* made by the rumble of the guns, the roar of the explosions, the piles of torn-up wet ice, the stones that fell from the sky after being ripped from the bottom of the shallow water by the exploding heavy shells; they would tell how their mouths went dry and their ears kept ringing for a long time from the searing whine of the lighter shells hitting the ice and ricocheting away in search of bloody victims . . .

The ice shuddered and broke, forming stretches of open water and ice holes.

The columns turned into lines, and nothing could hold back any longer the furious onslaught of the infantry soldiers who knew that if they survived at all it would only be there, on the island.

Neither the fortress walls, nor the barbed wire with electrical current, nor the land mines throwing the attackers up in the air along with the ice, nor the all-destructive fire of the twelve-inch guns, capable of shattering dreadnoughts and cities, could hold back the foot soldiers in their bloody cloaks and black faces, deaf from the crash of gunfire and rifle shots, as they walked with fixed bayonets right into hell.

At first only a few were wounded; after the ordnance explosions, they went down under the ice along with the living and the dead. The aerial bursts of the exploding "shimoza" shells struck them on the head and laid out those killed in almost perfect concentric circles. Encountering machine-gun fire, the troops began to suffer casualties—both killed and wounded.

At ten in the morning the fighting was rumbling throughout the harbor and streets of Kronstadt.

The enemy, chased into the stone casements, couldn't be reached; the majority of the hand grenades didn't explode; the artillery, confused because there weren't enough signal flares of the right colors, started to hit forts which had already been taken. The attackers quickly retreated with their losses, only to start all over again three hours later.

With a swift attack the Mints Regiment drove off the enemy and seized Fort Pavel. In spite of heavy machine-gun fire, especially on the right flank from the walls of Kabotazhny Harbor, the Nevel troops cut through the wire entanglements by the water's edge and, while suffering losses, seized the city ramparts, burst into the city, and engaged in protracted fighting on Citadel and Saidash streets. The Mints troops rushed along Alexandrov Street and Northern Boulevard . . .

By the time the number of killed and wounded in both regiments included ninety percent of the officers, control of the fighting was basically lost.

The wounded regiments began to retreat in their bloody cloaks.

What was left of the Brigade School was thrown in to close the right flank of the departing Nevel troops.

The school fought splendidly and was wiped out completely.

The retreating soldiers were met by horse sleds with provisions, ammunition, and empty sleds for the wounded; the horses were concealed in enormous covers sewn from army sheets with the indelible stamps of hospitals, clinics, and regimental storehouses on them. They appeared to be dressed up to participate in some kind of carnival.

They managed to gather together the survivors from the Nevel and Mints regiments who had reached the south shore; and they were formed into two incomplete battalions near the smoking ruins of the rescue station and transferred to the operative reserve of the Southern Group's commander. Three hours later, not yet recovered, not having had time to understand where they were, they were once again thrown into battle to save the broken United Division from being routed by pressure from the counterattacking mutineers pushing them toward the Petrograd Harbor.

The echo of artillery thunder rolled between the walls of the houses, and fires were blazing; the buildings, cleared of rebels, as if coming back to life, hit the attackers in the back with a dagger of machine-gun fire, and the surviving foot soldiers turned around once again to storm a broken-down house with gaping holes on all sides.

The situation of the units which had burst into the city was unstable. The commanders saw that the units were melting away due to loss of men, and could not attack successfully, let alone keep what they had taken.

The machine guns were of enormous service to the attackers, especially in the street fighting, and the same can be said about the machine guns of their opponents, which inflicted huge losses on the attackers. The mutineers had easily established positions on balconies which were convenient for enfilade fire on the streets. It was hard for the attackers to eliminate such firing points without field artillery. When he subsequently gave a theoretical interpretation of practical experience, the commander of the Seventh Army pointed, with reason, to the artillery and armored forces as the principal means for putting down mutinies in cities.

But here the street battles were still being run badly. The troops were dispersed into small groups, which in the absence of junior officers were practically on their own; such groups were easily destroyed. Scattered around the unfamiliar city, the Red Army soldiers grabbed their holsters whenever they caught sight of an officer: "Hey, Commander, command us!" The troops suffered great losses because of the muddle, the mix-up of the units, and, most importantly, the impossibility of establishing command. The casualties among the command officers exceeded fifty percent, in certain units they reached as high as ninety percent.

Under pressure from the counterattacking mutineers, units of the United Division started to stream back toward the Petrograd dock in disorder and it was here that the leader of the United Division, Comrade Dybenko, stumbled onto a platoon from the Fifth Company of students from the United Higher Military School of the Western Front; they were reserves and had arrived on orders of unknown origin. Each of the soldiers at once received orders to fight his way from the pier into the city and assume command of the groups of Red Army soldiers who had been left without commanding officers. After this lucky development the division chief himself went up to every soldier who looked like an officer and asked whether he was from the Military School . . .

Before telephone communication was broken off, command headquarters had ordered everyone to act energetically and to hold on to the occupied places no matter what, regardless of losses. There was no one who could reestablish contact, due to injuries; there were no telephone operators and any reserves had already been thrown onto the wobbly ice, which shook under the feet of the attackers.

Mutineers in automobiles were moving the units of sailors with machine guns who had mowed down the groups breaking into the city.

Remains of the debilitated units stretched toward the southern shore near Martyshkino and the Kronstadt colony.

By five in the afternoon the mutineers had pushed back the attackers from the city, but the latter held on to the fortifications in the harbors and nestled close to the edge of the ice.

The commander of the United Division, the main attacking force of the Southern Group, reported to the higher command his lack of confidence in success and raised the possibility of abandoning the city. The command immediately threw into the fire two regiments of the Seventy-ninth Brigade that had been gathered into incomplete battalions, and with battle order No. 541 they recalled the division commander, Comrade Dybenko, and the military commissar, Comrade Voroshilov, for rest in Oranienburg. It proved to be impossible to carry out this order since the division staff headquarters was located directly in the firing zone, nearly surrounded by a large organized group of mutineers. Comrade Voroshilov ran out from the staff headquarters and, in the thick of the whistling of bullets, he personally gathered up soldiers and organized the defense . . .

This was the hour of desperation and maximum application of force from both sides. And again—just as the prince's troops had come from behind Raven's Rock on Lake Peipus* and the Zasechny Regiment at the field of Kulikovo**—to the aid of the infantry that had been dislodged from the fortress across the ice came the cavalry from Martyshkino to slash and hack with their saber blades the sailors who were drunk with the specter of victory.

The strength of the attackers was exhausted. There was nobody who could take prisoners, occupy the battleships that had announced their surrender, and take over the schools of mines and machinery. There were no forces left even to pursue the fleeing mutineers.

At the end of the day on March 17, after finding out that their "leaders" had gone to Finland, the mutineers started giving themselves up.

By this time there were fewer victors than defeated on the island.

After the battleships had announced by radio that they were ready to lay down their arms, a painful, incomprehensible period began on board the *Sevastopol*, the time of the first and second watch from midnight until morning. In the city fighting was still rumbling, Fort Rif was resisting desperately—covering the escape of the "leaders" who had promised real freedom, real soviets, amnesty, demobilization, and regular rations; but the gray giants, the icebound dreadnoughts, seemed to be asleep, indifferent and abandoned.

Those who felt guilty set out for Finland; others, on the threshold of a new fate, took a bath and put on clean underwear if they had it, and some even tried to clean the deck, which hadn't been washed for ten days. It is striking that many, not only those who remained but even those who fled to Finland, regarded the entire event as personal, a family affair, a quarrel among relatives. Even the ringleader of the mutiny, Stepan Petrichenko, repented and returned to Soviet Russia in the mid-twenties after a short stay in Czechoslovakia.

The following morning at eleven, the cadets, worn out from the attack, started to climb the admiral's ladder at the stern boarding area,

*Peipus, the Estonian name for Lake Chud, where Alexander Nevsky battled in 1242.
**The Battle of Kulikovo took place in 1380 between Dmitri Donskoy and Mamai.

passing by the portholes of the commander's lounge on board the *Sevastopol*.

All the guards at the cabins with the arrested officers were replaced by cadets; the cadets posted guards at the conning tower, on the bridge, in the companionway, by the main engine, and at the shut and locked turrets of the main battery.

"What heroes!" the navy men said with a swagger, trying to retain their self-respect as they encountered the cadets.

"The heroes stayed on the ice and are lying by the forts." The victors were reserved and stern.

Pitiful, guilty, hungry, just yesterday intoxicated with the flattering epithets "pride and beauty of the Revolution" and "hope of freedom," but today called bell-bottoms, Georgie, or Navy-Ivan, the sailors tried to engage the cadets in conversation, but the latter hadn't recovered yet from the horror of the night's attack. They hadn't gotten over the death of their comrades and didn't have any idea which of their friends had survived and which hadn't, and they didn't feel like talking. It was strange to see soldiers' greatcoats on board a battleship, on the deck and by the gangways beside the sleepy and apathetic sailors, who were hanging around waiting for their fate, having suddenly become passengers on their own ship. If these same people as recently as two weeks ago, marching in straight columns on Revolution Square, had seemed like a monolithic, invincible force, then now they were like chaotically discarded parts of a machine which no longer existed; each part still continued its senseless spinning only from inertia, still continued to move inside the space defined by the armored hull of the ship.

Soon after lunch a transport unit of twenty scraggy peasant horses, harnessed to sleds, pulled up on the ice not far from the stern. They had been mobilized on orders of the rear staff commander of the Southern Group, Comrade Shtykgold. A commanding officer in a pointed cloth helmet and wearing felt boots with galoshes broke away from the Red Army men accompanying the transport unit. The officer ordered the guard by the stairway to summon a certain Raspopov. Raspopov came up from the depths of the ship rather quickly. The officer took ten steps toward the hull through the snow mashed down by the thaw, and shouted a request to Raspopov to let him have fifty or so men to work on the ice.

Right by the fourth turret they started to line up the first men they saw.

"Give me some artillery men! Let them look at their work!" shouted the officer, watching Raspopov's efforts.

Security men made out lists of those who were drawn up in formation, and the detachment went down on the ice.

In a column four men wide, accompanied by a convoy riding beside them on sleds, the sailors moved in a large arc toward the Petrograd Gate.

The heavy navy shoes soaked through after a hundred paces, and the sleds' runners left ruts behind them which quickly swelled with water. The horses were slipping and the whole train moved slowly. The sailors, stepping in the water, looked with envy at the sleds, each one with a driver and a soldier with a rifle, and continued to slosh through the loose, wet snow.

At first they walked around several enormous black ice holes; in the first hole the sailors saw a camouflage cloak turning around slowly with the sleeves sticking out—it had lost its owner and now seemed to be looking at him in the impenetrable darkness beneath the ice. Here and there lay the planks and wooden ladders with which the attackers had advanced over wide cracks and open stretches of water. In the ice holes broken ice floated, colored here and there with dark brown spots—hay from a sled that had gone down under the ice, bits of wreckage, trash . . .

In the snowy soup, trampled by a thousand feet, lay guns, clothes—greatcoats, some jackets, torn and bloody camouflage cloaks—then, more planks, newspapers, bandoliers, and machine-gun ammunition belts with unspent cartridges. Here and there you could see people calmly collecting and stacking arms in one place, but even with the arrival of the sailors and cart drivers on this enormous snowy expanse stretching from the barbed-wire entanglements by the shore to the forts which were hanging ghost-like in the unstable damp air, there were fewer living than dead.

North of the Petrograd Gate, just at the assault line of the Thirty-second Brigade of the Eleventh Division, the chief of the convoy gave orders to halt.

Without any preliminaries, the man in charge, who wore a Budyonny* cap, said, "Your assignment is to collect our comrades who have laid down their lives in the fight against the hydra of counterrevolution! Bring them over to the sleds—that is your assignment. The weapons of the fallen fighters aren't your assignment. Any man who takes a gun in his hand will be shot by the convoy without warning."

*A Budyonny cap was a woolen cap worn by the cavalry; it was named for the Civil War hero Semyon Budyonny.

When they began to fan out over the ice, one of the sailors saw a rifle under his feet and picked it up. Immediately a shot rang out. The sailor didn't even understand that it was aimed at him but had missed. He stood there holding by its sling a rifle with the bayonet knocked to the side from hitting the ice and looked without comprehension at the soldier who had shot at him. The latter cocked his gun and was about to shoot again, but hesitated.

"Throw it to hell! He'll shoot you!" shouted one of the prisoners.

The sailor spat emphatically and tossed the rifle to the side.

During the two attacks so many people had been killed that it was impossible to bury each in a separate grave. In the streets of Kronstadt alone five hundred corpses were picked up. In the fortress workshop axes and hammers were banging all day, putting together common coffins two meters wide.

The sailors divided into twos, since it wasn't feasible to pick up and drag the bodies alone.

Igor Ivanovich and the scalp-locked sailor from the No. 3 boiler didn't work as a team and didn't even notice each other; like everyone else, they just did their gloomy work silently, as if alone. Silence was the thing most suited to this work, even the convoy drivers spoke to each other in an undertone.

The snow and ice, just like brittle, weak paper, still preserved a record of the recent events.

Here is a man lying alone, holding in his outstretched hand a cap with the cotton plume torn off by a stray bullet.

And these were felled by a successful machine-gun blast, four of them cut down as by a scythe, but with one difference—one tried to crawl and did manage to crawl a little way, but the others died where they fell.

Here a well-aimed canister shot had come bashing down, and over there a mine had apparently broken through the ice and carried a few soldiers with it, since the edges of the five-meter-wide hole was so generously smeared with reddish brown.

Near the wire entanglements, which were almost at the edge of the shore, were the greatest number of dead: they lay not only in the snow but also on stakes, in the hammocks of barbed wire, on the rocks, and behind the rocks . . .

For those who were now floundering through the heavy wet snow, stacking on the sleds corpses frozen in the last movement of their life, unbending, swelling from each other—their only concern was to load as many as possible on each sled (there were only a few sleds and so many to be taken away). Only a few hours ago during the first and second watch, when the battleship was out of the battle and captured, these men had been hanging around the decks, languishing in the crew's quarters and on watch, incessantly and, for the most part, separately constructing a strong hold on their personal innocence or smallest possible guilt, in anticipation of the necessity of soon having to answer questions—not the howl of a hundred mouths but each one separately and for himself.

Never do people, not even the most dissimilar ones, seem so like one another as in that moment when they separate themselves from everybody, from the whole world, and become absorbed in their thoughts, in erecting in their imagination a fortress of their righteousness or well-being. Here all laws governing human destiny recede, losing their force and right, and only Charity, Justice, and Luck come forward together, helping each other. For the human soul is made like this: when hope doesn't find any support or help from anything anywhere, when the ultimate disaster, too terrible even to mention either aloud or to yourself, is approaching, depriving you of will and strength, then the soul's last resort remains faith in miracles. The price of miracles had fallen drastically on the public market, and therefore, each person was thinking of a miracle just for himself, as though afraid that there might not be enough of this rare grace for everyone.

Igor Ivanovich Dikshtein wasn't counting on a miracle and since he knew for certain that the mutinous crew wouldn't be left on the battleship, he had purposely dressed a little warmer, stuffed the most necessary things in his pockets and put on the sturdy boots which had been awaiting their moment.

After the work on the ice was finished, the officer in the pointed helmet started rushing around the higher command asking what to do with his men. The owners of the emaciated little horses, who had worked with all their might, staggering and slipping through the whole long March day until dark, were also complaining. Finally, the commanding officer succeeded in scheduling his men for interrogation out of order as it were, by tempting the higher-ups with the possibility of quickly sending this command off to the shore at Martyshkino, where the horses had been mobilized for transport duty. The commanding officer was concerned for his totally exhausted soldiers, thinking it was one thing to trudge in a convoy for ten kilometers on the ice along with the arrested men but another thing to ride beside them in the sleds.

Igor Ivanovich answered the questions clearly and without fuss: "I didn't leave my battle station because I could be of use to the Revolution there. Yes, the turret was firing. Only they hadn't removed the Radutovsky base fuse from the safety catch; they hadn't set it at the first or second delay. Therefore there was no damage at all from such firing. Who can confirm it? The entire turret." He said this confidently, knowing that he was throwing a life preserver to the entire turret.

The final question seemed strange. "Do you have any money? Show it!" He showed it. They quickly searched him, ordered him to pick up the money and—"Next."

It was the scalp lock's turn. When they heard that he was from the No. 3 boiler room they looked at each other and their first and last question was, "Do you have any money? Show it!" He showed it. Among the bills and coins glittered the heavy silver disk of Vilken's ruble. They took the ruble, and—"Next!" And no more questions, although the scalp-locked sailor had, like everyone else, as it happens, prepared a story which it would have been interesting to hear, namely that if it hadn't been for him . . . However, they wouldn't listen . . .

The sailors, who had gotten frozen during the day on the ice, had barely warmed up during the brief interrogation, when once more they were slopping through the soft snow accompanied by guards on sleds. It would have been shorter to go straight, to Oranienbaum, but they turned left to Martyshkino, evidently according to instructions.

They arrived in Martyshkino in the middle of the night. They were led to a tall wooden barn not far from the station and handed over to the local commandant or perhaps some sort of army command—actually no one cared about this for the moment. The barn was solid and dry with a plank floor, the walls, rafters, and floor were covered with flour frost—there had apparently been bran here, and possibly some kind of fodder, but now the premises were empty and retained only the dry, satisfying smell of flour. At first it seemed downright warm in there but that was only after being outside; after half an hour it was obvious that the temperature in the barn hardly differed from outside.

Those who still had some strength left took off their shoes and boots, squeezed out their footcloths, rubbed their frozen feet, cursing to warm themselves up. The pea jackets, damp from the day's work, had stiffened in the wind into a crust on the walk from Kronstadt and didn't give any warmth. The men lay down in the corners, along the walls, and beside each other, overcome with exhaustion, hunger, and cold.

Someone, invisible in the dark, announced loudly: "Mates, we mustn't sleep, no one will be able to straighten out in the morning, we will all freeze to death! If you go to sleep, it's curtains! Mates, hold out until morning . . . we've endured worse."

It was hard to imagine where this invisible man got his strength, his common sense, and his capacity to think for his mates. He walked around, chatted, swore, kicked those who had lain down on the floor . . . After lazily grumbling at him a bit, each man understood that if he did go to sleep he might not wake up, but for some reason it seemed to each man that this wouldn't happen to him.

Then he suddenly got an idea and started to sing: "The snowstorm was howling, the rain was roaring . . ." Those who understood what the singing was for, that it would help break the sleep of death, started to join in.

The guard pricked up his ears: singing in the middle of the night was suspicious. From the slanting roof of the barn the heavy layer of snow that had partially melted during the day came flying down with a rustling sound and hit the ground with a soft thud. At that moment a shot rang out: the guard had fired from fright. The singing stopped, the shot had awakened even those who were dozing.

The sentry came running, waving his Mauser, and five more cadets with rifles accompanied him.

The guard wasn't about to mention the snow, but said they had been singing.

"They should've sung earlier," mused the sentry, who left one more cadet as guard, had a cigarette, and left.

At about five in the morning light started to filter in through the cracks of the barn door.

The song leader who had quieted down was the first to awaken. Cursing softly, he started to shake the sleeping men. Those he was able to wake up recognized him as the commander of the fourth platoon, a member of the ship's Revolutionary Committee. He seemed to feel that he was in command here, too, and hadn't given up his responsibilities. There were two who didn't wake up, they had gone to sleep forever, having in their imagination warmed themselves with that last warmth which comes to a man who is freezing to death.

It was so cold in the barn that it seemed you'd get warmer if you went outside in the snow. The scalp lock sat hugging his knees with his hands stuck into his sleeves of his short pea jacket. Cold penetrated his entire body. Actually there didn't seem to be a body any longer, all that remained was a light suspension of frost in which everything was dissolved; he couldn't feel himself anymore, he couldn't remember anything, nor think, nor wait. All night and half the day he wavered between dream and reality, for a second or sometimes for several minutes sinking into oblivion, then again waking up from an icy burn. The pain in his feet had changed into a dull, nagging heaviness, he could no longer pull his hands apart, and only the sharp pain in his heart, as though a sharp piece of ice had fallen under his pea jacket and wouldn't melt, made him feel life in himself. As soon as the heart let go, he had no other sensation, and he slipped away somewhere as though there was nothing in him but frozen air. He didn't even know for sure whether he was lying, sitting, or suspended.

In the morning they had still tried to cause trouble; those who still had some strength left knocked on the door, demanding bread and tobacco, but now it had become quiet in the barn as though everyone in there had died.

Beyond the walls the life of the victors was bubbling. Singing the song "Ermak," a company of cadets marched by, sled runners crunched, drivers shouted, orders and laughter could be heard, people called to each other asking what had happened to their friends and chance acquaintances. From the station not far away you could hear steam whistles and the clanking of buffers when trains moved.

They started to call out names. People somehow straightened themselves up and dragged themselves toward the exit where a convoy was waiting.

When they called out the second group of five men, they called for a Semidenko or perhaps a Semirenko six times.

"He's asleep," said the song leader.

"Wake him up!" ordered the cadet from the door.

"Wake him up yourself. There he is," said the song leader, pointing.

The cadet left the rifle outside the door and walked into the barn. He went up to this Semirenko or Semidenko who was lying on the floor, grabbed him by the jacket, and tugged. He lifted from the floor a body which retained the shape of a curled-up sleeping man. He let go and the head hit the wooden floor with a soft thud. Then he grabbed the song leader by the shoulder and pushed him toward the door. He didn't resist.

At the end of the day they were given frozen bread and warm water. The food aroused hope that no more names would be called, and for half an hour the scalp-locked sailor felt as if he could see the light of freedom, but then he once again dissolved in frost.

In the morning the door opened and five names were called.

He could clearly hear his name, his last, first, and middle names. These words, these three words were pronounced, it seemed to him, louder than the rest, louder than last night's shot. He shuddered and made a movement as though to stand up. His body would not move. He once again strained to overcome this icy weightlessness, tried to make that incomprehensible mental effort thanks to which it is sometimes possible to break off a bad dream, wake up and turn over on the other side, punch the pillow and plunge into a new dream world. His last name sounded again and again. With his awakening consciousness he understood that this was the last thing that would be demanded of him and he even got frightened that he wouldn't be able to obey this last command; he pressed himself, his breath failed. The icy air was insurmountably solid. He once again tried to get up, he wanted to cry out for them to wait for him, but only moved his head with his mouth half-open under his frost-covered mustache.

"Aha," said the cadet by the entrance and walked into the barn without letting the rifle out of his hand, looked around, saw the good boots on Igor Ivanovich Dikshtein's feet, and pulled him toward the exit.

The rest of his life, those last hours which he was granted because of some unknown delay, Igor Ivanovich Dikshtein lived in an inconceivable, never before experienced, enormous, and feverish awareness of life. His consciousness, deprived of time to make his usual thorough deliberations, could simultaneously encompass what had happened, what he had seen, and what he had experienced. And all at once he came to the final conclusion, the final reality, that he would never again return to what had happened, to what he had experienced, and to what he had seen around him.

The man who had taken a liking to Igor Ivanovich's boots disappeared. They were led around from place to place for a long time, first joined up with someone, then again separated, were kept once more in some barn half filled with logs, and finally given over to new people, to a new guard . . .

The first thought, which at once forced Igor Ivanovich's consciousness to wake up and work at maximum effort as soon as the soldier's hand grabbed him by the shoulder, was—why? . . . how could they know? . . . who? . . . The answer came instantly, just as the receipt pops out of a National cash register when the cashier turns the handle and the machine answers with a cheerful ring.

The journal! The journal . . . The journal!!! He could see the journal of the turret section, the journal kept in ideal order, perhaps exemplary, not only for the brigade of battleships but also for the entire fleet, . . . the journal in which he, Igor Ivanovich Dikshtein himself, with his own hand, feeling that familiar sensation of satisfaction with a job well done, had for two entire weeks been writing his own sentence and had sealed it with his signature.

He at once dismissed the journal from his mind because he couldn't live stuck on something irreparable. But his life, over which he slid in a feverish mental glance, seemed a long series of fatal, irreparable mistakes . . . Everything had been a mistake—the fact that he hadn't gone over to the *Poltava*, that he hadn't let himself be arrested by those who were preparing to blow up the battleship. It also seemed to have been a mistake not to go to Finland as Kolosovsky had suggested. But the biggest mistake suddenly turned out to be his joining the navy and even his technical education, in consequence of which he had got the job with the ammunition. Whatever detail cropped up in his memory, it immediately acquired the aspect of a terrible and irreparable mistake. But worst of all was the realization that his whole life—all of it, as it turned out—had been given to Igor Ivanovich so that he could take just one step to the side, just one step, and none of *this* would have happened . . .

He walked along the icy road in the last group of the condemned, while around him the high spirits of the crowd of victors bubbled and boiled as they celebrated their success. The houses, the columns of soldiers, the trees in the park, Kronstadt, which briefly appeared on the horizon—he saw and perceived all this as something both familiar and alien: *there* everything went its course, there was no room *there* either for his presence or his participation. He walked like a man who was finally leaving a foreign city, a foreign planet where all was habitual, familiar to the tiniest detail, but senseless and alien. He had to leave, go back to himself, somewhere to the forgotten places that had been effaced from his memory but that he knew about . . . He tried to see, to remember this distant forgotten place, but the cold kept him from it. His body seemed to have become hard, rigid, impenetrable from the cold . . . The convoys at first ordered them to put their hands behind their backs, but later they didn't pay attention when the sailors, hunched over from cold and sadness, stuck their hands in the sleeves of the pea jackets and under their armpits.

Igor Ivanovich slipped. In a second he pulled out his hands which were stuck in his sleeves; by habit he grabbed with one hand his glasses that were about to fly off; the other he flapped in a funny way, trying to hold on to the damp spring air in order to remain standing on the earth that was slipping away from under his feet.

"Watch out, you'll break your glasses," one of the escorts walking beside him said with concern.

These were the last human words spoken directly to Igor Ivanovich in this world. He didn't reply.

The escorts fenced off Igor Ivanovich from all the rest of life with their rifles, the fixed bayonets pointing downwards, they separated him from the whole earth, from the enormous, bottomless blueness of the sky edged with gold near the cold sun, from life, united and moving according to rules and laws which hadn't been revealed to him. This incomprehensible life was now speeding away into its endless springs and winters, by itself now, without Igor Ivanovich.

. . . Three bullets entered the soft body of the mutinous noncommissioned officer together; one went through his arm, one lodged in his stomach, and only the third stopped the beating of his heart, which was trembling and thirsting for a miracle, thirsting for the impossible. Igor Ivanovich felt no pain and fell into the snow, already dead.

Properly speaking, Soviet power had no claims on Igor Ivanovich Dikshtein, and the scalp-locked sailor who had walked to the Arkhangelsk area in the spring was now riding in a train, amazing the summer passengers with the variety of blue pictures on his badly emaciated body; unfortunately the pictures didn't look their best—as if they were drawn on crumpled sheets of paper. He was going not to Petrograd, not to Anastasia Petrovna—Nastya—his still unwedded wife, but instead, to be on the safe side, to his mother in Moscow, where she had moved from Sergiev after the death of his father. She had sold the house and settled on Shabolovka Street and had been able to find a job nearby at Goznak, a factory where they made official government paper; at the time, this was considered to be a stroke of luck. Nastya was also sent for and she arrived with Valentina, who was born on one of the first days of July.

Nastya reasoned soberly: during the Revolution many people took new names, both first and last names. Now when the whole world around them was being renamed, when Tsarevokokshaisk, for instance, became Krasnokokshaisk, and Nevsky Prospect in Petrograd became October 25th Prospect, when they had abolished internal passports—that "rotten remnant of the police regime, an instrument for control and persecution," many citizens, even some in their Kolomenskaya district, had decided to begin a new life under a new sign. She mentioned numerous examples—four just from the agitation collective "The Red Kettle" at the city Department of Sanitation and Hygiene, where right up to Valentina's birth Nastya had been performing with her younger sister, pouring the boiling water of satire on dirt in all its forms and manifestations. Apropos, Sasha Smolyanchikov from the agit-collective had officially become Ferdinand Lasalle, Petka Govorukhin was too shy to call himself Trotsky directly and had modestly changed his name to Lev Bronstein. Konstantin Vedernikov kept his first name but thought up a unique last name, Klarazetkin, and it was all right; people were amazed for a couple of weeks but then got used to it. Therefore the appearance on Staropeterhof Lane of the previously unknown Igor Ivanovich Dikshtein couldn't attract the attention either of the authorities or of the few acquaintances and neighbors who knew about the on-again, off-again romance between Nastya and the sailor from the *Sevastopol.* But those who remembered the original name of Nastya's husband were given a very unoriginal and therefore quite convincing version: he had changed his name to immortalize the memory of the never-to-be-forgotten hero who had so early burned to death in the fire of the Revolution—without going into details.

During the long journey on foot to the Arkhangelsk area the scalp-locked sailor from the No. 3 boiler room became close friends with the former clerk from the Tenth Company of Torpedoes. The latter, in his turn, had sometimes pitched in for the clerk of the First Company, that is, of the main battery, and he retained in his memory valuable information which he shared for his and the others' benefit during the exhausting journey. For bread, tobacco, sugar, a dry corner in a leaky barn, and other important creature comforts, the clerk helped people—and not only from the *Sevastopol*—to prepare themselves for the serious discussions ahead at their destination.

The scalp lock learned the main thing: to answer all questions as briefly as possible, if possible with one word, and without details, emphasizing what everybody knows or what can be verified, and citing dead men as witnesses. From what little the clerk could remember about the first sergeant of ammunition for the No. 2 turret, they constructed a simple and beautiful life story: he descended from Russified Germans from Estonia, which was, incidentally, an amazingly correct guess. He was born and lived on the island of Ezel* (check this if you can: after the war Ezel was no longer part of Russia). His father was a businessman who traded

*The Estonian island Ezel is called Saaremaa in Estonian.

on the stock exchange; for political reasons he broke with his family and after the peace of Brest-Litovsk he stopped corresponding with them. The scalp-locked sailor had been to the turret of the main battery several times during emergencies when they received and unloaded ammunition, so there was no difficulty in establishing the basic points of "his" job.

During the three or four days' march to Kargopol they were able to get hold of some home-brewed vodka. After the "godfather" clerk had freely partaken of it, he saw himself surrounded by the honor and respect of his "godsons," he saw his fellow walkers' concern and love for him grow right before his eyes, and he became so brave that he foolishly started to brag: "I am already the godfather of about forty fellows, I might get a big reward from the authorities . . ." This joke was the end of him. Igor Ivanovich was inseparable from his savior, but once after a day's rest when he returned from the field kitchen with a small tidbit, he found his "godfather" with his head covered, already dead. The "godsons" who had suffocated him were there to watch how Igor Ivanovich would react.

Igor Ivanovich didn't refrain from rebuking them: "You can't take a joke," he said, looking over the "godsons," but after that he behaved correctly.

At the evening roll call they reported the clerk's passing away. The event wasn't unique, and the convoy didn't try to discern any particular meaning in it. All was noted down and buried according to proper procedures.

That most dangerous thing for which the stoker from the No. 3 boiler had prepared himself—the conversation at their destination—turned out to be simple and painless.

There were three interviewers. The one who sat in the middle and asked more questions than the others made a sinister impression. His head, as naked as a peeled hard-boiled egg, was unnaturally white and even looked soft; he had thick light brown eyebrows and an obviously dyed black brush of a mustache, in addition to a slitlike thin mouth with no lips and a gruff voice, all of which promised no good. The man sitting to his left was dressed as if on purpose in a civilian jacket and tried to indicate in every way that his participation in these conversations was almost accidental, since it didn't correspond to his rank, position, weight, and status. He was ironic and condescending, not so much with the changing interlocutors as with his own colleagues, stressing in this way their different status. To this end he directed his questions mostly to the one with the naked skull, addressing him familiarly: "What if he's lying?" "How you gonna check it?" "Hey, listen, let's go on to the next one. I'm hungry," and more of the same.

The third man was sweating over the minutes, and refrained from questions, since any question would inevitably increase the amount of writing.

The conversation was preceded by various formalities including photographing, during which process Igor Ivanovich Dikshtein obtained a new face. In a thin folder under the heading "Case No. . . . ." Igor Ivanovich's life was reproduced in the fictional version of the clerk from the Ninth Company in a most laconic account.

But the most fantastic feature of the events described above was the fact that after being separated from its original bearer, the name didn't transfer to its new owner as a revolutionary pseudonym but, on the contrary, pulled him away from himself, as it were. The combination of a new face with a new name resulted in features and characteristics of a new person who had nothing in common with either the stoker from the No. 3 boiler or the first sergeant in charge of ammunition for the No. 2 turret of the main battery.

Similar stories have happened since biblical times. After Saul took the name of Paul, he became, as we know, a strikingly different person; essentially, so do all monastics, hermits, lay brothers, and monks who abandon their former lives along with their former names.

For the scalp-locked sailor, originally it was only the thought of self-preservation that caused him to reflect on how he could conform to his new appellation; then he began to think more often about the previous owner of his name, and since the only person he could, without danger, discuss Igor Ivanovich with—the clerk of the Ninth Regiment—was no longer among the living, he had to be content with his own fantasies. His fellow prisoners in the barracks suddenly noticed that Igor Ivanovich, who had earlier been so willing to sing the malicious ditties and plaintive songs then especially popular among sailors, suddenly started to change his repertoire. He took up his mandolin less and less, and was seen more often taking guitar lessons from the warrant officer, Verbitsky. He became more demanding of himself and, most striking of all, he rebuked both noncommissioned and warrant officers several times for allowing themselves to go to seed in anticipation of their doom.

He easily refrained from habits which one might have thought had penetrated him as indelibly as the tattoo. For example, emptying his glass neatly, he used to let out three or four elaborate gasps so that his comrades could easily imagine how the invigorating flame dashed down, burning his insides in its search for its single predestined place. The scalp lock had learned this mannerism from the first sergeant of the No. 4 boiler, whom the men would go over to watch as he "partook." As early as the funeral feast for the "godfather," Igor Ivanovich had sensed that there was no point in trying to cheer up this company, and later he simply decided that there was no reason for a respectable person to make such a spectacle of himself. On the other hand, he would now sternly interrupt the man on mess duty: "Your tea, Barkalov, stinks like a dog." "You should have ordered coffee," the melancholy Barkalov retorted. Others remained silent or bit back without spite, but no one dared send him to the devil because they could sense in Igor Ivanovich an explosive force that was always ready to go off.

When Igor Ivanovich happened to hear his last name, or rather Dikshtein's last name, he responded almost instantly, as if afraid that someone might answer before he could.

You couldn't say that the scalp-locked sailor's sociable manner had changed completely. Just like any other person who plays the mandolin, guitar, accordion, or balalaika, he attracted people—generally speaking, there aren't that many wistful people in the world who play music for themselves alone. At the same time his behavior had become a little less open, not as noisy and cocky as before. He became sharp in his opinions, even categorical, and looked around guardedly.

During the first month after arriving he had a fair amount of leisure time and, firing up his imagination, he made himself into a petty officer and even tried to create for himself the mannerisms of the obstinate offspring of a stock-market entrepreneur from the island of Ezel. His ideas of the style and manners of such people were so vague that at times he felt like a man who had unexpectedly been informed that he was of noble descent, and he began to conform to his high rank to the best of his imagination.

However, at first Igor Ivanovich was convinced that he wouldn't continue playing this assumed role for long, that it was more like a game, like an interlude . . . He clearly remembered his own birth name, both first and last, and he knew that for him they would have the ring of a sentence. Not only did he expect exposure, he was even ready for it and understood that this game couldn't go on for too long . . .

But observing the audience of noncommissioned and warrant officers, all of whom were in this together, he came to an unexpected conclusion—one with which, I'm sure, psychologists and sociologists might have disagreed, if there had been any around at the time. On the way to their assigned place Igor Ivanovich observed how the signs by which people were distinguished on the ships and in Kronstadt forts were lost, how the importance of rank and duty was lost, although a short time earlier these things had given weight and strength to each man, and he decided that freedom makes people different and oppression makes them alike—whether oppression by fear, hunger, cold, or violence.

Once a warm ray of hope touched Igor Ivanovich's heart when he heard the news that all at once, noisily and conspicuously, the heads were rolling of those who directed the attack on Kronstadt—those who had led regiments and divisions, posted guns, and fired up the hearts of the half-shod and half-clothed soldiers. As he read in the newspapers about the fate of Putna, Dybenko, Tukhachevsky, Rukhimovich, Bubnov, Kuzmin,* and others, Igor Ivanovich suddenly started to feel again like the "pride and joy . . ."; his chest swelled and he was ready to tell everything that he had thought and heard about them earlier. It was just that the word "Kronstadt" for some reason never slipped out anywhere, and the wise Anastasia Petrovna who had already gotten used to the new Igor Ivanovich, restrained the impetuous stoker simply and easily: "Didn't they drag you around enough, do you want more?" Each time, for some reason, Igor Ivanovich remembered a head, soft and bare like a peeled hard-boiled egg, and he calmed down.

And the more relentlessly and ruthlessly the struggle went on against the counterrevolution which, as the years went by, took on the guise of anarchosyndicalism, or right opportunism, or leftism, or Trotskyism, or workers' opposition, or the trial unmasking the Industrial Party or the Shakhtinsk affair and the endless multitude of forms and shapes of saboteurs and wreckers, the more clearly the understanding grew in one's consciousness that the only way for a person to be spared, to survive, to save his family and friends, was to be exactly like Igor Ivanovich Dikshtein, against whom Soviet power had, as we know, no grievance.

Oh, Igor Ivanovich! If he had only suspected how much pain and difficulty he was adopting along with his new first name and patronymic and sonorous last name, he might never have accepted life itself with this weight eternally lying heavy on his heart.

*All executed during the show trials and purges of the officer corps in the late thirties.

Without intending to, he had acquired a role he had to play without interruption for his whole life—of a man he didn't actually even know. His imagination pictured him in different ways but only one thing remained constant—the unknown Igor Ivanovich was always—perhaps because he remembered those wire-framed glasses—smarter, more serious, noble, and honest than the scalp-locked stoker from No. 3 boiler room.

Experiencing sincere feelings of guilt before the trusting reader, I must admit that history most likely hasn't preserved all of the most interesting details of the long and laborious effort involved in recreating a true likeness of Igor Ivanovich Dikshtein. Long-suffering history has been burdened enough with inventions and fantasies.

Condemned to seeking all human strength within himself, the scalp lock created a saving image for himself on his own; but, of course, nothing elevates the soul like a talent for solitude.

. . . It is known that after just two or three years everyone sensed that an aversion to falsehood had become Igor Ivanovich's strongest passion. He had started to consider specifically this the most vile and unforgivable sin. Apparently sensing how truth suffered in this life and keeping in mind his own guilt before truth, Igor Ivanovich felt an unshakable loyalty to a new oath and he followed it unflinchingly—only the truth he had to deal with was minor and his heart, ready to serve honor, one could say was set on idle.

Igor Ivanovich's remark concerning the "nice frost" didn't go unnoticed and served as the impetus for a new wave of conversation in the line.

"You didn't forget your drawers, did you?" asked a nondescript man, looking all the time at the snow, the houses, and the road as though expecting to see something funny any minute. His question was so simple-minded that it would have been tactless to suspect him of indecency.

"I-I did put 'em o-on," drawled a woman on the steps indifferently, as if to suggest that when combating the cold, all measures were relative.

"It looks like the oven door will freeze stuck again!" And he looked around victoriously.

In the line people smiled politely.

"Oh, you just know everything!" the woman with three bottles said tongue-in-cheek.

"No one knows everything," the nondescript man said with the dignity of true modesty.

"It's damn freezing!"

"Ten below, they announced, and tonight it'll be minus twenty."

"During the Finnish War it was forty below—down to fifty-four below."

"No, it wasn't any fifty-four below."

"Yes, it was, on the gulf; I was there myself. We were just moving tanks over to Kokkola, then half of us ended up in the hospital, some for frozen noses, some for fingers, some for an ear, but mostly feet . . ."

"Here comes Anna Prokofievna!"

A woman was approaching the line. She was wearing felt boots and a frayed white garment like a camouflage cloak, with washed-out yellow spots. Naturally, she wore the cloak over a quilted jacket, and the quilted jacket, perhaps, over a coat, all of which gave her figure a monumental shape and inspired a certain authority.

"Are you last in line?" asked Anna Prokofievna. "Tell people not to get behind you. I don't have any money. Maybe there isn't even enough for you."

The first half of the line here noted the happy turn of fortune that had come their way.

"I don't accept jars," Anna Prokofievna tossed out as she walked up to the porch, more or less to the elderly owner of two large bags with crystal-clear jars sticking out of them.

"So where, then?"

"Hand them in wherever you want," said Anna Prokofievna firmly, and opened the door.

They started to console the sufferer, suggesting various addresses where maybe they took jars, or at least used to.

"Never mind, I have some bottles, too, under the jars!" cheerfully shouted the person who was standing firm against the blows of fate.

There was hardly anyone in the line who wasn't experiencing the warm joy of success. The sufferer because he had bottles, too, and the rest because they had managed to get in line before Anna Prokofievna's stern warning came. The right to return empty glass containers and receive either nine or twelve kopecks seems like a trifling one, but if you deprive someone of this right or make it complicated for him to use it, then at once a slight taste of bitterness and vexation is added to the joyful savoring of life. It's just that man is constructed in the very worst possible way: the happiness he gets when he manages to return his bottles easily is, like many other kinds of happiness—transitory. It doesn't leave an impression and doesn't light up even a single additional hour of his life; but mundane difficulties and burdens are capable of poisoning the entire day. And this continual blind game with fate engenders excitement in some, in others an enterprising effort worthy of admiration, and in still others a dull resignation and an unvoiced, unspoken resentment.

Sorting, counting, and placing the bottles in crates, Anna Prokofievna wasn't silent for a moment but was continuing a speech, the beginning of which the first person in line had heard and the end of which was obviously intended for those who would come after the renewal of her gold reserves, which were now running out, as she had frankly admitted.

"Vitka came home from school, he was kicked out of class. He said that they won't let him back in until his mother comes. What can one do?"

Money—clink—and the next customer.

"Wouldn't you go? You have to. After all, he's my kid . . . No, we can't accept Hungarian bottles . . . Like it or not, you have to go . . ."

Money—clink—and the next customer.

"He started sticking his drawing compass in the nose of a kid called Ivliev or something. Either during math or botany . . . My memory's gone, I don't remember. He and this Ivliev sit together, see. He must've really asked for it—to stick the compass up his nose! I think it's the teachers' own fault if the children aren't interested in their classes."

Each customer received his portion of Vitka's story: Vitka who suffered because he had no father, and because his mother was busy taking care of their home and working, and because he had mean teachers, bad friends, and was dumb himself.

"They call the parents to school, but they oughta be ashamed of themselves."

Igor Ivanovich waited for her to put the previous bottles into the crates.

"You should punish him," said Igor Ivanovich as he put up his oil bottles.

"Who asked you!" retorted Anna Prokofievna, staring suspiciously at the bottles.

Igor Ivanovich got tense and ready.

Coins clinked down on the table. While he was picking up the copper and silver coins, putting them in his pocket and walking out, he heard:

"Punish, punish . . . What kind of life does Vitka have with me? He has a lousy life with me."

Outside in the street Igor Ivanovich felt victorious.

Yes, say what you like, but if you could have found fault with the bottles, if it had been possible to find anything wrong with them, then Anka wouldn't have taken them, she definitely wouldn't have taken them.

This was fine work, no cause for complaint, no fault to find here, the bottles were washed just like they should be. No less important was still another reason for his sense of victory: the bottles which those impudent clouts had left, the "bombs" at seventeen kopecks, the ones the fast little guy had grabbed right out from under Igor Ivanovich's feet, Anka had not accepted. She had said, "I don't accept bombs . . ." Let him just run around. Igor Ivanovich even smiled, although his little smile was turned inward instead of outward. There you are!

Stepping firmly with his slightly warmed-up feet, Igor Ivanovich turned toward the grocery store; although it was possible to buy a half-pint closer to home, the grocery store was somehow nicer.

Those who have read the prominent French philosopher Charles Louis Montesquieu attentively would find it easy to notice certain characteristic traits which accompanied Igor Ivanovich through the major part of his life, which did not desert him even during the bottle expedition, as he stood in line in the frost, and possibly not even while striding toward the grocery store.

Let's agree that "man of honor" is a title—the highest badge of human virtue, which can be attained only if one is prepared to give up even life itself, not only its blessings.

Living something like a borrowed life which didn't wholly belong to him and being ready to return it under certain conditions, Igor Ivanovich was deprived of the main obstacle which prevents the majority from being men of honor, namely placing one's own rules higher than those prescribed him by the despotism of life.

The understandable feeling of guilt regarding the ammunition-store petty officer who had dissolved in the last frost of March forced Igor Ivanovich even unconsciously to observe the code of honor and to never lower himself to any actions which a noble scion of successful merchants from the island of Ezel wouldn't easily have condoned.

At the cashier's window in the grocery store there was a hitch. Having briskly ordered a small bottle of vodka and a pack of *Sever* cigarettes, Igor Ivanovich discovered that except for one ruble and twenty-four kopecks he didn't have any more coins at all in his pocket. Those thirty-seven kopecks which he had really counted on had probably been left behind in the kerosene jacket. He had to be firm with the cashier and instead get her to issue a chit for beer.

One way or the other it didn't work out.

They didn't have any Zhiguli beer and he only had enough for two bottles of Moskva. But it was too late to retreat, he couldn't very well march all the way home for those coins in the kerosene jacket . . .

This incident pretty much upset Igor Ivanovich. Since morning he had been living with the thought of how nice everything would be, and now he was already getting irritated both at this Moskva beer and at the pack of Sever cigarettes. The fact was that but for Nastya's order, which he could actually pretend not to have heard, he could have had three bottles after all. After all, he could have bought cigarettes separately in the little shop by the bathhouse, but he should have thought of this earlier, and when he was faced with the necessity of making a new decision right at the cashier's, he instinctively defended himself against everything he might have to hear if he asked the cashier for his money back.

He didn't feel like going home.

Once again all the petty misunderstandings, each of which in essence does not even deserve to be remembered, forced Igor Ivanovich to feel the border separating his life from the life he considered to be the real one.

In that other, real life everything resembled the strict clarity of a children's book—its correctness, simplicity, convenience, and above all the absence of numerous unexpected and ever-present annoying details.

That clear, simple life was somewhere nearby; sometimes he could even observe it.

At the bakery when he was thinking about buying an expensive loaf that he liked a lot instead of two French rolls and a loaf of plain bread, he heard somebody next to him, in the pastry department, say, "No, no, don't give me any *bouchées*, they're heavy. Two doughnuts, please, a couple of *baisers*, and two Alexanders, and you select the rest." This was a chapter from the kind of life where a person arrives at a railroad station half an hour before the train departs, goes to the ticket office and asks for a ticket: "First-class sleeper, please. If possible, the lower bunk. Thank you very much." Then, right in the compartment, he drinks strong hot tea with crackers or a couple of sandwiches bought from the hawkers, and goes to sleep on the fragrant crisp sheets, laid out by a smiling conductor. During the day he dines in the restaurant car, and at the station where he gets off, a porter in a white apron and cap carries his light suitcase and convenient traveling bag to a taxi. In all probability this fortunate first-class passenger would proceed to a hotel where he would immediately get a room with a bath, but even in his daydreams Igor Ivanovich would leave this pet of fortune at this point and would remain instead with the porters in white aprons, who in actual historical reality had thrashed Igor Ivanovich to within an inch of his life. They had beaten him to protect their jobs at all three stations—Moscow, Vitebsk, and Warsaw—where Igor Ivanovich had gone from Gatchina in the difficult years of 1949 and 1950 in order to make some extra money.

Rather quickly, after two, or at the most, three days, the porters recognized a competitor in this tall and very thin man who looked almost like an intellectual. Igor Ivanovich knew that they had the strength of the collective on their side and that his kind was doomed, so he changed stations, worked only for an evening or two, but this didn't help. The only thing he could do to protect himself from further insults was to avoid using the public toilets at the railroad stations where, as a rule, the porters would carry out their sentence on people like Igor Ivanovich. Each time they beat him, it happened outside. A couple of times they tried to take his money but, thank God, after two times in prison, he had learned to hide it on himself.

But it wasn't the reprisals performed by jealous professionals that were the most noteworthy of Dikshtein's railroad-station adventures. Rather often something almost worse happened—he would carry luggage, they would thank him . . . and pay nothing, and he was never able even once to ask for payment. The safest thing was to find clients at the streetcar stop. At first Igor Ivanovich picked out respectable people, older people who looked intelligent, women with kids. "Are you going to the train?" Igor Ivanovich would approach travelers who were getting off the streetcar. "Let me help you." "Are you going to the station, too? Oh, thank you." And taking him simply for a kind fellow traveler, they would be embarrassed to offer him money. After several such episodes Igor Ivanovich began to pick out simpler people; no misunderstandings usually occurred then. But nevertheless, Igor Ivanovich's respectable appearance sometimes gave people the wrong impression . . .

The outfit he wore for his railroad-station business caused Igor Ivanovich quite a bit of concern. Any of his shirts worn under his suit jacket might, to put it mildly, scare off clients, for they clashed with his image as an intellectual and carefree innocent traveler without luggage, so, therefore, when he went to the station, Igor Ivanovich wore a snowy-white knit scarf under his jacket which admirably hid the absence of a shirt. But to prevent this small defect in his wardrobe from being discovered, Igor Ivanovich had to be extra careful; it was hard to keep the heavy smooth material in place and avoid exposing the undershirt hidden beneath it, which, by the way, was always clean and had all its buttons.

It was at the stations that he saw how people left glasses with cognac still in them, and plates with half-eaten salmon sandwiches or even whole half-chickens—maybe it was a little tough. But even when he was ready to drop from hunger, even alone among these plates in the night buffet restaurant, he never permitted himself this final step.

Of the heaviest things which Igor Ivanovich had to carry, he was most afraid of suitcases full of meat. As a rule they looked rather small, more often than not ordinary wooden suitcases bound with rope for insurance, but they were as heavy as lead. Once when he picked up such a suitcase at the streetcar stop he instantly felt a sharp hook catch in his heart. He immediately got out a thick strap that he kept concealed, and threw the suitcase onto his back, forfeiting his respectable appearance, but the hook still stayed in his heart and under certain conditions and during awkward movements it would make itself felt, sometimes frequently, other times at long intervals.

Even suitcases full of books weren't as heavy as the meat deliveries going from well-supplied Leningrad to the unfed provinces.

And it must be said that Igor Ivanovich's aspirations to a better life, more suitable to his sonorous name, were almost unwittingly manifested in a pedantic attention to detail, in an ability to find a strict hierarchy of qualities in simple everyday circumstances, and he always preferred the best. So now, after considering the fact that he still had eleven kopecks, even more, left, he didn't immediately turn right after leaving the store— though he could see straight from the door that there was hardly any line at all outside the nearest beer stall—but set off instead in the direction of the market, to the Flatiron.

This haven for the thirsty was so cleverly named, not because of the fantasies of its patrons but rather because of the inscrutable progress of permanent architecture which had given the building an appearance the well-chosen word precisely described.

Say what you like, most people drink beer in a rather mindless way . . .

A German? What about a German? . . . Well, he sits keeping watch over his bottle all evening and rewards himself for his diligence and thoroughness with very small sips spaced out at such long intervals that you might think the meaning and pleasure of sitting with a bottle consisted of these intervals, this non-drinking. For a German, beer is either a means of killing time or a way of spending time. This was all alien to Igor Ivanovich.

Not being noted for greed or for love of luxury, Igor Ivanovich was able to transform beer drinking into a subtle and profound enjoyment.

Almost every one of us has in his life seen people drink beer, but far from every one has had the fortune to see a man who *knows how* to drink beer—those lucky enough to have known Igor Ivanovich personally can say unflinchingly that they did know such a man! . . .

Who else drank beer so beautifully! So cleverly! So lightly, openly, without embarrassment, hardly even noticing either the mug in his hand or the slowly diminishing life-giving drink . . .

Go and stand for an hour or two by a beer stand, look around, listen . . . It's the rare man who can maintain between himself and the beer that natural, unaffected distance which keeps the consumption of beer from becoming a commonplace quenching of thirst, or on the contrary, some kind of event; how many people constantly glance first down, then sideways into their mugs, contemplating the lowering level, and with such a grimace that it seems they aren't the person actually sipping but rather some old codger; and how many put aside the mug altogether or place it so that they barely touch it with their elbow and then fool around with some kind of papyrus-colored little fish, consisting for the most part of skin and desiccated fragile bones; while doing this they also manage to crane their necks and read something in a spread-out old newspaper, and only after they pick off some more or less substantial piece of fish remains do they hurry to wash it down with a sip of beer, as if they were taking medicine; and how many empty a mug in three swallows and then rush toward the little window, pushing aside their fellow citizens and asserting their right to a go-to-the-head-of-the-line happiness without showing any unusual honorary medals or a wounded veteran's certificate, but using the password understood by all: "Give me another!"

Not many have chanced to see how aristocrats drink beer, and there's no certainty that Igor Ivanovich had ever seen that kind of picture . . . How, then? How, dammit, did he develop this refined, casual, light manner of handling beer? Oh, there were times when fortune smiled on Igor Ivanovich with a generous face and without fearing the future he could allow himself to drink three or five or however many mugs of beer his heart desired. And wherever did he learn that beer isn't vodka and that one shouldn't get drunk on it, that one can allow oneself six mugs only during a serious conversation and not in just any company—with Shamil, for instance, a man of similar age and ideas, or perhaps with Yermolay Pavlovich, but with whom else would be hard to say.

The art of a man who knows how to drink beer is revealed in his first sip.

If he can bring the mug to his mouth, move his wide-open eyes about, and still have time to blink, too, I assure you he understands nothing about beer! . . . Take a look at Igor Ivanovich right now: after holding the mug at chin level for a suitable period of time, as though he had even forgotten about it, he lifts it to his lips with a quick, hardly noticeable movement, touching the brim like a clarinetist or expert bassoonist touches the reed before the intended sounds are extracted from the instrument raised to his lips, and then only after the instrument is finally ready ... Can the performance proceed now, do you think? No, one must, of course, also prepare oneself! Igor Ivanovich takes a tiny, the tiniest sip—this is like a gesture of acquaintance, a mutual greeting and exploration. And then the larynx, which had completely dried out while he stood in line, is rinsed, a cool and fresh sigh has filled his lungs, all senses have received the necessary information about the beverage's obvious quality and pungency, the instrument is ready, the player is ready, it can begin . . .

Igor Ivanovich drank down half the mug with his first swallow.

. . . It was like a first real kiss, deep and long: you lose your breath, your heart acquires a new rhythm, it turns the head, it makes the world around you slightly different than it was before, and it seems that everything is still to come, because after the first big swallow a new reckoning begins, the used-up page is turned over and a new, clean one is opened upon which there will be no blots and the marks will be entered according to a strict and meaningful system; the first swallow always washed all of life's minor vexations from Igor Ivanovich's soul, and perhaps the fact that he always had more than enough of them was the reason his swallow was so substantial.

With what a sweet weakness Igor Ivanovich lowered his hand with the half-empty mug, all the way down, as a duelist lowers his hand after a shot. Many who saw this gesture for the first time actually became afraid that Igor Ivanovich had decided to pour out the remaining half-mug on the ground, but it only looked that way. Igor Ivanovich didn't let the mug tilt. He looked at his neighbor, looked at his drinking partner, looked at the world with a soul filled with lightness and freedom, with a soul elevated by quenched desire, and his hand began to gain strength and slowly rose, coming to a stop at his chest, alongside his soul, if that really is located between the lungs and the diaphragm . . .

Denied his sip of beer, Igor Ivanovich's life would have been much dimmer, both in the sense of color and in the sense of the nuances of his mental condition.

During the last five or six years especially, one could see definite signs in Igor Ivanovich of fastidiousness, a strict meticulousness and even an ability to lose interest in an object instantly if it wasn't marked by some sign of superiority compared to other objects of its kind.

Specifically, Igor Ivanovich was a firm opponent of those who drink beer in winter, even if it has been warmed up, at a stall right on the street. He was convinced that only a lack of culture and a foolish hurry could force people to go to such extremes; at the Flatiron, even though there were no tables, at least there was in front of the counter a space of about forty-five square feet and an eight-inch shelf along the walls.

Nor can we pass over still another circumstance which confirms Igor Ivanovich's absolute aversion to lies. He was irritated by the hypocrisy of the sign "Beer—Soda Water" on the little street stalls where the only "water" available was for washing the mugs. By contrast, the Flatiron bore the enviably straightforward name "Beer—Beer."

The first person Igor Ivanovich noticed was Shamil—not counting two drivers in quilted jackets, which smelled of oil, who were washing down with beer some food set out on a newspaper.

On the narrow green shelf nailed along the wall and level with Shamil's chest stood a mug of beer which he had just started to drink. Shamil himself looked like a man who had forgotten about the mug next to him and was evidently deciding where to turn next. Still thinking about the main thing, Shamil slapped his pockets and found a pack of Zvezdochka cigarettes. Nina, who was pouring the beer and looking like she had dropped in just for a minute and was staying only because the patrons didn't have the tact to notice how bored she was with the whole thing—how right now she needed to be doing something else more important—shook her finger at Shamil.

Shamil suddenly remembered, nodded toward the sign "No smoking" and grinned guiltily. To show his repentance graphically he slapped his forehead and wanted to make some other grand gesture, but no one was looking at him any more.

There was a special rule about smoking in the Flatiron. Before four-thirty, before people showed up in the establishment directly from the day shift, Nina strictly saw that the stated rule was obeyed, but after four-thirty it was no longer Nina but the patrons themselves who watched the observance of etiquette regarding smoking. One had to smoke hiding the cigarette in one hand and carefully shooing away the smoke with the other hand, and although the tobacco smoke was hanging from floor to ceiling by seven-thirty, filling the entire premises like smooth thick batting, in different corners one could see men who were ritually waving their hands at head level.

Igor Ivanovich received his tiny little mug of beer and walked over to the wall farthest from Shamil.

"Are you carrying coals to Newcastle? A samovar to Tula?" shouted Shamil, nodding to the bottles of beer in Igor Ivanovich's net bag.

Igor Ivanovich, acting as though he had just noticed Shamil, smiled and walked over to him.

"I'm really in a hurry," said Igor Ivanovich. "It's one of those days. I thought I'd just swallow some beer on the run."

Shamil held out his hand, but Igor Ivanovich's hands were full. In one there was the net bag and in the other a mug, and there was nothing left to do but to make the gesture a surgeon makes as he is preparing for an operation—to stick out his elbow as a greeting. Shamil squeezed the elbow with his five fingers.

Although the two friends were probably about the same age, it had somehow come about that Igor Ivanovich was considered the older, perhaps simply because he stood three centimeters taller than Shamil's fur hat.

"I keep meaning to come and see you," said Shamil, "it's time to get a new fur hat."

This statement must be duly appreciated because Shamil after all was a genuine Tatar and in his mind he was of course dreaming of the traditional lambskin hat.

To a discernible degree Shamil's fur hat was Igor Ivanovich's pride. Five years ago Igor Ivanovich had constructed it from his own rabbits. When Igor Ivanovich had occasion to sell a rabbit or a skin, he always made sure to mention that they were especially good for fur hats and that he could provide the address of a man who had his fur hats sewn exclusively by him, Igor Ivanovich.

"I have one with a great big ear . . . I'm sure you'd like it. It doesn't even need to be dyed." Igor Ivanovich took a small swallow and in gratitude for the pleasant conversational start he added, "Only not today. I'm in a hurry. My nephew from Leningrad is coming. I just picked up some beer."

Knocking with his wooden leg, Mishka Bandaletov entered the Flat-iron. He was a real rascal, an old fox, capable of drinking a half-pint of vodka through one nostril for your amusement and, of course, at your expense. Understanding his special status in the town, he never recognized anyone first and never said hello to anyone first. And if the citizens of Gatchina themselves hadn't noticed and said hello to him, he could have lived that way, too, like a passenger who had arrived at an unfamiliar place for the first time. This guise of pride and dignity allowed him to address those very same people using words he might have read in some old book, or more likely had heard at the movies: "Don't let a noble man perish . . ." He didn't insist on friendship and didn't remind anyone of acquaintance, thereby showing a true nobility of soul, protecting his drinking partner from any demeaning equality, and therefore it was a rare day when Mishka wasn't already drunk by noon. Three knocks of his wooden leg on the floor, and Bandaletov stood before the drivers who were eating. Hearing the suggestion about saving a noble man, the drivers considered it best to curse at the supplicant, not from stinginess but out of a feeling of security and reluctance to participate in some kind of incomprehensible performance. Bandaletov bent his chin down sharply and the next second he jerked his head like an obedient aide-de-camp who had received clear orders for further action. He at once turned around and after carefully and deftly taking two steps, he stood before the friends. Bandaletov's noble soul would not disown acquaintance with Igor Ivanovich and Shamil.

"I wouldn't dare to interrupt the conversation of the smartest citizens of Gatchina," Mishka announced clearly.

Igor Ivanovich was glad that he still had seven kopecks left and he immediately tossed them into the outstretched palm. Shamil gave him eighteen kopecks. Thanking the donors with the same aide-de-camp bow, Mishka turned on his wooden axis and quit the Flatiron.

"Your nephew likes Moskva beer?" inquired Shamil, nodding in the direction of the net bag.

"What do you think? I wasted half the morning looking for it."

"That's good beer, I've drunk it. You and I have drunk it. On May Day they were selling it from a truck. They always sell expensive beer from trucks."

"Look what's happened to my hands." Igor Ivanovich put down the mug and held out a hand. "See, it won't stretch out all the way, only to here."

The fourth finger on the cracked and scratched brown clawlike fist did in fact assume an unusual position.

"You should try a calendula compress."

"I don't believe in homeopathy. Take offense if you like, but that's how it is . . ." Igor Ivanovich moved closer and announced confidentially, "It's the Buryats who thought it up, so it helps them."

Shamil thought about it, then remembering something, smiled, and said:

"Academician Pavlov wasn't a Buryat, I believe, but he was treated only by homeopaths."

"They did him in with their pills."

"It wasn't the pills—it was his wife . . ."

"His wife? But he buried her."

"By the way, science denies that Academician Pavlov believed in God."

"And where was your science when he was worshipping at Znamensky Church on Vosstanie Square? They didn't tear down Znamensky Church as long as Academician Pavlov was alive."

"I heard, on the radio, on the program "Atheists' Corner . . ."

"I don't need the radio when I myself . . . actually not me, but Nastya . . . her younger sister lived on Goncharnaya Street and used to go to Znamensky Church . . . So go listen to your radio . . ." His conviction that he was right prevented him from finding the right words.

"Marco Polo, the Venetian traveler, generally considered Russia to be a Chinese province . . . and called it Tataria. But that was a mistake! . . ."

"So there's no need to repeat nonsense . . . Marco Polo!"

"I only meant to say that great men make great mistakes."

"That's right. Because around each man there are lots of yes-men and they'll pick up any nonsense and repeat it! . . ."

Igor Ivanovich paused significantly and took a sip of his beer with pleasure, examining Shamil's face as though it were an inanimate object.

Except for a squeezed-in section near the temples, Shamil's face would have been completely round, and since the shape wasn't quite round, one was left with the impression of something incomplete or slightly irregular. For just this reason his eyebrows shot up one day and remained there, creating a look of surprise. This impression was strengthened by the narrow curve of his lips and the way his head leaned to the right, as if he were listening to some sounds coming from his right shoulder. The thin, hook-shaped nose on the almost flat surface of his face even looked somehow warlike, not exactly like a beak but something similar. Strictly speaking, Shamil's appearance could be considered arrogant, jeering, and aggressive but for the shadow of a smile which always seemed to hover around his face, randomly touching his eyes or his lips, the smile of a man who is always ready to admit defeat but with the kind of terms that would make a victor think it better to give up the victory.

"It's a disgrace, they're pouring nothing but foam," Igor Ivanovich lifted the mug to eye level.

"There's no beer without foam," said Shamil. "Here's a really strange thing: it turns out that the earth isn't explored at all."

"In what sense?"

"In a direct sense. Do you remember Rakiya? She's the daughter of

Ashraf, Hakim's first wife." Shamil unhurriedly sipped some beer. "Rakiya also has a daughter Nuriya. She's three years old. Makhuza collected some clothes—we had some shoes left from our kids, I took it all to Leningrad to give it to Rakiya. She lives on Kropotkin Street."

"Near the Evgeny Hospital?" specified Igor Ivanovich.

"It's Bakunin Street that's near the Evgeny, but this is Kropotkin near the Sytny market. I went there, she wasn't there, I had to wait two or three hours. You can't go to the movies with a big package. It was too cold for the zoo nearby. So I went to the planetarium. It was very interesting. See those eggs?" Shamil pointed to the stack of hard-boiled eggs in the showcase on the counter. "If you compare the earth with an egg, then it's the shell that has been more or less explored."

"But there's nothing more to explore. It's all melted slush there. Magma!"

Igor Ivanovich drained the last drops and firmly put down the mug. Without looking at his friend, Shamil poured some beer into the mug. Igor Ivanovich picked it up again.

"It turns out that they don't know yet where this magma is. If it's only where the yolk is or if it's also where the egg white is."

"Where the white is there's water and minerals, but where the yolk is, there's magma," said Igor Ivanovich with the certainty of an eyewitness.

"They say 'the road to a better life' . . . After some five or six billion years the solar system will turn into yet another uninhabited island in the universe . . ."

"Why an island?" asked Igor Ivanovich sternly without raising his eyes to look at Shamil.

"That's what the lecturer said, he meant something specific. There were questions afterward but no one asked about the island."

Igor Ivanovich was satisfied with the answer and nodded.

"Why am I bringing this up? If the sun sooner or later goes out, then how is it the 'road to a better life'?"

"You want life to stop?"

"That's impossible." Shamil smiled like a big boss who politely refuses some small request. "My thought is quite simple, I'm even embarrassed to tell you about it. If there's a beginning and end to everything, doesn't that mean that there must also be a middle?"

"Let's assume so," allowed Igor Ivanovich carefully, afraid that he was being led into a trap.

"So there is movement up and, whether we like it or not, down. That's how life is."

"I understand you." Igor Ivanovich regretted for a second that the drivers who were violently cursing the stupid management weren't listening to their conversation.

"If there's movement up, and then down, that means that this place, too, exists . . ." Shamil was describing flight and falling with his hand and his gesture could easily be understood. "We say, 'the top, the heights' . . . That's right, but is it worth striving for the top if the only road from there is down? I'm not against the top," Shamil clarified in an effort to keep the conversation in a loyal channel. "Don't think that I am against the top . . . I'm for the top."

"Do you see a way out?" Igor Ivanovich's voice was as stern as before, but an attentive ear could have definitely heard the flicker of a shadow of doubt.

"Just imagine—yes."

"What should be considered the top?"

"Exactly! I knew that you'd understand at once." Shamil burst out laughing happily, like third-graders laugh when they have solved an "impossible" problem. "What should be considered the top? For a tree it's one thing, for the sun it's another, but for humans? . . ."

"Are you talking about children?" asked Igor Ivanovich who, after thinking hard, had regained his confidence.

"No. Is human life meaningless just because you don't have children? And there's no top? Humans are not just about children . . . You can love your children very much, and still be a real bastard under the guise of loving your children . . ."

"So you believe that this isn't the top here?"

"That's just what I'm saying! We've known each other for twelve years. It's a long time. How far have you moved in twelve years as far as the top is concerned? You were a roofer? Or you moved twice—once to change apartments and once when the house was vacated for major repairs? So, is the conclusion that your life has no meaning? That's not how it is! That's not true. I don't know a single person in Gatchina who could say anything bad about you, and you know the sort of people here. I don't remember you ever offending anyone, and no one has seen your Anastasia Petrovna cry."

"And when Stalin died?" Igor Ivanovich reminded him.

"You've thrown me off the track with your Stalin. I'm losing the thread . . ." Shamil lifted his mug and looked at it as if he expected to see little fish in the transparent golden liquid. He saw none and took a sip. "Almost everybody cried then, and that has nothing to do with you.

To what heights should a man go if his conscience is clean, if he never did anything mean, didn't provoke people, didn't torture or insult anyone? . . ."

"And who says that?" Igor Ivanovich asked carefully.

Shamil again burst out laughing and looked with surprise at the unruffled Nina—why wasn't she laughing?

"You've never tortured anyone either," said Igor Ivanovich.

"Well, Makhuza doesn't think so," Shamil grinned bitterly, "but you've done good."

"To who?" said Igor Ivanovich with a start as though hearing about a lost purse. The word "good" in Russian has two meanings, and the very same letters can refer either to objects having exclusively material value—goods—which Igor Ivanovich couldn't deal with on his own—or to something positive in one's actions, which has no material equivalent.

"And Marseillaise?"

Igor Ivanovich admitted that this reminder was convincing, although his smile and nod clearly protested that only a small effort had been expended by the hero in performing this good deed.

Here the heroine of the narrative finally enters, the meeting with whom was promised long ago, the first one of the neighbors to become acquainted with Igor Ivanovich when he moved into the house at the corner of Chkalov and Socialist streets.

On that memorable evening Igor Ivanovich left the women to put things away in the chests and cabinets which had been moved to their proper places, and had gone outside for a smoke and to look around. He didn't hear Marseillaise Nikonovna approach from behind. Her voice, filled with that tormenting tenderness that had made more than one man's heart turn over, sang out confidently and passionately, "But how can anyone live with such short eyelashes?" Igor Ivanovich turned around at once and stopped, seeing before him a woman decidedly differing in every respect, as later became clear, from Yermolay Pavlovich's wife whom he also hadn't met yet. Marseillaise Nikonovna was embarrassed for some reason about her elegant name and instructed her friends to call her Mara or officially Margarita. And in fact, her eyelashes weren't anything like the whitish feathers of Yermolay Pavlovich's wife but were thick and long, and with a light shadow they tamed the fatal shine of her gray eyes; she had a thin tall figure with skinny legs with hardly any calves, but she possessed a bosom of magnificent splendor. No, we must stop, otherwise even a simple description of all the charms and accomplishments of Marseillaise

Nikonovna will carry us oh so far away. It's odd, but behind her back people always referred to Mara by her full beautiful name, with a certain inexplicable touch of irony even. Yermolay Pavlovich's wife, generally envious of Marseillaise Nikonovna's success among the male population of Leningrad and its suburbs, continuously reproached her for her unmarried state, and pointed out sarcastically that if she were to have her passport stamped* like all *proper* women, she would have to write out a document as thick as the Gatchina telephone directory. Her eternally unmarried state hadn't prevented Marseillaise Nikonovna from bearing a daughter before the war and the boy Lyonya during the war—in 1942. This woman who was so generous with love could never understand why all her desires and considerable efforts in the direction of Igor Ivanovich were in vain. Several times when they encountered each other rather closely during holidays, especially at spring and summer holidays in the open air, particularly on May Day and on Trinity, Marseillaise Nikonovna would come up to him with agonizingly inviting questions. On one such holiday at a time when the most blossoming time of her life had not yet passed, she ardently spoke directly in his ear, "Why, Go-o-osha, why? . . . Why is it that I bring people unhappiness? . . . It's so hard for me, Go-o-osha! . . ." In this way, looking within herself, listening to herself, and even seeing her listener only with the inner eye of her imagination, she would usually go to the edge of the precipice, and it was the rare man who didn't rush to rescue her . . . Then, as a rule, she'd start to punch her savior in the chest, but not for long. Although he was not sober because of the holiday, Igor Ivanovich said with sobering distinctness: "Just so there won't be any difficulties, Mara, call me Igor Ivanovich." This reply so impressed Marseillaise Nikonovna that she at once went around the cemetery—this was at Trinity—and started to tell everyone how Igor Ivanovich had answered her. She flitted from one group of drinkers to the next, until a new feeling and a new passion swept her off her feet and helped her forget herself.

One recalls that the Empress had rebuked the Gatchina residents for not knowing Greek and Latin. It is certainly permissible to ask, why twist your tongue with *similia similibus* when you could quickly and easily say "diamond cuts diamond." Exactly this method, well known both to those who speak Latin and to those who don't know any foreign languages, was resorted to by Marseillaise Nikonovna the next time.

Igor Ivanovich, of course, didn't know to what extent this unimportant incident, which had no witnesses, had elevated him in the eyes both

*That is, listing all her "husbands."

of the people who knew him well and of those who hardly knew him at all. It was precisely after this incident that Igor Ivanovich's presence or even a reference to him allowed Marseillaise Nikonovna to feel like a proper lady, protected if need be, and even in a certain sense inaccessible. But Shamil's words about doing good reminded Igor Ivanovich of an entirely different story.

This second incident, as we'll call it, was not even connected so much with Marseillaise Nikonovna as with her son Lyonik, and it raised respect for Igor Ivanovich even higher. The fact was that Lyonik, who had worked in the dye shop of the Gatchina furniture factory since he was sixteen, was a nervous fellow and often caused scenes with his mother, especially when in an intoxicated state. All the various pretexts for these violent scenes were reduced in the end to the strongest of accusations, the one most impossible to refute: "You got me from whoring with a German! . . ." To those observing such a scene for the first time he always explained, "I was born in 1942. Isn't that a fact? And I have no father, isn't that a fact?" Marseillaise Nikonovna cried and tried to make up to her ferocious son. Once when a periodic fight spilled out from No. 3 on the first floor directly into the courtyard, it spilled out with shrieks, noise, tears, harsh words in a loud voice, with the neighbors separating them and threatening to call the police. Igor Ivanovich who had just finished giving his rabbits fresh grass and changing their water as though nothing was going on, walked up to the hot-headed young fool and stood silently beside him. The fellow quieted down, the neighbors quieted down, too, and the tearful but still beautiful Marseillaise Nikonovna sniffed quietly and held on to the half-torn-off sleeve of her blouse.

"If you were a German," Igor Ivanovich said softly but yet so that everyone could hear it in the silence that had fallen, "you'd be smart—but you're a fool." Having said this, he went quietly to his apartment on the second floor.

The violent unmasker of his mother's moral, but mostly political, inconstancy wanted to say something sharp, but immediately realized that any continuation of the brawl would only confirm the accuracy of the strange neighbor's put-down, so he beat it to the apartment, and no one heard him ever make any more "German broadcasts," as they called it in the building.

"You bought the beer for dinner, or what?"

"I already told you, I'm expecting Nikolay, my nephew from Leningrad."

"It's nice here. It's nice in Gatchina, but nobody comes to see us. I call our relatives from Leningrad—Rakiya, Makhinur, Ganei, and Kerim—but nobody comes. Can anybody breathe the air in Leningrad? There's no air to breathe there."

"But the theaters . . ."

"Do you personally go to the theater much?"

"Not much. Very seldom. I don't like theaters because you have to dress, then undress. It's a waste of time."

Igor Ivanovich put his empty mug on the shelf and when Shamil made a move to pour some more, he covered the mug with his hand.

"The earth, you say." Igor Ivanovich started to button his coat and to bend back the fangs of his lapels. "At this point we ought to be interested in six feet of earth . . ."

"What are you saying? Now they don't dig that deep—you'll be lucky to get five feet."

"I like it in Gatchina. It's a nice place, dry . . . Is it true that Tatars are buried in a seated position?"

"Everyone is buried according to the law. Tatars too . . . Does our corpse belong to us, after all?"

Igor Ivanovich was in a hurry:

"Take care, Shamil. As they say, thanks for the company. I have to rush."

Shamil raised his mug with the rest of the beer in it.

The friends parted forever.

Since the relationship between Igor Ivanovich and Shamil will not be continued and will not be embellished by another word, gesture, or event, it's possible to sum them up definitively and make a conclusive characterization of this irreconcilable friendship of many years.

The word "irreconcilable" isn't used here to darken, to place in the shadow of history the great number of gestures of friendship and good will, sympathy and support, concern and attention to each other which had accompanied their friendship during all these twelve years. Perhaps both of them so appreciated the company of the other because in this exchange each one could confirm every time his very own rightness and his very own view of the things and objects in the surrounding world. All who had witnessed or participated in their arguments, discussions, or conversations—and that includes most of the people in Gatchina—were always amazed at the ease and unexpectedness with which either Shamil or Igor Ivanovich in the heat, at the very height of an irreconcilable conversation, suddenly agreed on some important point, but not the main point, and this very admission that the other was right was the pinnacle where their aspiring souls came together. The argument would seem to subside and both friends, finding themselves on the raft of friendship, suddenly stopped noticing the foaming unruly sea of irreconcilable contradictions around them. If among the observers of these moments there had been a witness to the meeting of the imperial personages on the raft at Tilsit,* who knows, perhaps this fortunate man might have been able to find similarities among people who are filled with magnanimity, nobility, and justice.

Igor Ivanovich went out on the low flat front steps and looked over the area. The two-story row of houses led his eyes to the end of the street where a 130-foot-high pile of red brick—the gigantic cathedral—stood alone, needed by no one. Among the houses large and small that lined the former market square—which had become yet another city wasteland—it towered much like a fortress, affirming through its appearance its non-participation in the bustling and sleepy life which flowed by.

Igor Ivanovich decisively set out in the direction of the courthouse.

As usual his glance touched on the Terek street clock, as big as a drum, which had for years testified with its drooping hands to the senselessness of keeping time in a place like Gatchina.

Igor Ivanovich's intention was to drop by the courthouse and find out more precisely when the case was scheduled to be heard and whether Nikolai had arrived, or whether the case had been postponed to another day, which could happen. This intention was quite well-motivated and promised to be a small but essentially necessary errand. But one would have to be very nearsighted not to notice that Igor Ivanovich simply couldn't deny himself the pleasure of entering a serious official institution on business and, moreover, completely without fear.

Igor Ivanovich's fate had been such that he hadn't had the slightest desire to get involved with a civil-service job.

The very word "service," which was so applicable to Nastya's work in the trade organization, or for Igor Ivanovich's sister's job in the book-keeping division, and generally for many jobs, didn't describe the many-faceted activities of Igor Ivanovich himself. Although one could, of course, perhaps say that the navy and the army—where he had served in the mobile bath and laundry detachment during the war because of his heart trouble—could be called service, but not in the absolute sense: it seemed

*A reference to the meeting between Alexander I and Napoleon in 1807.

to him that service could only be voluntary, chosen by oneself, that is civil service. After the war, in which he was wounded, he spent five years in camps in the Svirsk area for having been a German prisoner of war, which happened to all the laundry workers, owing to the regimental commander's forgetfulness—he hadn't warned the "louse-killers" deployed in the forest of the tactical change of position. So after the war he worked in Borisoglebsk in a sausage plant. But the name "service" would be too elevated for "that kitchen," as Igor Ivanovich called the plant, which featured emaciated frozen carcasses, bones, pus, and sausage almost liquid from an excess of starch. Nor would that name be suitable for his work in the carpentry workshop at the city trade office or at the oil depot, or at other piddling institutions like them. Service consisting of official activity did not resemble at all the roles which Igor Ivanovich had performed.

For instance, service implies a strict order, beginning with the need to show up punctually and to leave no earlier than prescribed. Even during the strictest of times, when you got time in prison for being late for work, Igor Ivanovich always had at his disposal some personal time, ranging from a few minutes to a few hours, which couldn't at all affect the progressive motion of the state mechanism as far as further development went.

Never during his whole life had Igor Ivanovich been in a position which might have permitted him to say, "There are many of you but only one of me . . ."; "I won't receive (give out, give permission, examine, listen) any more today"; "You see, there's someone here, let me finish, then come in"; "So what's this you are trying to give me?"; "You've come to the wrong place"—and the things like this he had heard all his life when he had to move in the *service spheres.* He could never feel himself as an element, or as they used to say then, cog, of that gigantic, highly complex, beautiful, and rational machine which embraced all of life in all its details, which is turned on at the same time (this is why people come to work on time), and is turned off at the same time, since there is no reason for some little cog to keep going if the entire machine is just resting and gathering strength for tomorrow's rotations.

And one more thing. In the civil service, as far as Igor Ivanovich knew, each person must prove himself, that is constantly prove to each and every one that he is worthy of his position and perhaps deserves a higher one. This is how the little cogs became wheels, the wheels became levers, the levers grew into driving belts, and these driving belts merged imperceptibly but very closely with the main flywheel . . .

But where Igor Ivanovich happened to work nobody expected or demanded any proof; just work and keep working.

When the time came for him to receive his pension there was real confusion. He collected almost all the essential documents with the greatest difficulty, and we have to consider that except for the documents about imprisonment and exile, all the others were really awfully difficult to collect; but it all proved to be futile, because in the end the social security office required a birth certificate or a legal copy from a church book, or at least some guarantee instead of them. And where Igor Ivanovich was born, what year, which month, in which books and in what language these corresponding entries appeared, this he himself couldn't guarantee, let alone find someone to certify it.

So that is how the dreams of a comfortable thirty-six rubles, which had kept Igor Ivanovich and Nastya warm during the last years before their retirement, collapsed completely and irrevocably.

And perhaps it was because he hadn't worked in the civil service that Igor Ivanovich retained a deferential respect for office mysteries, for paperwork, for everything involving work with ink, pencils, abacuses, and paper. Just observing that kind of work greatly impressed him and he saw only one way to express his respect and understanding of the complicated and important nature of the procedures he was observing—namely, by his desire to disturb and distract the people engaged in civil service jobs as little as possible.

The walls of the building to which Igor Ivanovich Dikshtein was headed were famous for being the site of the first experiment in commemorating contemporary history. This first try at using marble didn't turn out too successfully. In 1917 the Gatchina City Soviet was housed in this building, barely differing from other city structures which had been erected under the supervision of the architects Shperer, Kharlamov, or Dmitriev. In memory of this event a plaque was put up in 1927 and unveiled, accompanied by music and speeches. The plaque informed the citizens: "Ten years ago the first Gatchina City Soviet was located here . . ." In exactly one year what had been inscribed for eternity had become obsolete, and the question came up whether it would be necessary to renew the inscription every year or whether they should at once cover up the ill-starred "Ten years ago . . ."

After the war the People's Court was housed on the second floor of the building.

There are places which are indescribable. That's what people say, but it's hard to agree. It's another thing to say that there exist some places which are impossible to describe, and one could insist that the corridor in the Gatchina court house as it looked when Igor Ivanovich was there is one of those places.

The corridor is impossible to describe because of its utter untypicality, and rendering an account of it might easily lead one into historical error, since it can't be asserted definitely that this impossible place continues on to this day in its entirely impossible state.

Who knows, maybe it has become wider and a decisive hand may have rooted out its acrid infusion of tobacco and wet felt boots, fur jackets smelling of diesel oil, the sweetish smell of nursing breasts, the inescapable smell of the men's toilet, since the door had been torn off during certain memorable events and was at that time standing out in the corridor, leaning against the wall, so that it was still possible, if one desired, to use it to cover up the doorway.

Who knows, perhaps the Themis of Gatchina has already left these walls and moved into a separate building in a toned-down Corbusier style, a structure of glass and concrete, adding to the variety of architectural forms and styles in the little town.

But anyway, the two weak light bulbs could not fully reveal the entire spacious ugliness of the rather long corridor with its shallow recesses for stoves, nor could three little posters (about how to save drowning people, the collection of taxes, and about some holiday or other) cover it all. Most of the stoves were in the offices and in the two courtrooms. The firewood that had been dumped here rather carelessly didn't attract the visitors who were sitting on benches or simply standing along the walls. The logs were damp, but any interference in the heating process, even with the intention of somewhat decreasing the smoke which penetrated into the corridor, was met by the sternest and most jealous objections of the person whose job it was to see to the stoves.

To say that no laughter or mischievous children's voices were ever heard in this corridor would be as unjust as not mentioning that people often cried in this corridor.

Tears were seldom seen in the eyes of the people who had come here in groups or with companions or who had on the spot simply formed small parties of from two to twenty people. It was different for the individuals who had grabbed a comfortable corner of a bench with an unbroken armrest or by a stove ledge, forming rather cozy little nooks; here they could give themselves over to profound sorrow in privacy, accompanied as a rule by quick movements of the hand with a crumpled handkerchief by the women and loud noseblowings by the men.

There are places that are impossible to describe!

But what does all this dense, blatant shame matter in comparison with the disgrace and pain, hope and fear, filth and pride, in comparison with the anguish and faith in miracles, with the thirst for truth and fear of truth which people bring here, inaccessibly hidden within themselves and even more often from themselves, this whole muddle of life's thorny complications, which only yesterday had been your own private business but now suddenly are torn away from you, like a play you have written which is being leafed through by a yawning director who knows that he has to stage it anyway . . . a piece of your life fallen into the hands of a lazy, untalented cast.

Why is this fellow with the head of a new recruit standing behind the low barrier, trying to make out something over there beyond the window when he can't hear anything, and only the peculiar pallor on his cheeks gives away the fact that he is involved in the sentencing?

The simple and pitiless truth, pronounced by the prosecutor, can't be diminished even by his inarticulateness, inconsistencies, and incorrect stress on words of foreign origin.

Why doesn't this broken-hearted mother hear the words of the sentence? Why is she thinking that everyone is looking at her accusingly because she at the last moment decided not to sell the television and give the lawyer more?

And only a slight, disinterested, self-ennobling sympathy fills the souls of those who have crowded into the room, hoping to make the time seem shorter until their own case comes up.

Without any trouble, Igor Ivanovich found Nikolay in the corridor and noisily greeted and kissed his nephew.

Nikolay was barely taller than Igor Ivanovich, and his warm Chinese coat with a belt and a mouton collar made his figure more solid. The open newspaper in his widespread hands gave him the appearance of an independent man who didn't expect troubles from fate; he looked more like a witness than anything else . . . And actually he was a witness to how in Leningrad, on Borovaya Street not far from Obvodny, a drunken driver from Gatchina had started before the green light changed and run over a woman who was running across the street.

The nephew was looking through the open newspaper and in a rather coarse and playful masculine way salted his speech with such expressions as "slowdowns," "the devil knows why I did it," "they don't know what the hell they want." In Igor Ivanovich's opinion he looked splendid. Sitting down beside him on the bench, he also loudly, but with some restraint, cursed the procedures, the officials' inability to consider people's time, and all the annoyances, and he sincerely stressed the fact that this case was extremely clear-cut and it was simply ludicrous to fool with it for two months, remembering subconsciously that twice in his life his "cases," while much more complicated, had been resolved quickly and without any long, drawn-out proceedings.

The people in the corridor quieted down and started to look at the vociferous Igor Ivanovich and his strap companion in the Chinese coat.

Igor Ivanovich even got a little excited. He was ready to go somewhere, tell somebody something if necessary, and point out and mention . . . But his nephew stopped him, remarking condescendingly and wisely that the officials cannot be rushed, that if they did piecework, then it would get moving, and he gave out a laugh . . . A crazy thought suddenly flashed through Igor Ivanovich's mind; perhaps they were getting paid by the piece *back then*?

"Don't wait here, Uncle Gosha . . . Why sit here and stew? As soon as I'm done I'll come over to your house."

"Don't even think of eating anywhere! We're expecting you for dinner. How do you like Moskva?" Igor Ivanovich held up the net bag with two fingers. The nephew expressed as much delight as if he had seen Mongolian vodka.

"We won't start without you, you hear!"

On this note they parted.

Life had directed its not inconsiderable efforts toward suppressing the feelings, wishes and needs of Igor Ivanovich since his youth, but this had not only failed to blunt his lust for life but had, on the contrary, sharpened it to such an extent that Igor Ivanovich could no longer allow himself to neglect even the slightest chance of gratification, and he tried to experience every such possibility to the fullest, expending his energy without concern. Therefore, instead of choosing the shortest way home, he took a roundabout way—past the cathedral.

Turning homeward Igor Ivanovich again began to contemplate that very skillful creation, as common as could be, actually—namely, the famous Gatchina Cathedral of the Intercession—the whimsical translation of the Christian spirit into stone, which in appearance was a blend of church and barracks. No, this isn't the fruit of an artist's love, the kind of fruit which has, beyond the drawings and specifications, the secret aspiration of the artist to unite heaven and earth, to help the heart behold the light and harmony concealed in the inscrutable and the eternal.

The boarded-up windows and solidly shut doors imparted to the cathedral the appearance of a top security prison where, as everybody knows, the windows are not only traditionally covered with bars but also with those metal "muzzles," like gaping pockets, which let daylight in only from above.

Igor Ivanovich sometimes caught himself thinking, as he walked by the cathedral, that he was listening for something. His hearing really did get more acute by itself, not because Igor Ivanovich was hoping to discern a mysterious call, unheard by others, but because he simply couldn't believe that such an enormous building, with mighty walls and solid locks, didn't contain a single living soul. Perhaps it was that ancient instinct throbbing in his soul which doesn't let man accept uninhabited mountains, empty forests, the ocean depths, or even the transparent empty sky, but insists on populating that world beyond human eyes with mysterious creatures and spirits, both good and evil—the capricious rulers of human destinies.

But there was no soul in this brick bastion meant to be the habitation of the spirit. Since 1904, when the cathedral was founded and the construction began, Gatchina had lived in proud expectation, hope, and confidence, as if through the tall doors of the new temple everyone would enter a renewed life, cleansed of moral filth and even of poverty. They couldn't believe that so much labor, effort, and money wouldn't add goodness and grace to life. The brickwork was excellent (now they don't even lay tile that well). They took their time building—working for ten years. But before they had finished the exterior, they threw all their efforts into finishing the interior, and consecrated the cathedral hurriedly as though foreseeing its short lifespan, and opened it to the parishioners in October of 1914. The war had started and they couldn't possibly count on a speedy completion of all the work.

The tent-shaped belfry soared upward at a height of 160 feet, placed on the top like a small chapel, and at 130 feet the helmetlike cupolas bubbled out in the canonical five-headed cluster.

And why did the Vokhonovsky Convent, nestling with its poor daughter church at the foot of the gigantic cathedral, need to raise such a temple when the buildings of the convent remained unplastered until its closing at the beginning of the thirties?

Born at the wrong time, the cathedral started to crumble after less than thirty years, as if it had been raised just for the purpose of amazing— either by the foolhardy conceit or by the limitless credulity of human beings, or perhaps just to become yet another example of the transitory nature of a body abandoned by its soul.

So it had stood there for almost fifty years—dead to heaven, dead to earth, and dead to hope.

Just last year Igor Ivanovich was amazed to see workers attached to security ropes near the lopsided cupolas of which only the metal structures survived, making them look like huge cages for huge birds. But when only two of the four cupolas remained on their small drums everything was explained: the condition of the two others was considered dangerous, and they had only enough energy and means to guard against unnecessary misfortune.

Igor Ivanovich is no longer here and no one can say why he was attracted to this gloomy red-brick colossus with cupolas broken right through, the steep inaccessible walls, the silenced bells in a belfry open to the winds.

Perhaps this most imposing edifice of the municipality of Gatchina, standing among the squat, two-story, ugly little houses, reminded you of the gigantic battleship which had made even the large naval harbor in Ust-Rogatka seem small? . . .

And perhaps in a moment of spiritual weakness when you wanted a reasonable and just God to exist in this world, you would locate him right here, within the empty and cold walls, protecting his sorrowful wisdom from pagan fuss and incomprehensible verbosity, from flattery and cajoling in the unsteady candlelight and the glimmering gilt of the rich icon settings, from priestly importance and the competition of people in humble self-disparagement? . . .

Perhaps the wide flooring put together from sturdy planks, covering the roomy staircase at the main entrance, reminded you of one of those tiny Kronstadt piers where steam-powered cutters were moored, taking sailors on shore leave to flap their bell-bottoms all over the sidewalks of Petersburg and Gatchina, Strelnya and Oranienbaum (Rambov for short)? This flooring was constructed to make it easy to roll barrels into the cathedral and drag crates and bags into the city trade warehouse, which had long since occupied the vacant premises.

All that's left is to conjecture that the cathedral exerted an attraction because of its fantastic combination of mundane features and details, reminding Igor Ivanovich each time of quite different aspects of his life, which had flashed by so quickly: the fortress, the battleship, the dungeon, the storage room, and the convent which in its day had gone unnoticed by the sailors, and the pulled-down cupolas which had until recently risen above the people. One can only console oneself with the fact that Igor Ivanovich himself was a rather fantastic man, and so you can rack your brains all you want, but you will never guess what exactly attracted him to this gloomy edifice which had grown old without ever having started to live.

Oh, Igor Ivanovich, Igor Ivanovich, my abyss . . . my still waters! . . . No one will count the tears which life squeezed out of you, and who will hear the words which you didn't speak? . . . Birth was your beginning and death your end. You were rejected at birth, and you couldn't hold on to anything in your life, either . . . Either you weren't needed or you didn't find a way to fit in, to hold on to anything, not malice, envy, or desperation . . . The earth ripples beneath you, but strictness is your support. All that you touched took you over completely, for you had no other life than that very minute . . . You are like the first man who ever felt the need to understand the sense and meaning of his every word, his every deed and action, who immediately turned this understanding into a rule and a law, not permitting yourself to retreat from this law and expecting the same from others, expecting it and demanding it for their own good. And every injustice and even outrage you put down to a failure to know these strict laws and regulations, each time wondering why people live according to hastily concocted provisional regulations when even the blind could see that the time had come to cancel them, but no, they won't do it. And what kind of power and good fortune do those people have who make up all these provisional regulations for their own advantage while others accept them and implement them without question?

Since in a way he essentially didn't exist, Igor Ivanovich was assigned no duties by anyone, no achievements were expected of him, and therefore, with full confidence he could consider that he had fulfilled his main duty in life as he understood it. What can be more important than to prepare oneself for the kind of life where changes and improvements will no longer be needed, where everything receives its own name and place, where it won't be necessary to stand guard over justice and honor since no one will encroach upon them? So it came about that Igor Ivanovich's thoughts and advice relating to rules and laws about the just and strict arrangement of life weren't needed by anyone and went almost entirely toward constructing and preparing for a better life the one man who was in part subservient to him, who had for more than forty years borne the name of Igor Ivanovich Dikshtein.

Oh, Igor Ivanovich, Igor Ivanovich! . . . Who will ever be so lucky as to know a man whose existence would be denied everywhere—about whom people would say that no such person could ever have existed! You don't exist, ask anybody! And no matter how your boots crunch on the snow, no matter how you clank your bottles in the net bag, slam doors, and raise your voice at Nastya, you don't exist and you know this yourself better than anyone. And what kind of Igor Ivanovich can you be if even Nastya twice caught herself thinking she couldn't remember your real Christian name—she did remember it, of course, only not immediately.

Igor Ivanovich would probably be amazed to find out that his soul, filled to overflowing with strictness toward himself and with readiness to meet another, better life, because there was no room for him in this one, that his soul was perhaps that very abyss into which tens of states, hundreds of governments, thousands of little gods and tsars had vanished—an abyss that dissolves into itself century after century, saving from oblivion only those who were strict toward themselves and fervently yearned for another life.

Clanking the bottles, Igor Ivanovich passed the cathedral in a state of equality and independence, at this moment free from the burdens of concepts and of bodily sensitivity. And if it hadn't been for the excessive tension which was ever-present in Igor Ivanovich, he easily might have enjoyed in full measure a state conducive to bliss. Turning left, he disappeared behind a stone wall as though walking through it. And those few pedestrians who at that time were walking behind him along the former Constable Street couldn't see how the tall thin figure suddenly staggered, as though tripping or startled, like a man who suddenly wakes up and realizes that he has lost his way and, therefore, gazes all around him with a puzzled look, still trying to locate familiar objects, trying to understand how this happened and how he can get out of it . . . The net bag with the bottles slipped out of his hands and clattered down on the trampled snow . . . Here, 104 steps from the door to his house, the last merciful gift of fate awaited him—an easy death from a heart attack.

Igor Ivanovich staggered and fell sprawling in the snow. He was already dead as he fell.

The last thing that needs to be explained is the title *Captain* preceding Igor Ivanovich's name at the very beginning of the story.

Despite the fact that he went to the public baths only in the morning when it was almost empty and the steam was hot, it was impossible for Igor Ivanovich to conceal his naval background since he was covered with blue tattoos, like a medieval map of the night sky with Virgo, Lyra, and Aquarius. He firmly rebuffed all the efforts of his friends and acquaintances to find out the details of his service in the navy, which at first caused the concocting of legends, and later, no one knows how, led to the nickname Captain. The internal tension, sternness, and categorical manner which were constant features of Igor Ivanovich also strongly supported the accuracy and correctness of the adopted title.

It is true that Igor Ivanovich was called Captain only behind his back, out of respect for his serious and quick-tempered character, and for this reason he died without having an inkling of this—his third name, thought up by the friends and acquaintances with whom he had lived side by side for the last fifteen years of his life. A woman screamed as she saw the old man fall.

A young man ran to stop a car. Brakes screeched. A car door banged.

Someone cried out when he recognized the fallen man as Igor Ivanovich.

The noise of the city entered the hollow body of the cathedral in muted echoes but didn't remain there, dissolving without participating in the particular life of this petrified cry of hope which stood forsaken by the people and by faith itself, an unrealized gateway to the kingdom of eternal bliss and recompense, a dwelling of the spirit abandoned by the spirit and condemned to abide.

Leningrad 1977–87

Night Patrol

Nocturne for Two Voices, With the
Participation of Comrade Polubolotov,
Rifleman of VOKHR

*The main thing about the stories was the fact that he never told
a lie in his whole life, and whatever he said, that's just how
it was.—N. V. Gogol, "St. John's Eve"*

*Pray to God that we don't get infected with the disease of
truth.—J. Stalin, COLLECTED WORKS, vol. 12, p. 9*

I

"I'm crazy about the white nights . . ."

II

What a miraculous evening light that settles over the whole earth at
once, over all the houses, bridges, arches, cupolas, and spires! This light
casts no shadow; each creation of human hands takes part in a fair contest among equals, not deceiving the eye with reflections of the sun, nor
with the flying tinsel of moonlight.

Hanging above its own reflection in the countless water surfaces of
the rivers and canals, as though suddenly made weightless by magic, the
entire mass of the city seems to rock slightly from the light night breeze
entering the stone wilderness from the bay, asleep near the flat shores; it
rocks and trembles a tiny bit, gets fuzzy, and disappears as when your eye
is fogged up by a tear; the faceted features of history built in stone melt
when the unfathomably wide sky descends on earth . . .

. . . The silent waters are brought here by two Nevas, three Nevkas,
and countless Fontankas, Moykas, Smolenkas, Pryazhkas, Karpovkas,
Tarakanovkas, all of them losing their names and nicknames as they pass
the low, empty shores of the flat islands where the highest spot is only
three meters above sea level. For a long time the water runs silently
without being disturbed by oars or propellers, or pierced by heavy an-
chors, or even repulsed near the shore by the waves from some obstinate
cutter. Look how the reeds rustle in the shallow tributaries and fir trees
stand near treacherous swamps defaced by thick rust. Then come empty

open spaces and your tear-washed eyes can see the distant islets, retreating almost to the horizon to give the mighty and restless river more space to rest comfortably on the unstable swampy plain . . .

What a miraculous light and an unfathomable silence that drowns in its bottomless depth all the nervous rumbling, clanking, gurgling, screeching, and clattering of the restless city! Silence floods all streets and yards, pouring over the empty squares and deserted boulevards and hiding in the shadows under gates and fences, and were it not for the traffic lights winking to each other with their yellow eyes, and an occasional car buzzing across the washed asphalt and making a sticky splashing sound, if a flock of gulls didn't scatter over the motionless water with a screeching moan, the city would seem not just secretive and sleeping but dead.

But huge ghostly ships fly through the night, hardly touching the motionless waters, and they swiftly pierce the needle's eye of the opened bridges. Not a soul is on the wide and empty decks, not a soul in the doorways or on the sidewalks; it's only bits of broken glass that reflect what is moving past the palaces, and no human face or figure can be seen . . . But suddenly an iron door clatters open, a round porthole looking like a peephole in a prison door. A half-asleep galley orderly steps over the threshold and dumps a bucket of garbage into the black water squeezed between the steep side of the ship and the stone embankment, and then he again slams the iron door through which the loud breathing of the ship's insides escaped for a second.

The reflection of the palaces along the shores quivers on the water that is agitated but not yet roused from its sleep. A spire crowned with a lacy little ship floats in the water as though it had for a moment become soft and flat, and here, near the other shore, an angel is already swaying on a golden spire as though about to fall to the earthen bastions of the former prison, but after a moment the golden finger once again points to the opaque bottomless water along the shore beneath the fortress walls . . .

Why is he pointing?

This angel is raised toward heaven, his open wings touching the transparent clouds fragrant with roses, but where is he calling? What is he promising? . . .

. . . On such white nights* even the wild animal, long ago driven away from his birthplace, could believe that the long misunderstanding was

_____

*On summer nights it does not get dark in the northern latitudes where Leningrad is located.

about to end so that he could return to the land of his half-forgotten ancestors, to the land that had suffered so much and was almost beyond recognition, but that is still irresistibly drawing him back.

The speeding chain of wild ducks, their agitated wings rustling the dense somnolent air, moves quickly above the river like desperate scouts sent ahead to see whether the rich swamplands, expansive lagoons, and silent narrow channels haven't freed themselves yet from the imprisoning stones of the embankments. A moose sometimes wanders in, deceived by the silence of the empty streets, and stares at his magnificent reflection in the plate-glass windows. On such a night the roguish vixen, tired of running away from the city that is sprawling outwards in all directions, leads her trusting offspring out of the abandoned drainage pipe she has used for her den; they are first-generation city-dwelling foxes and she'll show them the sky, let them breathe the wind carrying a faint smell of the distant forest, promise them something, and tell them to arm themselves with patience. They are not frightened by the loud tapping suddenly breaking out all around; the beautiful black woodpecker has in defiance of all rules encroached on a territory that is not his; he props himself up on his tail as though cast in metal, just like the motionless horse beneath the bronze horseman, and he's beating on the desiccated trunk with his heavy beak. He beats alarm, scattering husks and small chips of bark on the few gaping people gathered underneath, examining, some for the first time in their lives and some for the last, this unfamiliar beauty who has flown in to save the fir tree, dying from the city fumes . . .

A wispy shroud of thin transparent clouds is spread out like a gigantic cover for the night. It doesn't quite reach the edge of the city where a wide, clear strip of sky shines with a golden glow near the horizon. The air seems freshly washed, there's no dust or soot. One can believe that the new day will come from that side and that it will be cleaner and brighter than all the days that have come to the earth before. This assurance pacifies the soul, and there's no need to urge time along.

III
. . . Well, I'm telling you, it's nice to go out on patrol or make an arrest on a night like this!

Now if I'm supposed to pick someone up, I'll leave the car and walk on foot down the street . . . Throw himself under the streetcar? No, the streetcars aren't running. Run away? Where should he run? There's nowhere to run. What about the instructions? You can't follow instructions all your life. Is all of life anticipated in some kind of book of instructions?

The white nights, perhaps? Well, try to hide them, cancel them, prohibit them. They can't be hidden. I know, "Route to follow," "Method of locating," "Preventive measures." Can every possibility be anticipated?

What kind of instruction could have foreseen me? Who made my life, who could foresee it? Even if it had been foreseen, it wasn't out loud. Now they pretend that nothing interesting or instructive happened in my life.

Possibly some people are renouncing their life, hiding it, but I'm not ashamed of mine. I didn't live for myself. I was a soldier. I was, as we used to say, a sharpened bayonet . . . Of course I wasn't perfect. Maybe not. But I had no glaring imperfections, and just think, I never had anyone escape from me, personally. You could always count on me to be conscientious and behave decently, and so I can say with a clear conscience: whether you like it or not, I can't be separated from my time! My duty was to become one with the times, and I did. And a splendid time it was; every day brought to the altar new successes, thanks to dedicated and hard-working cadres. I did my duty to the neglect of myself and my family, and I never asked any questions when they gave me different jobs, both hard and easy ones.

Yes, we had to trim away the rotten flesh and clear the road for the new world so that people could rejoice in peace and applaud their leaders. Now so much has been forgotten, but back then the question was clear: the mad capitalist dogs can't tolerate our triumphant achievements, and therefore they try to destroy the reputation of the very best people of our land. In remembrance of the times I lived through that have already become the property of the history that hasn't yet been written, I'll just point out one thing: when people gathered together in the mine shafts and pits, on construction sites, in the factories and workshops, in the dockyards, not to mention various institutions, and raised their hands all together to vote, let's say, for the death penalty of the Trotskyist-Zinoviev fascist agents, did they really want blood? Those nice girls, or young pioneers, or village bumpkins? No, they had simply become one with the times and created history . . . All together, with their own hands. Now they claim that somebody or other supposedly made mistakes. I don't believe it, though I admit it's possible, but that the people were wrong, now really, excuse me, even today such views wouldn't be tolerated. When Andrey Yanuarevich demanded that the guilty parties answer with their heads for every hair on the heads of the leaders, he was supported by all the people; I don't remember that anyone objected or argued. We had infinite love for the leaders, infinite! And now smiles, smirks, jokes . . .

Anyway, how long have you been at this factory? Three years? Look, they're already scheduling you to work on holidays. Well, the day before holidays, tomorrow is only the thirtieth,* but never mind. Just think, what an honor! Did they draft you from the reserve? I know. Telyukin was supposed to be on duty. He's pretty rotten, right? I know, many are stubborn and make up all kinds of excuses to avoid getting picked to work on holidays, but I'm glad to do it. Not because I can sit all night and day in the director's office with the telephones and the red folder. I've already seen my share of offices, bigger than this, and not this view of a crummy little garden and a factory fence, but, say, the main square of the northern Palmyra. From the Smolny . . . Say what you will, I've got a whole life behind me . . .

Have you noticed the furniture in here?

I had just started working here. It was my first year, I wanted an unpaid leave and needed the permission of the director, so I came for Nikolay Ilich's signature, and when I saw this furniture I almost cried out loud. Then I asked in passing, "Do you happen to know, Nikolay Ilich, where this furniture came from?" He said that he thought it had been there since before the war. But as it happened, I had inventoried it before the war. There's a little house on the embankment, almost across from the Academy of Arts. It doesn't look like anything special, but it happens that on the second floor of that little house was what they called the official residence of the police-chief general of St. Petersburg; and later, maybe for the sake of allegory, the head of the Leningrad militia lived there. One of the militia heads who lived in that apartment turned out to be part of the right-wing Trotsky block, so they took him away and confiscated all his belongings, and I inventoried all those objects, including this dresser with the bronze Egyptian heads; there was one head in each corner. Look, here one is missing and here two more. The sofa, this very one with the twisted wooden back and lemonwood trim, the little table . . . There used to be six armchairs, but now there're only two left. Even back then I really admired this piano of Karelian birch! Nikolay Ilich wanted to know why I asked about the furniture, but I was evasive and said that it was very pretty, especially the piano.

What a lot of informative stories I have under my blue VOKHR** service jacket. Storms came and went, you might say hurricanes, but I survived, and that makes the jacket really valuable. I look around sometimes and can't understand myself how I survived.

---

* April 30 is the day before May 1, a Soviet holiday celebrating the workers.
** VOKHR is the armed branch of the internal security police.

Before I came here I was at the prison; my boss sent me to the DPZ,*
where I was the chief supervisor. Well, what about it? A set routine, guard
duty according to schedule, not hard at all, but I really couldn't stand it
and left. Want to know why? It's the contingent of prisoners . . . Nowadays
the contingent isn't like it used to be, they can't compare. People used to
be nicer, quieter, a little dejected, their eyes staring out into space like fish
gasping in the air. It's true they loved to write appeals; where all didn't
they send their appeals? Well, most of all of course to Stalin, but all those
letters remained here; less often they wrote to other addresses, and those
reached the addressee of course, and they'd get replies . . . Yes . . . Earlier,
well, perhaps one out of five was dangerous, but now all of them are,
almost. Not even in prison do they calm down. At the slightest provoca-
tion, it's "Call the prosecutor! Call the prosecutor, you bastard!" You can
only give them five more days, that is, if they're waiting for their trial; well,
after their conviction you can add on ten days, see? That's all. What do
they do? Anything they want. First they try to break the light bulb in the
cell. When the light bulb goes out you have to call someone from housekeeping, and he sneaks them something to smoke and tells them the
news. What sort of discipline is that? Lately they have introduced dogs in
the Department of the Interior, dogs for reinforcement, but things stay the
same. They asked me why I quit, why I wouldn't stay, why I transferred
even with a cut in salary. There was only one answer; the contingent is
worse than ever. You know Pildin? He left the DPZ too; yes, it's gotten a lot
more difficult to work . . .

I won't say any more. It's not that I signed some oath of secrecy or,
like they say, don't talk out of respect for my uniform, but I'm not in the
habit of talking too much, and therefore, as you can see, I'm still alive and
well; I can't complain. I can look through the clean and clear windows and
admire the city washed by the spring storms. I retired and even got decorations and a pension, although as I said, it wasn't on my own, well,
initiative, but at least it didn't happen like with Pildin . . . Do you know
Pildin? He got a job in transport. And Katerinich from post No. 6? They
were pushed out, ho, ho, they were livid. It was just then that a directive
came that service in the organs** shouldn't be considered a special privilege when determining pensions. Those were some times, I'll tell you.
First they even managed to hold a few trials. You don't remember, proba-

*Pretrial house of detention.
**Organ is a common designation for the Soviet internal security administration,
known under different acronyms such as the KGB.

bly, but the head of the Novgorod administration was tried and got ten years. For what? you might ask. Well, that's what he got, but then they themselves started to think and realized that things might get out of hand. And so they put on the brakes. Then many of our men went on to VOKHR, and our director, Nikolay Ilich, looks at me funny to this day as if to say, "I'm not sure if you remember or not." He doesn't say anything, he's obviously scared he might be wrong, but I remember him perfectly well from '49. His real name isn't Nikolay at all, it's Narzan.* In his passport it says Narzan and on his order it says Narzan, and orders are made out according to the passports. He was orphaned during the revolutionary wars, and before he came to the orphanage he had no name at all, only a nickname; he had probably drifted in to Petersburg from somewhere in the Caucasus. Of course it isn't easy to live with a name like that, you have to explain it to everyone. Do you know the House of Scientists in Lesny? In the park near the Polytechnic? Well, in this House of Scientists, some kind of city officials used to have meetings in the evenings. What sort of meetings I don't know, but all of them were arrested later under Article 58.** Well, this Narzan Ivanich of ours, now calling himself Nikolay Ilich, he was the managing director of that house . . .

I really do love the white nights awfully. So much of my life is connected with them, but lately it's mostly memories.

Well, what's white, on the one hand, and night, on the other? Is it a mistake of nature? Or perhaps a dream? Honestly, perhaps it's a dream. Sometimes I sit and think that the city is sleeping and dreaming about itself. Then I look up and think, maybe life itself is a dream? What's left? I've lived my life, but I can't tell anyone about it. I didn't spare myself, I gave up everything for my work. Take those medals of honor. We used to have a General Poddubko. Once just before a holiday like now, only in November, he took me with him to a children's home he sponsored. He was wearing his orders for the parade, and I carried the goodies, a box of apples, candies, and cookies. Poddubko was a VIP; he had direct access to Lavrenty Pavlovich,*** everybody knew that. Yessir . . . He had figured it like this: the kids would line up one at a time; he'd give something to each one, pat them on the head, and shake hands with the older ones. But what happened? As soon as he stepped into the living room they were all over

*Narzan is the name of a well-known mineral water from the Caucasus.
**Article 58 was the law defining "enemy of the people." Under its many subdivisions numerous Soviet citizens were sentenced to prison terms.
***Lavrenty Beria (1899–1953), notorious head of the secret police from 1938.

him, especially the small fry. They almost knocked him down on the sofa, they climbed in his lap and grabbed his stripes and orders, of course. He had a lot of orders. Big ones. The little boys screamed, "He got that one for a tank!" But others argued, "No, the Order of Lenin isn't for a tank, it's for an airplane!" And the first ones again, as I remember, "No, a tank, a tank!" They clamored so loud he couldn't say a word, but if they had let him talk, what could he have said? The orders were for concrete things, not for long service and anniversaries, as has become popular now. What's he telling his grandchildren now, that some order is for a tank or an airplane? So it turns out that my biography doesn't interest anyone, either? And yet I lived as I was told, but where are those who gave the orders? They seem to have stayed in another life. But not everyone.

Our Pildin brings the bosses their cars, but why does he chew out people like he does? He was kicked out without a pension, it was an insult; you have to feel sorry for him. To tell the truth, he was a tough old veteran and it was usually him they sent when someone had to be taken away or brought here from another city, from Lodeinoe Pole or Kirishi. He doesn't like me, he never greets me, it's as though we never met before. But we have, and how! At this very factory he worked as an electrician in 1935, but he put more effort into the Komsomol. His father was a shoemaker and he had no more education than Vanka Zhukov,* that's why he tried so hard in the Komsomol. He hoped that they would notice him, and they did. An order came to the factory to send two students to the NKVD** school at Gorokhov, just two students; it's a well-known school. By the way, they only took Pildin, the other one wasn't accepted. It was in '36 that he went there, but he graduated in '37, ahead of schedule, on account of the desperate shortage of cadres, although it was a two-year course, or rather school. People were urgently needed for work, that's why they limited the teaching to one year, and he was an outstanding student. They had some kind of volleyball team, no one had heard of it, but Pildin really played great, both serving and spiking—you can't deny that. He *was* the team and it became famous. But famous where? Among us. Although they were young and no one knew them yet. There was secrecy, after all, so mostly they just had to play against their own older comrades from the Liteiny or with teams from the armed forces. They were young and enthusiastic and used to make it hot for their older comrades. The team had authority. Who was the team captain? It was Pildin.

*Vanka Zhukov is the young hero of a story by Chekhov.
**NKVD was the name of the secret police at that time.

By the way, he stayed in Leningrad and attained the rank of captain quite soon, the first from his graduating class, and even before the war he got responsible jobs that he fulfilled to the letter. For instance, they had to arrest Glushanin, the secretary of the Novgorod City Committee. Before the war there was no such thing as a Novgorod Province, and this Glushanin had some kind of dispute with the local comrade from the NKVD; they hated each other, and to order him to arrest Glushanin would be kind of unethical, there might arise suspicions of personal revenge, settling of personal accounts . . . No, he wasn't sent to Novgorod. I don't know if Glushanin was already here or if they called him to Leningrad for a conference, as they usually did, but just that day we were attending a cultural evening at the Maly Theater with our wives—a buffet, an unusual affair even for those times . . . During the second intermission we went out on the square to smoke. It was warm, the chestnuts were in bloom. We're standing there smoking, the weather is fine, our mood . . . Then an M-car drives up, they grab Pildin and off they go. It turns out that the order had already been made out, and at the Smolny they handed this Novgorod man over to him right after the conference.

By the way, the regional school was right next to Isaak Square, so for their evening walk the students walked near the former German embassy, singing. Their favorite song was "We Are Standing Guard." The song got a little embarrassing. Do you remember the words?

> We are standing guard
> Always, always.
> And if the country
> Needs our work
> Rifle in hand
> Supported by the strap
> We will repulse
> Comrade Blucher.

It's a lively marching song, but if my memory doesn't deceive me, it was precisely in the summer of '37 that the heads of the whole army command rolled, and Comrade Blucher's along with them. Then after several years I hear them singing it again. The words "support" and "repulse" remained, but instead of Blucher they sang, "The Far East, the Red Banner," and it sounded even better.

The flag with the swastika was flying on Isaak Square up to the very beginning of the war. By the way, I've met and shaken hands with Graf

Schulenburg.* He was traveling by train from Finland to Moscow. That was then, too, in '37. I was appointed to the open guard, open, that is in uniform. We met him at the Finland Station; there were four of us and how many secret ones I couldn't say. So this typical-looking German comes out of the car; you couldn't mistake him. We meet him, as we were supposed to, and surround him in a square; we're quite near him, like you, even closer. Even though he's a count, a real one, he smiles and shakes hands with everyone. He sticks out his hand to me, smiles, and says something in German. I didn't understand since we were only getting training in Estonian, Latvian, and Lithuanian, but not German. Later they repeated Schulenburg's words to me, and it turned out that he was joking: "You kicked out the counts, he said, and now you are guarding one." Well, I didn't want to look like a fool so I smiled, and this turned out to be the right thing to do. Schulenburg probably thought I understood him even without an interpreter. In '44 Hitler hanged him on a hook by the chin. If Hitler had known that already in '41 Schulenburg was warning Stalin that Germany was preparing to attack him and even told him the date, then he would have hanged him on a hook three years earlier. That's a count for you. He was the official ambassador to the Soviet Union but didn't consider himself Hitler's pawn; he had his own opinion and risked his life to prevent a war with us. He understood that Germany would break her teeth on us and he was actually committing treason, high treason from Hitler's point of view. That's where self-confidence can take you . . .

They often picked me for open-guard details because of my size. I'm over six feet tall, size Extra Large, and my back is as straight as a ramrod.

To return to Pildin, he and I had a small episode . . . Why don't you stay here by yourself next to the phone just in case. I'll walk around the area, then I'll return and tell you about this interesting episode.

IV

. . . On the boulevard here in the direction of the square, just a bit further down past the canteen, there's an arch, and beyond the arch is a shop where they fix ball-point pens. Have you been there? Well! . . . Did you notice that it's a small place with only one entrance from the street? The glass window takes up the whole wall, there's one door and a window, the

*Friedrich Werner Count von Schulenberg, German ambassador to the Soviet Union in the late 1930s. He was executed on November 10, 1944, after participating in an attempt on Hitler's life.

shop is no bigger than eighteen or twenty square meters, and there's no rear exit. It was behind this square glass window, in full view of all passers-by, that Pildin and I spent two nights and one bright day. That's the invisible front for you. Anyone who wanted could stop in front of that window and look . . . Actually the majority of people seldom understand what's happening before their own eyes. As Kazbek Ivanovich loved to say, "Our people have learned to see with their ears." Yes, the scene behind the window was strange, of course, but there have been so many strange scenes in our days . . .

In 1948, a Saturday in June. Train such and such, car so and so, seat such and such. Pick him up at Tosno* and bring him in; slightly shorter than average, the complexion of a sportsman, age thirty-seven, hair slightly curly, straight nose, lips, clothing, and so forth. Anyway, it would still be a long time before his hair got curly, it hadn't grown out yet. But he had one distinguishing mark: small hands.

Sure enough, when we arrested him I paid special attention to this characteristic, "small hands." He turned out to be a rather sturdy young man, well-built with a broad and pleasant mug but with the hands of a girl. They gave us a ZIS.** The ZIS 101 is an excellent car, not like the M-car; in the M you sit lined up like in a latrine, but in a ZIS you sit like on a sofa. We arrived in Tosno around six o'clock and went to the station, and after approximately half an hour the train arrived. It stood there for a minute . . . No, that's not true! The train stopped a minute just for us. The first stop was Malaya Vishera, which is past Tosno. So we pick up this character with the small hands. Our group consisted of three: Valdemar Khunt, an Estonian, so amazingly cold-blooded and reserved that he seemed almost stuck-up; later it turned out that he didn't know Russian very well, or he couldn't understand it well, but he was a great guy. I was the second and Pildin was in command; he was already a major although he had only gone to sixth grade and I had almost finished middle school. It was going smoothly, no hint of anything unusual. Around nine in the evening we arrive in the city and take him to the internal prison, the solitary for politicals, but they wouldn't accept him there. Imagine! Not accept him! You must give them their due, they had a lot of work; it's terrible to remember how they would arrest as many as five hundred or seven hundred people every night, but everyone arrested properly and according to

---

*Tosno is a town fifty kilometers east of Leningrad.
**ZIS was a car from the Stalin Automobile Plant in Moscow.

law—they kept exceptionally good order there. A Party member couldn't be arrested without the sanction of the District Committee, and for a member of the District Committee, the sanction of the Provincial Committee was necessary. Make an arrest without area committee sanction? A search without a warrant? No, never. And then to put someone in solitary without the proper documents . . .

But this happened to be a special case, one might even say exceptional. Neither sanction nor decree. We had arrested him after a call, following personal instructions given on the phone, an executive order. Pildin had assumed that things would be in order by the time we returned, but it was Saturday . . . It's hard to explain what had happened, but there were no papers and all we had was an oral command, so who could we hand him over to? Well, Pildin puffed up his chest and walked over to the commandant of the prison that is the solitary confinement place, and said, "Take the arrested, or you will answer personally for it!" But the commandant wasn't exactly timid and what was a major to him if he was on equal terms with generals? "If you yell any more, I'll take you instead. How could I sign him in? How could I squeeze him in? I'd have to pay for his keep, too!" They were shouting at each other and getting nervous. We were sitting in the car on Kalyaev Street and Pildin comes out like a beaten dog. We could have gone to the duty officer and asked, but Vakatimov, the man on duty, was a "friend" of Pildin's; he couldn't stand him and called him the "volleyball major," so that was out of the question. The chauffeur wasn't one of ours, he wasn't on duty, they had just grabbed him like they had us, right quick, and when he saw how things were going, he asked us to let him go. We let him go—what else could we do? So the four of us were standing there right on the sidewalk. Pildin kept running around for another half hour, trying to find someone or call someone, but it was no good. What should we do? Over there, across the Neva, is the Finland Station, but to take an arrested man on the streetcar was kind of embarrassing, so we tramped across the Liteiny Bridge. Four hundred steps, I counted. Pildin started to explain to the duty officer of the traffic police that since the arrested man had been taken from a train on the October Line, and the Finland Station is also called "October," he was more or less obligated . . . But the captain happened to be bright and understood at once that something was wrong, so he asked, "Why did you bring him here then; you could have put him in the Liteiny, or in Kryosty next door, or in Lebedev." We might have reached an agreement man-to-man, but Pildin got insulted. "I'm not obligated to report to you, comrade captain." He stresses the word *Captain*. And the captain replied, "I don't run a hotel, there are no guest rooms here, comrade *major*," stressing the word major. So we were in the street again.

It was getting to be night, although a white night and rather warm, but weird, somehow. If only we could have taken him home! But if we took someone like him home we'd spend the rest of our lives writing explanations . . . I'm carrying the arrested man's briefcase and Valdemar his suitcase. A nice suitcase with leather straps. Pildin and the arrested have nothing to carry. All around us citizens are strolling, young people are singing somewhere, ferries on the Neva . . . And we, like homeless dogs.

I say, let's go down Skorokhodov Street to the Petrograd District police department; after all, I used to work there before the war, perhaps they could help us for old friendship's sake. But they wouldn't. The police department was housed on Bolshaia Monetnaya in the rectory of the Lyceum Church across from the District Committee. They wanted to help me but couldn't. They're all so careful and frightened, trembling for their own skins, but the job is the least of their concerns. You see, we needed separate quarters for our prisoner; he couldn't go in a common cell. But on that evening their place was packed . . . I think they just didn't want to get involved. And perhaps there was something else, too. The Committee people generally look down their noses on the militia as though they are so high and mighty, and once in a while the militia enjoyed giving the Committee people a hard time . . .

So we are aimlessly wandering along Kirovsk Street, and here in front of No. 14 we come across a janitor; the boulevard was so clean and picked up. The last empty streetcars are going to the car park at Blokhin and Skorokhodov, and here is this janitor. He had come out to meet the horse-drawn carriage from the District Food Trade Center, and he's actually standing right there in a white apron. There were few male janitors left after the war, many more women, but this one looked as though neither the war nor the revolution had happened . . . Pildin assured him that the arrested man was a dangerous criminal and told him to place premises at our disposal at once so we could house him until Monday. The janitor didn't ask any questions. He at once set off to wake up the house chairman, who got up and unlocked the housing office that they called "the red corner."* It's where they repair ball-point pens now. The table was covered in red; that's why they called it the red corner; there were two chairs, or two sets of three folding chairs, each from some club; among the wall decorations were a short slogan, a poster about subscriptions for a loan,

---

*The "red corner" used to be the corner in a house where an icon was displayed.

and a portrait of Comrade Kaganovich.* But the main thing was the window that took up the entire wall right down to the sidewalk; there was nowhere to hide, no curtains, no blinds.

Well, it was good to have a roof over our heads and somewhere to sit, our legs were already aching.

The arrested had said nothing the whole way, he didn't let out a single word, and only when we were settling down, he says, "Give me my briefcase, I'm hungry." He takes out home-cooked chops, little sandwiches, and a bottle of cognac . . . So like comrades in misfortune we sat there under the cover of the white night and shared this bottle . . .

What sort of bird was the arrested? It was basically a trivial affair. It turned out that he'd had sort of a romance, actually more like hanky-panky, with the daughter of a certain . . . well, I won't mention the name. The daddy in question didn't like it; this prospective son-in-law babbled a lot. They gave him five years for talking too much and sent him to Vorkuta. When he was set free in '48 they warned him fair and square that if he as much as showed his face in Leningrad he'd get five more years. Well, this smart-aleck decided to arrange a ticket for himself *through* Leningrad so that he wouldn't, strictly speaking, actually be in Leningrad. By letter he arranged with his family to meet him at the railroad station since he had three hours between trains . . . In the meantime our people called each other, we were informed and waited for the decision, and in the end we practically had to catch up with the train, but they hadn't written out the sanction and the order as they should have done . . . Not good, don't you agree? On the other hand, he had a ticket to Penza, no, not Penza, Inza near Saransk.** Judge for yourself, couldn't they have sent him back later from there for his retrial? It's stupid, it really is. He who doesn't work makes no mistakes; well, there were mistakes, there sure were . . .

Well, so we sit there as though displayed in the shop window. The room was small, there was nowhere to hide, the window was huge and clean. Couples would stop and look. There weren't many passers-by, but there were some; it's Saturday, the weather's nice, a white night, and people were out walking. Was there anything strange about us? Four men, after all, with food on the table, it's a very common scene; but I noticed that at first people would look and smile, but then they walked away

*Lazar Kaganovich (1893–1957?) was a political leader and one of Stalin's supporters.
**Penza is a city in the Volga area north of Saratov. Inza and Saransk are towns north of Penza.

quickly as though a wet rag had wiped the smile off their faces. He's dressed in civilian clothes, we too in civilian; one is asleep, two are chatting, it's all very ordinary, but people shied away a little. Maybe because after the war the Leningraders' nerves were shot. Of course, people had lived through a lot; it was still sort of empty in the city . . .

All right, then. This man wanted to go to the toilet, he was in custody and he had that right. I tell Pildin that at the streetcar stop not far from here there's a luxurious public latrine at the corner of Gorky and Kirov streets.

By the way, this toilet is famous, it's shrouded in legend. It was constructed to look like a villa, with scrolls, turrets, spires, fancy brickwork, the devil knows what all. A castle from a German fairy tale. Here's the history behind it. On the place where we're sitting there used to be an amusement park that belonged to the owner of the Central Aleksandrov Market. He was unbelievably rich, and he donated to the city a charity hospital for tuberculosis and paid for all the equipment with his own money—it's standing to this day, it's where we have fluoroscopic tests . . . You know the red house to the left in front of Kamenoostrovsk Bridge, at the end of Kirovsky Bridge? Aleksandrov was supposed to be a millionaire. Well, they say that he fell for a certain high-born lady, let's say a baroness. At first she giggled and wiggled, led him on, accepted his attentions, as they say, but when it came down to action, no way. I don't know exactly how he tried to prevail upon her. He wasn't a simple shop attendant in a general store, he didn't wear greased boots, he was a capitalist, had manners, an automobile, had been in Europe! . . . But she didn't give in and that's that! They had a frank conversation and she called him a peasant straight out. "You're a peasant," she says, "but I'm a baroness." End of conversation. "You can have my hand, but only up to here, no further." Mister Aleksandrov tried to control himself. What's interesting is that the lady wasn't all that inaccessible, so they say, and this made it especially insulting to him. He took his revenge. She lived in the house at the beginning of the boulevard, beside the Witte mansion; later it became the Institute for the Protection of Childhood, with the windows on the corner of Kamenoostrovsk and Kronwerk, as the streets were called then.

The suitor contacted the city government. "Since I'm concerned about the health of the people I want to build a public facility in the garden of the People's House, of the *sortie* type, at my own expense." The city fathers—that's what the City Soviet was called—accepted the gift with gratitude; it was a useful project and a busy location. Everyone was astonished at how luxurious it was; it looked something like a castle or an old Russian fortress. And this castle was an exact replica of the suburban villa of this same Baroness who was inaccessible for the successful man of humble origins. Please come and admire how every resident in the city uses your hospitality!

Well, of course she left at once, changed apartments and moved to a place near Nikolaevsk Bridge, Lieutenant Smith Bridge. And he put a john there, too, under her windows. It's true, a simpler one. She, poor thing, quickly retreated to the other end of Vasilevsky, to Tuchkov Bridge, and there, too, he built a villa for public use beneath her window . . .

After the war there were huge open spaces for nightingales in Leningrad. For example the little garden of the Aleksandrinsky Theater, named for Pushkin, which is, as you know, straight across from the Eliseevsk store on Nevsky! And around here, the garden of the People's House is like heaven for them. There's water nearby at the Kronwerk, there are bushes . . . They sing, answer each other—it's really beautiful.

At night any sound becomes special; it has a different weight than in the daytime, and because sounds are few and far between at night you listen to them, try to guess their meaning. Take the sparrow, an insignificant bird: in the day they chirp and you don't even hear them, but just before morning they give a concert . . . Sometimes I listen with great interest. I keep listening and think of the life of those birds with only a small voice and not a very interesting one at that, but when they all come together, how they all carry on—they can outdo any nightingale. That's power! The nightingale, I tell you, isn't a fashionable bird either, a little pointy beak and a body like a spindle; that's the entire bird, but he knows his worth. Most songbirds seek a place for themselves rather high up— well, take the starling, even the titmouse and the oriole—they fly up in a tree to the very highest twig. But the nightingale settles in a bush or on an unimportant branch, or even right on a stump; he doesn't need to be high up, he can be heard anyway . . . When he starts to sing it's like the sky moves, as though the earth becomes wider . . . I've heard a southern nightingale, and so what! Our northern one has a smooth, strong, clear voice, it's like silk, as if icy nails are going into your soul. Honestly, you stop breathing, it seems to be your breast, not his, that's filled to overflowing with the chill of night, and the song feels crowded and wants out. It's beautiful!

Yes . . . Well, this establishment with the spires and turrets, it's only open until one, then it closes for the night, but we got there in time. It was already after one and an old lady with one of those oilcloth aprons was cleaning out . . . I showed her my document and she let us in, all cultured-like and honest.

In those days the nightingale was special to me. I had different kinds of duties; I also had to attend burials . . . Naturally not real funerals, we just threw them in a hole. Coffins? What do they need coffins for? Anyway you don't need to know all that. It wasn't all that far from the city that we threw them in a hole; you wouldn't believe how near it really was.

I'll tell you, there were nightingales at that place.

First there's a small hill with houses, then very wide fields, and these fields run up against a range of real hills covered with forest. It's un-inhabited there. In the line between the hills and fields, in the fold, so to speak, there's a creek and by the creek there's willow and osier. It's really a delightful place for nightingales, you couldn't think of a better one. That's where we used to go. Our work wasn't noisy; we didn't disturb them, but they disturbed us. I'm talking about the nightingales. I went to that place in winter and fall and in summer when it rained, but the first time—I remember it clearly—was just at the end of May. I mentioned in passing how I loved the nightingale's song, but Gesiozsky, our commanding officer at the time, said that he personally preferred the oriole. You don't argue with your boss, but I didn't change my mind.

What's the most interesting thing about a nightingale? Huh? You never know what trick he'll play next, in which key he'll sing . . . He taps and whistles back, taps and then suddenly it's as though he rattles dry little boards, like castanets, tra-ta-ta-tra-ta-ta-tam and suddenly without breathing, with such a long, fine, fine whistle, that it goes right through your heart . . . he is tearing at your soul, tearing . . . You start feeling uneasy; it's night, after all. In one direction it's empty, in the other direction everyone is asleep, and he is drawing out your soul, out . . . and when he finally gets tired and stops it's as though everything drops and spills out . . . it's really serious . . . it's gone, it's gone, life's worth nothing . . . A rattle and his special call, the silence, then it rattles downhill, uphill, all around . . . once! And he stops, the dog. At the most unexpected place he breaks off, the bastard, and catches you by surprise, as though he stopped to hear if your heart is beating or not. And this silence, the silence between two perfor-mances, for me it's the most dismal . . . It's good if you're listening to a distant nightingale, otherwise it's like falling into some kind of hole, and what kind of thoughts come into your head then! . . . Dead silence. The shovels are clanking, when the ax hits the roots it sounds like bones breaking, and all you can hear is the gurgling water in the creek as though somebody is gargling softly all the time. In this silence you begin to feel like the last human being in the world; when we return to the city there won't be anyone there and there's nobody in the rest of the whole wide world either, daylight will never come, there will only be white nights like this and an endless silence. Such thoughts would creep in, especially if you had to dig holes for your own people. According to the rules we didn't talk about who and what it was—that's not our business, of course—but when it was our own people it inevitably leaked out. We, too, had our disturbers of the peace, why deny it. While I made all those trips out there our composition changed more than once, and during that time we had a high turnover rate too, just like the Executive Committee and the City Soviet . . . Take that Gesiozsky, for example. He had a girl friend, a sweetheart, the well-known prostitute Dublitskaya, a citizenness not involved in anything or noted for anything, and she denounced him to us. He had dragged her girl friends off the street, threatened them with arrest, and even got into fights. His living habits compromised him seriously, as far as both his virtue and morality were concerned. Once when he was drunk he bragged to her that he had been awarded an order by the Emir of Bukhara in 1920. And there was an interesting coincidence: Dublitskaya's apartment was near Karpovka, in the very house of the Emir of Bukhara; the entrance was on the second courtyard with the columns. Thus, combining major and minor clues, they forged a chain heavy enough to destroy him. And he was destroyed.

What else can I say about the nightingale?

He sings both in rain and fog. Have you even heard a nightingale in the fog? It's only one bird singing, you understand with your mind that it's only one, but the sound comes from all sides: it's white, white all around you and you're not sure if you're still alive, maybe it's you they're digging a grave for . . . Who sings in paradise? Maybe nightingales? I'm joking.

Well, one more small addition to this picture, a short conversation at the establishment with turrets and spires; the seats inside are open to the front, there are only partitions on the sides. The arrested man is pulling up his pants and suddenly says, "Yes, there's an inexplicable delight in solitude." This expression is ambiguous for a person in his position. I pricked up my ears. People are unpredictable when they come from solitary confinement—you can expect just about anything from them and they themselves don't realize what they are capable of, they might say anything at any time. This one was supposedly from the camps, but circumspection has never let me down.

So we leave. I say nothing. Then he says, "Let's stop a little, for five years I haven't heard the nightingales." According to instructions this isn't allowed, of course, but I thought it better not to irritate him; it would be better to stop a minute . . .

V

. . . 1948. In the empty night the nightingale's song sounds above the Kronwerk Channel, above Lenin Park and Revolution Square that's being changed into an enormous garden planted with flower beds in the very center of the city . . . They are heaping up dirt, excavating trenches, pulling up something, transplanting something else, pyramids of sand and gravel are piled up; maybe here, the site of the very first city square, they're looking for some missing links in the unbroken and clear chain of history, or maybe they're filling in something to hide it from view . . .

No trace remains of the Troitsky Cathedral whose bells pealed to the glory of Peter's victories while the sonorous bronze from other empty bell towers, recast into guns, tore out those same victories from the hands of the brash foreign enemies along with their flesh and blood. The Troitsky bells also rang at the burial of the violent-tempered earthly ruler who had, with whips and canes, driven the people, handed over to him by the cowardly boyars, toward some kind of new happiness only he knew about.*

The nightingales are ringing. Their light, easy trills gurgle gaily and knock on the granite plaques and silent walls of the bastions and parterres of the famed fortress. This fort never fired a single shot at the enemy but became a threatening bulwark of supreme power in its endless war against its own unreasonable subjects. The sound dies out and the nightingales' trills don't come back as an echo; they stay in the damp empty casemates that guard secret and unimaginable grief, fear of death, and torture by loneliness and silence.

. . . It's the rare fortress in Europe that can brag that beneath its walls a hundred thousand men have fallen—but not during storms and sieges, neither of which this famed fortress has experienced during the two-and-a-half centuries it's been standing firmly planted by the sea, but, rather, during its own construction under the direct observation and guardianship of the chief inspector of both constructions and constructors, His Majesty the Lord Emperor Peter Alekseevich himself in person . . . For fifteen years they drove workers hither, dragged, carried, and imported them from all corners of Russia, rapidly exhausting the insignificant strength of foreign and who-knows-what-other prisoners, since it's a well-

*Peter the Great used harsh methods to modernize Russia.

known fact that after the surrender of Nienschants,* the garrison was dispatched straight here, still armed, and given bullets in their mouths ... Creating a New Amsterdam at the edge of his vast fatherland, the emperor forbade the erection of stone buildings in the rest of the empire, but faster than digging canals the builders had to dig holes where they dumped the exhausted construction workers, faster than they could build the fortress walls grew the mounds over the bones of slaves. Meanwhile, the government was dejected not over the destructive nature of the locality and not over the absence of housing and food for their industrious subjects, but only over the slowness with which the grand plans were taking shape, and it didn't realize that the work could be completed easier, faster, and better with free contracts and hired labor.

Where else, what other country could brag that the capital of the empire had become a place of exile for its subjects?

They were traveling with broken hearts, too afraid to disobey, dragging themselves along and biting their tongues, merchants, artisans and noblemen ... People of various professions, trades, and arts from inside Russia were sent to live in the capital, and in the first place those who had a factory, business, or trade. Runaways from the capital were caught and returned there. The name of the last exile to the capital is known; he was, admittedly, exiled simply thanks to his own whim. The metalworker Aleksandr Kastorych Skorokhodov was caught and sentenced to exile for agitation and insubordination and for organizing strikes at the Nikolaevsk naval factory, but he wished and even demanded that the place of exile should be St. Petersburg, the city that had just been renamed Petrograd because of the quarrel with the Germans. The historic cablegram, sent by the Petrograd police chief general, got lost in the police archives; in reply to his colleague at the Nikolaevsk factory who was desperate because he lacked power, the police chief sent his most gracious benevolence: "One scoundrel more or less; let him go." This took place during the cruel war, September 1914.

Many solemnities, feasts, celebrations, holidays, and victories have shaken the unsteady ground of Troitsky Square and the oldest streets leading away from it, a busy area surrounded by the houses of the tsars' favorites until it obtained its present proud name and sank into quietude and silence, only rarely broken by bursts of salutes from the beach below

---

*Nienschants was a fortress at the confluence of the Okhta and Neva rivers built in 1349 to replace the Kantsy fortress. During the Great Northern War it was replaced in turn by the Peter and Paul fortress.

the Peter and Paul fortress, or by some ruffians like the ones who supposedly hung a four-meter-high wooden cross on the facade of the House of Political Prisoners, bringing tremors of unrest to the troops preserving internal law and order, who had until then been dozing in permanent battle readiness with all their mortars, machine guns, and recoilless rifles . . . Much gaiety has taken place beneath the low firmament, many cheerful sounds and shouts of exultation have risen to the sky, but on the ground and also under it remains all the blood that had splashed on the executioner and from the executioner to the ground, the blood of those broken on the wheel and quartered, then hanged from iron rods conveniently arranged in a circle to exhibit both these quartered bodies and the bodies of those graciously allowed to be decapitated with a single blow.

The bells rang for weeks during masquerades and holidays, and drumrolls could also be heard drowning out the frantic screams of those presently undergoing punishment. Isn't this where the new capital held the first of its many executions, one of the first being conducted with the same geometrical strictness as the basic plan according to which the city is constructed? Justly and graciously, only four were chosen by lot from the twelve captured malefactors, who with the intent of theft had burned the two-storied wooden shops of the new Gostiny Dvor Market next to the Kronwerk Canal; and they were hanged on four gallows immediately raised neatly and symmetrically on the corners of the still-smoking ruins . . .

Having strayed onto the Russian throne over the universally impassible roads, Emperor Peter III may have remained in the memory of his grateful descendants as the emperor who destroyed the torture chambers and the secret chancellery; his spouse, Empress Catherine II, went even further and abolished torture, although it's true that Aleksandr I abolished torture again . . . The plan to abolish the knout as a widely used means of upholding order and morality was in 1817 entrusted to a secret committee under the leadership of Count Arakcheev.* The fathers of the fatherland spent days racking their brains over two tricky questions: "Is it possible to abolish the knout?" and if so, then "What can it be replaced with?" Prince Dmitry Ivanovich Lobanov-Rostovsky was racking his brain, which had been shot through at the capture of Ochakov; he was an infantry general who was appointed minister of justice; he held to the reasonable rule: Beat nine to death and put the tenth before a firing squad. The bastard son of

*Aleksey Arakcheev (1769–1834) was a general and a strict but efficient advisor to Aleksandr I.

Count Stroganov's sister, Nikolay Nikolaevich Novosiltsev, also racked his brain; it was he who had prepared the revolt of March 11 which brought him extremely close to the emperor and allowed him to become famous by establishing the secret chancellery in the Polish Empire. Aleksandr Nikolaevich Golitsyn also uttered his weighty words; he was the weather-vane at court, known for his cheerful temperament and daring entertain-ments, and he had by some strange accident become both the head of orthodoxy and the minister of spiritual affairs; he also gathered up under his wing public education for the convenience of persecuting the univer-sities and imposing the fiercest censorship. Neither Count Tormosov nor Prince Tsintsianov nor Senator Plotnikov had enough mental and moral strength to advance the problem of the knout. It's true that the progress made in the organization of domestic guards and the practice of transport-ing convicts by convoy enabled the government to abolish the slitting of nostrils (or "placing marks") to discourage escape, introducing instead "commercial execution," namely knouting, and this outlived the nostril slitting by a remarkably long time. Thus the knout, introduced by Aleksey Mikailovich the Silent to the rank of state instrument in the Code of 1649, remained in force, except for four years, until its bicentennial. It was abol-ished only in 1845.

The last big bloodletting on this square took place in January 1905, that memorable year when soldiers, quickly redirected across the brand new and very conveniently placed beautiful bridge, efficiently sprayed bullets, from the Vyborg side of Petrograd, over the citizens who had come to ask the tsar for mercy.

The nightingales are trilling above the quiet Kronwerk Canal, above the steep shores of the embankment. A hundred steps from the parade ground lies the so-far-unidentified location, not yet adorned by an obelisk with five profiles, of the wicked and unskilled execution* when rotten ropes choked the throats of the five madmen who wished a different destiny for their fatherland than the one meted out by the single ruler, even though he may have been anointed to tsardom by Lord God himself.

Beat, nightingale's song: beat on the silent stone walls, beat on the thick prison gate, beat on the prison bolts that have locked up thousands of souls, some from the light of the world and others from the light of truth

---

*A reference to the execution of five leaders of the 1825 Decembrist Revolt, namely, P. Pestel, S. Muravev Apostol, K. Ryleev, M. Bestuzhev-Riumin, and P. Kakh-ovsky.

and goodness. May God let your whistling wake up someone who will start moving under the ooze of life's cares, let someone's soul be roused from its gray sleep and try to make its own life meaningful, strong, and bold, and begin to abhor its own muteness, timidity, and endless chase after petty advantages. Let someone respond with sweet pain to the song of this bird, fearless in the ignorance of its own fate, having perhaps been sent to the stone city as an example for us or as a reproach.

Ring on, nightingale! It's your night, your truth.

VI

. . . What was I saying? I and the arrested are standing by the rest-room. We had stepped just a bit to the side, as I said, to listen to the nightingales. It's interesting that I could listen to them in the city and not be afraid at all.

"I don't remember that there were so many nightingales here before the war." This is me speaking.

He says, "There's no cats, that's why there's so many. The night-ingale's nest is low-down and in the city his worst enemies are the cats."

And really, after the war there were hardly any cats left in the city; they yielded their place to the nightingales. What kind of an animal is the cat? Aren't there enough rats for him in the city? And mice? No, he has to eat the nightingale! . . .

I can't remember how, but from cats we got to talking of love.

I didn't want to stand there like an idiot so I said that the nightingale is actually very small but it can feel such great love and expresses it so beautifully.

The arrested man says, "That's only a preconceived idea. What kind of love can it be if his chicks hatch only a few days later? It's amazing, of all the animals, the birds are always before our eyes; we hear them and see them, but we don't understand them. Obsolete and basically incorrect opinions stay alive . . ." An interesting conversation starts between us.

To avoid irritating him I ask calmly, "You seem to doubt that the nightingale sings about love."

The detainee doesn't look at me as though it wasn't me he wasn't talking to. "People are strange, someone tells a beautiful lie and others only repeat it, keep on repeating it without even moving their brains, so help me God . . . What's love got to do with it? It's a guard song! A warning: here's my house, my family, my nest . . . don't get closer, or you will have me to deal with. It's a call!" "Does it also warn the cats? Does it call them, too, as you say?" Here the arrested looks at me and answers chokingly, "Cats, too." "Let's go back," I say, "so they won't accuse us both of trying to escape." It was a joke.

He places his hands behind his back and walks three steps before me. But I recognize this posture.

Just as we came out on the boulevard from the red corner, he at once put his hands behind his back and moved three steps in front of me. I caught myself wondering what command I should give to make him walk normally. There's a command: "Hands!" They understand at once and put their hands behind their backs. But this is a street, not a prison for politicals. Bystanders may look through the windows, they may come out of any front door; after all, there's no curfew. But I knew what to do. Just as he started walking with his arms back, I said just like that, in passing, "You must be a little more modest, citizen." He turns around, doesn't understand. I can see that he really didn't understand. I say, "You mustn't draw attention to yourself like that, keep your arms more relaxed," I say.

I'll tell you, he was not the only one who did this, he really didn't have any evil intent. It was explained scientifically to us. It's called a reactive condition, when in certain situations the organism itself reacts from habit, as though not controlled by thoughts. I've also been involved in rehabilitations. I was filling out questionnaires for financial aid; they used to pay those who were released three times the estimated salary at the moment of arrest. No, the length of imprisonment didn't matter, whether ten or fifteen years. You wouldn't believe it: this old man, a professor, came here after his rehabilitation, you ask some completely trivial question, like place of birth, and he jumps up and replies. "Sit down," you say. You smile. He smiles too, but when you ask your next question, well, let's say, where did you reside on the day of your arrest, he again jumps up and replies. That was an interesting old man. Why did they put him inside? He wrote a book about the British commandoes, summarizing their activities in the Second World War, and therefore he was accused of admiring foreign things as well as of carrying out counterrevolutionary propaganda and agitation, again Article 58/10. That's scientific research for you; you see, he wanted to bring it to Russia so it could be used here, too. He jumped up and down as on springs, and yet, according to our information, he was seriously ill. So this one with the "small hands" didn't do it on purpose but from habit. We're walking along the boulevard, and to make the situation look natural I decided to continue the conversation about nightingales. "A careless bird," I say, "is the nightingale, however. If it sat silently, fed its chicks, guarded its home, then perhaps it could even get along with the cats." "For two hundred years nightingales and cats have lived in the city. They haven't learned to get along but they live. The birds sing and the cats miaow, they watch out where and how they live, the birds fly and the cats hide." On the whole, we're walking along nicely; if you saw us you'd think that two friends had stayed out too late on Saturday night, missed the last streetcar, dropped in at the public toilet, and were now walking down the street, talking, all is proper and not at all conspicuous . . .

On the following morning people came into the store, bought this and that, called home on the pay phone; we had to put up with it. There was a market next door and I went there to buy some smelt; my favorite food from childhood is smelt. There's smelt from Belozersk, from Pskov, and from Chud Lake. I personally prefer the Pskov kind, although smelt from Belozersk is also very good. The Belozersk smelt is larger and more fatty, and it has a slightly different color. I can tell them apart by their taste with my eyes closed if, of course, they aren't too heavily salted. You can kill any fish with too much salt. But the Pskov smelt, if it has been dried correctly, has both a special flavor and a special kind of odor. Smelt isn't just any food but a delicacy in its purest form. Sunflower seeds? No, brother. With smelt you need beer, of course . . . The beer plays a special role, it's absolutely indispensable if you want to enjoy all the specifics of the smelt, that's when you need beer! If the smelt is just a little too dry it's covered with the thinnest mist of salt, but this doesn't matter and the beer will remove this cloud instantly, and the salt gives the beer pungency, it rejuvenates it, this is how they influence each other . . . Yes, and another thing, you mustn't keep smelt in your mouth too long. If you drink beer with roach, for instance, then you place a piece of the fish in your mouth and filter the beer over it. You can't do that with smelt. You need to hold it in the beer for just a second, let it breathe, don't suck it in, chew it a little and then swallow it with your second mouthful of beer . . . If you keep the smelt in your mouth too long it's not as good any more, it's tender to begin with but gets too soft and loses its taste; it's not the same any more . . .

I was lucky with the smelt and got the Pskov kind and there was no problem with the beer either. There were three shops nearby; at the corner of Bolshaya Posadskaya they had Martov beer that doesn't go with smelt, and at No. 26/28 where Kirov* used to live there's an excellent little food shop in the basement. I got Riga bread there. A third shop is on the

*Sergey Kirov (1888–1934), Soviet political leader and aide to Stalin, was assassinated under suspicious circumstances.

corner of Divenskaya and we got other things there. Good. How the day flew by we didn't notice.

We had to take him out during the day too, you had to take the beer into account . . .

Early Monday morning Pildin got down to the station, filled out all the forms, came with a car, everything done properly. He was put in the solitary for politicals, and I never saw him again in my life.

Incidentally, he told me some other interesting things. It turns out that birds don't live in their nests, their nests are only to raise their young in; otherwise they live out in the open. People think of a nest as the bird's home only because they look at the bird through their own eyes. The bird doesn't fly to its nest when it rains or to escape from danger, and at night it doesn't hide in the nest. The bird has its own life, its own habits. It needs no nest. It carries its bed with it, sticks its beak under its wing and sleeps.

I got interested; where had he learned all that? From his cellmate. They had swilled the same slop for three months, and he was a real specialist on birds.

Actually, I've acquired quite a bit of education in the course of my work. It's amazing to think what a lot of people I've had to deal with.

All kinds of people, all kinds. I can't mention them all but here's one, he died later in solitary; he didn't even last until the Special Conference, his heart gave out. I can remember him although I only talked with him two or three times, no more; it's funny, he was a university professor and I usually got simpler people, as a rule. This professor was interesting. He must have hated our science or culture, because otherwise why did he carry out research activity hostile to our regime, both in writing and orally, straight from the speaker's platform, so to speak. What did he and I talk about? Who had directed him? Whose instructions did he carry out? Accomplices? Where did they meet? What were their goals? . . .

People are usually rather disconcerted when they come directly from freedom, but this one seemed to be not exactly grinning but calm, as though he was questioning me, not me him. He had already been burned; it turned out that already before the war he had served time in prison, but not very long, just three years. We had this kind of conversation: I ask him something, and he says, "Why are you so muddleheaded, my friend?" I asked him politely to leave my head alone and answer my question. Then he up and says, "Let me tell you about two cows who came into a shop and wanted to buy a pound of tea!" Well, it's not uncommon to pretend insanity. I answer calmly, "Have you decided to act like you're insane?" Then he laughs out and says, "Sorry, but you didn't impress me as being well read. Sorry." It turns out that I hit the nail on the head, this professor was some kind of famous specialist on Gogol, and Kazbek Ivanovich later explained that this piece about the cows and tea comes from Gogol's "Diary of a Madman." I had read other works by Gogol, so I went and got this "Diary" because I wanted to check up on Kazbek Ivanovich. Yes . . . How they used to write! They could write whatever they wanted! Gogol didn't like the French and he writes it, too: the French are stupid, I'd like to give them all a beating. I understand that it wouldn't matter so much if you write like that about your own people, but it would be rather embarrassing to do it about the French . . .

But the most interesting and best informed people, those that I learned the most from, as far as my education is concerned, were the refusers. They were the ones who refused from the very beginning of the investigation. "What you can prove I'll pay for, but I won't incriminate myself or anyone else." . . . You can explain to them in all kinds of ways that their refusal to confess guilt and cooperate with the investigation shows a lack of faith in the organs, and a lack of confidence in the organs already constitutes hostility to the socialist order; it seems that you have convinced them but then they start all over again. Our commissar, what did he use to tell us? Every Soviet citizen is a collaborator of the NKVD. If you don't want to collaborate with the NKVD, what does that mean? This and that, but they didn't see it that way.

. . . And formalism, we had that, too, a damned lot of it! You go on a search, and well, under his mattress you find a Nagant revolver or a pistol, you'd think you could write in the protocol "pistol TT." No way. "From Tula, construction Tokarev, length of barrel 116 mm., four threads, in the magazine eight rounds, the shells bottle-shaped, the bullets in casings . . ." Why is all this necessary? And the interrogations? This is formalism in its purest form. The Special Convention didn't read these protocols but they put pressure on us to fill them out. To be honest, they didn't put too much pressure on us, actually. Do you remember the law of December 1. No? An excellent law that one was, signed in 1934 by Kalinin and Enukidze.* There was such a person as Enukidze. Incidentally, Kalinin's wife was convicted according to this law, and Enukidze's son, too. This law stated that all cases concerning assaults on Soviet power and its best representatives had to be sorted out within ten days, no more. A summary of the prosecution's case was given to the accused one day before the court hearing. But

*Mikhail Kalinin (1875–1946), a revolutionary and politician; Avel Enukidze (1877–1937), a politician and editor.

if you look at it soberly, what good is this summary to him if the Special Conference would already meet the following day? According to this law of December 1, 1934, the sentence had to be carried out immediately because appeal wasn't allowed, and to reverse the sentence was illegal. Why then, you may ask, were these stupefying interrogations necessary? That was a good law, it simplifies the formalities considerably, otherwise I can't imagine how we could have processed such large quantities of people . . .

But formalism is a living thing. They introduced the fashion of interrogation at night. I don't even know where this fashion came from, but it got so that if you didn't haul them out at night it meant that you didn't work well. The result was that protocols weren't all that necessary, but you had to drag them to interrogations . . . I used to especially call in refusers for night interrogation, they are supposedly the most difficult ones, but in fact it was like rest for me because they were already known to be refusers, and if someone should suddenly want to look at the protocol, there you are, I've got a clean paper with ten or so questions. I did it so well that you couldn't find any faults with it. Just to sit there all night was boring, so I would at once establish a direct and frank contact with them. I say, "We'll sit here until five, that is I'll sit but you'll stand. But if you want to tell me something, I'll permit you to sit. Tell me anything you want, you can talk about your life, your childhood, your work, anything you want, or you can tell me about interesting books if you can remember them . . . No names or addresses or dates, I don't ask for anything and I won't write down anything." This method worked without fail, and it was seldom that anyone agreed to stand there silently all night. So word by word, a little at a time, you see, I learned interesting things about the French Revolution. One man recited poetry all night. At first I listened and could almost understand what it meant, but then I was simply amazed at how this man could remember such a lot of verse! Mining is more interesting; I might say that I've heard lectures about energetics, all different kinds, and about electrical engineering, and building the power network, and conversion substations, and I don't think I'll ever confuse oil rectifiers and those with mercury, I could tell them apart by the way they hum, although I have never actually seen either kind. And take bookkeeping . . . Awfully interesting, that. Banking, credit financing, how savings and loans banks differ from commercial banks, if you please . . . I got this from Kondrikov. Don't you remember? Well. What a character that was. Kirov found him in a Novgorod bank or somewhere and made him his authorized commissioner on the Kola Peninsula. Kondrikov became famous, he was the "Prince of Kola!" . . . It was funny when we came for him. Along the way between Kandalaksha and Murmansk he had little apartments, not really residences but little houses, since he had to move constantly between Apatiti and Monchegorsk, and along the Neva and Tuloma rivers. He had a kind of little house right by the station at Zasheek. The fast and efficient housekeeper there was Finnish. The house was always prepared for him. She'd look out of the window when some train went by, even a goods train, to see if her employer was on it. One day she looked, the train was just arriving from Kandalaksha and Vasily Ivanovich comes walking up to the house with five or six men. Instantly, in the span of three or four minutes, she sets the table. There was grayling, mushrooms, and lancet fish straight out of the oven, as though she had been expecting him. She opens the door, smiles, mumbles something cheerful in her language . . . When we walk into the apartment in silence she sees that Kondrikov isn't himself, and since we happened to be in uniform she understood everything instantly and started to clear the table. Bandaletov of the Kandalaksha NKVD tells her, "Don't hurry, leave it there!" She mutters at him, angry as a witch, and takes it all away, but she pours Kondrikov a glass of vodka and gives him some salmon. Actually this wasn't permitted, but what can we do; it is, after all, an unusual case, and then the woman understands absolutely no Russian. I can't remember now why he was arrested, it seems it was because of the right-wing Trotskyist Center. The man remained steadfast, he was a total refuser and didn't mention a single name the whole time, but he told me a lot about banking.

Well, shipbuilding is my special interest. First, there's my youth in the navy, and second, I could understand this much better than other subjects, of course. And medicine. That's more complicated. While they're talking I think I understand, but when I try to recall it later, maybe at home, I get nowhere, I get all mixed up. I asked a professor why this is so. He said that I have no basic preparation, no foundation, I don't know anatomy and physiology. Well, perhaps, it may very well be true. How the skull of the accused is constructed, this I really don't know. But I did notice one thing. The greater the specialist, the easier it is to understand him, and I thought that if someone's a professor, then only other professors can understand him, but that's not the case. A certain Sawbones from the infirmary at a wood-processing factory—it used to be called Maltser, not far from Karpovka—he once tried to explain to me how a human hand is constructed. I got very confused, but later we got some doctor called Bekhterev from the Institute of the Study of the Brain in the Grand Duke's mansion on Petrovskaya Embankment, and he explained it amazingly well. What a hand is. A German came through, his name was Worms, a very famous gynecologist; he was here because of the Syzransk Bridge affair. He was one of that group—who knows if they were really planning an explosion—but just before the war he came here because of that affair. We had to send him under escort to Saratov, where they held a well-publicized show trial that was written about in the papers. My gynecologist got fifteen years. I receive an order to get a preliminary confession from him, but he refuses. At first he had a round beard cut short, and glasses with half-lenses like a half-moon lying on its back. He, too, was dragged out at night. I'm on duty. He stands. He stood for an hour, a second hour. He sees that I'm not asking him about anything but writing something, then he asks me, "What are you writing?" I frankly admit that I'm writing a letter to my sister, it's been four months since I wrote, she isn't getting along too well with her husband, and she has three children. I had six sisters before the war. He begins to get nervous. Then I say again, "You may sit down, this chair's for you, and you can tell me anything you like." Basically, we started chatting, I explained to him straight out why we hauled him out at night, and he told me how it's all organized in there with women, in the sense of females. All this mechanism, hidden from the male sex, he presented it to me very well during two interrogation sessions. Before that time I might say I was a wild man, I didn't differ much from animals. In this matter culture isn't a bad thing. He explained to me so that I could understand it, what's going on with them, with women, and what they need . . . What surprised me most of all was that it turns out that they have everything we have, only it's the other way around! I couldn't even imagine this at first, but then it turned out it's true.

After this I started to take greater interest in women, even my wife, and treat them more gently, I really did.

. . . The more you know, the more interesting life becomes. In this respect my work gave me much, otherwise just think what would have become of me? I've lived my life with people who disappeared who-knows-where and I'll go there too, either with them or after them . . . I can't even use any of my vast but haphazard knowledge.

Many view the world differently than I do; that's OK, I'm used to it. There used to be more who looked with my eyes but now there are fewer. Maybe it's inevitable.

Why I came to earth, this I have figured out. Why I lived, what I served, this I know, too. But why did I get the rest of my life? As a reward? Can old age really be a reward? Perhaps so I can share my rich experience with the new generation?

Our service didn't attract with showy uniforms; people joined not because they were talented but because they were eager and mentally strong, but not everyone could stand our work. I remember that three years before the beginning of the war I was sent with a group to Arkhangelsk as reinforcement, a major investigation was going on up there and we would take along local young activists as witnesses when doing arrests and searches; they might themselves be recruited into the organs later. Among the ones that our local cadres had their eyes on was the Komsomol secretary from the Arkhangelsk dramatic theater. It's true his profession was acting, but he was obviously talented and had a great inclination for organizational work. Everything about him was good: at various meetings he spoke very well, he had excellent recommendations, he was an orphan, altogether a young man with a future. They had looked him over and decided to test him, so first they enlisted him as a witness at the arrest of Serkachev, the director of the Arkhangelsk harbor, a gray-haired old man, well-known in Arkhangelsk; he had got the partisan movement going in the war, and it seems he had seven Lenin Orders. We arrive. This and that, a search, like it's supposed to be. He had a large apartment with many books, even in the hall there were shelves. The most troublesome thing in searches are papers, letters, manuscripts, and books. Junk, stuff that doesn't take very long to sift through, and to turn over furniture and knock on the walls, all this is nothing. To look in the vents, stoves, and trap doors doesn't take much time—but books, here you waste your time and effort, you pick up every one, leaf through it, shake it. Well, then, everything is going normally, we get to the books. But here are his two daughters, you might say young ladies, and his wife . . . Suddenly this old gray-haired uncle starts to sob. He's sobbing and can't stop, sobbing convulsively, like. Both girls were in tears at this point, but they had been crying quietly in their handkerchiefs; that's OK, but the old man is actually shaking. And he calls himself a partisan! His wife wants to go with him, but she isn't allowed to, she might hand him something or there could be some element of coming to terms, anyway it's not allowed. I look at our Komsomol youth, he's leaning against the lintel. I can see that he is holding his face up all the time as though he had a nosebleed. I go closer to him and it turns out he's sobbing like a hysterical woman, only without a sound . . . Such a militant boy, and here you are! I calmed him down, spoke to him like man-to-man; he seemed to calm down, drank some vodka, wiped his face. But ten minutes later he's in tears again, kind of moaning quietly . . . No, brother, I can see that you're not fit to become a Chekist, you're wishy-washy, no substance. Go home, go to hell. It's one thing to talk from the speaker's chair at meetings, anyone can do that, shout and brand the enemy; but to root him out you need to be tough and firm and perhaps something else, too.

Generally it was easiest to catch them for agitation. A certain engineer came to us for investigation, someone had reported that he had seen his cousin during a trip to Finland—he had gone there to get some equipment for the Baltic plant. He hadn't listed this relative on his application, or they wouldn't have let him go. The report was true, but we had nothing else. He insisted on negatives; he wasn't there, he didn't see, he didn't know. I brought him to interrogation several times and was present once. The investigator was Sekirov,* who was an excellent man and had been through a lot—his very name always made an impression—and he tells him straight out and without any tricks, "Sign or don't sign, you'll do time anyway. Just name a single person who got out of here without a sentence. Just one! Do you know anyone?" He says he doesn't. "How are you better than them, fuck your mother? Are you really stupid enough to give me a hard time? If I let you go it's like I failed in my work, can't you understand that? You're an enemy of the people, that's written on your forehead. And you will go to prison." Sekirov was helped by a coincidence. One morning the engineer wakes up in his cell and tells his dream. He had dreamed that he was going around in Finland unescorted, and there was something about going shopping . . . But there was an informer in his cell. This was at once made out to be counterrevolutionary agitation, and he went to fell trees, according to the law.

They say that the intelligentsia is polite. On the one hand, there's an element of truth in this, but on the other, it depends. The criminal contingent, I have noticed, is more attentive and tries to find a common language with us. But not those intellectuals! Like that "bridegroom" I told you about, what a lot of trouble he was; how many times I had to take him out personally and let him do little extra things, like listen to those nightingales. But did he thank me?

Here's another example.

Few people know of this place behind the goods station of the Moscow railroad station, on Konstantinogradskaya Street. Across the street, literally fifteen meters away, there's the lumber depot of the Moscow District Residential Administration. This firewood is lying there, it's been there for years, decades. It has turned black and gray because it's not used; it's to discourage people from looking closely. A railroad branch goes to the lumberyard, and at night wagons would come there—only it

*The Russian word *sekira* means "ax."

wasn't wood that they brought in and took away. There was a transit prison at the Konstantinogradskaya—not actually a prison but a reloading point. During the day it was filled up and in the night a group was quickly herded across the street to the lumberyard and loaded, and then shipped in sealed red cars to sorting stations . . . The difficult part was to bring the contingent to Konstantinogradskaya. They would bring them in Black Marias, three tonners; the back doors are shod with iron, on top there are two ventilation holes, and immediately inside the door to the left and right there are two little closets called "cups," intended for especially dangerous prisoners or those condemned to death. But how many can you put in a car at one time? Well, twenty, twenty-five if you cram them in, but sometimes we had to load sixty. Once a group was brought into the yard for loading and I saw an old lady, very beautiful, she looked like an empress and seemed extremely cultured. This was in February, at the end of the month, it was a sunny day and everything was melting. Hey, I think, it's true it's not very far, maybe half an hour, but how will you look then, tsaritsa, because after the previous trip I inspected the car and found an aluminum flask that looked as though the devil had danced on it, chewed it, and spat it out. I take this woman first, lead her to the car, help her in, and install her in the "doghouse"—that's this closet, so she wouldn't be trampled in the crush. How she screamed! How she started to knock. She screamed that she was only going to retrial. Fine, I think, she'll thank me yet. We start to load. As always there were curses, screams, groans, uncensored expressions; somehow or other you have to stuff people on top of each other, clear up to the ceiling. But they don't know that it's only a short way and they can put up with it . . . I tell you, it's hard work . . . I escorted the car, so it was I who unloaded it at Konstantinogradskaya, too. I dragged out this lady last of all. She's pale, not a drop of blood, she's gasping for air and doesn't look at me, or rather doesn't seem to recognize me . . . You'd think she'd thank me. No, I didn't expect it. And she was of the intelligentsia . . .

A criminal, now, he never behaves like that, he appreciates even the smallest sign of attention. "Citizen Commander, thank you," "Citizen Commander, thank you very much." They seem to be thanking you all the time. Generally there are all kinds inside the zone, literally all kinds. Including money and vodka . . .

. . . What else can I tell you about the intelligentsia?

For the most part these people are careless and therefore dangerous. On the radio and in newspapers and books they talk about the times we're living in, how we're under siege, and the internal enemies are just waiting for us to disclose our weakness. Not for a minute must we lose our vigilance and sense of responsibility. It's the same for everybody. Here, for instance, we have Air Force Marshal Vorozheykin, a general during the war. He survived the war but later he got twenty-five years; and his wife Aleksandra Aleksandrovna got twenty-five years, too. Why? The fact is that after the war some important person died, very important he was, and the funeral was of course very solemn and mournful, with high honors. But this Vorozheykin up and says, "This is fine." He says, "But when Stalin dies, that's going to be some funeral." That's all! You may be marshal ten times over but you won't get a pat on the head for talking like that. No one believes in God, sooner or later even Comrade Stalin might die, but why talk about it where people can hear you? Why? Could he have avoided saying it? No, answer me, could he or couldn't he? I'm asking you personally, because nowadays they love to dump the guilt on someone else. Someone is guilty. No one? Who asked you? Those who loved Comrade Stalin and couldn't think of living without him—and this was our whole people—they found this outburst insulting and it had to be answered with the utmost severity. He was guilty! But he was, after all, a marshal and he was given his due: as soon as Comrade Stalin died he was set free, literally the day after. He was inside for only three years, this is three out of twenty-five!

I can give you as many examples like this as you want. I don't have to go far. Over there, diagonally across, you can see the mansion of Count Witte, he was prime minister in the time of the tsars, minister of finance. They say it was he who introduced the wine monopoly into Russia; before him anyone who wanted to could distill both for himself and to sell. But we're talking about something else. The Institute for Protecting the Health of Children and Youth is housed in his mansion, but at elections its naturally an agitation point. The commandant of the mansion saw them nailing up a sign on a door that was carved of pearwood and laquered; the sign said, "Election Precinct Number XX for the Election of People's Judges and Assessors." When the commandant saw this he had a fit and yelled: "What idiot put this up? Take it down instantly," and he himself ripped down the sign. But the head of the election committee, a labor union representative, was a very serious comrade. The commandant had to answer to two accusations simultaneously: slandering the Soviet labor unions and attempting to disrupt the election of the people's judges and assessors.

There's one more story about Witte. In the Pharmacological Institute pharmacists are trained. I can't remember if it was a fourth- or fifth-year student, but this pale and weak-looking fellow read two volumes of this Witte's memoirs. You say it's in three volumes? He only read two, the third wasn't involved. Well, under the influence of what he had read he started to speak well about Witte, but the times were severe—it was 1950. He was accused of disseminating propaganda of monarchistic ideas. He even started to argue . . . All the things that have happened just in this Witte mansion—there are too many stories for just one evening—but if we were to talk about the House of Political Prisoners? One of our men estimated that in the 142 apartments, 134 people were unmasked and rendered harmless . . . I remember myself how five cars used to be detailed every night to come to this house. What kinds of cars? M-cars, sedans.

VII

. . . The low location of the former imperial capital deprives those who thirst to contemplate its grandeur and magnificence in its entirety of the kind of convenient elevated vantage point that St. Petersburg should possess, as Paris and Moscow do. Adapted for viewing as though from below, the city attempts to overwhelm the beholder not only with the uncommon height of its spires and enormous cupolas raised toward the sky, not only with the multitude and grandeur of its columns, hewn from solid stone, cast from bronze and iron, or fashioned from marble, granite, polished stone from Pudok, or Afghan azurite, but also with the sound of bronze chariots flying high in the sky, rendering the gaping traveler breathless . . .

. . . Above the city horses are flying, only momentarily touching their weightless hooves to the magnificent arches above the dark square or on the pediment of the temple of Melpomene in order to push off from the skyward-pointing stones and continue their eternal flight.

Not for nothing are these horses placed all over the city, tamed by mighty riders or frozen in the strong hands of nude athletes, unconcerned with frost, rain, or wind. The bridled and subjugated horses on the bridge that at one time marked the city limit were a welcoming sight to those entering the capital from the Arkhangelsk, Vologda, and Yaroslavl areas! . . .

Many beautiful monuments and symbols have been collected in the city beneath its dull sky . . .

Yes, the heart of the true amateur and specialist in beauty will also in other cities and in other lands find many columns and angels hovering in the unreachable heights. Arches, spires, palaces, and cathedrals generously adorn many proud capitals, but where else, except perhaps in Rome, can you find yourself captured within such ensembles of stone, astonishing in their elegance and in the perfection of their execution; luxurious palaces consisting of whimsical combinations, endless squares, countless bridges, obelisks, public gardens, buildings of differing styles cleverly joined together as though they were twins, mirroring each other from the opposite sides of one and the same street . . .

It's all the more surprising and mysterious that in the very center of the city, its navel during the first years after its foundation, there should be an empty space, dejected like an abandoned stage strewn with unfinished scenery; now it's called Revolution Square. The infinitely large park constructed on this square doesn't attract or delight the citizens with its abundant light or the fresh winds blowing in straight from the Neva, or its vast space, or even its seclusion. One of the sides of the square reaches straight down to the embankment, to a gigantic bridge crossing the Neva at its widest part with seven leaps. On the other two sides streetcars come flying down from the steep bridge and encircle the square, and the fourth side of the square touches the foundations of two enormous buildings, extending in one line as though continuing each other, as though in their conception they were intended to be joined together. But for over thirty years they have remained unjoined, separated by a space that's filled by nothing.

With their facades overlooking the square, the two gigantic buildings symbolize the discord between two epochs and the paralysis of the administrative decision-making power as far as joining them together is concerned. Totally open to sunlight and all the winds, containing only straight lines and unadorned surfaces, rejecting the tinsel of decoration and unburdened by details, the geometrically precise facade of the House of Political Prisoners is dotted with balconies placed like swallows' nests along the upper floors, and on the lower floors the balconies are joined into tribunelike terraces, as though the designer knew that the inhabitants of this house would grieve in the closed spaces of their dwelling, earned by suffering and hard labor, unaware of the possibility of stepping out on the balcony at any moment and delivering a speech full of life and rage, addressing the crowds of people below who are thirsting for light and truth, exhorting them to struggle and sacrifice themselves to achieve great feats.

The house beside it is completely different; it's described in the newest guidebooks as a "house of highest monumentality, conceived and erected around the middle of the present century." The facade is decorated with a multitude of pseudo-Grecian columns, arranged in two rungs, one on top of the other. The bold artist challenged the ancient masters who could erect a single Parthenon, for example, but were unable to build a second one. In the resuscitated language of the ancient Greeks, the majesty of the present time is expressed by a grand portico with numerous columns, marking the center of the two buildings that haven't been combined into one. Raised on an enormous and in a certain sense also grand parallelepiped, the portico is ornamented with windows both semicircular and traditionally rectangular, in which, in the spirit of elevated monumentality, there are no transoms but instead beautiful columns two meters high. The viewer is also impressed by the rough-hewn foundation three stories tall. But the portico has no pediment, or rather it does have one, but it's unexpectedly flat and humble, the shape of a modern sailor's cap, the kind you get from the sergeant at the supply depot, and you turn it around in your hands and begin to wonder what part of it you're supposed to pull up and what part to push down to make the line along the stiff edge with the white ribbon look like a wave rising on your head but frozen in time. Perhaps this flat pediment is only a stage on which our plaster contemporaries haven't entered yet, carrying in their hands tokens of triumph and heroism. The countless columns covering the facade are separated from each other by tiny little semibalconies on which you couldn't place both feet, should you desire to do so, and you couldn't scream to your neighbor, cut off from you by a grandiose prominence, even in case of fire.

Anyway, the dwellers of the "House of Highest Monumentality" are expected to have an elevated morality, which precludes certain actions, possibly permitted to a few individuals even in our current times but reprehensible from the point of view of the future. The epoch of monumentality ended before the House of Political Prisoners lost its original face and could become a symmetrical reflection of the left part of the structure, in accordance with the monumental plan. It should have another twenty-eight columns along the former Great Court Street, known as Prospect of Peasant Poverty during the construction of the House of Political Prisoners, but renamed Kuybyshev Street during the construction of the House of Highest Monumentality.

Thus these two buildings ended up standing beside each other, but not together, since the short side of the House of Political Prisoners reaches out toward the House of Highest Monumentality with a kind of rounded shape that could easily be taken for a clenched fist, or maybe a seven-story-tall conning tower on some armored battleship from the time of the October Revolution.

The portico above the square and, incidentally, also the cube on which it rests, houses the design office that was unable to complete its own mansion but is now sending designs to near and far regions for further building projects on locations not yet occupied but already cleared of old structures.

How did it happen that Revolution Square, in the center of the city, famous for its harmonious architectural ensembles, has turned into such an obviously ambiguous stage?

However, it's time to quit the habit of asking questions of history, since I fear that you would in any case have to keep the answers to yourself.

Behind the streetcar tracks running away from the square, hidden behind trees and tall clumps of lilac, stands the mansion of a grand duke's favorite ballerina, whimsical like an expensive toy and executed in the most fashionable style of the beginning of this century. The grand duke himself, however, was maintaining close connections not only with Terpsichore but also with Euterpe, and he made his name almost immortal by giving to the simple people the wonderful song "The Beggar Died in the Army Hospital," and he bequeathed to those of more refined tastes and feelings the romance "I Opened the Window." His pompous mansion—the last construction by the tsar's family in the capital—is rightfully occupied by the Institute for Research on the Brain and stands behind the House of Political Prisoners not far from the little hut, enclosed in a brick case, of the founder of the city, and a seven-minute leisurely stroll from the famous ballerina's mansion.

Another corner of the square touches the park where beyond the transparent stage scenery of tall trees you can just discern the arena, known by everyone, where during the white night of July 13 one of the most famous of all tragedies was played out without any spectators, but agitating the souls of contemporaries and plunging the fatherland into a silent torpor for many years.

A brick horseshoe as mighty as a fortress then occupied Kronwerk Square, where in accordance with the inspired composition by the emperor himself, who also planned the procedure of its implementation, ninety-seven officers were subjected to civil execution and public dishonor for daring to doubt that tsars are appointed by God and for wanting to communicate to others the original meaning of the words "legality" and "justice." They had weakened and changed terribly from half a year of imprisonment, but without trembling and even triumphantly they went to meet their fate on the earthen banks that had settled and were crumbling, on which a scaffold had been constructed with two posts and one crossbar for the five whom the tsar had graciously granted hanging and delivered from quartering. They saw how some youth grabbed a noose on the almost completed scaffold and hung on it to test the strength of the rope from which five hours after the execution they would remove the dead bodies that had before death been wrapped in white shrouds; but the strangled Russia would keep dangling who knows how long . . . The tsar, who had started a new historical epoch of petty despotism, saw himself as the heir and follower of Peter the First who didn't know the meaning of the word "petty," and he had not only drawn the plan for the disposition of the troops during the execution but also decided who should come out at what time, who should go first, how many guards should be assigned to each criminal, who should read the sentence, and how many drumrolls should be beaten for extra effect after everyone had reached his place.

The fires were smoking and ready to receive and consume the glorious uniforms of the heroes who had saved the fatherland from foreign invasion but couldn't save it from the homegrown tyrant . . .

On that early morning there were no spectators at this perhaps most luxurious of all the executions that Troitsky Square and its surroundings have ever known and remembered. It was only the anointed organizer of the brutal spectacle who was awake at Tsarskoe Selo and received messengers every half hour, steaming from the long gallop, who reported on the premier performance.

VIII

. . . I only saw the performer in Novogorod, he was always drunk.

IX

. . . Since ancient times people have always raised crosses, shrines, and temples in remembrance of shed blood, in remembrance of exploits of the human spirit that defy the despotism of everyday life.

So also here, between the former Kronwerk Square and Revolution Square, then still called Troitsky, a temple was raised in 1906, presumably thanks to the oversight of those called to guard the spiritual peace of the autocrat. It was a temple of mercy, an army hospital, whose geometrical design repeated the disposition in two squares of the officers of the guards and of the army who were condemned to exile and hard labor.

The ever-alert eye of the spiritual pastors must have been clouded, because the Vladimir Mother of God is looking down at us from the high hospital wall with the black eyes of Princess Volkonskaya,* thanks to a

*Princess Volkonskaya was the wife of one of the Decembrists, and she followed him in exile to Siberia.

whim of the young iconographer Kuzma from Khvalynsk, who rejected the thousand-year-old Byzantine canon that prescribes that the intercessor for the human race should be pictured with pale blue eyes.

The merciful Vladimir Mother of God is concealed by soot and dust from the eyes of the swift knaves who would be prepared to denounce even the mother of God herself if it helped them maintain and augment their brainless devotion, their only capital, to anything or anyone at all.

X

... From all these arrests and searches there isn't much to recall. You think that they were all unique dramas? Nothing of the kind, they were all the same. You get the house chairman or the yardman to come along as a witness, you send them ahead to find out whether the citizen or citizenness of interest to you is at home, then you come with this house chairman; people would calmly open their door when they heard his voice, even at night ... There were, of course, unpleasant incidents when people shot themselves. You ring: "Open up!" and there's a shot. On the one hand, of course, this is a failure at work, but if you look at it from another side ... well, if he wasn't guilty, why shoot himself? If you come and knock on my door at night or in the morning, I won't shoot myself, nor will you ... It was harder to work in communal apartments, especially large ones. We come in, but the person we need isn't there. What to do? The squad leader calls the officer on duty over the official line, this and that ... But what can he say, just think of his position. He can only say one thing, "You botched it, so stay and wait!" That's called ambush. Once we waited in ambush for two days, and it was a trivial matter; we were arresting some lady librarian. What sort of procedure was there? They sent lists to all libraries, such and so books to be taken out of circulation, handed in or destroyed. They were granted a certain time, twenty-four hours; it could be extended to seventy-two hours at the most; that's three days, no matter what. What's on the shelves can easily be removed and liquidated, but what about the things that have been checked out and are circulating? Then they run like rabbits, sometimes they had to run around to lots of people and collect everything during a single night. And you know what people are like. They might borrow a library book and take it on vacation or on a trip to read on the train. People would also take library books to their summer houses. Or a person may be in the hospital and leave the book at home. Then you had to find him in the hospital, ask for his key and make him explain where to find the book. Some would give you the key but others wanted to think about it. If the time limit was up and the book on the list hadn't been turned in, we'd arrest the library workers.

So we spent two days waiting for this particular library director who was chasing about near Siversky or Vyritsa, trying to find some journals, while we were waiting in ambush. Terribly boring. To make it clear to you how difficult our situation was I'll mention that I'm by nature sociable and not at all mean. I always did everything in a cultured way, politely, I never took any liberties; I know that others may have behaved in an unseemly manner but I didn't. But friendly relations weren't encouraged among us workers, it wasn't approved, and I think it was the same thing upstairs. They gave orders, you carried them out and reported. Don't wag your tongue. Well, we weren't silent while we worked, we are human, after all, but our conversations were brief: you know, about fishing, you could talk about that as much as you wanted; soccer, "Dynamo," that's fine, when our team was doing well; and the movies, what actors you liked best, we had discussions about this, some liked Lemeshev, others preferred Kozlovsky; just as some were for "Locomotive," the big bruisers, and others for "Food-services."* Such conversations were not really enough, sitting there together for two days, nose to nose, you know, and to sit silently is also kind of embarrassing. When people sit silently together it's the first sign of hatred or stupidity, a normal person would die from boredom, sitting silently like that. Try to solve that problem. On the one hand, they liked you to be close-mouthed and reserved, but on the other hand, you don't want to look like the village idiot. I didn't like those ambushes, to hell with them, precisely because of that silence and the artificial conversations.

There was a funny incident with the telephone. Suddenly some girls started calling on the duty officer's phone. I was the assistant to the duty officer. Ring! I answer calmly, "Seryozha isn't here, you've got the wrong number." Another ring. "But aren't you Seryozha?" "No, I'm not Seryozha. Girls, you're interrupting our work." Giggles and a stupid conversation, something like this, "Do you have whiskers?" I patiently asked them again who they were trying to call, what number, and they gave our number. Then I tell them, "Forget this number once and for all and never call again." And they say, "But then we can't hear your voice!" I really do have a nice voice, they weren't the first to notice it. I also sing well, and in our amateur group no one could sing Ukranian songs better than I . . . "The Sun Is Setting, Evening Is Near." But back to the phone. Those girls kept calling, talking about my voice. Then I told them angrily, "Stop this calling or I'll take away your telephone." A couple of hours went by, maybe three, then they called again but by now I had their address and sent an M-car to

*Names of professional soccer teams.

pick them up. I told them to wait in the corridor. They sat down. I went out specially to look at them. They look awful, they're pale, they're too scared even to cry. I think, it's lucky for you that I'm not Kazbek Ivanych, he wouldn't have let you off so easily. I wasn't going to do anything about them. After three hours I signed their passes and sent them away. I didn't even say anything. Kazbek Ivanych had this method of prevention, and we had it too. We pick up someone, there are no accusations against him, no evidence, but I simply tell him nice and friendly, "Comrade, you should be more careful in this and that area. We're warning you and hope that this is our first and last conversation. You're free to go now."

I noticed how Kazbek Ivanych invited people for preventive talks, but often he didn't even talk. He kept them in the corridor for four or five hours and then let them go. Once I mentioned in passing, "We haven't had time for preventive talks, there simply aren't enough working days." "No," says Kazbek Ivanych, "it's my method. What can I tell him during a conversation? Very little. Don't blab, don't bother such-and-such at work, leave so-and-so's wife alone . . . But imagine what all he is thinking, feeling, and suspecting while he's standing waiting in my corridor for four hours, or even if he's sitting. He's probably taking apart his entire life, recalling everything, going over it a thousand times, thinking about more things than I could tell him during ten conversations. The main thing is that he leaves without any idea of what I know and don't know. He leaves, firmly convinced that I know everything, and this is why I brought him in." An amazing person, Kazbek Ivanych, stern and difficult, he didn't spare anyone, including himself, and he was very clever. When we used to bring in between fifty and two hundred people every night, there was always a meeting in the evening with instructions. Everyone was good at giving these instructions, the department chiefs, their deputies, but Kazbek Ivanych was better than anyone; after he pumped us up with his pep talk, we could almost fly.

You want me to tell how we spent days and nights in the department without going home for weeks on end? As soon as you start to talk, you have to watch out so you don't say too much. Because it's not only us but also those who went free, they too had to sign a pledge not to divulge anything. To divulge nothing, everything was secret, the investigations, the discipline in the camps, the transports, everything in general. I think that the repeated sentencing according to Article 58—that's when they tack on a second term as soon as the first one is over—that was done exactly for this reason, to keep them from divulging anything. If a person survived and was released, could he really restrain himself and not blab?

Perhaps it was precisely the "too much" that was the main thing in his life, as it was in mine, so in the end both his life and mine have been cut off. He's an enemy, a criminal, but how about me? Why should I have to hide my whole life?

Take Valentin. His mother was my wife's godmother. He finished the Institute of Rubber Technology; he was enlisted into the NKVD in '35 and spent days and nights in the "Big House."* After a promotion he went to Sakhalin where he advanced to lieutenant colonel. Yes, lieutenant colonel. Ryumin was promoted from lieutenant colonel to deputy minister, just like that. What about Valentin? He was cold and honest, hard-working, conscientious, but rather limited . . . He returned from Sakhalin quietly, no stripes, no pension, and started working at the Red Triangle plant as assistant foreman, then he became foreman and died, it seems, as the deputy director of his section. No matter how many times I tried to worm things out of him, he never cracked. Even to me he said nothing. You have to keep secrets from the enemy, I understand that, but ourselves, why hide things from each other, relatives, family . . . Or the orders. Now it's 1966, right? A few years ago they were going to take back all orders. So they were given for nothing. No, here they don't give something for nothing. We started to complain about our personal pensions when the District Committee sent us this impersonal form letter: "Service in the organs does not constitute a privilege." . . . All your life you've been surrounded by the respect and love of the whole people, but when it comes to pension, then it "does not constitute." Tell me, is it fair? I remember this commandant at the "Big House" before the war, with one of those long Jewish names—he had four orders of the Red Banner. He liked to sign his whole name, and when he got papers to countersign—like subscriptions to a newspaper or journal, nothing big—there wasn't enough room for his signature, no place to spread out, but he still managed to squeeze in his entire name down to the last letter. He signed many such receipts, but then they signed one for him . . . Didn't he realize that his work didn't go unnoticed, that he was walking on the edge, right on the borderline, taking risks, and after all that, "it does not constitute a privilege."

On the whole I'm pleased with my fate although I didn't rise in the ranks, but like they say, I'm still alive . . .

They say that any work is honorable. They talk and talk, but did you ever hear a song about, let's say, prisoner transport escorts, or convoy services? The kids don't read poems about them on holidays and there're

*The "Big House" is the NKVD headquarters in Moscow and Leningrad.

no plays about them. Actually I do remember one play about reeducation on the Belomor Canal project.* It wasn't true to life, but from an educational point of view it was very useful; the government approved highly and it was playing at all the theaters.

I don't follow the theatrical life very attentively, mostly it's with the kids that I go to the Theater for Young People or the opera. We have seen the *Nutcracker*, but most of all I like *Sleeping Beauty*—I've seen it three times. I carefully follow the career of one director, his name is Zhulak. He used to work with us. He spent four years in the internal service, then worked for a short time as an operative, but all he did was organize amateur performances for holidays, short funny skits and so on and so forth, then he entered the Theater Institute, or perhaps they fixed him up there, I don't know, but he graduated like anyone else. I met him once. He used to have such a mean expression on his face, like a vicious pug dog, and he didn't laugh like normal people but like a chirping sparrow: khi, khi, khi . . . But when I saw him later he was cheerful and happy, his coat unbuttoned, and right on the street he flings open his arms: "Hello, my friend," and he laughs so loud that the passers-by look at him, he's laughing for them. But after all, I'm an old infantryman and tomorrow I may have to face the enemy again, so there's no need to attract attention right in the busy street like that. I'm a little over 180 centimeters tall** but I know how to melt into the crowd. Never mind. "Well, howdy, how goes it with you over there?" Zhulak wanted to know. What does it mean, "over there?" Did he actually expect me to tell him about the operatives, or what we're doing about "discipline," or news about the staff? I ask him, "Be more specific, where is 'there' and what, precisely, are you interested in?" He laughs. "Do you remember me?" he says. This is different, of course. I answer, "We're observing you closely." He got up on his toes and whispered in my ear, "You mean you've put me out to pasture" and laughs again. "Cut it out," I say, "tell me instead about your successes." He had staged a play by Shakespeare, maybe *A Midsummer Night's Dream* or *Twelfth Night.* I asked just to get him riled up, "Don't you want to put on something about our life?" "No," he says, "My gifts are in the comedy genre." Yes, perhaps those with a gift for comedy should do plays about life on the kolkhoz or about scientists . . . Later he put on yet another play, *Turmoil at Night.* Our investigators took note of the fact that he liked titles containing the word

*The Belomor Canal was built by prison labor; the project was notorious for its high cost in lives.
**Equivalent to six feet.

"night," like a memory from those times in his youth when he worked after dark.

XI

. . . Look through the window . . . Yes, the white night is given to man for some reason, perhaps we don't fully understand it yet.

I made my first arrest, as it happened, on a white night, in late April. There was much work, there were still problems with transport and there weren't enough operatives; it was long ago.

How is an arrest made? It all depends on the person you're arresting and what you might find in the place where this arrested person lives. If he has a small room, two men are more than enough. Yes, and a witness. If it's an apartment or a villa, a palace somewhere, then the entire brigade works. Here the brigade wasn't needed.

My very first prisoner, I even remember his name, I remember everything down to the tiniest detail; right now, if you like, I could walk the same route blindfolded . . . His name? That's not important, he had a name like everyone else. Brown hair, medium height, steely gray deep-set eyes, a tendency to corpulence, possibly wearing a dark-blue suit with a double-breasted jacket. Among his characteristic features was a habit of shrugging as though a bird sat on his shoulder and he wanted to push it off. Round face, smooth-shaven chin, straight mouth, thin lips . . . And so on. All this after almost forty years. I felt anxious as I set out independently to carry out this responsible task. Of course I worried. I wasn't actually high-ranking enough to be in charge of an arrest detail, but as I said, we didn't have enough people but had to do everything as best we could.

There was no time to spare but I nevertheless managed to run over the route the day before.

What do I remember? In the daytime, when I looked over the route, there was a strong smell of pea soup near No. 61, Griboedov Canal. When I took him that way at night, past the same No. 61, there suddenly came a strong smell of mushroom soup . . . and both times I thought, "Look at the quiet life, people are cooking soup, but I'm armed and have orders to confront the enemy."

This was the address: 9, Bolshaya Podyacheskaya, a plain-looking entrance from the street to the right of the gateway in the middle of the house, that's the main entrance. I entered, three steps down immediately to the right, the door to the janitor's, then a landing, turn left, and there you are at the bottom of a wide flight of stairs. On the landing there were two low windows to the courtyard. I made a mental note of this circumstance; it happens that people try to use windows . . . From the house to Podyachesky Bridge across the canal it's 125 paces, then on the way to Kokushin Bridge there are two gateways . . . I told the janitors to close them. Between Kokushin Bridge and Haymarket there's one gateway, between Haymarket and Demidov Bridge also one . . . A completely satisfactory route, we could go that route. The most difficult part was between the canal and the Moyka. From Demidov Bridge to the Moyka it's four hundred paces, count it yourself, and five gateways, two entrances through the house and four double courtyards, one with an exit to Stolyarny Lane. This was especially bad. OK, I can see that you're not interested. Well, to cut it short, we arrive. Up to the third floor; the floors are far apart in that old apartment building. There was an interesting doorbell: they don't exist any more, a bronze sort of little knob on a kind of bronze moon lying on its back; you pull the knob and inside the apartment a little hammer beats on a small bell. Another type of bell was a metal sign, "Kindly turn," like on a bicycle. These two types of doorbells were most common in the city, although sometimes we had to knock. I didn't like to knock, a bell is better, cultured and neat, and no extra noise.

I ring. The door opened quickly although it was already one-thirty at night. Did I mention that? It's a man who opens: not tall, on his head he has a handkerchief with knots in the corners—you couldn't tell if he tended toward corpulence—horsefaced, undershorts, undershirt, on his feet peasant shoes with cut-off tops . . . Later it turned out that his head was wrapped in a handkerchief because he had shaved it and cut himself in three places. I look at him and don't understand anything, there's nothing to identify him by. Had I really got the wrong apartment, had I got mixed-up because I was nervous? But the possibility that the apartment was full of other people who were listening at the doors right now—this didn't enter my mind. What a greenhorn I was! This seems funny to me now, but then it was nothing to laugh at. I was ashamed. If he slammed the door in my face right now, then what? But my heart whispered to me, No, it's no mistake, no mistake . . . Just to make sure I ask, "Does so-and-so live here?" He silently points to the door where the matte glass had been painted with decorative flowers, a pretty design, and a light was burning behind it. The apartment was interesting. The entry is like a room with six doors leading from it, but there's no corridor. I open and go in. The room was large but empty; an iron bed, a shelf with leftover food, a board had been placed across two chairs to make a table. The general impression was that the owner had left, and very recently, too. My heart sank. We were too late, it was empty, no one was there. And yet someone had just been there.

The cot was rumpled, it smelled inhabited, there were cigarette butts and empty bottles, all was in place but nobody was there . . . Brother, you're making a great start in your independent work, you should still be running in harness. But now the man with the handkerchief on his head comes in, shuts the door, and explains, "I'm so-and-so . . ." Can you imagine? That's how fate can sometimes turn around! Well, it was a real pleasure to conduct a search in that place. Before he had finished dressing we had already filled in all the forms and made up a protocol. Do you have a weapon? No. Literature? No. Letters, valuable papers, money? No, no, no.

But this wasn't the end of the excitement.

My "godson" dresses, I look and can hardly believe my eyes: a dark-blue suit, a double-breasted jacket, inclined to corpulence, and his height really is average. When I had looked at him out there on the stairs, from my height, he of course looked smallish, but now when I'm sitting on the chair by the table made of a drawing board, bent over my protocol, I look and yes, he's of average height. He was dressing and suddenly shook his shoulder as though a bird really did sit there and he wanted to chase it away. For me all this was like a receipt, a final check, it's he! Never have doubts, brother, march bravely forward. Forward march! We go out.

To the right on Sadovaya is a fire tower, to the left beyond the canal is St. Isaak's golden tent. He wanted to turn right on Sadovaya, but I took him along the canal that I had already measured. Why is the embankment better? The number of escape routes is halved, there are only half as many courtyards, front doors, lanes, and side streets as on any other street. When he saw that I wasn't taking him across Podyachesky Bridge but down this side, since the other side has more gateways, although it's a little shorter, he asked perplexed, "Are you cutting off my escape routes?" I say, "No talking," but I'm surprised. We start to talk, and would you believe? It turned out he was one of ours . . . Not quite ours, but a prosecutor . . . That's why he had already shaved. His family had left just in time and the room was empty. Obviously the man had gotten ready. Jump in the water? How could he jump in the water? Don't make me laugh! There's water there now, but back then the entire embankment was lined with launches full of firewood, barges with bricks, fishing nets, rafts, the devil knows what all, so there wasn't very much open water even in the middle, let alone along the sides.

So I walk behind this older man, and I'm getting nervous. I only have one guardsman with me, and he's straight from the village. As far as physical strength goes we were sort of OK, but as for intelligence, all the responsibility was mine.

We are tramping along the canal, behind us the guard is striking his hobnails on the heavy white stones, but we walk side by side, like friends or colleagues, only he's more experienced than I, lots more! . . .

Why did he shake his shoulder? A bullet was lodged in his shoulder and it bothered him. He said that the bullet was a personal gift from Ataman Grigorev. I remembered someone telling us what a good shot Grigorev was, and I mentioned it. He objected: "If he had never missed, he'd have lived longer." He told me how Nikolay Alekseevich Grigorev had been laid low by Nestor Ivanovich Makhno with one shot in revenge over Maksiuta . . .*

We came out on Pevchesky Bridge and stopped to smoke. I wanted to hear the end of his story, and he told me two more instructive cases of making arrests without committing excesses. He was dressed in civilian clothes and so was I, we're standing there talking. The bridge, the water, a white night . . . it's possible that also Pushkin and Onegin stood on the same spot where we were standing.

Oh, youth! Everything seems important, it's all new, you remember everything. This first arrest I often recalled later, not because it was the first, because it wasn't really the first after all. To tell the truth, my first arrest, the very first man I arrested, he shot himself when we rang on the door, and so the advice of this man with the bullet in the shoulder turned out to be useful. I still remember another observation he made, or a thought, it has nothing to do with our subject but I'll tell you anyway.

He was older than I and more experienced, he could see that the greenhorn was beside himself with worry, all tense, so he decided to defuse the situation. He said, "At first I was afraid of taking my finger off the trigger, but then one time I fired foolishly; I almost shot myself in the foot and got seven days in the stockade. After that I relaxed and got smarter. Why does one lose one's cool? Because there are so many of those people and they're all different, each one thinks his own thoughts. Each one has his habits, physiognomy, and secret thoughts that others can't read. How can you help losing your cool?" I agreed with him. "But now I've lived, I've observed and spoken with people both like this and at interrogations, and I've realized that there isn't such an awful difference between them. They don't differ all that much from each other. What are the instructions based on, the rules, the methods? Why, on the fact that the overwhelming majority of people behave almost the same way in certain situations." Did you hear, not the same, but almost. This is how he

*These military leaders were fighting against the Reds during the revolutionary wars in the Ukraine.

warned me of stereotypes. He said, "Those who really aren't like the others, those who simply don't react to the common approach, you can tell them a mile away, that's number one, count it on your fingers. And here's number two, in general each person only wants to eat, sleep, and live. Just think of it! . . .

I didn't understand then what a key my first prisoner had given me. Basically, I was still under the impression that people were all different, but with time his words keep floating up in my memory . . . He spoke the truth, "Every person only wants to eat, sleep, and live!"

This is the end of the story about this anonymous man. We finished smoking, this was already on Pevchesky Bridge, and I said, "It's funny, I was supposed to pick you up and here you're teaching me, huh?" Then he confided in me. He said, "When I noticed that you didn't have a car but were going to march me away, the thought flashed through my head that this beanpole with a baby face would bump me off . . . After all, you came without witnesses . . ."

I slapped myself on the forehead. Holy mother! I was so nervous that I had forgotten. A greenhorn is always a greenhorn.

So we turned into the yard of Pevchesky Chapel and found a secluded place. I got out the clipboard, and he himself signed as a witness. We laughed, of course, but then we marched away solemnly again. I handed him in without a hitch and never saw him again in my life, as they say. He was an interesting person, he had higher education. Many hide this fact and even provide certificates to show that five or six grades is all they have. But our chaps keep digging and searching, and look, they do have higher education. So why hide it? They all hide something, and then they're surprised that we treat them severely . . . By the way, Pildin only finished sixth grade, and just look, I'm standing here checking passes and have to walk around the place three times every shift like a dog, while he sits in an office with three telephones, and all that with only six grades. He has a friend among the higher-ups, and I happen to know just who . . ."

XII

. . . How I ended up in the organs? Well, in a funny way, and again the white night was my godmother.

I can't say that I had been spoiled by fate at the end of the twenties, but I hadn't been mistreated either. I was born in Porozhkin. When I was still in my teens, I went to Oranienbaum to look for work in the harbor or at the station. Gradually I got more jobs. The port and station are in the same area. Then I managed to get into the navy. But what kind of navy was it then? Even the Baltic Steamship Company had changed its signs and names after a year and wasn't exactly a strong link in our system of water transport.

I served on the *Dekret* and *Frants Mering* and *Sofia Kovalevska*, and I must say that those little steamers were impossibly worn out. What did I see? The crew's quarters, the hold, engines, and deck. There wasn't much to see, but there were some legendary triumphs and famous battles that make us proud to this day. The return of the *Ermak* after her refurbishing! And every new timber cargo ship! . . . The famous *Krasin, Yan Rudzutak, Smolny* . . . Lots of things. People pass on and all is forgotten. . .

The state of the navy was so bad that they even pulled ships from their "watery grave" and tried to salvage them. Instead of Cardiff coal we got ours from the Donets, both more expensive and worse, and instead of lubricating oil we got the devil knows what . . . On the other hand, the absence of good management was obviously harmful . . . That's when millions of our workers' rubles slipped through our fingers and into the pockets of foreign steamship companies; part of this money, of course, ended up in the hands of the proletarians of the capitalist countries and gave them work; this is a consolation, but it didn't make our state grow any stronger. As they say, putrid pimples started to break out on the body of the Soviet merchant fleet. It was obvious that many of the crew regularly visited pubs. There was some talk about the fact that the physical condition of the navy didn't really permit us to fulfill the plan for transport without endangering the vessels and crews.

To counter this defeatist attitude the following slogan was proclaimed: "When the technical condition of the ships is not good and the material basis is old, the role of socialist discipline becomes greater." But on a number of vessels and in certain sectors of the shoreside services there were incidents when discipline broke down, I saw some myself. They tried to stress discipline and responsibility even more, and conceal the fact that the principal reason for the accidents and the failure to fulfill the plan of transport and repairs was the fact that the crew was undisciplined and the officers completely incompetent. It came from both sides, no one could of course condone increased criminal activity; the struggle had started and, as we used to say then, it was every man for himself, dog eat dog.

I wasn't going to wait for history to take care of this problem, and as soon as an opportunity arose I went ashore. My posting was to the Tolbukhin lighthouse; the watches and duty hours were fine, the mechanical equipment was, so to speak, nonexistent, and this meant that you couldn't be accused of wrecking anything. You could live there.

I liked to stand watch during the white nights, this was perhaps the brightest period of my whole life.

That was a long time ago. I was on the one hand a peasant, of course, but on the other hand my dad kept a tearoom in the village. It was a pretty bad one, dirty, small, crowded, only half a cottage in size, but what can you do? I had six sisters, but our land—if the dog sat down it couldn't even stick out its tail. How could you feed them all and give them dowries? At first, I remember, we used to weave baskets. Father took them directly to Petrograd and sold a lot of them to institutions . . . Then we bought a second cow, and a third. In the fields girls don't work very well, but father made them go out; they obediently both plowed and harrowed, but at harvest they didn't use pitchforks but worked with scythes . . . I was the last one, my sisters teasingly called me "Your Lordship," and Father spoiled me a lot. My childhood was on the whole quite happy, but even as a child I wasn't attracted to the peasant way of life; I was more inclined toward the proletariat, if you can put it like that. In Father's tearoom I started to hate people. I was just a little boy, but in my presence they would pinch and squeeze my sisters. Father acted like he didn't notice, but I was ready to fight, even to bite like a dog. Even then I started to hate the "spawn of lackeys" and have continued to do so my whole life. We would probably have been dispossessed as kulaks* although we weren't rich; they gave us twenty-four hours to pack, but Nadya was at that time working at the courthouse as secretary and lived discreetly with the assistant prosecutor Andrey Ilich Barsov. He was a very rightminded and cautious man and later rose very high in the ranks. So he arrives at the courthouse and Nadya is lying there like this, her head resting on her hands, shedding tears on some protocols. Barsov says, "Nadya, Nadya dear, what's the matter?" He was scared. She said through her tears, "We've been dispossessed." They did close our tearoom but didn't touch us personally; we managed. Even after Andrey Ilich was transferred to Leningrad, Nadya would go and visit him."

XIII

. . . I've noticed that during the white nights all disorder in life seems to die down, it's not in full view but hides, it's invisible, stillness descends on both people and nature . . . During the white nights rain, strong winds, and storms are very rare. You yourself know the weather here in Petersburg! Or take the silence . . . It's perhaps the most profound thing in the

*Prosperous peasants who supposedly employed hired labor.

world. Back then I was vaguely interested in God—I was in love with a nun, so I started to imagine all sorts of things in this silence. I thought that if I held my breath I could hear the prayers of many people rising from earth to heaven, the prayers of those who have such limited minds that they no longer wish for grace and justice on earth. The tiny waves lap the stones by the shore, and in this splashing I hear the prayers of my departed grandma; she used to spend a long time kneeling on the little rug in front of the icon, and she squelched out the words of a prayer with her wet mouth. No matter how hard I tried to catch the words, I couldn't understand anything besides "Lord, have mercy" . . . I used to tease her that no one could understand what she was saying, so she wouldn't be saved. She glared, threatened with her finger, and said, "God hears everything, everything!" . . . I remember thinking once as I stood guard, that on such a night God probably lets the souls of the righteous in purgatory look down on the earth that they had left, and they are consoled; there's no room on earth for the righteous, their place is in the Heavenly Kingdom, and I imagined with what inexpressible mercy and sorrow these souls would return on the first rays of sun to their heavenly abode to await the Last Judgment.

Or take the sea gull, the most stupid and unimportant of birds, you can't even compare it with the sparrow, but in the night even they are immersed in some other kind of life, they don't quarrel but stand on the stones like marble elephants on a shelf. Suddenly one flies up, makes one or two turns, squawks, and back to the stone . . . I was already used to their short little nightly flights, but then suddenly one took off and flew higher and higher . . . The gulls only fly high when they migrate, otherwise they fly low like chickens, but this one went up, up! And it cries and cries! . . . Well, I think, it's somebody's soul. I had barely thought this when it turned completely red all at once as though its heart had burst, and it flew screaming, drenched in blood, higher, higher, higher . . . Oh damnation, it felt so creepy. But its comrades are still standing there, they don't stir, they stand all bunched up. I raise the binoculars to my eyes, but it had already turned white again. It was as white as though a light had exploded inside it and made it transparent, shining white like the Holy Spirit . . . I felt as though something under my uniform was moving, as though I myself was leaving the ground and could fly, fly—there are no limitations or obstacles, I can fly to the sun if I want, or even farther. I moved the binoculars to one side and then the other . . . There was my fate! Six or seven something or others were bobbing along a cable in the water. Now you could see it, now you couldn't. A light breeze blew, there were no waves but only ripples in the water as though it was shivering from cold. The things seemed to have disappeared. I looked for my gull up high, but no matter how I strained my eyes it was gone. I looked at the water, was there anything there? Not quite like a head, maybe a drowned body, that often happened. There were two of us. I say to Frolov—we were on duty together that night—"I'll go and have a look." I took the dinghy, it drifted a little. I had taken approximate marks but then the wind blew again, almost a gust . . . I found it! A small sort of buoy. I pulled. The rope stretches, it's a Swedish one. A long rope. I pulled and pulled, it got heavier. I pulled it out of the water. Five jars were made fast to the rope. I knew these jars, it was Estonian contraband. The jars were of soldered zinc and inside were wooden vats. Wonderful alcohol. In short, four jars Frolov and I hid in the coal bunker and one I took in and reported. So-and-so, we've found contraband. They reported it higher up. We expected congratulations and thanks from the working people, as they used to say then. But from up there, from the person in charge, they ask about the four remaining jars.

It turned out that they had put them there themselves, the bastards, to test our alertness on duty.

They called me in, and it started. I just stood there and listened. While they were cursing me up and down I had time to think it over and decide what to do. "They were torn off," I said. "What d'you mean, torn off?" they yelled. "They were too heavy and broke off," I said.

A short silence. Then while I was there they started to discuss how to recover their loss, arguing with each other. Then one of them looked at me, his name was Pizgun, a man with a checkered past. He glares and glares and says, "How could you tear off the rope, you son of a bitch?" "It had caught on something on the bottom," I say. "No," he says, "I don't mean that, don't look at me with your big baby eyes! This rope is strong enough to tie up boats with, so how could you tear it off?" "Like this," I say, and show with my hands how I jerked. "Well, we will have a look now at how you tore apart a rope like that with your bare hands!"

I'm not exactly a timid guy, but I got scared and started to sweat a little. They were all staring at me. Pizgun went out and came back with a roll of Swedish rope. "Is this it?" "Yes," I say. Even today I'm no weakling, and I was younger then. I was big and I could hammer in nails with my fist, but I was scared. I pulled the rope with my hands, I pulled and pulled, but couldn't rip it apart. "I have to jerk it, like I did then."

They started looking for something to tie it to. What could they find in the office? Not the safe, not the table. The stove in the corner, couldn't use that. One of them suggested tying it to the doorhandle. It was a strong handle of bronze or iron (the house was an old expensive villa). The handle was quite solid. They tied it there and stood looking at me. No, I think, you won't catch me, even for twenty rubles. "You shouldn't have doubted me," I said and jerked. I jerked with my whole soul and didn't hold back. Can you imagine, with one jerk I pulled off the handle along with a big part of the door. A whole panel came clean off. They shut up, but I act like it was nothing and say ironically, "You should've tied it to something stronger. What's the matter with you?"

You think this was the end of the affair? I wish! I was afraid of going to the coal bunker. I had a fortune so close by, but had to stay as sober as an angel. And I was nervous and couldn't sleep. I was expecting the worst, waiting for things to explode, and I couldn't relax.

It was resolved very simply. The one who had decided to test the rope came to see me, Pizgun, and he says that he and I should be shareholders. "I want two jars," he says, "the rest doesn't interest me. You won't be sorry. You see that sandbox?" Well, yes, I see it. "Tomorrow very early in the morning I'll pick up two jars there. Two, you hear." He turned around and walked away.

I started to weigh the situation. If I went near the sandbox I'd get caught red-handed. No good. If I didn't carry out the order, it was no good either. I'm not greedy, and what's this alcohol to me, I can't sell it! On the other hand, I don't feel like sticking my head in a noose. I called Frolov and said, "Such and so, there's plenty of it, but they have their eyes on me. We need to hide it somewhere else. Why don't you take some of it?" Two jars I hid elsewhere myself and told Frolov to hide the others. At the appointed hour they were in the sandbox. No one stopped Frolov or reprimanded him. I could have done it myself, but caution hasn't hurt me yet. You mustn't split hairs in these matters. A month went by, I was already thinking that I had fooled them. No, they call me to that office where I had broken down the door and ask how I would feel about serving in the organs. I answered that it's a solemn duty and an honorable obligation for every citizen.

They started to ask me questions. "What's the main slogan of the period of reconstruction?" I answer smartly, "Attack on all fronts." "What's death for the attack?" I answer, "Indiscriminate motion forward is death for the attack." "What's repression in the area of socialist construction?" There was plenty about all this in the newspapers. "Repression in the area of socialist construction is an element of attack, but an auxiliary one." I also remember the last question. "Where does our Party live and stay active?"

I knew at once! "Our Party lives and is active in the very thick of life, subject to the influences of the surrounding situation." "Who said that?"

A question from the examination of pioneers. "The words of Comrade Stalin."

They looked at each other, nodded, leafed through my thin personal folder, and but for the wink of Comrade Pizgun I honestly wouldn't even have suspected any connection with the sandbox . . .

So this was the beginning of my new fate, new wanderings. I've been in the North and the Far East, but not much; I've met different people and experienced many different and surprising events. Perhaps it wasn't even the sandbox that was the cause. I had gone on a trip to Igarka two years earlier. There was unemployment in Petersburg, so to keep order they were removing policemen, that is, former tsarist policemen, prostitutes, and those arrested for belonging to the nobility. None of them came back. But the trip was unforgettable in its own way. Really, you could easily write a novel based on my biography.

XIV

. . . The sparrows, the sparrows are starting to chirp. Oh well, soon the streetcars will start running. We had talked the night away.

Why do I like to be on duty on days before holidays? At the end of winter they always wash the windows before the holidays, both here in the factory and in office buildings. And I can see that they don't put back the curtains right away. Maybe they're at the laundry? For three or four days the newly washed windows are always left without curtains. I can think of nothing more beautiful than newly washed windows! As though it's not a wall but your soul that's clean and transparent. Through the clean pane, life outside looks both bright and happy.

No, say what you will, there's something exceptional about the Leningrad nights, like some dream is poured over the city . . . There's silence. As though nothing is bad, nothing gloomy. It's as though everything is still to come, life is starting over again. Look, the paper-thin clouds are settling on the ground like clean sheets of paper, you could sit down and write your life on it . . . To make us think of what we're doing and where we're going, this is why we have the white nights. Sit down and think, but not in the gloom of night, not in smoke-filled rooms, but here in the silence before daybreak when you can see everything and the day is about to start.

What's that, our relief is calling downstairs. Could my watch be slow? Look, it's actually stopped! . . .

Leningrad 1988

Petya on His Way to the Heavenly Kingdom

"Are you alive? . . . Strange, very strange,"
said the corpse and shrugged.
—M. Zagoskin, A CARNIVAL OF DEMONS

The short but significant life of Petya took up four days in the life of the Niva III settlement. By the day of the funeral the old news had lost its interest since there was nothing mysterious in it. Much more interesting was the death, shortly thereafter, of Colonel Boguslavsky—who has yet to dash out onto the pages of this story, out onto the snow-covered Kirov Boulevard, at exactly one-thirty in the afternoon of March 26, dressed in his military breeches and bedroom slippers and carrying his TT.* After the news of Petya's death had become less interesting in this large town three kilometers from Kandalaksha, it made the rounds of the barracks and two-story wooden houses where the engineering and technical personnel lived, and then it came back to the army base. But now it wasn't Petya who was the interesting person but Private Cheremichny, an insignificant soldier who looked a little scrofulous. According to the company commander, Captain Topolnik, this Cheremichny wasn't even fit for parades; after three years in the army he still couldn't fill the uniform his fatherland supplied him with the substance of a fighter; the tunic, pants, and greatcoat hung a little too loosely on him, as though he had just gotten out of a hospital where extreme weight loss had made him unrecognizable. The most amazing thing was that Cheremichny, who couldn't hit a waist-high target, either lying prone or kneeling, not to mention standing, had felled Petya with his very first blast; true, at a very short distance. Events with a fatal outcome live only for a short time in the oral traditions of garrisons if no one has to answer for them. The history of Petya's life and, above all, his rather interesting death migrated to the city of Kan-

*A Tula Tokarev pistol.

dalaksha that lay beyond the army base, and after a week all of Lower Kandalaksha was repeating some absurd nonsense in which time and events had been turned around and had nothing to do with Petra any more. And the story, already faded by the sea, continued all the way to Luvenga,* where Anastasia Pavlovna Lopintseva's sigh, "It didn't happen here but over there, thank goodness," constituted the final touch and put a full stop to the earthly memory of Petya's life and death. Petya was remembered slightly longer, about a month and a half, at the train stations Ruchi and Prolivy, located just south of Kandalaksha on the Kirov Railroad.

From the Ruchi railroad station the pockmarked and sinewy Valentina Repisheva would travel to Kandalaksha, or rather to Niva III, located three kilometers from Kandalaksha, to wash and clean at the ITR** houses. She was a young, strong mother of three. As a rule she brought with her as many cranberries and cloudberries as she could carry, and she took back home groceries, clothes that people gave her, and gossip that would for a short time enliven the social life in the neighboring stations Ruchi and Prolivy.

If historians should ever tire of the noise of victories and marches, campfires, tocsins, thunder and lightning, and would in their spare time feel called upon to describe Petya's brief life and unexpected death, they would be very well advised to regard Valentina Repisheva's stories as a firsthand and completely objective source. She knew Petya personally and had heard from the ITR ladies how Petya had been killed and buried. After she had done their laundry and cleaned their houses they would feed her, and since she was a visitor to the suburb they also treated her to the most interesting gossip. "How long has it been, Valechka,*** since you were here last? Two weeks? So much has happened, it's absolutely awful . . ." Valentina was sweaty from working and during that winter she was also emitting the smell of the milk filling her breasts to overflowing. She quickly exclaimed in horror but didn't listen very attentively; instead she was trying to figure out how to get to the station and what stores she would have time to go to, and, brushing away the obligatory tear, she managed with the same gesture to pat down the reddish tresses of her not very thick hair, quickly tied up after work but already crawling out in

*All the places mentioned are located on the Kola Peninsula in northwestern Russia.
**Engineering and technical staff.
***A diminutive of Valentina.

all directions. Valentina remembered that three or four times Petya had stopped cars on the way from Niva III to Kandalaksha and instructed the driver to take her, weighted down with impossibly heavy bags, to the station. Valentina wasn't paying much attention to the story about Petya's death, but not because she was callous and had forgotten Petya's help and wouldn't need it anymore; she simply didn't have the luxury of succumbing to sorrow as the settlement ladies did; she had to guess quickly what they would give her for the children out of all they had promised her, since they always promised just a bit more than they actually gave. "It's lost, Valechka, I'll find it for next time and have it ready." She also had to figure out whether to carry whatever they gave her to the store and then to the station, or to leave it here, go to the store, and then come back for it and run to the train. They were talking about Petya in all the six apartments that she had taken under her patronage. The striking thing was that all the stories agreed even in the details, and this is the best evidence for their authenticity; that is, none of the ladies telling the story had the slightest interest in improving on Petya's life and death or even to brighten the colors. Here we can discern the—let's call it positive—influence of the best literature of the early fifties. Presumably there simply wasn't any need to twist the truth, and therefore they told everything just like it was; otherwise they couldn't have restrained themselves and would definitely have exaggerated in one direction or the other. The tenets of good taste didn't allow the settlement ladies to add color and exaggerate what had happened.

Everybody stressed that "the poor fellow" was killed on the very same spot where Mishka Elzenger had killed his father. Two summers ago, the police chief of the local district No. 6 took his son out to shoot a Melkashka rifle, but as he was putting up a tin can to aim at, Mishka fired and killed him. Valentina had heard this story many times and knew it well. Now, in connection with the death of "the poor fellow," the ladies always insisted "almost at the same spot . . . ," "at the very same spot . . . ," "literally in the same spot," saying this in order to impart some mystical and unusual feature to an event that was otherwise of no educational value. Mysteries are necessary for ladies who have all the moral and physical resources to be carefully protected from all the dangers of life, including inexplicable dangers. Yes, yes, the passion of real ladies for the mysterious, secret, and unexplainable is completely unconscious; just like lots of other passions, this one is dictated by the instinctive need on the one hand to announce their own fragility and vulnerability, and on the other hand to remind their protectors of their duty, responsibility, and obligation to protect, defend, and shelter them in their defenselessness from all unpredictable and enigmatic elements.

Dear ladies, I understand your wish that it should be "literally in the same spot," because then the place would become ominous and you might almost feel real horror. I must, however, distress you by inserting a necessary correction. Unlike numerous other historical characters, Petya has no need whatsoever to have the facts of his biography distorted, at least not the scanty details that have been preserved. It's not in the interest of politics, high morality, or even poetry itself to tolerate lies, even lies fabricated by the minds of the most clever ladies of the settlement. Mishka Elzenger killed his father near Bear's Valley, while Petya was felled way down below stream No. 14 beyond the glade, far beyond the huge bald patch rising steeply toward the foot of Cross Hill. To the east it slopes down to Bear's Valley, but to the west its smooth saddle joins with a round hill called Woman's Navel. Admittedly this name isn't very original compared to Big and Small Karakvaiisha, which means no more or less than Big and Small Bosom in Finnish or Lappish. Anyway, Petya was not killed behind the explosives dump on the uninhabited bank of the River Niva, a kilometer from the bridge; the explosives dump was much farther back and to the left. He was killed where the glade ends and the high and dense fir forest starts at the foot of Cross Hill. Robust trunks stand there, one beside the other like a wall, up to the middle of the rather steep slope, but further on comes a completely bare stony field with dwarfed birches, mashed down and licked smooth by the strong polar winds. In the cracks of this completely open hilltop that seems round from the settlement on the other shore, one can see patches of last year's snow in the real and not allegorical sense even in July and August.

This description of the place where Petya was killed by a machine-gun blast is absolutely necessary, but not just to find inaccuracies in the fleeting traditions of the Kola land,* which harbors numerous secrets. It is necessary so that one can picture how far they had to carry Petya back, since there were no roads, only paths, and the nearest road, really a log-path,** started near the explosives dump that is at least two kilometers from where the event took place.

Now then, except for this detail we could rely for all others on Valentina Repisheva: from her we could find out that Petya's mother really felt

---

*The Kola Peninsula is located east of northern Norway in the Arctic Sea; Murmansk is the best-known city in the area.
**A log-path is a temporary road built of logs over swampland.

that the military should bury her son since it was they who killed him, but she could think of no other convincing reasons besides the fact that from the hospital morgue, where Petya was temporarily placed, the shortest way to the cemetery lay precisely through the army base. In the end she received a promise that the army would help with the coffin.

The commander of Private Cheremichny's company ordered him to make a coffin with his own hands for the dead man as punishment for his mistake. Cheremichny was sent to the garrison carpentry shop, where he put together something absurd from unplaned planks, amid the derisive remarks of the real carpenters who knew their business. This pine sarcophagus was not destined to be used, since at the same time the guys in the Niva GES* garage had made an excellent coffin of light dry boards from the flatbeds of two written-off, one-and-a-half-ton trucks; the planks smelled of gasoline and the road. Petya couldn't have hoped for anything better. So in the end the garage took care of the funeral and even the funeral feast, although not officially, of course, and not everybody came—only those who couldn't pass up what might be called a legal excuse for taking time off and an even more legal excuse for drinking. Anyway, more people came to the funeral feast than to the funeral itself. In addition to the seven from the garage, two from the militia—Kopytlov and Mnogolesov—were invited to the sad commemoration, with the joking observation, "It's your man we're burying." They couldn't figure out how to avoid inviting them, since such friendly relations with Kopytlov and especially Mnogolesov were both appropriate and timely just before the annual technical inspection in the spring.

It was strange to see Petya's mother running around to the authorities in the settlement and on the army base, trying to arrange things for her dead son, because it was strange to see her without Petya. While alive, Petya often appeared without his mother, but no one would have noticed Petya's mother without Petya, as tall and flat as an evening shadow, walking beside this ageless and faceless woman as tiny as a little bee, usually not dressed right for the season but almost always wearing a worn-out dress or a padded jacket the color of granite. The comparison with a shadow leaves much to be desired, as all comparisons do, and it would be simpler to compare this pair, so familiar in the settlement, to an exclamation point where Petya was of course the vertical stroke and his tiny little mother the point. If you remove the vertical from an exclamation point, you could never guess what the point had been part of—a question mark,

*GES is an abbreviation for "hydroelectric station."

a colon, or perhaps an exclamation point. A dot is only a dot. To confirm this it might be mentioned that no one in the settlement noticed what became of her after Petya's death, although in fact—this is especially interesting—she didn't go anywhere. She remained right here in Kandalaksha, but she moved from Niva III; well, not actually Niva but Lesny, on the road to Golovnoy, and moved straight to Kandalaksha, where she found a rather good place to live in a hovel between factory No. 310 and the timber exchange on the bay shore. Now and then she turned up in Niva III or Lesny, but hardly anyone recognized her without Petya, and thus she gradually and rather tactfully sank into nothingness and total obscurity.

Sopki, Ruchi, Prolivy, Valentina Repisheva, all this is just beating about the bush. It would be better to meet Petya himself at some triumphant moment. In his short life Petya had two such moments, and both deserve detailed description.

If one were to follow an invisible thread connecting the world-famous people's artist Cherkasov* and Petya, one mustn't overlook the club called Twenty-fifth Anniversary of the Great October, located on a stony knoll—strictly speaking on Vysokaya Street—with a wonderful view of the vast railroad-junctionyard, where they stored basic materials for the GES under construction.

Everything started out very gradually and didn't promise any triumph for Petya; on the contrary, no one thought of him at all. The existence of someone like Petya couldn't possibly have occurred to those men, perhaps right there in the Moscow Kremlin, who decided to have the beloved people's artist Nikolay Konstantinovich Cherkasov elected to the Supreme Soviet to represent the Polar Territorial District. What a lot of people crowded into the Twenty-fifth Anniversary of the Great October Club where the pre-election meeting with the deputy was held! It's absolutely impossible to calculate just how many: the 600 seats were overfilled; in the back rows there were instances when 2 people sat on one seat, even 3 if you count the children; in the aisles there were maybe 150 persons, and 27 people were hanging on the walls, twisted in very unnatural poses. Plus 30 people on the stage and approximately 35 in the wings. As many were left outside, ready to freeze if they could only see the great performer and beloved deputy with their own eyes when he left the building.

*Nikolay Cherkasov (1903–66) was a Russian movie actor, perhaps most famous for his role in the film *Aleksandr Nevsky*; he was in fact a deputy to the Supreme Soviet from 1950 to 1958.

What unprecedented passion and unimaginable enjoyment there can be in a meeting with the candidate for deputy! Especially at a time when conventional wisdom had reached perfection but politics had lost its living essence and had ceased to be a power struggle, and had instead acquired purely fictional features and was terrifyingly strong. A deputy of such stature was a reflection of that higher and limitless power that each person knew and remembered; but to actually touch him, even just with one's glance, that was a rare opportunity.

People could, of course, remember how in early 1943 Comrade Shvernik had traveled through Kandalaksha to some negotiations in Murmansk; the train consisted of only four cars but was equipped with two SO* locomotives and two flatcars with antiaircraft guns. Since an aerial attack on the local station had just started, the train didn't stop at Kandalaksha and they canceled the meeting at the railroad depot where people had been waiting since early morning; only four barrels of choice salt herring, especially prepared at the fish cannery for the leader, remained as a pleasant souvenir with the city leaders, who had been unable to hand over this gift and even failed to catch a glimpse of the prominent guest.

It's easy to explain why people piled up in human pyramids in the club that, I would like to point out, was built very artfully in the best traditions of prewar polar architecture, with verandas, wooden porticos, and intricate little turrets. At the time of the meeting and speech at Kandalaksha, those who couldn't get in had no other hope left. They hadn't been able to squeeze into the Pobeda movie theater; they had tried to sneak into the Railroad Workers' Club but were driven out; they had tried in vain to force their way into the Red Army Club on the base. But this speech at Niva III in the Twenty-fifth Anniversary of the Great October Club was the last one, and if they didn't succeed in seeing their deputy there, they would have to go to Zasheek, thirty-six kilometers away— that's where his next meeting was—and if *that* didn't work out they would have to continue on to Apatity or Monchegorsk, although people from Kandalaksha weren't welcome there.

It was winter and Petya stood in the aisle on the right as seen from the stage, squeezed on all sides by the furs, overcoats, and other clothing impervious to polar winds and temperatures, worn by visitors from various distant hick towns. Petya's whole head, neck, and even the top of his shoulders stuck up above the citizens crowding him. He was clothed in a padded jacket, pulled tight by a sword-belt with an empty holster for a Na-

*SO stands for Sergo Ordzhonikidze Locomotive Series.

gant revolver. Petya understood that he should remove his blue peaked cap with the red cap-band, since the majority of the people in the aisles were without their headgear, but it's one thing to remove a three-flapped cap or a Lapp hood with earflaps a meter long—you could stick them in your pocket or inside your jacket—but where can you put an army cap if you can't move your arms? You could, of course, take it off, but it would be ruined, perhaps forever, by the pressure of all the people, and not even the remarkable lacquered peak might survive. The nimble and loving hands of his mother had sewn it onto a police visor that Petya had got hold of. Petya also had a uniform Kuban cap with an NKVD emblem.* He wore it in the winter according to regulations, but for attending this solemn historical meeting the peaked cap was much more appropriate.

Once Petya had forgotten about his peaked cap he felt like he was in a sanctuary. The words coming from the podium were solemn, festive, and exultant, although not very easy to understand. They glorified the happy epoch, the joyous life, and the creators of our happiness, and they expressed love for the worthy son of our fatherland, the candidate for deputy, Nikolay Konstantinovich Cherkasov, the great artist and prominent fighter for the peace and happiness of the whole Soviet people. In all the speeches the mandate of the voters—to let them see more movies and to hear their dear deputy more often on the radio—was supported by the public with outbursts of applause. The absence of other wishes and requests from the voters reflected their profound understanding of creative labor and their desire to protect the artist from all that might interfere with his great service to art.

Their eyes were glued to Cherkasov. They felt the sweet anticipation of the opportunity to hear him, too, to hear his voice, that incomparable voice, thundering as though emanating from some fabulous cave, to hear with their own ears, not just over the radio, what the upper classes of society think about them, the simple people, who are building their future with their own hands right here, beyond the Arctic Circle, struggling against nature and adversity. As they heard this, many forgot that society wasn't yet prepared to see the masses in the politically correct way.

Sitting on the stage, Nikolay Cherkasov seemed to be profoundly engrossed in sweet thoughts as he sat turned toward the speaker and listened attentively, but actually he wasn't thinking about anything and heard nothing; whenever he had to yawn he quickly leaned over his note-

*Kuban is an area around the lower Don. A Kuban cap is made of Astrakhan sheepskin. The NKVD was one of the predecessors of the KGB, the secret police.

pad and jotted down something. The trip had really been very exhausting and the overwhelming majority of his appearances had not been notable for their variety.

Never in his life had Petya seen so many leaders and administrators, and he was no less excited than those who had the opportunity to sit up there on the podium at the same table as the people's artist. When the actor turned and directed a question to his neighbor Nikolay Ivanovich, the chief of the Niva GES project, Petya's heart missed a beat. It didn't even occur to him that these people should gossip somewhere else, that they didn't really have to do it on the stage sitting near the dais covered with red calico. Nikolay Konstantinovich whispered to Nikolay Ivanovich politely and quietly to avoid disturbing the current speaker, and the chief, adjusting the paper in front of him, replied with the kind of restraint suitable for a conversation onstage, half-turning toward the actor while looking out at the audience. Petya knew that, thanks to this brief conversation and the smile of Nikolay Ivanovich's he had witnessed with his own eyes, life would certainly get better. Furthermore, it was obvious that Nikolay Konstantinovich wasn't listening to the flattering speeches, interrupted by loud bursts of applause, praising his outstanding work and great talent. He was looking at the audience intently and thoughtfully, trying to commit to memory forever each face turned toward him, taking note of all the hopes and aspirations that people had brought with them.

Petya wasn't listening to the praise addressed to the eminent political and artistic personality Nikolay Cherkasov, and precisely for this reason he could feel and understand the profound and total truth contained in every word spoken in this hall, and he no longer felt crushed by the numerous bodies that seemed unusually hard in spite of their soft winter wrappings. It was as though he stood on a peak from which he could see the Kremlin and all of Moscow glittering beneath the red Kremlin stars, and the whole country and all of the people in the whole world making all their hopes known to the staunch ranks of well-dressed fighters for peace.

He was looking unblinkingly at Cherkasov, and only once did a poisoned stream of envy pour through his heart, quivering with intensity. During the program, some man in a sweater and jacket came out of the wings and, treading carefully on the stage and without disturbing anyone, he bent down, crossed the stage behind the first row of chairs, and stopped behind Cherkasov. Over his shoulder he handed the deputy a piece of white paper and stood still, waiting. Cherkasov read it and smiled, and half the audience couldn't help smiling with him, then he turned around to the messenger, completely hidden behind him, and nodded in agreement. "Just think, that could have been me bringing him a message," thought Petya, as though a great happiness had just slipped from his grasp. The great Cherkasov might smile like that to him, Petya. How was Petya to know that this man from the construction committee had asked the guest's permission to place some salmon, salted specially for him, in his car?

The man from the construction committee walked back through the rows on the stage almost without bending at all, or even brushing against anybody, and he was carrying the seeds of a certain greatness in himself that would invest him for the rest of his life with the right to tell at length the true story of how Cherkasov came here, how he, the narrator, attended the meeting, how he then went up to the guest, gave him the message, and so forth, with all the preceding and subsequent circumstances.

This bitter envy pricked Petya like a sharp nail and lacerated the place under his jacket and shirt, soaked with sweat, where his soul had taken refuge in his dreams and fantasies. But at that very moment the impossible happened: Cherkasov looked around the hall and his glance happened to meet Petya's.

Petya's eyes shining so ardently and desperately, his head damp with perspiration, his mouth half open, his hair completely soaked—all this gave the impression of a drowned man whose head suddenly emerged for a moment from the surface out of the hopeless depth, only to vanish again into the abyss. Either because of the stuffy air or from exhaustion, Cherkasov felt as though he had stumbled and was falling slowly, slowly, and the round bulging eyes staring at him and the black panting mouth suddenly looked like a chasm pulling him down into it. It happened quite often that looking out at audiences, he noticed faces that he didn't want to see. Sitting on a stage, he liked to look at people and guess who they were and how they lived; sometimes he made up bits of their biographies. He was repulsed by certain barely noticeable features, and he would reshuffle couples sitting in the front rows, creating awfully funny combinations of young girls and old men trying to look young, or of fading beauties and their younger competitors following in their footsteps, but that was a game, like solitaire. This was different, and he was losing control. He was frightened by the gloomy, unhealthy joy shining in Petya's eyes; he had realized long ago that people shouldn't look at him like that. He had already noticed this boy's head with the military cap sticking up over the other heads, and he had tried to avoid looking at him, preferring to turn his eyes to the walls where people of various ages, though mostly young, were glued like lizards sunning themselves on a warm stone slab. How they could stay up was beyond his comprehension. He remembered his trip to India with Pudovkin;* in a hotel in Calcutta some kind of nightmarish bird had looked in through the window, a bird with a huge beak and a long wrinkled neck without feathers. The bird looked at them sideways like a cock. He looked puzzled, or perhaps he was selecting his next victim. Without hesitation Seva Pudovkin had grabbed a shoe and thrown it at the bug-eyed monster with one of the juicy oaths that sometimes escaped from the great director's lips even on more humble occasions. Recalling that long red wrinkled neck like an old man's, Cherkasov forgot himself for a second and met Petya's glance.

Seeing that Cherkasov was looking at him, straight at him, Petya was overcome by a cold and senseless desperation, in spite of the fact that he was faint from heat. His eyes opened even wider but his arms and legs were constrained, and he couldn't explain and express his love and admiration for the beloved artist, even though this was probably the only chance he would have in his life. He wanted to cry out but the cry didn't reach his throat, it stuck between his diaphragm and lungs.

The great artist attempted to look away but couldn't. He could see the thin whitish eyebrows that reminded him of dusty grass on the edge of a precipice, he saw the dark circles around the excited colorless eyes, he saw the drops of sweat that the crowded man couldn't wipe away, and it seemed to him that the hall started to move and drip, and all the other faces dripped too. The walls with the figures stuck on them moved upwards like scenery during the set change between acts, and the eyes of this crazy man in the militia cap were the only stable points that he could clutch at to stop all this madness. He looked at Petya and was afraid to look away, feeling that his own body had become weightless and would fall if he lost this last point of support.

Petya suffered unbearably when he saw Cherkasov looking at him without turning away, as though waiting or perhaps even asking for something . . .

And Petya winked!

Petya winked with his left eye from under the army cap that slanted sideways; he winked as to an old buddy, an old friend or neighbor. And now the entire audience noticed that Cherkasov winked to somebody, winked dashingly, cleverly, knowingly, in a word, like Cherkasov. The people in the audience, continuously staring at the beloved face, following

*Vsevolod Pudovkin (1893–1953), a famous Soviet film director.

every gesture, every turn of the head, every movement of the fingers on the table—how they had needed this greeting, this gesture that tore down and swept into oblivion the barely noticeable, almost transparent wall that was still standing between the people's artist and the people! He had winked! The wall was gone as though he himself, all of him, so huge and so dear to all of them, had touched it with his hand, just like that, in his own way reminding them of their precious and longstanding friendship.

In that second hundreds of heads turned as one in the direction of this inimitable gesture, the brief lowering of the left eyebrow, the closing of the eye, and the friendly jump of the eyelid. They turned toward the person Nikolay Konstantinovich recognized and greeted.

The few who had missed this exchange of winks turned at once to their neighbors with impatient questions, but some things can't be put into words; the neighbors only smiled as though they had been initiated into something greater than a mystery.

From the way Petya looked at Cherkasov and smiled, there could be no doubt that the friendly gesture was intended for him and no one else. In this audience everyone knew Petya.

This triumphant moment of Petya's that we have just described had a public and almost national character, but no one witnessed the second high point of his life, the point to which he ascended and where he remained completely alone in such a feeling of pride and bliss as he had never experienced before. Loneliness is, after all, a trait characteristic of exceptional people.

Born to various ordeals and disasters, Petya could handle these disasters and ordeals with relative ease. In any case, they didn't burden him as much as they would you and me, in fact considerably less. His childish mind didn't permit him to fully grasp the adversity that devoured his life, let alone to understand it and to look beyond its borders, even in his imagination. For this reason he didn't experience tragic events to their full extent.

It's not for me to judge how he differed in this respect from the people of higher mental capacity who had assumed the roles of teachers and leaders of at least part of humanity, although they probably understood less than Petya what was happening to them, what they were doing here, laying out roads with desperate energy toward a blessed vision of an assured future happiness, and more such stuff that we can't talk about today in simple and clear terms.

Petya had things to do that he found extremely enjoyable and that didn't burden his delicate nature at all, and his daydreams didn't complicate the lives of the rest of humanity. The second moment of triumph in his life was precisely connected with the fulfillment of a secret dream he had long cherished.

Hardly had the first Pobeda car with the amazing color known as "café-au-lait" appeared in the settlement than Petya started to languish with an ardent, inexpressible desire to inspect this car. If we add that this Pobeda was the first one not only in Niva but also in Kandalaksha—where the administration and Party bosses had to ride in the worn-out shabby old M-cars that dated back almost to before the war, while the director of the 310 Factory traveled around in a BMW (the spoils of war) totally unsuited to the rough arctic roads because of its low-slung undercarriage—then Petya's wish can easily be understood.

Grisha Vartanian was promoted to driver of the Pobeda; he had been the trusted driver of Nikolay Ivanovich's Kozlik, an old car that had a heated, wood-trimmed interior with red carpet runners on the seats. He had kept it running in exemplary condition for four years already. Nikolay Ivanovich and Grisha differed in appearance, but they were very similar in certain other ways. For one thing, Nikolay Ivanovich had a high sloping forehead and was bald all the way to the back of his neck, while Grisha's brow wasn't as high, and he had thick black hair; for another, Nikolay Ivanovich was white both on his face and body, and after recovering from tuberculosis he didn't even burn in the sun, whereas Grisha was swarthy and looked sunburned even during the polar winter when the sun doesn't emerge over the horizon at all from late November to early February. As for rewards received in the war, Nikolay Ivanovich had not only the Medal for Defending the Soviet Arctic but also one for the Victory over Japan. Grisha had no medals. Grisha had been a prisoner of war, and to expiate his guilt before the fatherland, he was sent to the Arctic when he was repatriated. The two men resembled each other mainly in that Grisha never let anyone know that he was the driver for the head of construction, and Nikolay Ivanovich never stressed the fact that he was the construction chief and a member of the Bureau of the Provincial Committee,* which allowed him the privilege of being driven around by Grisha. Petya knew none of this, because he could observe the life of such enormously high government officials only from a considerable distance.

Not once had Petya inspected Grisha's Kozlik and there were many reasons for this. In the first place, there were quite a few such Kozliks in the settlement, admittedly somewhat simpler ones, less elaborate and lacking homemade interior heating and, well, red carpet runners on the

---

*The Provincial Committee is the principal local Party organization.

seats. The chief of the Kandalaksha construction group had such a car. Others were owned by the chief of the not-yet-completed aluminum plant and by the chief engineer of the Niva GES, Anatoly Fedorovich Vasilev. Vasilev's driver was incorrigibly foulmouthed; his children learned curse words first and only later real words. For this reason Petya inspected this car only when he saw Anatoly Fedorovich himself sitting beside the driver. The engineer's narrow toothbrush-moustache inspired Petya with respect and confidence. When Vasilev's driver saw Petya standing beside the road with his hand raised, he glanced at the inscrutable and serious Anatoly Fedorovich as he put on the brakes, and since he didn't dare to curse in front of his boss, he asked, "Well, what's the matter, you silly scarecrow?"

"It's Inspector Petya," said Petya as he introduced himself, touching his military cap. "Comrade driver, where are your license and work schedule?"

The first time Anatoly Fedorovich nodded to his driver, who happened to be called Petr too, and the driver got the license from his shirt pocket at once and reached with his other hand for the schedule behind the sunshade. But when Petya stopped the car for the second time, a year and a half later (this was last winter) Anatoly Fedorovich declared at once, "Comrade Inspector, we're in a big hurry."

"I understand," said Petya seriously and sternly, and to keep the inspection from seeming trivial and annoying he glanced inside the car. "There're no other passengers? You may proceed." Thus went the inspection of Vasilev's Petr, a daredevil and drunkard, the complete opposite of Vasilev himself.

We must, of course, explain the strikingly odd juxtaposition of this Vasilev, an English type of person, an engineer with advanced training who tried to surround himself exclusively with people and things of the highest quality, and his chauffeur Petr, a drunkard who used profanity and whose driving was both rude and hazardous.

The connecting link between these men, so far-removed from each other both in interests and in personal development, was a dog. Alma, a German shepherd of the best pedigree, acknowledged only three people in the world as having supreme power over her: Anatoly Fedorovich himself, his wife, and the chauffeur Petr. In spite of her ferocity, Alma also nourished a truly inexhaustible amount of devotion and love (enough for half of humanity) toward Petr, who permitted her to jump up and lick his nose. When the chief engineer's wife went to Leningrad to visit her sons, who studied at a special section of the Department of Mathematics and Physics at the university, there was no one to walk the dog; the master spent almost all day at the administrative office or the vast construction site. When the master left on a business trip or if the whole family went on vacation, Alma's problem stood out most acutely. The dog had attended an excellent obedience course at a special facility; she didn't wish to repeat the course or change her habits, and she refused to tolerate anyone besides her masters and Petr. She barked fiercely at everyone else and repeatedly tried, if not to maul people to death, then at least to bite them, regardless of sex and age, so they would remember her. Especially fierce was Alma's hatred for beggars and all shabbily dressed people in general. There weren't really many beggars in the settlement, fewer than in Kandalaksha, but some were always going begging from house to house, mostly older women or more rarely old men. Why beggars would choose this gloomy province for their trade is impossible to say. Perhaps they stayed in these semi-penal colonies because of an unconscious conviction that people share poverty more easily and willingly than wealth or comfort.

On those occasions when Anatoly Fedorovich was away at the building site, Petr usually showed up quite drunk, whether on foot or in the car, to take Alma out. Sometimes his condition was so serious that it looked as though it wasn't Petr taking Alma for a walk but a clever guide dog taking a man seriously injured by mustard or chlorine gas out for some fresh air. At such times Alma didn't pull at the leash or bark furiously at others but tugged the leash carefully to avoid knocking down her sovereign lord, helping him to move from the front porch to the post and from the post to the shed where Alma had a checkpoint. Sometimes she even sat down on the ground to let Petr gather his strength for the next short move, and cutting down the walk to a minimum, she would drag him back to the house, understanding in her soul that as long as she was there, nobody would dare try to help him. This little performance would attract quite a few spectators, admiring equally the dog's intelligence and Petr's faithfulness to his duty to walk the dog twice a day.

In this way, the chief engineer himself and his family were to a certain degree dependent on Petr, but because of his mental limitations Petr didn't understand this. Instead he was sincerely convinced that he and Anatoly Fedorovich were friends, perhaps even close friends.

With the chauffeurs of Kazov and Kandalaksha, Petya had strictly professional relations that didn't blossom into friendship, only because

Petya himself didn't permit himself to cross a certain boundary or dividing line beyond which he could no longer be fair but only stern.

When the men in the garage wanted to catch him being a coward and asked if he had inspected Nikolay Ivanovich's car yet, Petya ignored the baiting and, adjusting the empty holster on his right side, remarked in a loud and clear voice, "I'll do it soon." Petya wasn't just pretending, he really meant it. His confidence grew, especially after he had happened to eat with them. Sometimes with his mother, sometimes alone, he'd go to the Orsov dining hall at the railroad station to buy food for two or three days at a reduced price, maybe 15 percent off, and it was on these excursions that several times he had happened to see Nikolay Ivanovich and Grisha eating. At the green wooden shanty, built on a rocky hill where it wasn't possible to build either workshops or warehouses, or even an air compressor shop, Nikolay Ivanovich would charge across the high wooden porch, wearing a cloth cap with a large visor, an American leather coat flaring out like a bell from the waist down, and canvas boots spattered with mud and cement. Grisha followed his boss, and while the boss washed his hands, both the soup and goulash were brought to his table. Nikolay Ivanovich also got a glass of vodka, but only one. The vodka was sold freely at the dining room, and he drank it like medicine, without making a grimace, after which he ate his meal, not greedily but quickly, much faster than Grisha could manage his food; and while the chauffeur finished the main course and was messing with the jelly or stewed fruit, Nikolay Ivanovich would smoke calmly. Sometimes during dinner Petya could hear Nikolay Ivanovich reply to greetings, exchange remarks with his fellow diners, or tell jokes, all according to his mood, and while putting on his coat he might say, "Hey, Grisha, let's fly down to the harbor" or, "And now, Grisha, to the Golovnoy sector," but Petya never heard Grisha's voice. So if you were to ask Petya what terms he and Nikolay Ivanovich were on, he would have no trouble answering, but it would have been much harder for him to explain his own relationship with Grisha. This is why Petya lived with all his mental functions strained to the utmost for a certain time after the Pobeda turned up in the settlement.

The Pobeda that was delivered was, as though a joke, a convertible with a removable canvas top. Grisha waited a long time for hot weather when he would finally be able to use this remarkable feature, and finally in the heat wave at the beginning of August, for the first time in history, a car rolled along Chkalov Street and Kandalaksha Road with the roof down—a convertible! The top was obviously designed not just for a warm climate but also for asphalt roads, neither of which was at that time to be found in

Kandalaksha itself and certainly not in the surrounding area, and after spending half the day beating out the dust and cleaning the car, Grisha pulled down the top of his luxury sedan forever. To Petya's regret, he didn't see the car with the top down, but he fully believed the eyewitness accounts.

There were no idle vehicles in Niva III; the transportation situation was difficult, and everything that could roll was repaired, patched up, and repaired again; old cars were already in their second, third, and maybe fourth life beyond the grave in this land, on these roads, where even the first life of our cars can enjoy a very short span. Slightly longer was the life expectancy of postwar Dodges and Studebakers. Typical Russian ingenuity combined with the absence of spare parts gave birth to hybrids and monsters that could drive a sane person crazy were he to see them.

Why was it then that the constantly speeding drivers of dump trucks—desperately struggling uphill from Kandalaksha to Niva—and even the drivers of the faster, regular one-and-a-half-ton trucks stopped submissively at the stern gesture of the crazy militiaman?

Whenever a car drove by without reacting to the imperious gesture of the tall ridiculous-looking man in a police cap and an empty holster on his sword-belt (holding together his padded coat), Petya became angry and bewildered. The noise of the passing car remained in his proudly raised head and was transformed into a rustle, whisper, babble, and ringing inside him. Standing thus for ten or fifteen minutes, as though hoping that the driver would come to his senses and return, he would listen to these faint internal noises and suddenly set off in a hurry, his arms flapping, in a completely unpredictable direction. He would stride along with his feet pointing outwards, driven by insult, bewilderment, and the many indistinct voices whispering evil things in his head, leaving his mother, two garages, and the entire militia unit that was housed in half of one of the barracks on Third Polar Street to the mercy of fate. A few times he was seen striding as far as Kandalaksha; once he crossed the river and was stopped near the explosives dump by women picking cloudberries. But further out in the hills there was no one to stop him; people brought him back both from nearby places like the bakery, and from distant ones like the Golovnoy Junction, and no one knows where his sweeping, decisive strides might have led him were it not for the spiritual kindness of the free population, most of whom hadn't come of their own free will to this land of forced labor. Someone always stopped the striding Petya.

Luckily, most of the roads in the settlement led to the store, a two-story building constructed before the war of blackened timbers that housed a grocery store on the first floor, a general store upstairs, and offered year-round trade in sunflower seeds from a sack beneath the club's bulletin board in the corner. Some roads led to the tearoom, a large light-blue wooden house with a verandalike porch and columns of squared timbers by the entrance, and other roads led past the little dining room next to the militia and on to the beer hall on the Lesny Highway that was always crowded all day long, regardless of the weather.

No one could recall when Petya showed up in the settlement, but obviously it must have been after the war, during the difficult time in which the Niva GES construction group and some of the equipment had been evacuated to Oblaketka near Ust-Kamenogorsk, leaving the settlement deserted. Nobody could remember seeing Petya at that time and no one knew anything about him.

The incoming population consisted of a complex mixture of people, classes, and ethnic groups. Among the engineering staff there were some who had sullied their youth by getting involved with the Cadets; there were also one Bundist, some defeated leftist Social Revolutionaries,* one inveterate monarchist, and a well-to-do draft dodger from the Desiatnichenko railroad-engineering school. Naturally none of these people were part of Petya's circle of acquaintances.

Technology and slave labor, or actually slave labor first and technology second, were the principal concerns of Nikolay Ivanovich. He hadn't participated in the evacuation but remained here for defense work, and only the ITR part of the collective had stayed here with him. To get the work done he needed one thousand laborers every day; the Obkom bureau had to come to his aid and transferred to him special forced settlers from various places in the vast Kola area, including Apatity and even Kirovsk. The German and Italian POWs arriving in late 1945 couldn't adjust to this area, but then our own prisoners were repatriated from German camps and arrived here at a very convenient time, precisely at the early construction period. They constituted a very good contingent, for instance this Grishka Vartanian, who came with this group. Although Rodchenko, the assistant chief of the construction project, didn't leave Moscow, Leningrad, Zaporozhe, and Kharkhov, he could get hold of anything—starting with the Pobeda, one of the first produced. He also got

*A Cadet was a member of a prerevolutionary party, the Constitutional Democrats; Bundist, a member of the Jewish Bund; Social Revolutionary, a member of a Radical party competing with the Bolsheviks for power.

hold of building materials and hay all year round for the auxiliary agriculture, since there were no local grazing areas. For example, through the
Construction Bank, Rodchenko was able to obtain a carload of items of
intimate masculine hygiene to use as waterproofing for the detonators on
blasting jobs. But he organized the recruitment sloppily, and the question
of slave labor kept the construction in a permanent state of tension.

Mordvinians, Armenians, Ukrainians, Udmurts, ordinary Russians
from Vologda and other places near and far—all were mixed up in a huge
pot and dished out in random scoops to the thousands of construction
projects that were bringing socialism closer. They felt like temporary residents on the frozen and stony land and didn't look upon this land as
theirs. It's all the more surprising that this whole ill-assorted and embit-
tered crew, representing a mixture of customs and races, all down to the
last man showed indulgence and kindness to Petya.

Like a chip from a rock or a drop of floodwater, he settled here with
his mother in the club barracks in the settlement of Lesny, and no one
knew where they came from.

If we had to dedicate a couple of pages of our laconic narrative to
Nikolay Konstantinovich Cherkasov, a truly great person and one so famous that it is enough just to mention his name, then it's necessary to
speak in a little more detail about Nikolay Ivanovich, with whom Petya's
second moment of triumph is connected, although there are many who
may already know of him and may even have seen his photo on the front
page of *Pravda* among those awarded the Stalin Prize, first degree, for
completing the first subterranean hydroelectric station in the world.

The construction of Niva III was naturally surrounded by official silence. For this reason there was only one radio station that reported when
the plant was started up, namely the Voice of America, and they mercilessly garbled the facts and called the station Nivo III instead of Niva III.
Evil tongues from among ourselves claimed that the Stalin Prize was given
only because the station was started up on December 21, 1949.* But then
everyone bit their tongue when a machinist on the railroad loading crane,
Vasia Popov, was boiled alive on Nikolay Ivanovich's orders. The problem
was that the Sandor floodgate units were delivered from Leningrad to the
construction site after a delay of two months, and Nikolay Ivanovich personally gave the order to begin unloading them immediately and to bring

*December 22 is the Day of Energy, commemorating the founding of GOELRO in
1920.

the equipment to the Golovnoy Junction to be installed at once. They were to be transported on sleds specially prepared by the mechanical workshops. The work was begun on a Sunday, but not a single one of our decrepit tractors could drag those monsters over our roads. Nikolay Ivanovich then made a deal with the army tank drivers, who brought their T-34s, and Vasya Popov carefully removed the turrets and placed them on pallets, built beforehand from railroad ties, to remove the unnecessary weight from the tanks. Then they started to unload the Sandor units. The work was very risky; the wind was gusting at twenty-five meters per second.* Nikolay Ivanovich was present at the Golovnoy Junction along with the commander of the tank regiment, Colonel Golik, who had come to watch this unusual work performed by his own vehicles. Incidentally, the excellent brigade leader of the scaffolding builders, Volodya Moiseev, twice had to drag Golik's tanks from swamps with nothing but compound pulleys; he didn't allow the metal sheets to catch the wind and the unloading went normally until the next to last sheet, the fifteenth, caught the wind. Perhaps the dog-tired and frozen, one-eyed Volodya had overlooked something, but the railroad crane was holding the enormous reddish metal sheet at the full extent of the jib when the sheet suddenly yielded to the wind. Vasya should have pulled it in immediately and dropped the load, but he couldn't see if anyone was below and he presumably decided that it would hold, but it didn't. The crane crashed down. It was over in two or three seconds. The steam bursting out of the broken boiler cooked Vasya Popov alive, hiding its crime in a dense boiling and burning cloud. When the steam dispersed, everyone could see the face, full of dark blue patches, of the crushed and boiled Vasya Popov. At the weather station, Nikolay Ivanovich placed a Golden Label chocolate bar before Nastya Bocharov and received a certificate stating that the gusts of wind on February 27 had reached only fifteen miles per hour. The inspector of steam boilers, Pavel Ivanovich Zmeenkov, who came up from Leningrad, was secretly and hopelessly in love with Nikolay Ivanovich's wife and would himself never bring the matter to justice, and even if he had wished to do so, his bosses would not have permitted it. Zhemerin, the minister at the time, would never have allowed the project to be decapitated just at the critical point when they were prepared to start up the plant. One might add that a short time earlier, in the summer, at one of the Sunday picnics by the shore of the Niva, Nikolay Ivanovich had decided to con-

*Twenty-five meters per second is approximately fifty-five miles per hour.

quer the river one-on-one as it bubbled madly over the stones for the last time; but as he was swimming across it, he was carried three kilometers downstream. Vasya Popov, who was at the picnic, cried a whole bucketful of tears while they were looking for Nikolay Ivanovich.

Besides his heroic and selfless subjugation of the Niva, we must relate at least one more characteristic episode from Nikolay Ivanovich's life; it dates to the winter of 1941 when he evacuated the whole collective but personally transferred to the Oboronstroy* to preserve the construction project. We must remember that for several years before the war conditions at the construction site were extremely worrisome; people lived in a constant state of uncertainty, and the times were cruel. First Dumlerov disappeared, then Vereshchak was arrested. The matter dragged on and on, and finally Migalovsky was released, after all. Ivan Gaponenko ranted and raved. He had come from the Dnepr GES with an Order of Lenin but couldn't do anything, he sat in the central administration and babbled for a year before being transferred to the Kandalaksha NKVD. But after a year and a half he was himself bumped off, as they say. This is why Nikolay Ivanovich decided to acquaint himself personally with all staff matters contained in the archives of the Personnel Division, when he had decided to save the construction project. Leafing through one folder after the other, looking through literally everybody's biography, especially of the ITR cadres, he reached the firm conclusion that these documents must never fall into enemy hands, and he mentioned this to Anna Ivkina who was responsible for the personnel records. "Hey Annie, let's draw up a little document stating that in view of the imminent threat of enemy invasion we have liquidated this dangerous material." According to this document, the number of files retained should be drastically reduced, and this would also cut down on the maintenance work. Anna Ivanovna agreed to set up the document in three days, and while the well-known battle of Moscow was being fought near Moscow, they sat by a little stove in the empty administration building of the construction project and burned one fat file after another, leaving in the cardboard folders with red tapes only enough excerpts from the employment papers to make it possible to determine length of service and arctic bonus pay and to decide vacation time.** Even the cleverest enemy who might come into possession of this

*Defense Construction.
**Soviet workers north of the Arctic Circle are entitled to higher pay and longer vacations than workers elsewhere.

information could hardly cause much harm to the country and its long-suffering citizens who were building a hydroelectric dam under the bleak arctic sun.

This brief digression into the construction chief's biography is introduced to enable the reader to appreciate the substantial nature of Petya's hesitation and the mental obstacles standing in his way when he decided to inspect the café-au-lait Pobeda and to explain why it took him so long to get up his courage.

By the summer of 1952 Petya was already an experienced inspector; he knew a lot and could anticipate much. Planning this important step, he tried to take into account every possible surprise and act only when the time was right.

First he had to decide whether to inspect just Grisha or Nikolay Ivanovich too. Petya decided to go for broke because he secretly didn't quite trust the taciturn Grisha.

Now he had to pick a day.

Petya made a small concession for himself; he decided to do it on a Sunday. Perhaps in his confused brain he somehow recognized the need to carry out the most complex and risk-filled tasks on Sundays. On the one hand, it would be best to stop the car in the settlement in the full view of everyone, but on the other hand, this was quite risky; if the car didn't stop many would laugh at Petya; the chief always has the right to refuse to stop, but not everybody knows that. For this reason he chose to do his inspection on a certain section of the highway between Niva and Kandalaksha, running for two kilometers from the Military Registration and Enlistment Office at the outskirts of Kandalaksha to the foundations of the new club that was to be built at the approach to Niva. Approximately half of this road went uphill in the direction of Niva. It wasn't a good idea to stop cars going downhill; one might, of course, check whether the brake system was in good working order, but this could get very expensive for a negligent driver and a careless garage manager. To stop a car going uphill when it's surrounded by a cloud of dust isn't very good either, but it isn't any better at the bottom of the hill, since the car has to speed up and gather momentum; thus there remained only a short stretch of road, about two hundred meters, between the foundation of the new club and the top of the slope. The road curved there, but it was plenty wide enough and convenient for conversations.

Two Sundays Petya spent in position; six times the beige Pobeda sped by with Nikolay Ivanovich, but Petya's arm was fettered by hesitation and refused to rise. Learning at the garage that the chief of construction was going on vacation at the end of July, the inspector finally made up his mind.

With his sharp eyes Petya already noticed the Pobeda when it passed the commissariat; in a couple of minutes it would come flying up the hill and around the curve. No, they mustn't see you from afar; a real inspector turns up suddenly and pounces unhesitatingly. Petya adjusted his sword-belt and pulled the cap down on his head as though he wasn't just planning to stop the car according to the rules but to jump up on its roof while it was in motion.

The car had barely come around the corner, having lost a fair amount of speed up the hill, when Petya strode out on the road from the curb and gestured commandingly with his arm. Rolling up to the inspector, the car came to a stop with the engine still running. Grisha lowered the window and looked inquiringly at Petya.

Nikolay Ivanovich's heart just about stopped, but he collected himself and glanced sideways at Grisha, worried that he would do something wrong. On the back seat sat the chief's eleven-year-old son, a fifth-grader with a crewcut that spared only a small tuft of hair. The boy at once slid across the seat behind his father to the left door so that he could see Petya better, and he even lowered the window.

"Your license, comrade driver, and your work schedule," said Petya, not even looking at Grisha but off into the distance, watching out for possible trouble on the visible part of the road.

Grisha started to get out his license.

"You didn't introduce yourself," said Nikolay Ivanovich sternly.

"Sorry," said Petya, bent over and looked in through the window with his hand to his cap. "Inspector Petya."

The little boy in the back seat snorted and turned his laughing face to his father. The father didn't hear the laugh.

"Nikolay Ivanich," said Grisha after he had given his license to Petya. "I don't have a schedule."

The patriarchal ways of Nikolay Ivanovich permitted Grisha to spend more time in the car than in shuffling paper.

"Now we've really been caught," said Nikolay Ivanovich and his bushy eyebrows shot up.

"Where's your schedule," repeated Petya impatiently; he didn't hand the license back.

"All right, all right," the boy's threatening little voice could suddenly be heard from the back seat.

Nikolay Ivanovich turned to his son but didn't say anything; he threw open the door and came out to Petya.

Petya's heart beat so strongly that he couldn't hear the engine that was still running.

"Comrade Inspector, this is more my fault than the driver's. I wasn't exactly sure if we'd only go to market or also drop by the barber's. You understand? You'd have found fault with the schedule either way."

Petya was triumphant, his soul was singing, he slapped the license on his palm and looked past the shortish man who had had such a hard time thinking up this clumsy justification. There was nothing he could say to this man. Petya looked at the hilltops beyond the river and returned the license to Grisha through the window without looking, saying sternly, "You may proceed." Only then did he turn to the man in a leather coat, standing beside him.

"Thank you very much," said the building chief a little too quickly. He hesitated for a second and repeated, "Thank you," confirming this phrase with a brief and somewhat fussy nod.

It's funny, but Petya possessed the grace of a real GAI traffic inspector* who stops you and punishes you, or possibly even forgives you, but in a perfunctory way, showing no concern and hardly even paying attention, and thereby forces you to realize your complete insignificance beside this person so infinitely superior to you with all your infringements, excuses, oaths, and thirst for freedom. Never, not for his Stalin Prize, not for his appointment to chief, or even for being accepted into the Party after a trial period of nine years—before the war such things did occur— never had Nikolay Ivanovich thanked anyone like this, admitting both his guilt and insignificance.

The boy in the back seat looked at his dad and didn't understand a thing; he knew that his father was able to act the fool, but what was this nod, this "Thank you, thank you?"

"Well, Grisha, you'll have to pay up," said Nikolay Ivanovich as he finally got into the car.

"Why did you make explanations to that idiot?" came suddenly from the back seat. The son had heard his father talk on the telephone with the minister and even the secretary of the Obkom. He had seen his father communicate with higher-ups whom he respected, and even carry out their orders while showing profound reserve and dignity; but now he

*Ordinary traffic police; GAI stands for State Car Inspection.

suddenly saw his father being insulted and made to confess his guilt, even when it wasn't his fault. And by whom? By this gangly imbecile!

"Stop!" said Nikolay Ivanovich softly. He got out of the car and opened the back door, hesitated for a moment, assuming that the son would guess; but the boy only blinked, so the father pulled out the puzzled young scoundrel by the hand. "Get some fresh air and think." Both car doors slammed and the car rolled off.

Petya hadn't collected himself yet and didn't notice what was going on around the curve. But now you want to know why Petya took his time, why he stood there slapping Grisha Vartanian's license on his palm, Grisha's only valid document, and why he was in no hurry to forgive the transgressor, although the construction boss himself interceded for him? With his sharp eyes Petya had seen Colonel Boguslavsky's car flash by the school, shining like a polished black boot—an Opel Kapitan, one of the spoils of war. He could hardly have hoped that the car would pass by at the very moment when he was inspecting the construction chief's Pobeda. The Opel of the camp chief, Colonel Boguslavsky, was off-limits for Petya; the car had a military license number and the gloomy driver came from the labor camp. When he was waiting for his boss on the street and people started to talk to him, he answered in monosyllables or not at all, pretending that he hadn't heard, perhaps because he appreciated his cushy job or because he felt like he was still inside the camp zone, even on this side of the fence that had been extended so far that you couldn't quite tell where the camp ended and freedom began. Petya had examined the car a few times with approval when it was standing near the polyclinic in the hospital where Irina Konstantinovna, Boguslavsky's wife, worked. Petya communicated to the driver his approval of the car's exterior and the tread on the tires; the front tires were made of better rubber than the back ones whereas only the back tires had matching tread patterns. In response to Petya's praise the chauffeur said "Thanks" very quietly, without moving his mouth, and Petya at once became aware of the vast power he had over this quiet man and decided not to bother him any more. Many people didn't understand why Boguslavsky wouldn't allow his chauffeur from the camp to let his hair grow out, at least a couple of inches. It was, of course, very chic to keep a zek* from the camp like this, without a guard, without letting him look like a civilian. It was just like taking a wolf around

*The word zek is an acronym of the Russian term meaning "prisoner." It refers to the inmates who worked in labor camps.

the settlement without a leash, keeping him controlled and subjugated with nothing but will power. But actually it was simply a matter of jealousy. Thanks to his many years of service and a profound understanding of the life in which he was a far-from-insignificant little wheel, Colonel Boguslavsky was ready to suspect everyone of everything. Irina Konstantinovna was born and grew up in Sumy as the eldest daughter of a very important Chekist.* Knowing the present and past life of his beautiful wife and mentally admiring her irreproachable biography, he could suspect her of only one thing, namely marital infidelity; but he regarded this infidelity in futuristic terms and admitted it only as a possibility. Once he had allowed his chauffeur to let his hair grow out, but when Irina Konstantinovna said to him, "How nice you look in longer hair," Boguslavsky at once ordered the chauffeur to be shaved down to zero, remembering his wife's pathological fear of shaved prisoners.

Faithfulness to her husband was her wish but not her duty, and although she was not a dissolute woman by nature, she gradually became debauched in her attempts to avoid the suspicions, spying, and hypocritical attention of people who were dependent on her husband or wished to be useful to him. Irina Konstantinovna knew that she was being shadowed and was occasionally unfaithful to Boguslavsky, stunning all her chosen ones by her sudden and overwhelming passion, demanding immediate satisfaction. The clever Boguslavsky had learned to easily identify the man most dangerous in that futuristic sense in the hospital or polyclinic where he found a job for Irina Konstantinovna, and he would invite this man to a confidential conversation on the subject of state security, and at the same time, as a sign of special favor, he would entrust him with guarding the moral order, including the way in concerned his wife. Their frequent changes of residence, and consequently, places of work, had soon engendered in Irina Konstantinovna the ability to easily identify her guardian within the first two or three months, and then in one of the examination rooms, once even in the linen closet, she would in a couple of minutes, with totally convincing arguments, convert her enemy into her closest and most faithful friend. In contrast to all other wars, this secret war deserves all possible encouragement since there were no victims, only victors, sometimes three, and in Olenyaya and on the Yov there were even four, since Boguslavsky had managed to enlist several observers in those places.

*Sumy is a town in the Ukraine between Poltava and Kursk. Cheka was the name of the secret police immediately after the Revolution.

Thus changing enemy into friend, Irina Konstantinovna could every-where fully experience and enjoy the liberation and freedom she needed, not just for coquetry. The rhythm of her life, her behavior and activities were far removed from concerns with love affairs, and the unbelievable goings-on in the examination rooms or linen closets, sometimes even without sequel, demanded a detached approach free of petty moral preju-dices. No, no, don't hasten to avert your honest and truth-loving face from Irina Konstantinovna. A woman doesn't lie! When telling you an untruth she is simply expressing her concern for you; she only wishes you well and tries to save you from grief and annoyance as best she can.

You must agree that a woman's power is the highest kind of power, and what high power doesn't have the right to a secret that everybody usually knows but pretends to ignore? This is the strength of power!

Unspoiled by the pleasures enjoyed by other happy and cheerful youths, in fact somewhat cheated by the wicked caprice of fate, Petya fell in love instantly and entirely—well, he didn't exactly fall in love but just started loving—and became completely immersed in this totally serious feeling. Irina Konstantinovna became for him the land of beauty and hap-piness from the first moment of their acquaintance, from the very minute when he had scalded his arm at the garage and was brought to the poly-clinic and left in the doctor's office. Petya was overcome by an immense irresistible rapture when she touched his hand and asked him to roll up his shirt sleeve.

Her every movement, glance, and walk, the touch of her hand and the way she applied to his burned skin some ointment that smelled of smoked fish, all this was the incarnation of that ultimate fullness of relations that is the only one a determined lover strives for. She belonged to him com-pletely and fully by her smile and voice, in which there were no words but only the sound of her breath, and by her feminine knee showing beneath the white smock where the edges parted in front; he could swear that he had seen nothing like it before in his whole life.

There are writers who enjoy talking about themselves and their near and dear, revealing things that shouldn't be told at all, especially affairs of the heart. But Petya! No, Petya's romance was pure and selfless, not a single moment of it could offend even the sternest taste, and it's only a shame that history has preserved so few moments.

All the time his hand was healing, Petya had to go every day, and later every two days, to get a new bandage, and he was immeasurably, irresisti-bly in raptures over Irina Konstantinovna. His cheeks, pale from emotion, combined with his burning eyes, gave him a certain beauty. His short and laconic answers to all her questions awakened Irina Konstantinovna's curiosity, and one day she asked, "Have you been in the army?" Petya regretted that his padded coat, sword-belt and holster, and the Kuban cap were in the cloak room. In reply to the question he said with dignity, "I'm still in the military to a certain degree," and when he saw that Irina Konstantinovna's eyes lit up, he quickly explained, "I serve in the State Car Inspection." Irina Konstantinovna suddenly bent down and blew on his unwrapped scalded arm and quickly started to rebandage it.

Every minute for the rest of his life Petya could feel this blowing, this breath given to him by his beloved. Many people make punctures on their arms so as to extend and preserve the joy they have experienced, supposing that the blue ink injected under their skin can prolong and make indestructible the euphoric feelings they have savored. In the garage the former sailor Sergey Parkhomenko made pretty good tattoos, and he offered to tattoo "Valya" on Petya's arm when he noticed that it was precisely the red-haired Valya from Ruchi who had caught Petya's attention. Petya refused at first, but nevertheless he later asked if the sailor could tattoo both Valya's first and middle names. Sergey was drunk and refused to do the middle name, and then later forgot the whole thing. Petya didn't remind him again but contented himself with the more meaningful scars on his right arm that were healing slowly and badly because of the lack of vitamins in his system.

An elevated love is free love, and Petya's passion was absolutely free of any demands whatsoever, including the need to possess; but like all happy lovers he was totally enraptured by delirious fancies.

Petya couldn't even understand or explain the desires tormenting his soul, desires that normal people call fantasies.

The impatience of a heart striving to enjoy happiness as soon as possible was alien to Petya. That first elevated moment of love when he who is doomed to love doesn't yet know his fate, but is already bewitched and lives in the joy of his fascination, this happy moment when he doesn't yet know the grief of crumbling hopes, the pain of jealousy, the empty despondency of separation, this moment fated to last only a few brief hours or days in hearts thirsting for reciprocity, this moment remained frozen for Petya at its highest peak and lit up his entire existence, just as the never-setting arctic sun shines around the clock.

When Irina Konstantinovna leaned toward him the first time she bandaged him and he could feel the scent of her hair, he realized that such a bright and joyous fire had never penetrated his soul before; it was stinging like the little sparks from the Bengal lights that are lit for New Year's at the club, and the smell of her hair, light as the sap of fir trees, reminded him of the smell of the forest and the purest water, a big lake like Lake Ples. Later in the spring he recognized this scent when the whole settlement was sparkling in the sun and flooded by the roaring, gurgling torrents of melted water and when he stood on the bridge over the Niva and watched the water flying, boiling, bubbling over the stones.

The purer the river looked and the louder the water gurgled, the more clearly Petya was reminded of Irina Konstantinovna's hair sticking out from under her white cap. He couldn't say what color it was, just as rushing, living water has no color, as eyes have no color when all you can remember is how they shine and the joy you feel when seeing them before you.

The whimsical lustful little feelings that sneak into a lover's soul never inspired Petya with the recurring desire to even for a brief moment experience complete union with the object of his rapturous adoration, but nevertheless he did experience it once when he saw Irina Konstantinovna in the rain.

One end of an enormous rainbow was propped up on the sea, perhaps right on the prow of some little ship in the bay, and the other end had flown halfway to the sky above the hummocks, touching down far away in Lake Ples, and it made the rain, penetrated with the red light of the setting August sun, look festive but a little bloody. Irina Konstantinovna had been surprised by the rain as she was walking along Chkalov Street in the glory of her beauty, but not shrinking from the red-tinted streams. She wasn't hurrying, and Petya noticed her from where he was sheltered under the small overhang of a green kiosk boarded up with planks.

He licked little drops from his cheeks, listened to the thick rustle of the rain; at this very moment he had been thinking of Irina Konstantinovna. Noticing her from afar, he at once jumped out in the rain and moved toward her, plunging through the slanting downpour colored by the setting sun and shimmering with red reflections. He walked quickly, as a man in the rain should walk, and he looked continuously at her: her soaking-wet hair, her clinging dress, her legs, breasts, arms, all suddenly standing out in stunning visibility.

The water, the ancestral source of all life, simultaneously embraced and joined them, and the light disturbing dreams borne last winter by the scent of her hair, nurtured and sustained by the scent of pure water, and pursuing him for over a year, these languorous desires, tormenting in their elusiveness and exceeding even fantasy itself—were fully and triumphantly realized . . .

The reader has of course already recalled the history of the incomparable Arethusa* who threw herself into the sea trying to escape from the persistent Alpheius. The enterprising Alpheius then changed himself into a river, dashed into the sea and reached his beloved . . . But Irina Konstantinovna didn't seek to be rescued and Petya didn't attempt to ravish her. As Karamzin* said, "The delights of love are incalculable."

Just as we don't want to appropriate the beauty of the sky, sunset, or snowstorm and make it our property, so also did Petya refrain from converting his delight in feminine perfection into a thirst for possession. Every moment spent with Irina Konstantinovna was for him a moment of complete possession of the object of his love; and anyway, it's not for us to understand this, although it's easy to imagine Petya's feelings when he saw the Opel Kapitan just as he was inspecting the construction chief's Pobeda. That was on a Sunday, so it was quite likely that Irina Konstantinovna would be riding in the car. This was actually the case. Petya saw a familiar beautiful face leaning forward from the back seat and casting a hot glance in his direction.

It only seemed to Petya that the glance thrown out of the window of the passing Opel was directed at him.

"I wish he'd get sick, the devil," thought Irina Konstantinovna.

Boguslavsky always sat beside the chauffeur.

The decorative plumage of Irina Konstantinovna, hidden inside the speeding boxlike black Opel, part of the spoils of war, was less suited to the dreary skies of the arctic tundra than to the Vienna woods or the assembly rooms in Baden-Baden. Incidentally, these very clothes had in fact been sewn for the ladies of those places. By the time these events took place, the Viennese fashion had probably changed, but Irina Konstantinovna had to shine in costumes from the late forties in whatever place she found herself at the blossoming of her perfection.

Well, quite often those army officers whose job it is to receive consignments of convicts from the depths of Russia, distribute them in different security zones, and vigilantly maintain the contingent in strict conformity

*In the Greek myth the nymph Arethusa was pursued by the river god Alpheius.
**Nikolay Karamzin (1766–1826) was a Russian writer and historian.

with the prescribed regime, have wives who must serve as adornments in places so far removed from civilization, so it's easy to see how these wives must suffer from not being appreciated according to their worth. This feeling is both natural and justified. If only some Austrian baroness had shown up in Niva III or Kandalaksha, the local population could have seen with their own eyes that the Austrian baroness had nothing to brag about compared to Irina Konstantinovna, but no baroness ever came to Kandalaksha, and not even Colonel Boguslavsky could correct this situation, although they do say that he brought in groceries for Irina Konstantinovna straight from Leningrad in a special railroad car hooked onto a passenger train. As a consequence of this he had some unpleasantness with the new administration, and in late 1953 he was put behind bars in a camp where he soon became the victim of an accident; that is, to put it bluntly, he was brutally murdered.

To make it more graphic we should add that Irina Konstantinovna was tall and blond and had a rounded figure, even a certain tendency to plumpness which, however, hadn't turned into excessive corpulence. Her large features were regular and well proportioned and she shone with freshness and health. Colonel Boguslavsky was only ten years older than his wife. Irina Konstantinovna didn't conceal her poetic fictions, fabricated in order to justify her advantageous marriage, and she willingly talked about Boguslavsky's immense superiority over men her own age who wouldn't make her happy. This fortunate husband was, so to speak, big-boned and looked quite dashing since he dressed as foppishly as his strict service would allow. As for his height, with his service cap, sewn by the sorcerer Aleksey Deomidovich Kyrf of the Kandalaksha army store, he was no shorter than his wife walking beside him. A blank and stupid expression could sometimes be discerned in Irina Konstantinovna's gray eyes, but it instantly disappeared as soon as she was inspired with some thought or intense wish. At the time of her meeting with Petya she hadn't lost her youth yet but had already acquired that experience and assurance which permits the flexible soul of a beautiful woman to satisfy all her desires and yet remain true to her own high principles of morality and rectitude. Not only her friendly face but also her sturdy back, enveloped in a pretty dress, frequently invited the glances not only of men but also of women.

The feeling that possessed Petya was boundless and had the amazing capacity of igniting at the mere scent of pure water, as has already been described; nevertheless it didn't burst out but remained entirely contained inside him.

It was another matter with Irina Konstantinovna's feelings; they were ready to explode and demanded instant gratification but couldn't find a way out, and this caused Irina Konstantinovna, unaccustomed to suffering, to suffer deeply and unreasonably.

A large number of provincial love affairs and romances in godforsaken places begin with music accidentally heard through the windows of an unknown house and affecting the soul, heart, and whatever else of the hero or heroine.

The above-described Nikolay Ivanovich liked to play music at home for his own enjoyment. Boguslavsky had an apartment on Kirov Boulevard where most of the residents were administration people. He didn't live in the same house as the construction chief, the chief engineer, and the director of operations, Gennady Alekseevich Volokov, but in a similar two-story house next door, with eight apartments, constructed of exactly the same kind of timber. It was therefore completely natural that one time when Irina Konstantinovna heard piano music wafting through the open window into the street, she wanted to know, "Who's playing so nicely?" "That's our Nikolay Ivanovich playing," said her neighbor Mina Lvovna Bykova with a certain pride; she was the wife of the head of the Technical Division. Irina Konstantinovna became flustered and even felt guilty for saying "nicely."

Curiosity lightly tinted with a feeling of guilt; what could be more promising than such a seed? If planted in the soil of an empty female heart it could yield not just sprouts and shoots but the most amazing fruits. "How well he plays," Irina Konstantinovna at once corrected herself.

Home for his lunch break, Nikolay Ivanovich was actually playing badly; he had just received a photocopy of the sheet music for one of Monti's czardas, but the copy was too small to read. Nikolay Ivanovich stared unblinkingly at the sheet music, made a mistake, got angry at himself and therefore made more mistakes. Nikolay Ivanovich's spouse possessed an exceptional musical pitch and she corrected him by singing the melody exactly right; but this only angered her husband, and she got angry too because she couldn't deflect his attention away from Monti and onto the lunch that was getting cold. However, the sheet music, ordered long ago, had just arrived, and in accordance with Nikolay Ivanovich's nature, the czardas had to be played at once and without mistakes.

Maybe Irina Konstantinovna was favorably impressed by the fact that while he was trying to figure out the music, Nikolay Ivanovich was playing, as the French say, *du bout des doigts,* with his fingertips; such performances can be impressive by their lack of polish, lightness, and promise of future passionate but vain outbursts of emotion.

So this music, drifting out from the house, dangerously inflamed Irina Konstantinovna's curiosity which could so easily grow into alarming and unsatisfied desire.

The construction of the hydroelectric plant was accomplished without help from prisoners; it had been sufficient to use special settlers and repatriates.* Therefore their professional relations that might easily and almost inevitably carrying over into personal and friendly relations, never caused Nikolay Ivanovich and Boguslavsky's paths to cross. Introduced into a social circle of friends and comrades from her husband's service, Irina Konstantinovna suddenly felt cut off from people in the free society where subordinates don't pride themselves on the high connections of their immediate superiors or on the ability of these superiors to show kindness and patronage—or, as Boguslavsky put it, "to move things"—but instead praised their ability to play the piano.

Most of all Nikolay Ivanovich liked to play the accompaniment to violin sonatas; His father had played the violin and he remembered accompanying him when he was only a boy of thirteen. He recalled the poignant pauses that he strictly observed when he played—pauses for the violin solo parts—yawning with an enigmatic emptiness that his listeners could fill in according to their own imagination.

In order to show that the forty-two-year-old Nikolay Ivanovich with his Rachmaninov and Monti didn't stand out like a white crow against the background of the arctic building project, we might mention, for example, Aleksandra Ivanovna Zemliakova, a graduate of the Petrograd Conservatory. (Incidentally, Rachmaninov was sincerely impressed with her marvelous contralto and promised to write a romance for her, but in the confusion of his departure this promise remained unfulfilled. To be even more convincing we can also mention Elena Anatolevna, the wife of Skorodumov, deputy chief of the Technical Division; she had studied ballet, and on the stage of the Twenty-fifth Anniversary of the Great October Club she danced *The Dying Swan* at holiday concerts in a tutu and au-point shoes, leaving half the audience profoundly mystified; they hadn't expected so much exposure in a classical ballet. The wife of Vasily Kondrikov, the so-called Prince of Kola, formerly Kirov's** right-hand man in the arctic

*Special settlers were prisoners released from camps but forced to live in restricted areas; repatriated prisoners of war usually had to live in "internal exile," often near construction projects, but many POWs were sent to labor camps.
**Sergei Mironovich Kirov (1888–1934) was a revolutionary and a politician who was assassinated under suspicious circumstances.

region, was also a ballet dancer, from the Maly Theater in Leningrad; it's true that she had already left in 1938 for Tobolsk with other wives of enemies of the people, then had gone on to Kolyma from where she returned in 1948 with a new name (no, not to Monchegorsk but to Leningrad).

Thus it is only at first glance that the arctic tundra seems like a wilderness outside the mainstream of the life of the country. But even so, the life stories of almost half the tamers of this rigorous land could serve as the basis for real dramas or even tragedies, so desperately lacking in our dramatic theaters.

Petya's biography, or indeed his life, isn't very long and it would therefore be wrong to omit significant events from it, even when they have neither instructive nor educational value.

When tourists, especially alpinists, reach their intended goal, they rejoice, make merry, and congratulate each other—in a word, celebrate. When the builders of a hydroelectric plant reach a certain point in the process of the construction—draining a coffer dam, flooding the foundation pit, dismantling a coffer dam, starting up the first generator, and so forth—they of course celebrate too. But building an electric plant so far underground had of course no analogy in the world and involved numerous unusual stages, intermediate peaks, as it were, and the conquest of each one justified a victory celebration. One of these peaks in the construction of Niva III was reached at a depth of fifty meters.

In late winter, actually the spring of 1948, the subterranean part of the drainage drift was finally cut through. The drifters approaching each other from the railroad station and the Moscow Canal blasted the last meters of rock with ammonal, and when they met, they embraced and started celebrating. This driftway didn't go through moraine, nor through the kind of permafrost that can be found near the surface, but through the bedrock—the famous rock of the Fenno-Scandinavian Shield that has never been above sea level, not even when the world ocean had expanded to its fullest extent, so it's the very oldest dry land on earth. It was in the depths of this dry land that they met. The axes of both tunnels met so precisely (thanks to the considerable skill of the chief mine surveyor, Zentsov) that several crates of vodka were brought directly to the tunnel to polish and strengthen it, and there were also some snacks and then more alcohol. It actually seemed that an inexhaustible well of alcohol had sprung up somewhere down there, because after the satisfied chiefs had each drunk a symbolic glass of vodka in the damp underground, they drank another swallow with the most deserving heroes of the day, and then they suggested that everyone should go to the surface to avoid getting locked in, but people were unwilling to leave. Anatoly Fedorovich Vasilev, whose involvement with alcohol was quite moderate and highly disciplined, was among the first to come up and be naturally headed straight for his little Kozlik, where his faithful servant Petr was already asleep, dead drunk behind the wheel. How Petr had managed to reach that condition, even though he found himself at a distance of at least two kilometers from the celebration deep underground, remains to this day an unsolved mystery. (The car stood next to shaft B, which supplied the underground crews with air and was equipped with a large cage for lowering and raising people.)

Nikolay Ivanovich walked by and saw that Anatoly Fedorovich was angry at his cheerfully snoring chauffeur, asleep with his mug resting on the steering wheel, and he shouted, "Overcelebrated, huh!" He continued to his own car with the sober Grisha at the wheel, but changed his mind and returned to the chief engineer's car. "Hey, men, let's send him down below," ordered Nikolay Ivanovich, and loosening the brakes he leaned on the car to push it to the elevator.

After fifteen minutes of hilarious effort, the car with the sleeping Petr in it was not only lowered seventy meters underground but also rolled a hundred meters down the underground tunnel away from the shaft.

The chiefs drove off and the chief engineer's chauffeur, Petr, remained below for the amusement of the victors.

No one wanted to leave now; everyone wanted to see the look on Petr's mug when he woke up.

At this point they also thought of Petya-the-Inspector. It took them only twenty minutes to find him. Petya and his mother were at the Orsov dining room at the railroad station, since the entire settlement had spent the last days in anticipation of the imminent juncture, and the speculations about improved supplies for the station dining room also concerned this little family that had no direct connection with the construction and the victory. The drunks literally pulled Petya from the table and dragged him to the scene, confusedly but earnestly explaining to him the essence of the situation.

Petya understood the main thing: there was a drunk driver. He didn't like drunk drivers; a drunk driver means threats, curses, rudeness, and a complete lack of respect for authority, and if people actually turned to him for help it must mean real trouble. Petya didn't overestimate his powers, he was aware of his meek character and was sadly conscious of the empty holster on his right side.

When Petya shook his namesake awake, the latter didn't believe his eyes. He let out a few curses and tried to go back to sleep, but the faces behind Petya and the peculiar booming sound of their voices, like clanking iron—all these unfamiliar tunnel noises forced him to try to open his eyes. "Your license and work schedule, comrade driver," uttered Petya with suppressed excitement. The chauffeur seemed not to have heard the question. "Why don't you tell me this instead, weirdo—where am I?"

The grubby audience in overalls, padded jackets, and rubber boots, mostly drunk, gleefully watched the spectacle in the faint illumination of the lamps, hastily strung up in the rough-walled tunnel that hadn't been smoothed over yet with cement.

Petr turned on the engine and realized that he had to move backwards and shifted to reverse, but when he got to the engine room and didn't see the exit he tried to go forward and asked, goggle-eyed: "What's this place?" and "How did I get here, can anyone tell me?" The chief's order not to tell Petr how he had got there was cheerfully carried out to the letter.

Because of the state of his health, Petya-the-Inspector was completely indifferent to wine and even disliked it after the repeated efforts of his friends the drivers to get him to indulge; in his soberness he was superfluous at the underground celebration. After playing his brief role earnestly and conscientiously and making everybody laugh, Petya retreated to the background and was forgotten; he started to worry about his mother back in the dining hall and hurried off to look for the exit. At first he thought he knew where the lift was, but he ended up somewhere else, and in his confusion he rushed along the many-leveled forests of machinery and reached the lifts of the third and fourth pits, where instead of passenger cages there were only tubs for lifting rock. Now and then someone stopped him and asked what he was looking for. He was ashamed to admit that he was looking for the exit, so instead he said earnestly, "You haven't seen a 2GAZ62, license number MF62-33?" "Uh huh, it's over there, the one you want; look lower down." And again Petya ran off into the labyrinthine crossings and galleries and got totally lost among the five levels of the engine room.

Meanwhile, in his "Kozlik," Petr was speeding away from the rock face where the festive juncture had taken place, toward the ventilation shaft, perhaps just as terrified and desperate as the unfortunate inspector.

They were both liberated at the same time.

Vasilev's Petr took recourse in the universal way of overcoming grief; he was offered a drink and naturally accepted it, and since they had struck a spring that wouldn't dry out the whole day, he could partake freely. After an hour they put him on the back seat in an irresponsible condition, rolled the car to the shaft, and sent it up.

Petya's sensitive ear had heard the familiar sound of the lift engine and he reached the lift in time. He found his mother walled in with white unplaned planks in the heated cabin of the derrick, where Vera Makolkina was on duty this evening. Petya rushed home through the sleeping settlement, plowing through the snow with his long legs, but even so he couldn't keep up with his mom flying before him like a lark before an eagle; she had grabbed her son by the hand and dragged him along, treating him in the same way she had done for over fifteen years now, her grown but nevertheless not adult son.

For about a month this story didn't leave the lips of the settlement. It was retold with new details and accretions and became a legend, and at the official reception held when the station was presented to the Government Commission, it was told at a suitable moment to Kandalov himself, who unexpectedly found himself underground. Descending to the machine room in the lift, the first things that caught his attention were the humble two-armed bronze bracket lamps placed on all four walls. "Is this all the illumination, these lamps?" remarked the knowledgeable commission chairman at this first inspection. He remembered perfectly well that each of the eight chandeliers in the auditorium of the new Moscow University building contained 150 fluorescent lights. Nikolay Ivanovich had to explain very tactfully that the six tall "windows," placed along the wall near the oil regulator, were the principal sources of light. "But that's in the daytime. What about when it gets dark?" insisted the government representative. "Here it's always night, Comrade Kandalov," said Nikolay Ivanovich politely. "We're underground, in point of fact seventy-five meters." With an imaginative curse, the commission chairman refrained from expressing further angry irritation and instead laughed and praised the light, smooth and soft as the arctic sun, pouring in over the whole machine room with its four nests of reliably working generators.

Petya-the-Inspector had dropped out of the story Kandalov was told during the banquet, about how they lowered a car wih a drunken driver into the tunnel; Petya had dropped out not only because the guest might get the two Petyas mixed up but also because half a year had already passed since Petya had been buried, and he was forgotten, not having left any mark behind him.

In his lifetime, however, not a single social activity took place without Petya's participation and attention; he took an active part in funerals and always marched in the columns of demonstrators, although the chauffeurs didn't trust him to carry the most responsible portraits and slogans. (Incidentally, he walked in the demonstrations wearing his "civvies," as the military men called them, that is without his belt and holster.) He regularly took part in the summer outdoor fairs on Chkalov Street, the central street in the settlement, along its most fashionable section from the post office past the tearoom, the store, and other major buildings, and so on to the hospital, built with its facade across the far end of the street on Hospital Hill. When the barns on Second Arctic Street burned, he was among the first to come to the fire, and he dashed into the flames to save a goat. But when the twenty-five-meter-tall wooden pile driver at the No. 5 mine pit burned, then, like all the others, Petya was only a spectator; the firemen couldn't reach the shaft and had nothing with which to put out the flames almost a hundred meters high. Nor did Petya fail to observe, and to a certain extent also participate in, the traffic of the huge gray mass of people proceeding twice a day, there and back, past the club in Lesny.

It's no secret to anyone that builders for the most part live in temporary quarters, something like barracks. They don't really need anything better, because after living there for five to ten years they move away anyway to new uninhabited lands, new tents, new temporary housing, new barracks. It's different with the living quarters of the citizens who come here to take up permanent residence after the departure of the builders. The hydroelectric station, for example, had just been completed, and right beside it one could already see the 150-meter-tall smokestacks of the KAZ* aluminum factory and some kind of industrial wood or paper complex to which a thousand people wanted to dedicate their lives forever. In order to meet the legitimate demands of these residents at the times we are describing, a piece of land near the outskirts of the inhabited area was enclosed with barbed wire, and the necessary number of barracks were put up and populated by the future builders of the well-constructed stone-and-brick housing for the workers of the factory or factory complex. Luckily, or perhaps not so luckily, the criminal world placed at the disposal of the national economy exactly as many desperate criminals as were needed for building canals, arctic railroads, industrial complexes, and other remarkable and necessary structures, both in the center of the capital and in the vast outlying areas of our country.**

*Kandalaksha Aluminum Plant.
**For example, forced labor built the notorious Belomor Canal, which cost hundreds of thousands of lives in the course of its construction. Certain apartment

Everybody can remember that an outflow of slave labor from Niva III could already be noted in the early fifties: the peak of the work was over, the station was running, the workers had begun the final stage of decorating and were preparing to hand it over to the State Receiving Commission. But at the same time a new construction project was begun, the last station along the rapids, Niva I. Part of the collective didn't want to part with Nikolay Ivanovich and their polar bonuses, so they moved to Zasheek to work on Niva I; another group went to the hydroelectric construction projects on the Kama or near Gorky, where it's warmer; and the rest went to work at KAZ. So it was absolutely impossible to find builders for the permanent stone settlement, or rather, the town. But then as though by magic a small camp grew up; there were no more than four barracks. The camp nestled on the rocky bald area beyond Lesny on the far side of the Niva settlement and facing toward the Golovnoy Junction.

In the winter of 1951, in December, the commission approved the zone, giving it the high grade of "Satisfactory"; the proviso about the unsatisfactory lighting of the high enclosing wall was removed at once; the walking path for the guards was equipped with additional wire and firewood was even brought in for the initial period. And then the little camp received a contingent of zeks, something on the order of a thousand souls.

The residents of the settlement rejoiced when shortly before the completion of the little camp the authorities not only installed street lighting but also used remarkably bright lamps along Kandalaksha Road, Kirov Boulevard, and First and Second Kirov streets. It now looked cheerful and bright in the settlement. (In the impenetrable polar darkness any kind of light is welcome.) It hardly occurred to anyone that all this was done only to make it easier to impose the regime on the zeks, who had to walk both to and from work in complete darkness.

And so every day, shortly after eight in the morning and after six in the evening, except on days of rest, holidays, and when work was canceled because of frost or fog,* a column strode along the stony road, crunching in the snow, stomping in the mud, or raising thin clouds of dust; they walked six abreast and were accompanied by only fifteen guards, not counting two German shepherds on long leashes. They walked past the

---

buildings in Moscow were also built by convict labor (Solzhenitsyn worked on one of these projects). One of Stalin's unrealized plans was a railroad from west to east in the northern part of the country.
*Prisoners did not have to work outdoors when it was below −40°C.

Lesny club building (frankly speaking, disgracefully ugly), where the extremely tall Petya's tiny mother lived and worked as a cleaning woman with the rights of a commandant, or as a commandant with the duties of a cleaning woman.

Some mornings Petya went out on the club's front porch overlooking the road and watched this orderly and almost military procession. The observant chief of the convoy, Captain Kapustin-Iarkin, brought up the rear of the procession, walking with the resilient and independent stride of a man who is quick on his feet, and an automatic PPS* the size of a big toy invariably hung on his back with the barrel pointing down.

Before making his decision Petya deliberated for a long time until he finally realized what he was expected to do.

One morning by the white light of all the stars in the sky and the frozen blue full moon, the convoy guards and zeks saw a tall figure in a Kuban cap standing on a boulder beside the road. The guards got nervous, but the prisoners were only sorry that they couldn't discern the face of the man because the moonlight was falling almost vertically. When the column came up even with Petya, he threw up one hand and touched his cap in a military salute. Kapustin-Iarkin involuntarily moved his automatic from his back to his side, preparing for a surprise. He never had to think long before firing in the air and giving the order "Down, you motherfucking sons of bitches." If he preferred this way of addressing his subordinates it wasn't because the Russian language doesn't offer a wide enough selection of vocabulary for such occasions; his choice primarily revealed his respect for the leaders, his desire to uphold traditions, and many other remarkable qualities that recommended Kapustin-Iarkin in the very best sense of the word. Veterans of the Belomor Canal Construction used to quote the shortest speech made by the legendary Firin at the Sorozh sector, to convince the workers to complete their section ahead of schedule: "A Russian peasant doesn't cross himself until he hears thunder. We'll give you thunder. Cross yourselves, you motherfucking sons of bitches!"

And the Sorozh workers completed the plan. At the time, this story made a great impression on Kapustin-Iarkin, and he incorporated the experiences of his elder comrades in his own fighting arsenal.

Kapustin-Iarkin's concern was unwarranted, and in spite of their excitement no one in the column gave him any pretext to make everyone lie down in the snow. The zeks were obviously experienced and nobody

*A submachine gun with folding stock.

wanted to lie bellydown on the road with their face against the boots of the citizen in front of him.

When the column had passed, Kapustin-larkin nimbly jumped over to the curb in his felt boots and ran up to Petya: "Get the fucking hell out of here or I'll set the dogs on you!" Kapustin-larkin spoke with great force, adding to his words some sounds that aren't part of any known language, and these sounds imbued even old familiar words with a certain quality that froze the soul.

Petya stood there with a foggy look in his eyes, seeing himself, the road, the stars and the moon, and the German shepherds, always ready to jump, as though from the outside, not actually belonging to his own world. He was quite surprised when he saw Kapustin-larkin in front of him and heard his malicious voice. On his behind, he slid down from the slippery boulder, adjusted the empty holster, touched his hand to his cap, and rapped out with an amazingly steady voice, "Carry on!" Then he turned a sharp left and strode off to the club, where his mother was waiting for him on the porch, her bare feet in felt boots and a rug thrown over her shoulders.

What can we say about the crowd of eight hundred souls floating by before our eyes on the brightly lit road in the pale bluish reflected moonlight? Not a lot; there was extremely little variety in this type of people. Perhaps the most characteristic and distinctive feature was their way of lacing up their heavy but nonetheless cold workboots—but this couldn't be discerned from afar. Shoelaces were extremely hard to find in the zone; they could be seen only on the strongest and boldest camp dwellers, those who would do anything to defend their position in life. Good string could also be considered a mark of great fortitude and stamina in the struggle for survival. Bandages or strips from old sheets converted into laces revealed a certain cunning and skill in management. But wire used as laces was a bad sign, frankly; from wires it was only a short step to no laces at all, and there were some like that, too.

Or take headgear. All the caps were of light cloth and didn't provide good protection from the cold, but also here one could judge the character and fortitude of the prisoner. Those who still cared about how they appeared to the free world would leave the camp area to walk to the construction site with the earflaps up and risk getting their ears frostbitten. It was necessary to make the decision when lining up inside the camp, because while walking nobody was allowed to take his hands off his back to adjust or tie anything. Those who no longer cared how they looked to the outside world tied the ragged earflaps of their caps under their chins at once, and this made them look like they had a toothache, or like sick children carefully bundled up against the cold. Kapustin-larkin wouldn't let them wear the earflaps down without tying them; once he had been reprimanded for this by Boguslavsky, although he didn't quite understand why, and after that he was strict and permitted no deviations from the uniform prescribed by his superior.

For the sake of justice we must not describe only what separates people, differentiates them, makes them unlike one another but also what brings them together. For example, among the hundreds of participants in this winter parade there was not a single one at this moment who would have noticed that all the actors were enveloped exclusively in padded coats. The only exceptions were the five screws* whose faces were hardly visible behind the raised collars of their coats in which they would later take turns standing guard all day on raised wooden platforms that by their design vaguely and distantly imitated some of the less well-known towers of the Kremlin. The tall and skinny man with a pinched face on the slippery boulder wore a padded coat. The convoy commander who dashed up to him was also clad in a padded coat that enabled him to move and maneuver easily and quickly, but his was new and green and had a collar, while in the column all the convicts without exception were shivering in short padded jackets without collars. For additional but very doubtful warmth they wrapped their necks, covered by boils and frozen stiff in the frost, with their rough towels, not too freshly laundered and furthermore not quite dry after the morning wash-up.

How, by what coincidence had this identical clothing been acquired by all the participants in this unforgettable encounter.

These observations about the uniform garb may cause the reader to suppose that Petya's story, at first appearing senseless and crazy, might be an allegory, developed with some kind of grand and secret intention. Unfortunately, no; this simple story contains neither political allegories nor a hidden meaning, it's only the simple truth, or perhaps only fragments of the truth that have survived only partially on the millstone of history turned by the burden of everyday life, just as the traces of many other civilizations on earth have rotted irretrievably in the abyss of ages.

During the night of March 6, 1953, Petya felt uneasy and hardly slept at all, nor did his mother who was silently mumbling prayers about health,

---

*"Screw" is camp slang for sentry.

interspersed with weeping.* When it was announced in the morning that it was all over, Petya burst out crying, but his mother had already cried herself senseless and only let out a moan that sounded more like a shriek, fell face-down on her pillow, and went to sleep instantly. The previous night Petya had inquired offhandedly in the garage whether mourning flags should be displayed if the doctors didn't succeed in saving Stalin. The drivers refused to answer, but at the militia, where Petya dropped by later on, the frank and garrulous Mnogolesov stated firmly that not only would the "country dress in mourning" but the factories would close down and the transportation system too, and therefore Petya set off at once for the storage room in the club where flags and the holiday inventory were kept. He found a box of black ribbons left over from the Day of Lenin and taken down literally on the eve of the Day of the Red Army and Navy. Petya tied twenty-seven black ribbons to a flag but couldn't make up his mind where to hang it up, not even over the door to the club, recalling what Senior Lieutenant Mnogolesov had said the day before: "If anything happens, the strongest discipline will be enforced all over the country."

Petya went out on the porch of the club and looked at the sky. Almost two months after the end of its winter imprisonment below the horizon, the sun was shining on the residents of the polar lands in silent splendor and with growing generosity, and each day the duration of its heavenly promenade was extended a little more.

Not counting the sun's standing low and directly above Women's Navel, the whole cloudless sky was empty and seemed hopelessly deserted, fully corresponding to Petya's feeling of immeasurable loss. High up, higher than the sun, he could see a jet fighter dragging a white tuft of wool, perhaps coming all the way from Afrikanda,** and he thought that there was no sense in flying now, just as the snow made no sense or the houses around him or the solitary sun that didn't give out heat. The white flourish in the sky seemed to Petya totally senseless and out of place.

Higher up, toward KAZ but just to the right where the road turned toward Golovnoy Junction, a black ribbon was coming into view, slowly spreading out and occupying the whole width of the road. Petya had many times observed the slow, viscous motion of this black column, and on the downhill slope he always expected it to start sliding and slipping, or at least to increase its speed just a little to help it more easily slide

*Stalin died on March 6, 1953.
**Afrikanda is a town thirty miles north of Kandalaksha.

up the next hill that ended near the club. But the long black caterpillar crawled downhill and uphill at the same speed, and it seemed that if a straight wall should block its way it would just as unhurriedly ooze up its side, go over the top edge, and as slowly make its way down the other side step-by-step.

Today, the depressing motion of the black ribbon along the road, powdered by snow overnight, corresponded more than ever to the infinite sorrow that had gripped the hushed earth. Petya felt so sorry for these men who not even today, on a day like this, could remain within their camp perimeters and weep in their sorrow.

He went into his hovel beside the boarded-up ticket office and quietly, without waking his mother, put on his belt, holster, and army cap and went out again. His boots broke through the thick March crust and dug into the snow, grainy like sand; he reached that same boulder where Kapustin-larkin had made him come down in the winter, and he climbed up on it again.

Now he could be seen by everybody, the sun shone in his face as he stood on the stone, severe and sad, ready to greet his orphaned countrymen with a military salute.

At the front of the column two soldiers in thick army coats walked slowly and not in time, carrying their rifles with the bayonets pointing down as though searching for mines. They quickly glanced at Petya and smiled. Petya interpreted this greeting as conveying sympathy and approval, but his transparent mind, receptive only to simple facts, could not comprehend what he saw afterwards. He saw hundreds of faces turned in his direction, but not a shade of sorrow, not a sign of grief, no eyes red from weeping . . . Earlier they had resembled a flock of corpses that had for some reason been raised from the dead and were driven from one large common grave to another, but now Petya could see quite clearly that they were living people; these were real faces floating by. The cheerful, youthful faces looked out at him from the filthy cocoonlike shells of the earflaps and the towels around their necks, and even the scabs of frostbites on their cheeks, the black circles under their eyes, the crimson blisters of lupus, everything was washed clean and didn't look terrible any more. Eight hundred pairs of happy eyes, yes, precisely happy, were looking at him, and some of them even winked, hinting at some secret mutual understanding that couldn't be openly expressed yet.

Petya was horrified, he suddenly understood with unwonted clarity why these people had been brought into the camp, why they were removed from life and placed under convoy, why the guards and dogs were necessary.

Kapustin-Iarkin, bringing up the rear of the column as always, only threw a quick glance in Petya's direction but gave no sign of recalling their first meeting. The little automatic weapon of black metal with a folded-in butt-stock, hanging on Kapustin-Iarkin's right shoulder, seemed to Petya completely inadequate for subjugating these perfidious scoundrels who only appeared to be human beings and could actually smile and rejoice on such a day, at such an hour as now. Following Kapustin-Iarkin with his eyes, Petya was cheered to see that in addition to the automatic he also had a Nagant revolver on the belt that firmly held together his short green padded coat.

Petya's approving glance followed Kapustin-Iarkin's Nagant pistol, in a polished militia holster with a rounded cover and a brass cleaning rod with a ring; he would soon see it in action. Kapustin-Iarkin would use the handle to hit a zek between the shoulder blades, and the muzzle to fire live ammunition, since he found it insufficient to hit the zek on the spine with the handle, no matter how hard. The man on whom it was inflicted didn't seem to fully comprehend the blows, so Kapustin-Iarkin decided to fire the gun. For the first time in their lives, Petya and a few adults, not to mention the children who came running to see what was going on, would see a living man be shot. It was frightening but interesting. Actually this extreme measure was, you might say, provoked by the man who was guilty in the first place. When Kapustin-Iarkin began to belabor his back with the Nagant, hitting him mostly on the spine, that jerk for some reason covered his face with his hands, although he wasn't hit in the face, and started shouting, "Don't kill me, Uncle; don't kill me, Uncle!" More than likely it was these very screams that made Kapustin-Iarkin realize how useless his blows to the spine were and that he must finish the business with a shot.

The event that occurred was in fact quite simple, even trifling, but we all know that other people's troubles never seem very difficult or complex.

On March 26, a Thursday, Petya was walking along Kirov Boulevard, where there were two-story ITR houses only on the left side. This street marked the end of the settlement, and on the right side, as you go from Kandalaksha Road toward the Construction Administration, there were hardly any structures. There were only three houses, each with eight apartments on the right-hand side of the boulevard; but in contrast to the houses on the left they were not plastered, and for some reason they were turned with the side toward the street and not facing it, unlike the houses on the opposite side. Further, between these houses that were standing sideways were several foundations laid in the ardent prewar years, but the construction hadn't progressed since then, and by the early fifties there was nothing there except sickly birches and puny alder bushes (it's true that every autumn beautiful baby-pink rose-bay blossomed both inside the foundations and along the edges). These foundations were, however, used by the local school children. After watching films about savages, students from the first six grades would arm themselves with sticks and jump from one stonewall to another, chasing each other as though possessed and letting out penetrating screams, also borrowed from the films that were among the spoils of war. When some old ladies who didn't understand that active games in the open air are important for children's health asked the kids what they were doing, they replied, "Tarzan!" as though this explanation was sufficient. We have to mention the school-age children because they, too, witnessed how two desperate escapees were caught and how Kapustin-larkin lost his self-control and had to use his weapon.

Returning to these foundations, we must mention that soon after the little camp beyond Lesny appeared, the foundation nearest Chkalov Street was surrounded by posts, and these posts were joined by five or six strands of barbed wire, part of which the dexterous owners of suburban vegetable gardens managed to steal to protect their plots, too attractive to the unsupervised roaming goats; at the four corners of the foundation stood wooden towers of white pine boards with pretty tent-shaped roofs over the platforms.

It must be pointed out that even if the barbed wire had been stolen earlier from the building site, which was left unguarded at night, there still wouldn't have been any escape attempts for a year and a half. But after the tragic death, mourned by the entire people, speculations about a possible amnesty started instantly and only a complete nincompoop would decide to escape then. It is completely erroneous to suppose that the prisons held only farsighted people who undertook well-considered and carefully planned actions. There were different types of people in the camps at that time, all kinds, and it's surprising that people later came to suppose that the flower of Russia's manhood was in the camps. Take for example the man Kapustin-larkin would soon shoot: he was just a snot-face and looked no older than seventeen, and how he broke down and started to beg. That was really a sight! The other one who crossed the River Niva and then went toward the explosives dump, I ask you, was he a genius! And these are the best people in Russia! Don't make me laugh! Just remember, for instance, the famous Kargopol* breakout when 176 got out at the same time. Now that was something! At the Pin Lake camp six men escaped, but one was caught in Kotlas and another in Obozersk; a third was caught when he went on a drunken binge, and three were never heard of again. Those were real men! I think it's absolutely necessary to say this because the reader who's used to works of socialist realism might try to generalize after each concrete incident to get the total picture; but one mustn't judge all the ones who reached 1953 in a convoy, figuratively speaking, by these two dupes** who'll be mentioned in passing later on.

It wasn't by accident that Petya was walking along the Kirov Boulevard on March 26, although he lived in the opposite end of the settlement. He liked to walk on this last street of the town toward Kandalaksha, because here he might meet either Valentina Repisheva from Ruchi, whom he tried to help quite openly and unselfishly, or Irina Konstantinovna, whose mere appearance made his blood freeze and his heart pound.

The Pin Lake camp was more severe than the one in Lesny, and Boguslavsky was its chief too, but the conditions there couldn't be compared with those at Niva, and it would have been inhuman to make Irina Konstantinovna live there.

Petya had become accustomed to seeing the sluggish screws stomping on the towers in their sheepskin coats with the beautiful fur collars guarding their faces from the arctic gusts like a wall, but now he was more than a little surprised when he reached the tower on the corner of Kandalaksha road. He couldn't understand it: first he thought that the guard was jumping up and down to stomp out a cigarette butt. Petya couldn't understand why he had dropped the butt on the plank floor instead of tossing it from the platform in the snow, and only when the guard had got free from his sheepskin coat and stood on the platform in his jacket did Petya begin to see what the problem was. It all became clear when he saw a man in boots and a cloth cap with earflaps running from the wire fence toward the two-story houses, while another climbed through a wide gap in the barbed wire. It wouldn't have been very difficult for the guard on the tower to shoot down at least the second one; he could almost reach

*Kargopol was a prison camp complex in the Arkhangelsk area.
**The word *dupe* is camp slang for "newcomer."

out and touch him, as they say, because he was only twenty-five meters away, but it turned out that the long bayonet on the rifle was caught inside the roof of the watchtower, and there was no way the guard could pull it out and point the barrel in the right direction. The problem was that the soldier on the watchtower had got snarled up in his sheepskin coat and lost some precious seconds, maybe even a minute, and he couldn't use the rifle at all. Thank goodness he realized he shouldn't shoot after the second man, who was already through the wire and had taken off on the heels of the first, so he simply shot where the barrel was pointing, that is straight up in the roof. The shot didn't sound very loud to Petya. Finally, this lout on the guard tower worked the rifle loose, but now there was no one to shoot at. The clever men in the building zone had all hidden, some in the supply sheds, some behind the brick walls that were already up to first-floor level, and some in the cellars; Petya couldn't see a single man, and he worried that perhaps those two were the last and all the others had already managed to get away quietly.

The entrance to the zone was on Chkalov Street. There stood the commandant's temporary post and a sentry box and all the necessary things, and it was from there that Kapustin-Iarkin came running, already holding the Nagant revolver in his hands. Even before reaching the tower that had given the alarm, he asked the guard in unprintable language what had happened, and the guard answered with the same friendly banter, expressing anger, alarm, and willingness to defend the zone to his last round. He explained that two men had broken out, and he claimed falsely to have shot straight at the fugitives. Even though this intense dialogue wasn't exactly a state secret, it nevertheless cannot be printed, and there's no need to repeat it either. We can selectively reproduce only the end of the conversation where Kapustin-Iarkin gave further orders: "And if a single . . . sticks out his . . . no warning shots at . . . do you hear me, Frolov?" Petya noted to himself that the name Frolov was a good one and that a soldier with such a name ought to be capable.

From the nonplastered house standing edgewise on Kirov Boulevard three boys and a girl came running straight up to Kapustin-Iarkin; huffing and puffing and waving their arms, they cried, "He's over there, he's over there! That's where he ran!" Kapustin glanced at the house, put the Nagant under his arm for some reason, pulled out a pack of Belomor cigarettes from his pocket, and lit up. Only after two short puffs did he seem to notice the children. "Where's the other?" Kapustin-Iarkin's question sounded like a command. The children hung their heads guiltily and started to argue among themselves; realizing that they still had a long way to go before they would be real heroes, they tried to remember, "You said . . . I said . . . didn't I tell you!" and so on in this manner, but in whispers so they wouldn't disturb Kapustin-Iarkin while he was smoking and thinking.

From the plastered house across Kirov Boulevard, Colonel Boguslavsky himself came running to the scene of these events. He was wearing his tunic without a belt, a deerskin cap, riding breeches, and worn house slippers, and he was carrying a TT.

"Why are you standing there? Why, you . . . ?" Boguslavsky found a vividly profane expression to describe Kapustin-Iarkin, a shortish man, although Boguslavsky himself, God knows, was at best of average height. To emphasize his decisiveness, Boguslavsky shot twice in the air.

Petya definitely appreciated the shots from the TT more than the rifle shots, perhaps because they rang out much closer to him.

Hardly had the first shots from the guard towers rung out than several curious busybodies came running, forming maybe not a crowd but a small bunch of spectators consisting of ten boys, two girls, and three poorly clad, ageless women with dull faces and eyes staring drowsily as though someone had just awakened them and brought them by force to watch the events. Boguslavsky's shots aroused fear in the sleepy women, but also a growing eagerness to watch the coming spectacle to the end, no matter how terrifying it would be. Regardless of the fact that the spectators were few and there was lots of room, the children managed to scuffle and even fight among themselves, whereupon the adults told them to behave themselves and tried to impart to them respect for the serious event, and thus they finally came to realize their role and obligations.

Petya hurried as fast as he could to the center of action, and he kept moving around so that he could see the face of the convoy chief and guess from his expression the direction of his thoughts and predict the coming events. Dragging his long legs through the snow, he circled Boguslavsky a couple of times, almost tripping over the children who were fighting over the hot cartridge cases that had flown out of the colonel's pistol. If Kapustin-Iarkin and Boguslavsky were the principal characters on this stage of trampled snow (let's give them their due), then Petya, with his intense interest in literally everything and everyone, resembled a director who unceremoniously climbs up on the stage during rehearsals and walks among the actors as they play their roles, to check that they are correctly carrying out the instructions only he knows.

Petya's reason had developed exactly far enough for him to understand that the life surrounding him was the only possible one.

One must admit that three grades of primary school in Usmynsk* is not a lot of education, and thus one may boldly say that the absence of a proper education—plus the absence of fantasy that could take wing and permit him to imagine a more or less just life even without an education—made Petya indistinguishable both from those who had organized the life he knew and from the many famous singers who glorified this life and didn't let anyone imagine any other way of life.

The little boys who had hurried there, some on sleds made from bent pipes, some with shopping bags (on their way to the store), some on skis that were, according to the fashion this season, almost as short as skates, and some only half dressed, like Boguslavsky: all these people gathered to see what the grown-ups would do, as they came out into the street ready to use their weapons. Different voices pronounced the word "escape" with different intonations: fear, excitement, hope, and horror.

For each of us there are things beyond our understanding. For some it's God and for others a lack of God, but Petya was unable to understand what escape was, and he was not the only one. Running, escaping—this is one of those unfortunate problems that render even serious researchers unable to remain objective and avoid extremes. It's like dealing with the profane and the sacred. A runner—used as the word for young shoots of plants—is an affirmation of life. To escape is like being born again, but better.

At our first birth we can't understand very much; there are feelings but no memory, and there just isn't any way to understand what's happening. Our first birth is more or less forced and there's not much we can do about it. But the second birth, escape? If you haven't taken the time to wind up the spring inside yourself that must one day throw you across the prohibited line and even farther, beyond the checkpoint, if you lack the will to do this like that snotfaced kid—the second one who jumped over the barbed wire today—then it's better to sit quietly from the beginning to the end of one's term.

Escape isn't life itself but the elixir of life.

If you break out beyond the barbed wire for just one minute or ten minutes, then you understand with your whole being, not with just your mind and eyes, that everything, all that you used to see when you were marched down these very same streets between these very same houses—all of it was sheer deceit and illusion. The light will pour forth even if you escape at night, the world will expose its face to you and

*Usmynsk is a village 250 miles south of Leningrad near Velikie Luki.

remove that curtain of blind indifference that had for so many years separated you from all that's on the other side. The whole unembraceable space of the earth that a minute ago was not intended for you, it becomes yours in one moment, in the first hallowed moment of freedom, it's with you and for you, and for the sake of this single moment it's perhaps worth taking the risk. In that hour, in those blessed minutes when there's no one to tell you what to do, no one to help you, you'll see your decisiveness and presence of mind grow to equal the increased danger.

The debilitating and fervent thought of escape doesn't leave you for a minute, not even in your dreams; it makes your soul desperate, your enervated interior voice no longer asks whether you can escape or not, is it reasonable to do it, are you strong enough, daring, lucky? Your brain is deafened by all the sounds reaching you from over there. All doubts are silenced and your reason recognizes only those arguments that favor escape.

This is what I say: escape is a disease, a mental disease, it's that life within you that hasn't accepted its own prescribed slow death, it demands its own, and the only cure for it is escape.

Different kinds of people make their escape, and therefore there are not only different methods of escape but different feelings, hopes, and passions behind it.

It was fear and not love of freedom that forced the first young man to escape, and for this reason he simply planned to run to the nearest house. There's not much to say about him. It isn't even interesting. Briefly, a certain citizen, Dmitry Filippovich S–ky, born in 1918, had four convictions and was currently working off his punishment on four counts. He had lost at dominoes, and the stake was this boy; if the boy didn't get away, Dmitry Filippovich as the loser would have to "soak him," that is, kill him with a knife. Aleksey Nikolaevich Br–n, aka "Beaver," born in 1921, with three convictions and two attempted escapes, found out about this and proposed to the young man that they escape together; he promised that he too would "soak him" if he should as much as squeak to anyone. Aleksey Nikolaevich reasoned soberly that if the young hawk got mixed-up or lagged behind, or even if he got shot, it would nevertheless take the pressure off him, because the boy would draw away the pursuers, at least for a while. If they both succeeded in getting away, it would be incomparably easier later on if there were two of them; take for instance sleep, they could take turns napping. This is important.

Escape for citizen Br–n wasn't the same as for the youth who had unscrewed two light bulbs in the kolkhoz office where he lived and where he was caught red-handed by some important Party organizer from the Machine and Tractor Station.*

No wine, no vodka, no card games, no games with girls, no games with knives could make Aleksey Nikolaevich Br–n experience those acute and instantaneous feelings of renewed life that come crashing down on an escaping person all at once, like an ocean wave on a man frying in the desert and thirsting to death in the sand. Escape, like the ocean wave, refreshes and imparts renewal to all senses of the body, but the bitter-salt liquid can never quench the thirst burning in the soul.

I am certain that you didn't even suspect that you had the capability of developing this acute perception that forms during those first few unbelievable moments of freedom. No matter how long and passionately you may think of freedom, during its first moments you understand and feel how confusedly and foggily your imagination had depicted this hallowed goal. And really, it's one thing to imagine a girl dressed in something flimsy, but quite another thing to embrace a living girl, submissive to all your desires.

Captivity is painful and tragic; freedom isn't sweet, either; but escape is an art.

Just like any art, escape requires a desperate self-assurance.

If we accept the view that art isn't the depiction but the alteration of life, then escape is undeniably a work of art; it changes captivity to freedom and it also alters the author-performer and the whole world around him.

Have you noticed that the imprisoned zeks call the wall-boards in the cell "the horizon," the ceiling "the sky," and the bare light bulb "the sun"? This is a very significant detail, stressing the fact that the real horizon and sky don't seem to belong to them but exist in a totally different world, just as the real sun, judging from its name inside the zone—"prison lamp"—only shines on the free, the lucky chosen ones. Nothing, absolutely nothing, seen from the ranks in the marching column, looks as it does in reality. For example: if while running away you notice some totally trivial thing that you had already seen many times that day, say this hoarfrost on the wires, you would certainly be as amazed as if you had made a discovery.

What should a runaway wish for?

More flexibility and a sharper perception of the unforeseen and unexpected!

*The system of MTSs, intended to make available machinery to the collective farms in an area, was abandoned in the late fifties.

This formula could also refer to a person freezing in captivity, but if a dejected man were to follow it, he would turn utterly into a worm.

If you haven't reached the point yet of forgetting yourself but want to experience some enjoyment in life—then escape! It isn't necessary to cut through the wire with a band saw;* you could push a bribed convoy guard into a ditch with your hands or dive under the barbed wire if you wait for a good snowstorm. Freedom is freedom, after all, and if Pushkin was already thinking of escape near the end of his short life, if the writer Leo Tolstoy ran away even at an extremely old age when his health wasn't very sturdy, this shows that freedom counts for something.

I mention all this for one single reason: in case you should ever have to shoot an escaping man, before you press the trigger you should consider for a second the fact that he really has nowhere at all to run; any life, no matter how you twist or turn, is like prison.

Beaver walked away correctly, that is he ran a little but then changed to a quick pace, at first to avoid drawing unnecessary attention to himself from the local bag ladies and dogs loitering in the street, but then mainly to save his strength. A novice wastes it all in the first ten minutes of exuberant joy over the fact that he got away unhurt, but then he starts to gasp for air like a carp and is surprised to find his lungs full of cotton and his legs numb from lack of exercise . . .

"We'll get him soon," said Kapustin-Iarkin curtly, as though not recognizing at this moment the superior rank of the colonel in slippers.

Two soldiers were already running from the sentry box carrying rifles with fixed bayonets.

"How many got away?" asked Boguslavsky in an ominous and threatening voice.

Having such a young and charming wife as Irina Konstantinovna, Boguslavsky felt obliged to be a *bon vivant*, cultivating the habits of a man exclusively concerned with organizing his life in a pleasant way. He had a barber brought to his apartment, and if there were to be guests for a birthday or the October holidays he also had cooks brought in, chosen from the chefs who were doing time for theft; in the six camps over which Boguslavsky extended his patronage there were brilliant representatives of Moldavian, Muscovite, Caucasian, and Ukrainian cuisine.

These menials, dragged by Boguslavsky into his private life, surprised him with their naive simple-mindedness. Rewarding the barber, for exam-

*A band saw can be made from the chain of a pocket watch.

ple, with an opened package of Belomor cigarettes, even while realizing that in the prison camp zone it's worth exactly a hundred times more than the price in the store, he considered the barber's rapturous thanks unnecessary. Anyway, not burdened with excessive knowledge of the life of those under his guardianship, the colonel could only guess what advantages the camp craftsmen gained from the brief but profitable trips to the settlement to do laundry, clean the apartment, and perform other services. But if he had realized the enormous advantages the barber would have earned had he let his razor slip on his neck, he might have preferred to shave himself.

If the operative situation permitted it, Boguslavsky always dined at home, dropping by the polyclinic for Irina Konstantinovna or simply sending the chauffeur for her, as there was an eight-hundred-meter walk from the hospital compound to the house if one cut the corner at the obstetrics department. Boguslavsky was enticed home not only by dinner but also by the company of Irina Konstantinovna and the chance to have a comfortable rest after the meal.

But now, right near the end of lunch—*entre la poire et le fromage*, as the French say—the colonel heard booming rifle shots, one, two, after which he decided to jump out in the street, if only to impress Irina Konstantinovna, who had for over a year tactfully refrained from noticing that on his broad and fat chest there were repulsive supernumerary little nipples. He decisively grabbed the pistol that he kept under the mattress, removed the safety catch, and for a second displayed the shiny fang of the barrel hidden inside the pistol. After tossing out a curt, "Lock the door behind me," he rushed to her defense even though he had only his slippers on. The ability to see himself objectively led him to the correct decision: there was no point in wasting time fussing with his boots, which would have diminished the sense of haste and youthful boldness so precious to aging husbands. The box-calf upper part of his everyday boots were particularly tight and could be pulled on his rather stout calves only with great trouble, as was also the case with his patent-leather boots for parade dress. Showing up in the street wearing his slippers and losing a little stature in the eyes of the crowd had definitely earned him more respect in Irina Konstantinovna's eyes.

At the question "How many got away?" Kapustin-Iarkin retorted briefly, "Two," not deeming it necessary to justify himself or cringe before his chief. Service, not fawning, was expected from the head of the convoy. For those serving on the supply staff, deference and respect toward their superiors must come first, but the convoy chief's job is to catch runaways. That's all very good, but if they escaped he'd be lucky to get away with a punch in the face, and no amount of saluting would help.

"Where's the other?" bellowed Boguslavsky.

"We'll get him too," said Kapustin-Iarkin as though the first had already been lassoed and laid before his feet.

The informality of this conversation between the officers may at first glance seem reprehensible, but in certain situations it is frequently noted.

Kapustin-Iarkin realized perfectly well that the title of convoy chief didn't protect him from having to respect rank, but at the same time it permitted him certain liberties in his relations with arrogant officers who enjoy ordering people about because of their own superior rank. The convoy chief took into consideration the fact that his superiors were directly dependent on the efficiency and intelligence of those junior to them by rank and duty. Colonel Boguslavsky, unquestionably most deserving of his rank and post, and credited with many successes in his work, was nonetheless an absolute schoolboy in such things as organizing manhunts and pursuing and capturing runaways. Even Boguslavsky realized that the single laurel leaf so promptly snatched by Kapustin-Iarkin didn't yet constitute a wreath, and that he would definitely need another leaf, and he had faith in his fellow officer who had proved many times that he would always be ready to resort to illegal measures for the sake of the cause.

In the final account, Kapustin-Iarkin's superiority consisted simply in his understanding that the *disorder* of a pursuit is in fact the precise order necessary for capturing a runaway, whereas the government had everywhere grafted on regulations, rules, and laws and was quite incapable of trusting the elements; that is, the government didn't see the capture of a prisoner as an art form. It has been noted that to exaggerate the organizing factor in an undertaking that demands intuition, daring, and experience is necessarily prejudicial to its success. Either much time is wasted, or the runaways themselves specifically design their criminal plans and maneuvers with the express purpose of overcoming a logical and elegant pursuit and capture, since as a rule they imagine their pursuers to be as highly organized as the guards in the restricted zones and the troops serving as convoy guards.

"How many people do you need?" Boguslavsky changed his tone and was beginning to freeze in the tunic that he had put his arms through but hadn't buttoned up.

"We'll see where he went," said Kapustin-Iarkin in a businesslike way, tossing away his cigarette and yelling "Follow me!" to the approaching soldiers. They ran to the house where the children had said that one of the escapees was hiding.

The subsequent events occurred like this.

The house where the escaped prisoner had hidden stood turned sideways to the street. It was constructed on an uneven plot and the back porch had a wooden overhang and seventeen steps, while the near porch had only six. Kapustin-larkin led his soldiers to the back porch.

Boguslavsky's star had at this time reached its zenith and was shining brightly, but his star was about to start setting; it would actually start very soon, by midsummer. He seemed to deliberately ignore Petya, so on purpose Petya kept walking around right in front of the half-dressed Boguslavsky who had been promoted to colonel just a year ago, and Petya was able to examine the officer in detail. The colonel was of shorter than average height, and on the one hand, his body displayed a very obvious tendency to corpulence when it wasn't pulled in by a belt or hidden in a tunic closed in front by buttons and hooks. On the other hand, his swollen face with heavy bags under his eyes was too pink for his age. In a word, neither Petya nor more observant people would get the impression that he was a man with a tendency to refined and elevated feelings, even romanticism, but he explained that unfortunately he "hadn't found the time yet to cultivate all that." However, he did possess a definite talent for carrying out orders and displaying firmness, and he had developed this talent to its full extent.

But Boguslavsky was no more interested in Petya than in the lamp-post beside the road, blackened by rain and frost, as Petya with a dashing gesture straightened his Kuban cap with the NKVD emblem and tucked in the folds on the back of his padded jacket under the belt on which an empty holster was hanging as a reproach. Petya was secretly hoping that the colonel would notice that his "agent" had no gun and give him his own TT, if only temporarily, or in some other way correct the situation. Incorrigible dreamer!

Petya decided that he had to act on his own. He rushed to the back porch and ran up, slipping on the steps where the snow was cleaned off only in the middle, but he realized that he was too late; the detachment of three men had already disappeared inside the entrance door. On the stairs he could smell warm-scented boiling soap; someone was doing laundry and boiling the clothes. Petya returned to the street in case someone should jump off the roof or run out of the second entrance.

It took Kapustin-Iarkin only a couple of minutes to ask the residents whether an unknown person had come running. The left-hand apartment on the second floor was locked, and the grandmother in the opposite apartment said that her neighbors had gone to a wedding at Oleniaia and taken the kids, since they would soon be out of school anyway.

Now started the most sensitive part of the operation. They opened the trap door to the attic and there were wet footprints on the ladder, so one didn't have to be a dog to understand the danger threatening the first person to stick his head through the opening. Whether the escapee was armed or not would most likely be shown by a hole in the head. In order not to make the soldier nervous, Kapustin-Iarkin nodded indifferently toward the ladder and gave the order, "Lagofet, you lead."

Lagofet, sweaty after running from the sentry box to the house, turned around as though looking for some other Lagofet who was supposed to climb up. His glance fell on the old woman who huddled in her apartment, her head sticking out of the door that she was holding with both hands. "What are you looking at?" yelled Lagofet suddenly. The head disappeared and the door, covered with something like a padded mattress sewn into a sack, slammed dully and softly. "We could call that tall guy and let him look." The soldier's voice trembled uncertainly as though he was hoping that his commander would think of some way to save him, or that like Chapaev,* he would go himself.

"Go on, you crud . . . !" the convoy chief hissed through his teeth, emphasizing his order with a mighty oath and a gesture with the Nagant, pointing in the intended direction of motion. "People are watching you," he said in the same way, without moving his lips, possibly referring to the woman hiding behind the door and watching through the keyhole, or perhaps implying, according to tradition, the People, the Fatherland, and all men of good will. Not surprisingly, this last argument seemed to calm the soldier, it did its work, and Lagofet got on the ladder and, slowly, stepping on every rung with both feet, moved upward with his head turned back, ready to fly down at any moment.

The three-lined rifle with a long, fixed, three-edged bayonet was totally unsuitable for fighting in the attic, but Lagofet had no other weapon. Halfway up the ladder the soldier realized that with his next step he would expose his head, so he started to stick his rifle up the hatch. His com-

*Vasily Chapaev (1887–1919), a daredevil revolutionary hero; incidentally, his sidekick was called "Petya."

mander saw that the soldier was nervous and afraid, that he worried and did stupid things, but he didn't stop him. He was waiting for a shot; the main thing was to find out whether the runaway was armed or not.

Not without difficulty Lagofet got the rifle through the trap door and lay it across the opening. If the criminal was nearby it wouldn't be hard for him to grab the weapon, or, to use their clumsy language, put a horse collar on this moron—that is, grab him by the throat from behind.

Before sticking his head up, Lagofet pulled the trigger and jumped back, then he nimbly and quickly jumped up into the attic. The attic was full of slag between the beams, and the crunching of his own feet prevented him from hearing whether there was anybody else up there. Lagofet looked intently into the dimness, and near the trap door to the other ladder he saw a man in a gray padded jacket sprawled face down, his feet, in unworn canvas boots, sticking out.

"Ready," Lagofet shouted victoriously and put his no-longer-needed rifle on his back. What a lot of thought and feeling he expressed in this triumphantly careless "Ready!"—the pride of victory, a certain vague reproach for his commander, gratitude to fate, and pride over his own well-aimed shot. And he even seemed to include in this brief expression the tired sigh of a man who had accomplished an important and difficult job.

"Where?" Kapustin-Iarkin instantly flew up into the attic.

"Over there . . ."

The commander and the soldier went over to the killed man.

"Where did you hit him?" asked Kapustin-Iarkin, officer of the internal army, generously forgiving past errors and changing his voice into a comradely businesslike tone.

"How the fuck should I know," said the victor carelessly.

The second convoy guard also clambered up into the attic, realizing that they would have to drag the body down and he might as well not wait to be called up.

But Kapustin-Iarkin was very interested to know "where," and he touched the prone man's shoulder with the tip of his boot in order to turn over the body and take a closer look.

The killed man raised his head and said, "Please, Uncle, don't kill me, please don't kill me!"

The shout was so unexpected that there couldn't even be any question of killing him.

"Where are you hit?" asked Kapustin-Iarkin, who hadn't satisfied his curiosity and still had his doubts as to the accurate aim of his soldier.

The seventeen-year-old fellow got up on his haunches without turning his head, and, still expecting a blow, he straightened himself and raised his arms like a captured German in a movie. He was looking past them at the rough unplastered chimney pipes with mortar sticking out between the different-colored bricks, he looked at the clothesline with two forgotten wooden clothespins on it, but he was afraid to look at the convoy guard as though thinking that if he looked at him he would die at once. He was aware that they had every right to kill him now.

"Uncle, don't kill me; Uncle, don't kill me!" The young prisoner rolled up his eyes as though he wasn't asking the guard but God himself.

"Yes, he's alive," said the soldier who had gone near him, adding his two cents' worth to the arrest.

"Get downstairs," bellowed Kapustin-Iarkin at him. "And be quick about it. You should pay attention and not think of women up there on the watchtower, or you won't stay 'alive' yourself!"

The convoy chief quickly frisked the runaway to make sure he wasn't armed, then he hit his raised arms with the Nagant to make him put them down.

To the complete surprise of Petya and the other spectators at the scene, the prisoner, without any warning, came flying out on the lower porch—the one nearest the street, not the one where the soldiers had gone in—like a gray lump of dirt, as though shot from a boy's slingshot, and after sliding on the snow, he at once got to his feet.

Then the officer and the two soldiers came out on the porch. Going past his soldiers, Kapustin-Iarkin skidded off the porch, ran up to the captured runaway and hit him as hard as he could between the shoulder blades with the pistol grip.

Petya expected that after this blow that would have broken the back of most men and could have felled a horse, the runaway would fall flat in the snow and not get up again. But the young prisoner only shuddered as though swallowing the blow and covered his face with his hands, although no one was hitting him in the face. He started whining again, choking on saliva and tears: "Uncle, don't kill me; Uncle, don't kill me!"

Kapustin-Iarkin was at first happy with the quick victory, and in the attic and on their way down he felt a certain satisfaction that Lagofet hadn't killed this retarded runt so that they didn't have to drag him down. But on the porch when he saw the colonel, still standing in front of the house, he started thinking of the long and hard chase after the second man, and anger instantly flamed up in his heart and scorched his reason.

He leapt at the captured runaway and bashed the rifle stock between his shoulder blades a few more times, but the prisoner only shuddered and howled: "Uncle, don't kill me . . ."

No longer in full possession of himself, Kapustin-Iarkin let the prisoner get five steps ahead and then shot right at his back. Petya couldn't understand how the captain could have missed, but the guard walking in front didn't even jump aside when the bullet tore a lump of ice out of the solid trampled path right by his feet.

The young prisoner seemed not to hear the shot, because when a second one rang out he cried out his invocation, "Uncle, don't kill me!" in the same way as before, without turning around and without removing his hands from his face.

Missing for the second time, Kapustin-Iarkin got even more blazingly furious, but now the convoy had reached Kirov Boulevard, and from Chkalov Street came the gengas-powered car of the chief of Sea Canal,* the chains on the back tires clanking cheerfully. Petya knew and respected this car as the last gengas-powered vehicle in the entire garage.

The convoy had to move aside.

"Put him in the shed," ordered Kapustin-Iarkin to the guard walking behind him. Petya, walking two steps behind the convoy chief and prepared to be at hand whenever necessary, thought at first that the order was meant for him, but when he saw the commander stick his Nagant in the holster and walk toward Colonel Boguslavsky, Petya decided to turn back.

"The idiot," said Kapustin-Iarkin as if speaking about a naughty schoolboy, forgetting that he had just fired his Nagant. "The second one is more serious, but this one, he's just an apprentice thief."

"Mobilize the duty shift! Get dogs. And get your own noses on his track, he must be caught by dark, dead or alive! Have you understood!" screamed Boguslavsky suddenly, as though figuring that his voice and screaming would be heard by his superior officer to whom he would have to report the escape, if it hadn't already been reported.

"Kandalaksha is closed. They've already been told," said Kapustin-Iarkin, as though they were equals and paying no attention to his shouting. "He won't get through the army base, either. Perhaps he'll cross the river."

*For lack of gasoline during and just after the war, cars ran on gas generated by burning charcoal in a trailer pulled behind the vehicle. Sea Canal was the run-off canal between Lupcha and the Kandalaksha Bay.

"So he can croak under a tree," said Boguslavsky angrily.

"Well, there are skis in every house, Comrade Colonel," remarked the captain reasonably. "The garrison will have to be mobilized."

"OK, do it. Mobilize people, dogs. If you croak there, it's your own fault." During this conciliatory speech Boguslavsky removed the cartridge clip from the handle of the TT, then he pulled out the safety catch and caught in his palm the shining brass cartridges with short, fat bullets that Petya thought looked a little like the colonel's own head.

The adults and two dozen school kids who had come running and were observing this scene weren't especially chosen but were picked by chance from the general population of the settlement; all of them spontaneously displayed an amazing and incredible lack of compassion.

From where did the children acquire such hardened indifference? And where did the adults get this inhuman coldness? Can it really be that the practice of selling one's soul to the ruler of darkness, until recently considered to be the stuff of ancient superstition and ignorance, is indeed the sheerest truth, and that poetic fantasy only softened this truth by exaggerating the gifts received in return for the soul?

It's hard to say what benefits the residents of Niva III received from their pact with the devil. Considering the fact that they didn't possess any immeasurable riches and that aside from the arctic bonuses added to their pay they got no magic gifts—they were in fact rather badly supplied with food and consumer goods—one must conclude that in the secret deal with this all-powerful being, the payment was simply life itself.

The most remarkable thing wasn't actually the silence of the soulless public, but the fact that the victim himself, walking on the edge between life and death, shot and beaten with the convoy chief's Nagant, saw before him a crowd of people but didn't even think of appealing to them for protection; instead he pinned all his feeble hopes for prolonging his life exclusively on Kapustin-Iarkin, as though infinite goodness and generosity were concentrated in him alone. Where were the crushed, enslaved, and abducted souls of Petya's contemporaries while this solemn public murder attempt was taking place? Who was their all-powerful master? And why did this master need their souls? What did he plan to do with them?

There's no answer.

It's as though we are talking about a dangerous disease that no one wants to call by its real name.

Although the first escapee had been caught quickly, almost incidentally, and nothing remarkable had taken place, Petya figured that he wasn't doing badly. He had, after all, helped them catch the first one, and Boguslavsky had seen it and would surely tell Irina Konstantinovna; the women standing here had also seen him and could confirm that he had almost been there and almost helped surround the man. But he decided to take a greater part in the capture of the second runaway; then he could leave the garage where he worked as a car inspector and become an operative in the section.

"Petya! Just what we need," said one woman. "Look what's happening."

"Petya should get an order," sniggered another, probably remembering how on May 9 the guys at the garage had put twenty orders and medals on Petya, and he, the lucky guy, had walked around and congratulated everyone on the holiday.* He had lost one medal, for "Victory Over Japan"—or maybe some boys had snitched it—and Petya had to apologize to the distraught drunken owner of the medal and promise to earn one himself and give it to him. "Petya, Petya," grieved the conqueror of Japan, "when will we fight Japan now? Just think a little." After this event, whenever they had nothing else to say to Petya in the garage, somebody would ask how things were with Japan—was some serious conflict brewing?—and everyone would laugh. "Our Podoliakin taught them a good lesson; they won't stick up their tail any time soon."

As a joke, of course, they suggested that Petya should sign up as a volunteer in Korea, as the Chinese were doing, and when he had made up his mind to do so they explained to him as one friend to another that Japan wasn't taking part in the military action; the Japanese sympathized with the Syngman Rhee** clique, but only from the sidelines. Nevertheless, Petya attentively followed the events in Korea in the newspaper displayed in the post office window to make sure he wouldn't miss the moment when he might be needed, and in the meantime he kept tally of how many American airplanes were downed by the People's Army antiaircraft troops and chasers. This happened so often that they just needed to ask Petya, "How many today?" "Two" or "Three" answered Petya readily. When four or more were hit they would congratulate Petya. They blamed him in a friendly way for permitting the Americans to bomb Panmunjom during the peace conference; shells were exploding near the buildings where the negotiations were taking place. Sometimes, in the garage, they asked

*May 9 is Victory Day, commemorating the end of World War II.
**Syngman Rhee was president of the Republic of Korea, 1948–1960.

Petya about the American mine-bombs that preoccupied the former front-line fighters; the bomb doesn't explode when it falls, but later when some-one touches it, it sprays shrapnel. They asked why Pusan was given up, why the liberated Seoul was abandoned, they pestered him about both domestic and foreign politics. It was in the garage that the wants and cares of his bleak existence disappeared and he lived a rich and full life. Even in the militia he didn't feel so happy, and he understood that he hadn't deserved to join them yet; it would come in due time.

Petya had turned up one day at the garage himself and no one wanted to deprive him of this harmless pleasure.

With a distressed look he would examine the cars, and sometimes he lay for hours under some worn-out dump truck on a sheet of veneer, as though he were an auto mechanic trying to solve some complicated prob-lem. He enjoyed testing the lighting systems, and the drivers would some-times let him turn the headlights on and off himself; then he would get out of the cab, mutter something, and wipe the glass on the headlight and the light over the license number, if it wasn't broken. Petya loved to check the brakes, the clearance of the steering wheel, and the weight per axle, and he would kick the tires with his boots. No one treated cars and all that concerned them more seriously than Petya, and they all respected him for it. Sometimes he spent half a day checking old orders that had already been paid and the money partly spent or drunk up; he looked through stacks of old bills of lading and last year's dispatcher's journal, and he made discreet inquiries.

Surrounded by his beloved smells and sounds in the garage, Petya sometimes also asked stern questions; the replies as a rule consisted of comforting protestations and promises to correct the mistake, but he never asked the same question twice, perhaps because he forgot or was afraid to be a nuisance by persecuting a particular individual with his reprimands.

In the smoking room the men talked with Petya about the most varied subjects, and his replies were often unexpected. Petya didn't know that he was a simpleton, so he didn't try to seem smart.

"Petya, do you want to become the garage manager?"

"For that you need more knowledge and a different kind of character. You know me." He didn't mention his meekness aloud because he under-stood that he had to act strict in order to preserve the necessary disci-pline here.

"Petya, do you want to be head of the militia?"

"First I'll have to join them," said Petya with a sigh, but his eyes lit up. What unlucky star had caused him to be seized with rapture over the militia cap, sword-belt, and holster? This remains unexplained.

"Petya, is the world round?"

"I don't know," said Petya seriously, but he enjoyed discussions of this kind.

"Petya, do you want to live long?"

Petya never replied to this question but smiled guiltily and looked in silence at whoever asked him this as though he knew how little time he had left and didn't want to distress them with his answer; or perhaps the other way around, he thought that he would survive them all but didn't want to distress his friends with this news. Or possibly he was smiling because he didn't know the purpose of life or what to do with it.

Since he didn't smoke, Petya never sat very long in the smoking room; besides, he considered it unsuitable in his capacity as inspector to spend too much time there. He liked to go outside.

"Petya, where are you off to? Stay here with us a bit longer!" they'd say when he began to slap his knees, a sign that he was ready to go.

"I sit, but work doesn't stand still." For the hundredth time Petya repeated this catchy phrase that he had heard somewhere. This caused general merriment and everyone laughed, but he left quickly and resolutely, although he didn't go very far, only to the dispatcher's area or the repair shop, and he might return after fifteen or twenty minutes, or he might be gone for a week.

Boguslavsky hastened to set the military in motion, not just because most soldiers fight better when somebody is watching them, as observed by the partisan Denis Davydov,* but simply because in the evening when he made his report by telephone to the Kola Camp Administration he should be able to say that he had lifted the state of emergency from transportation, the city police, and the local authorities, and that the runaways were locked up and awaiting retrial.

It's well known that distant camps have special duty details, similar to the emergency patrols in the Border Guard, only not so large; there are two or three men with light firepower, carrying food for three days and standing at constant readiness to pursue escapees. There's no point in keeping such units in densely settled areas that offer the runaways nu-

*Denis Davydov (1784–1835) was a poet and a partisan in the war of 1812; he was also a character in Tolstoy's *War and Peace*.

merous routes, and although general methods have been worked out based on extensive experience and an enormous number of facts, it's understood that there can be no routines in such events and one must always act according to the particular concrete circumstances.

To catch this common railroad-station thief, a pimply character armed only with a razor and a shift key* hidden in his boot, Boguslavsky got an entire infantry company from the garrison, but it was not at full strength. In this company there had recently occurred an unfortunate incident that was followed by an investigation, and in order to present the company commander and the commander of the second platoon in the very best light before the tribunal, the higher command offered him this chance to distinguish himself by apprehending a particularly dangerous armed criminal; this is how Boguslavsky described this petty thief, capable at the most of stealing a suitcase or the hand luggage of passengers waiting for a train.

The direct impetus for the decision to escape was an incident that took place on February 23** and infuriated the inmates; their breakfast slop smelled slightly of kerosene. Thirty-two men refused to eat the mess; the rest chowed down, although everyone could smell the strange odor. Even the events of March 5 and the consequent conversations about amnesty could not stop the flywheel from going out of control, since the circumstances of the escape were fanned by many different facts.

Of course it might be interesting to look from the outside at the escape, chase, and capture of a runaway, but to participate in such a mess is not interesting at all, even considering the fact that for the most part no two cases are exactly alike. This may be so, but Petya was an exception, since this was the first and last time he took part in such an unexpected and absorbing incident.

The fact that the company, commanded by Captain Topolnik, took part in the pursuit, is also in a way connected with February 23. To mark the holiday, they had organized shooting competitions between the companies, and the victors in the garrison-wide socialist competition would be congratulated at a solemn ceremony. Topolnik felt confident of winning the machine-gun contest, since his company was to be represented by a certain Fedotov who loved machine guns and could fire them pretty well. The shooting match was organized more like a sporting event than a military practice; this explains the fact that the little soldier who was

*A small crowbar.
*February 23 is the holiday called Day of the Soviet Army and Navy.

changing the targets happened to be right in front of the machine gun at the very moment when Fedotov started to load it. As he put on the second ammo-belt, the machine gun began to fire wildly and cut both legs off the little soldier as he was walking away from the target. A public outcry followed the incident, Topolnik's company was removed from the social-ist competition, and an investigation was started, during the course of which the company commander, Topolnik, and Fedotov's immediate su-perior, the platoon commander, were to go before a courtmartial. The fault turned out to be in the worn lower detent and the worn condition of the sear as well, causing an unintended blow to the firing pin by the sear notch at the moment the handle was lowered onto the roller. This was confirmed by the commission. Everyone understood that neither Topol-nik nor the platoon commander, nor even Fedotov, was responsible; it was the head of artillery materiel that was at fault for not distributing new RPG's at the shooting competition as had been requested; no, they were stored in grease, but instead they got ancient "muskets" of the Maxim type.

Because of their sympathy for the unjustly suffering officers, the high-er command decided to leave them at their normal duties until the court-martial.

The troops under the command of Captain Topolnik, sent to recap-ture the escapee, didn't look elegant at all when reporting to Kapustin-lar-kin. Fifty-two bayonets and a unit with submachine guns were mobilized by Topolnik for the military emergency; to avoid possible criticism from above, they were ordered to go fully equipped; that is, each soldier carried a gas mask and the engineers had shovels. It was stupid, of course, but one must understand Topolnik; nobody would want to be in his place. The soldiers started to object, but the company commander soon found the right words to convince them to carry out his orders without complaining.

By the time the company arrived in the settlement, Kapustin-larkin had already got some kind of orientation. The runaway was at the water reservoir on the hill outside the settlement, and had taken the lunch belonging to the guard there, Galina Pavlovna Shestiperova, and also the dagger that she kept to serve various needs. He took the grub but re-frained from rape in spite of the fact that Shestiperova was, as they say in the zone, "the goods"—a plump and attractive woman, even in her work-ing clothes. After grabbing the skis of Shestiperova's son, good skis with semifirm bindings, easy to adjust to the foot, he followed the water pipe down toward the railroad, and then to the river.

The wrinkles gathering on the bridge of Kapustin-larkin's nose gradually smoothed out and even disappeared altogether when the dog found the scent, but he could only follow it to the water tower, he couldn't follow the ski trail.

Petya saw the chain of skiing soldiers stretching out along the outskirts of the village, and he joined them. They had greatcoats, gas masks, rifles, and skis—wide and flat, rounded and slightly raised up at the tips. The local boys called them "coffins" and bought them from the soldiers for between five and ten rubles to make sleds. The skis naturally increased the mobility but didn't contribute to the speed of the moving company, so therefore Petya had ample time to catch up on foot with the soldiers moving slowly in a line. The soldiers' bindings were soft and their canvas straps with metallic buckles were of the most primitive design. Their boots rattled around inside these bindings so that it was quite out of the question to brake or turn when going downhill, but it was possible to just shuffle along a ski track on a flat stretch. Not surprisingly, after two downhill slopes the nonmilitary losses started to pile up: Private Urazbaev twisted his foot so that he could hardly move, and along with Private Alimbekov* he was sent back to the barracks. Petya asked for Alimbekov's skis, promising to return them without fail, but the friendly Urazbaev offered him his, insisting that his bindings were better and the tips more bent. Petya took Urazbaev's skis. Now he felt fully part of the group, as ready as everyone else to fulfill his duty and render an especially dangerous criminal harmless.

At 16:10 hours the company crossed the Kirov railroad and moved toward the bridge over the River Niva, since the guards at the explosives store (the only building located within a few kilometers of the bridge on the other side of the river) had reported over the telephone that they had seen a man crossing the bridge and moving through the forest downstream, that is, in the direction of Kandalaksha.

To the left the hills piled up, snow-covered, huge, and enigmatic, and to the right the river was roaring incessantly. It was busy with its own affairs as though trying to run away from the dam about to trap and kill it.

The Niva gurgled over the stones and didn't freeze over even in the worst frost, so it could be crossed only at Kandalaksha, over the bridge near the prison, or seven kilometers higher upriver, on the frozen Lake Ples. The fact that the runaway was moving downriver significantly simplified the task; his goal must naturally be the bridge at Kandalaksha since

---

*These two names suggest that the soldiers came from Central Asia and were unused to snow.

the nearest habitation was located twenty-five kilometers through the forest and over the hills. Such was the geographical situation.

Like a coin, the winter forest has two sides. If you are full of strength and energy and want to escape from noise and worry, you should fill your lungs with the frozen air and go into the legendary thick forest where the birches and alders, bent under the weight of snow, form peculiar arches; every stump is adorned with a white fluffy boyar's cap, and beneath the weightless snowy blanket a little stream murmurs, barely audible as though carrying on a secret conversation. The enormous firs, clad in white fur coats, have become slender because they are under a heavy snow cover; not even the thick lower limbs can stick out in all directions but are flattened down as far as they can go, just as a trim soldier presses his hands to the seams of his pants. And, the whole army of white giants is prepared to repulse any attack with their very presence and motionless stance. They inspire the most poetic feelings and make one forget everyday life (although not for long), where there are no giants, enchanted grottoes, or hidden rivers carrying the restless water under the snow to the rapid, roaring river that acknowledges neither frost nor winter but fills the surroundings with the warm sound of boiling water.

It's another matter if it is necessity or some trouble that drives you into the winter forest. Well, you might forget your trouble for a moment or two because the forest demands such concentration, attention, and strength that the struggle will absorb you—maybe just for a short time, but absorb you it certainly will. If you want to move forward but remain unseen, you must stay close to the trees, but that's where the soft snow will drag you down almost to the waist, like a quagmire; a twig inadvertently disturbed will dump an entire snowdrift on you, and if it's not just a twig but a whole birch that's straightening itself up, it will almost bury you in a snow coffin, or it will slap you with its naked twigs and knock off your cap. And woe to you if you didn't hear the gurgling stream under the snow and the treacherous snowy blanket collapses under your weight; you're lucky if this disaster befalls you where the water isn't very deep and if only one ski and one leg go through; in the unfrozen streams there may be holes where trout spend the winter, and you could sink up to your waist there.

Kapustin-Iarkin was followed by Topolnik and the detail from the camp guard. They sewed through the white space like a steel needle on their light and sturdy skis and dragged behind them, stretched out over almost half a kilometer, a thread of armed soldiers.

Petya didn't have any heavy equipment or weapons, and Uruzbaev's skis turned out to be well waxed, which was perhaps the reason why the soldier had gone downhill so fast, crash-landed at the bottom, and twisted his right foot. On the open field where he could move over the crust, Petya overtook the slowly moving soldiers and approached the advance group with the commanders.

Beyond the bridge there were tons of ski tracks turning to the right along the left shore of the river, but not too many fresh ones, and only five or six completely new ones from today. Sending soldiers along each track, Kapustin-larkin had already identified the right track after one-and-a-half kilometers. An arctic wolf-hunter like Kapustin-larkin, strong in spite of his short stature, had little difficulty in distinguishing children's tracks from those left by the smooth motion of an adult male; there was only one such track. When they reached stream No. 14 he found that the skier had had trouble. The prisoner hadn't espied the danger but fell through the treacherous snowy fluff covering the stream, getting his skis wet. Here he tried to continue, but the ice build-up slowed him down. Aha. Here he had figured it out, and took off his skis; here they are, the lumps of ice he knocked off; here he stood on one ski and rubbed the other one with snow, wiped it off, and put it back on, and he had to hold them in the frost to let them dry . . . Aha, he rubs the other one. He won't get far now on those skis.

"It would be good if we could intercept him from the left and above," said Kapustin-larkin, sticking down both ski poles in front of him and almost hanging on them from his shoulders, the familiar pose of a resting skier.

Petya heard his wish, and he moved away unnoticed by the command group and continued slightly to the left. His wish to carry out the encircling maneuver by himself made him act boldly and decisively.

This maneuver also cost Petya his life, essentially.

A large number of armed people is not needed to catch a mere dupe, as real thieves say, and for this reason the twenty men that Kapustin-larkin had with him were quite enough to encircle and catch the runaway. There was no need and no time to wait for the others; it was already beginning to get dark. They decided to capture him alive, because Captain Topolnik realized that the criminal may come under crossfire and this shooting might be fraught with new unpleasantness, so he ordered them to fire warning shots in the air and shoot point-blank only as a last resort. He warned them, "Screw him, let him live, the bastard, only don't shoot each other!" The only ones who heard this order were his twenty soldiers plus the five guards that Kapustin-Iarkin had gathered, not waiting for the rest to straggle in. There were many lagging behind: one man had managed to break his skis; two were limping because they couldn't brake going downhill and hit the tree stumps with the pretty white hats; and seven had, in spite of all their caution, got their skis wet when crossing the streams and were now forming a hopeless rear-guard.

The little soldier Cheremichny had fallen behind his platoon of sub-machine guns, but in contrast to the rest he tried to catch up with his group. He kept asking the soldiers in front of him where the machine-gun platoon was. One of their inexact arm gestures pointed to Petya's fresh track. Afraid of another dressing-down, Cheremichny raced on along the track.

They say that in this twentieth century, when humanity has been enriched with various wonderful adaptive measures, a nerve gas has been invented that paralyzes the human mind and ability to act; one must conclude that it's a very good gas, because under its effect a person would never commit any horrible, base, or despicable crime; but even earlier people had invented, used, and perfected more dangerous substances that paralyze morality. If a man's conscience is paralyzed, he will act unpredictably, so to speak, in different circumstances. It turns out that under the influence of the substances paralyzing morality, people who consider themselves "proper" forget that this label doesn't last their whole life, and talented people forget what their talents serve and are inspired by God knows what; in a word, things happen that weren't predicted by the citizens themselves or those around them, and so in the end the border between reason and insanity becomes completely movable, flexible, and imprecise. Consequently, those guarding these borders have to close their eyes, or else keep changing their position rapidly.

The elements that paralyze morality and hypnotize the conscience are numerous: hunger, for example, and fear; poverty in its many manifestations is also extremely favorable to the birth of moral dystrophy; literature crowned with laurels also adds a weighty contribution; but power is, nevertheless, the main source. The elements are, as it were, natural by-products of power and more or less serve to reinforce its basis.

Earthly power is temporary: before departing and giving up its place to a new power, the old one declines, yet lingers on for a long time.

Any power tends toward excess—that's the catch! And a second catch is inside those possessing power—their love, devotion, and enthusiasm is the leaven for its self-destructive extravagance, excesses, and lack of restraint.

The seven-league strides made by science have led scholars to the most unexpected observations. Do you remember that in 1948 a certain Simson edited a collection of studies, published under the title *Psychic Changes in Alimentary Dystrophy of People Under Military Occupation.* A most interesting work for its time! But if some scholars should ever want to collect studies on the theme of *Psychic Changes Under the Moral Dystrophy of Power,* who knows, then perhaps even Petya's unimportant life could serve the progress of science.

What makes Petya interesting as a *"Homo insanus,"* an insane man? Well, maybe the fact that he was faithful to his craziness at a time when his contemporaries tried to prove their eminent sanity by constantly changing "points of craziness" whenever it was to their advantage.

It seems to me that Petya's insanity was really nothing other than a variety, perhaps without medical interest, of "Korsakoff's psychosis," affecting the part of the brain called the hippocampus, or "sea horse." In this condition the sick person loses his long-term memory, but this doesn't prevent him from retaining enough operative memory to solve immediate problems, reach immediate goals, perhaps even a complex victory in chess or the acquisition of power. The hippocampus is located not in the frontal lobes or the occipital areas but in the cerebral cortex, in what is called "the knowing brain." It's interesting to note that the hippocampus is one of the most useful parts of the brain, since it's the oldest, and if it weren't such a useful instrument it would have died away long ago, like the tail or fangs that aren't needed by *Homo sapiens* for pulling down branches and gnawing bones. Not for nothing is the hippocampus positioned in the brain like a master with all conveniences at hand; with one end it goes deep into the temporal cortex and with the other it's supported on the brainstem in the subcortex.

It's my opinion that when virulent infectious psychoses are spreading, people lose their memory as though the hippocampus were damaged; the consequence of this disease is that submissive narrow-mindedness triumphs and people deliberately but unconsciously abstain from developing their minds. The moral flexibility of the human soul now demonstrates its endless potential; the unconditioned reflexes are artificially extinguished, either instantly or gradually, but they are compensated for by the extreme development of the conditioned reflexes, and this guarantees a high survival rate in circumstances where the unripe fruits of the promised prosperity can be replaced by flattery and lies, shamelessly propagated by the powers that be.

Thus the "Petya phenomenon" shouldn't be examined within the framework of traditional psychiatric research; there should be some science like "historical psychopathology," and if such a science hasn't been developed yet, it needs to be established immediately.

Being a law-abiding citizen with a profound respect for power, I don't want to cast aspersions on the various political organs that have assumed the task of organizing everything in our lives. In addition to many remarkable fruits, every living organism can also produce both bile and slag, even extremely repulsive sludge and sewage, but our task can be reduced to this: don't get confused, make a clear distinction between what serves the affirmation and continuation of life, its embellishment and blossoming, and what must be considered unavoidable waste, the cost of universal happiness and prosperity.

Looking at Petya from another point of view, one might of course ask, "Doesn't this man have a fatherland and why did it give him such a fate?" We must, of course, reply that our fatherland is our fate.

At first sight it seems that citizens who have, metaphorically speaking, been beaten like dust-bags and can stay alive only thanks to their minds, which, differing greatly from the minds of people around them, must be similar to the minds of people like themselves in other countries—similar as, for example, flu, hemorrhoids, or middle-ear infections are similar. But no!

Sickness is, of course, always unpleasant, but this sickness reflects like a mirror not only the imperfection of human nature, its inability to resist viral infections, but also the face of the fatherland and the epoch, at least in part, and sometimes even the current moment.

Is it possible to separate Petya's Kuban cap with the NKVD emblem, his belt, and holster from his love, cultivated since childhood, for the Party and the government, his love for power, the best and most just of all powers? His feelings were nurtured by orchestras, slogans, and holiday toasts, painted outdoor signs that are displayed not only on holidays but all the time in our cities and towns and on railroad embankments, and by the radio, of course, buzzing continuously for five or six hours a day from a pole by the post office. All these considerable means of propaganda helped concentrate in Petya's mind energetic feelings that demanded to be transferred into heroic actions.

Power is irrational, but Petya didn't understand this, and the people as a whole also failed to understand it; they hadn't yet been embraced by the advance of reason but remained in ignorance, and therefore they were convinced in their souls that it was possible to reach unimaginable happiness very soon, and they remembered only one thing—the need for sacrifices, their duty to endure countless sacrifices—and nobody asked their opinion!

Since the human personality can be elevated only by values higher than personal ones, and while preoccupation with one's personal welfare destroys the personality, as it were, it's clear that Petya was the ideal embodiment of unselfish service to higher goals, since his personal welfare was of absolutely no account to him.

Petya was fully convinced that he himself and his tiny little mom, and the vast premises of the club in Lesny, and also the settlement itself, the river and the hills located on the other side of the river—all this belonged to the state, and he thought of himself as property of the state.

Petya had a secret that not only Sherlock Holmes but even Dr. Watson could have discovered without difficulty; however, no one wanted to know this secret and it died with Petya.

The secret was of a mathematical nature. Petya had a very special way with figures, nothing like the majority of people with nothing but basic education.

Petya is asked to chop wood.

"Petya, you have to go and chop wood!"

When people addressed Petya, he felt impossibly important and clever, just like everyone else who claims openly or only to himself that the world couldn't possibly manage without him.

"You said chop wood?" Petya invariably asked again.

"Yes, chop," answered the first one, enjoying this intelligent conversation.

"Chop wood?"

"They brought a load of firewood and it's blocking the door."

Petya didn't pay attention to these evasions and excuses but came straight to the point.

"How much will you pay?"

"I'll give you thirty."

Petya's eyes narrowed to a penetrating squint and he looked at his interlocutor as though he could see right through all his clever tricks. Although Petya had never had a moustache or a beard, he was convinced that at this moment he looked like the portrait of Dzerzhinsky* in the militia reception room.

*Feliks Dzerzhinsky (1877–1926) was the founder of the Cheka, the prerevolutionary secret police.

"Ye-es," drawled Petya, and to make it more expressive he started scratching his head. "Well, but it's going to take all day . . . You said thirty!"

"Thirty it is."

Petya shook his head and looked expectantly at his employer, waiting for him to raise the figure, and then he waved his arm boldly and decisively.

"Twenty-five! Do it my way or not at all," he said and looked expectantly at his despairing employer.

"All right then, twenty-five," said his confused employer.

"That's it, twenty-five," insisted Petya. "Twenty-five, and no more haggling?"

And the deal was settled.

Usually people didn't cheat Petya; sometimes they would add to his pay five or ten rubles or pay for his dinner, or they might even give him salted cod and bread or perhaps potatoes to take home with him.

If somebody had attentively examined Petya's math exercise books he would at once have noticed a lack of confidence in zero, beginning in the first grade. This lack of trust had penetrated deep into his soul. Once he had learned that zero didn't actually mean anything, he didn't allow himself to be tricked again but regarded further explanations as ruses to lure him away from the truth that had been revealed to him. No power on earth could convince Petya that thirty was more than twenty-five, or that three hundred was more than 146, more than twice as much. In his mind's eye Petya saw a number consisting mostly of zeroes as without any significance, and beside it a number with real digits, and he didn't let himself be fooled. The kind and helpful Vasya Baskov, a metal worker in the mechanical workshop and a sincere lover of mankind, tried several times in the cafe or the dining room to help Petya take the first steps into the world of mathematics, but he couldn't overcome Petya's iron logic. Petya explained to the thick-lipped Vasya Baskov the drift of his reasoning. It went like this: to find which number was higher, he added up the digits of the number. Three plus zero is three, but two plus five is seven! So it turns out that thirty was next to nothing but twenty-five was real money! Because of his special friendship with Vasya, Petya suggested to him in a whisper to count the same way.

If we were to speak absolutely logically about Petya and how his tiny family had been plunged into poverty and despair by the accidents of hunger, cold, and homelessness, these problems would also be state property and must be kept under guard until instructions arrive as to how and where this state poverty is to be used.

We must note that the Twenty-fifth Anniversary of the Great October Club hadn't been used for its original purpose for two years, with the exception of election campaigns, when it was actually used as an agitation center, being smartened up and coming alive for a month. The Niva GES no longer needed this barrack with the loose plaster, and it wasn't needed yet by the aluminum factory that was still under construction. The head of the Municipal Division, Tikhomirov, who was responsible for this gloomy building, reasoned correctly when he decided to let the commandant-lady live in it without a residence permit; an uninhabited building starts falling apart almost instantly, and meanwhile it serves for a long time as a public toilet. Thus Tikhomirov managed, at least in this case, to harmonize the public interest with the personal interest of the citizens.

Petya's family found itself on that level of human development where the distance between happiness and unhappiness looks so infinitely small, hardly even noticeable, from the vantage point of those who have attained a higher level of life's advantages. Thus in December 1947, at the time of the currency reform, all the shelves in all the kiosks and shops of the settlement were empty, and if there were still some goods available, those hoping to buy them were prepared to trample each other. Squeezing in one hand all his mother's savings, put aside for a rainy day, Petya fought his way to the counter in the state store where they had only an extremely limited choice of goods of three of four designations, and he spent almost all his money on twenty-five axe handles; he could have bought another five but there were no more. He came home with only twenty-three, having lost two on the slippery road, but he felt a happiness that no one would have begrudged him, neither in the Niva III settlement nor in the rest of the world.

Petya's feminine soul was continually seeking union with power, sensing with a kind of animal instinct that only power holds truth, justice, and order. And thus, walking past the halls of power, the Construction Committee, the Construction Administration, even the houses where the leaders lived, not to mention the two-storied institutions with red flags in Kandalaksha, he always secretly hoped that he would be noticed and called in. Living in ignorance of what was going on around him, Petya had fallen in love with power poetically and unreasonably and wished not only to adore, revere, and admire its boundless and unchanging glory but also to serve it.

That which a normal person can figure out only with enormous effort and from bitter experience is accessible to those poor in spirit as a simple and obvious truth. You couldn't say that Petya knew, since he hadn't known any other life than the one surrounding him, but he felt with all his being that there hadn't been in the past, nor were there in the present, other equally enormous and unlimited powers that encompassed such vast spaces and countless peoples regardless of climates, languages, and faiths. To belong to such a power means to share in its glory and fame and heroic achievements.

This isn't really very strange; after all, these events took place at a time when life had assumed an almost unconscious character, and consequently power had almost lost its limits and each one who possessed even a tiny drop of power could be certain that his little drop gravitated toward infinity in at least one direction.

Cheremichny was an incompetent soldier and interpreted a rather nonspecific sweeping gesture, pointing in every possible direction, as a clear indication, and he set out in Petya's tracks. If Cheremichny had been a little more sharp-witted and less trusting of someone's word and gesture, he would, of course, have followed the wide and well-worn track without even thinking; but why the devil led him along the higher path, this he couldn't explain later when he was reprimanded for his precipitate and irreparable action. It seems impossible to mix up the track of two or at the most three skiers with the tracks left by Kapustin-Iarkin, Topolnik, and the whole avant-garde. When Finns go through the woods, you can't tell if it was five or a hundred and five . . . But twenty of ours leave tracks looking as though two hundred had gone there and dragged a few on the ground for good measure.

Ever since the company had been alerted and the battle gear handed out, Cheremichny hadn't stopped feeling afraid, afraid that he'd lose his clips. He knew what that meant. After firing the new automatic Kalashnikovs, they had to crawl around the shooting range, picking up and accounting for the spent cartridge cases of the "secret" unitary cartridge, and when they were shooting while running in the winter, hunting for the cartridge cases was like hard labor. He could just imagine what they would do if he lost the magazine with live cartridges, even of the old type. Not even in a military emergency was the chief of artillery permitted to distribute the new assault rifles. At this time there was in the company two sets of weapons: the old and the new. They only rarely took out the new ones—on parade and inspection they marched past the grandstand and carried out demonstration fire with them, but usually they marched on field drill and fired the 93-pattern, three-lined rifle from 1930 and the automatic PPSH which were easily produced during the war by the little factory in Kandalaksha where they normally repaired navy artillery.

Of course it would have been more practical to throw the submachine gun over his back, and if Cheremichny had in fact carried it on his back, then perhaps while he was fussing about, moving it from back to front, this way and that, he might have got a closer look and seen that his victim was Petya, not the terrible criminal that a whole army had been mobilized to capture. Or, if Cheremichny had put away the clip, perhaps the accident wouldn't have happened, either, but Topolnik constantly wanted to see that all the weapons were in order and all the clips in place, and he had given orders not to unfasten them and put them in their pockets. But what about the magazine pouches? It's like this: they are issued, as everyone knows, when the soldier receives his full equipment—three clips in the pouch and one in the weapon—but pouches aren't issued with just a single clip in them. Cheremichny would have liked to put the clips in the pocket of his greatcoat, but he realized that during their ski maneuver, involving a large number of falls in the snow, he might lose them, so he rejected this idea even though Topolnik was nowhere near. Therefore Cheremichny skied with the submachine gun on his chest like a partisan on well-known monumental canvases. The barrel and the butt got in the way of the ski poles, but the barrel knocking on the strap buckle sounded like a snapped bolt and inspired the soldier with calmness and confidence.

Moving uphill and to the left, Cheremichny found himself on the third terrace, the highest of three clearly discernible steps on the left shore of the Niva.

The stupid soldier had reached the home stretch, as the saying goes, but for Petya it was near the end of the race, and although this "straight" home stretch was winding, as a ski track should be, they had no other way to go.

People no longer understand the phrase "straight road" as geometrically straight or as a road leading directly to hell, straight into the abyss, to destruction, to the collapse of the family; in life it isn't quite as simple as a straight line on paper. In past times, baseness of soul guaranteed a straight path to success, but to prove that baseness is unselfish you need twisting, strange, and winding paths.

If you have been told, "Go straight this way," it doesn't mean that the road will be straight, it means only that you have been shown the shortest way to your goal. Therefore even winding roads are commonly called "straight" if they are the shortest ones.

There was only half a kilometer between Cheremichny and Petya; we will soon say farewell and I won't add much to what I have already said.

Well, maybe a couple of words about the "third terrace" on which the tragedy will be played out. These terraces stand out especially clearly at the mouth of the Niva and enable a person with an idea of the geological history of the earth to see how the ocean has receded and the land has risen.* It's rising even now, the whole Murmansk district rises five to ten centimeters out of the sea every year, and I must say that this is a crazy speed, a hundred meters in a thousand years! Just use your imagination and the hillocks, standing in endless rows from the sea to Imandra along the Niva shore, will appear before you as islands, only recently emerging out of the cold ocean. Moving downriver along the third terrace, one could have found a dwelling of the original humans one kilometer from the mouth of the Niva, if a fish-packing plant had not been built there before the war. But there's no need to regret this too much; not only was the archaeologist N. N. Gurin able to salvage the skulls, scrapers, stone arrowheads, almost the whole legacy left for us by those unknown inhabitants, but another fifteen such settlements have also been found between Kandalaksha and Umba. Quartz scrapers and stone axes are, of course, no treasures, but it's the moral that's important; these objects seem to support our contention that it's possible to live and get along with nothing but the barest necessities.

This digression to such ancient times perhaps confuses the reader, but not for long; it will soon become clear how close those primitive communal times are to us, especially on the Kola Peninsula.

The Lapland cockroach and the northern dentated butterfly, easily found in the Monche tundra on the Kola, could tell you, if they had memory and could speak like humans, how the first vertebrates came out of the ocean where life was born. That improbable and tragic bird, the loon, remembers the giant lizards ruling the world in the Cretaceous period, but it's still completely unchanged; also human society was preserved here in an amazingly pristine state until the very threshold of the twentieth century. In spite of all this rich history on the Kola Peninsula, and in spite of the distinction of the name Kandalaksha, first documented in writing five hundred years ago, one must nevertheless admit that the main history of humanity touched this land only on its periphery.

*The whole Scandinavian peninsula and adjacent lands are rising, springing back from the latest glaciation, most rapidly in the north.

Incidentally, we must disperse the widely held erroneous opinion that the name of the city Kandalaksha derives from the word for shackles, "kandaly," and that a fettered and burdensome life with elements of coercion was always the lot of this land and its inhabitants. Perhaps people need to dig out something dark and gloomy from the past in order to see the present in a happier light, so they also tried to show that the name of that little town, Kem,* was an ugly-sounding abbreviation. No, it's only today's inhabitants who find the climate and soil and all the conditions here favorable for organized forced labor; earlier, during the time of autocracy, this never occurred to anybody. As far as anyone can remember, this land and her people were always free; no Mongol yoke, no serfdom, no colonial rule ever left their imprint here, either on the souls of the residents of the arctic tundra or on their way of life.

Swedes and Finns came here to rob and burn, they burned monasteries and salt factories and wrecked the fisheries, slaughtering many people. On May 23, 1589, the Swedes killed 450 people in Kandalaksha, and in the autumn a new gang of 700 led by that great master of pogroms, Sven Peterson, came with fire and sword to the Lopskaia land; but as early as 1615 the Kandalaksha monastery defended itself successfully, setting an example for centuries. On September 23, 1919, Uncle Vania Lopintsev and five of his comrades met a landing party of an English punitive expedition near Luvenga with machine-gun and rifle fire. The blow was so heavy and the losses of the punitive force so great that after several days an English aircraft carrier sailed into Kandalaksha Bay, escorted by torpedo boats, and looked for the partisans from hydroplanes. At this time the Kola land was covered with labor and concentration camps, there were camps at Pechenga, Aleksandrovka, Murmansk, Kandalaksha, Kem—yes, everywhere. And when there was no more room, a floating torture chamber was installed on the warship *Chesma*. Having begun their history in the stormy times of the struggle for a happy life, many prisons and labor camps will be famous for a long time. The triumphant strides of civilization, characterized by progress and taking the form now of slavery, now of feudal monarchy, now of the all-powerful rule of a trade-and-industrial aristocracy, didn't bring anything attractive to the inhabitants of the oldest land on earth who had adapted to the land and lived in small communities.

Civilization burst in here with the railroad built from Petrozavodsk to Murmansk in twenty months, between March 1915 and November 1916.

*A town in Karelia.

This instantly placed the area at the boundary between two eras. After existing for five centuries, the fishing village Kandalaksha had attracted barely 410 inhabitants, according to a census report at the end of the last century, but now it suddenly found itself in the midst of the latest political conflicts. Arriving agitators, including the Menshevik Tikhomirov, the Socialist revolutionary Koshelev, the representative of the Temporary Government Gorsky, and two Bolshevik leaders—the railroad electrician Kurasov and the stevedore Loiko—all of them complained that the local population astounded them by their terrible social and political backwardness, their spiritual poverty, their total inability to understand not only the slogans of the day but even such a simple word as "union." They didn't know the meaning of the word "union," and therefore it was possible only with the greatest effort to found the local fish-production union and have its committee elected. One can imagine how far removed they were from such issues as constructing socialism in one country separately, since they had never even experienced the terror of slavery, the oppression of feudalism, or the tyranny of trade and industrial capitalism. Life wasn't easy; it was hard, no matter how you look upon it, but a person depended more on luck and his own ability to work than on politics. For many centuries even the very concept of power had in this land carried a somewhat mythological character.

A dissertation has already been written about the construction of the Murmansk railroad; this undertaking was admittedly unique—in its scale, in the speed with which it was accomplished, and with regard to the difficult natural terrain—even for the late twentieth century, but if some day the history is written of the relation of humans and power on the oldest land of our planet, I'd like to think that Petya's history would occupy a humble but well-deserved place.

The great bright spring day was slowly sinking into nothingness.

With profound indifference to the fate of the runaway, nature placed her snow and open expanses at his disposal. Three hours earlier Aleksey Nikolaevich Br–n, the forty-two-year-old prisoner who had escaped, had from one of the hills seen the vast horde of soldiers pursuing him, and now he had only one thought, namely how to surrender with honor—that is, surrender and stay alive—and he decided to wait in a place where he had an unobstructed view of the progress of the pursuers. He knew from experience—he could feel it in his bones—that this hunt wouldn't end without a kill, so there was certainly no need to goad them on to excessive cruelty.

Dusk was slowly creeping in and it was no longer possible to get away or to hide properly. In the dark they shoot to kill, that's for sure, and they wouldn't check first to see if you're armed or not. How he would surrender Br–n wouldn't know until the very last minute.

In the first moments of flight the entire immensity of the earthly sphere takes you into its languishing embrace, in the first minutes of flight you can't get enough of the huge mass of fresh air embracing you from all sides, you gulp it in, suck it through your mouth and nostrils and with your whole being, and this air of freedom, intoxicating like liquor, burns your soul. But already after an hour the space around you begins to curl up and tighten into a cone at the tip of which is that single crack, hole, path that leads to freedom; you're alone now, you must decide everything yourself, for the first time in many years you have no one with you, no one is twisting and turning you every minute, but this is no longer freedom, you can't go where you want and do what your heart desires. No, bondage didn't stay behind the barbed wire, it sits on your shoulders and you have to drag it with you, you can't throw it off, it urges you on and makes you break out in a sweat, it drills into your brain; but the air, this life-giving drink that you couldn't get enough of an hour ago, it gets stuck just below your throat, and only with difficulty can you pull it into your lungs that are already full of acrid tobacco smoke, and it spills over like a cold fever into your whole body.

If we turn our attention to the geologic formations defining the relief of the right-hand shore, the convict Br–n moved along the second terrace, and therefore Petya, who had gone higher up, could rather quickly catch up and pass him. Up on top there was a crust on the snow; at the end of the winter, the snow is always packed down in open places and where the forest is thin. The climate in Kandalaksha is mostly damp thanks to the predominant southeasterly winds that blow almost the whole year round. The damp air forms ice on the roads, and on the snow fields the wind is conducive to the formation of a crust. On this crust Petya had now pulled ahead of the runaway by almost half a kilometer and would perhaps have gone even further, to the "Small Side," as people in Kandalaksha call the other riverbank. However, a completely trivial event forced him to turn back and run into Cheremichny's automatic fire. Cheremichny in his turn hadn't stopped wondering why he hadn't caught up with the unit's avant-garde ahead of him.

But before describing the last moments of Petya's life we must finish with the convict Br–n.

When you place a bet and wager your life—not just any life but your own—your heart doesn't agree with your reason. The head carefully stews it over: "If I do everything right, I'll be fine, but only then!" But the heart leaps like a toy on a rubber string, it jumps in every direction as though wanting to run away from the stupid idiot who can't save himself but places it, his palpitating heart, under fire.

The convict Br–n let Kapustin-Iarkin and Topolnik follow his track across an open space among the undergrowth. A few dozen burned trunks were sticking through the snow and there were some stumps and fallen logs.

Kapustin-Iarkin moved easily and effortlessly on his officer's skis, and his light bamboo poles made him look like he was actually skiing for fun. After him came Topolnik, also in a padded jacket and with a submachine gun on his back.

At first Br–n must make them stop: "Stop. Not so fast, Sir!" No, that was no good. What would do the trick was whatever came out of his throat at the time, or his agitated memory, or perhaps his great unhappiness and his wish to change everything into a game.

"That's it, Station Berezay. You can get off here." This desperate cry surprised both the hiding runaway himself and his pursuers.

Kapustin-Iarkin really did stop, and Topolnik slowed down and almost ran into him.

"Here we go," said Kapustin-Iarkin to Topolnik without turning, unwilling to give up his role as master of the situation; he moved his skis to the side to give the other officer more room.

Seeing that Kapustin-Iarkin didn't take out his weapon, Topolnik didn't prepare to shoot either.

"I'm yours, Chief, I'm yours. Here I am!" shouted the runaway without showing himself.

"You're surrounded, Br–n. Come out!" shouted Kapustin-Iarkin, perhaps to the convict or just for Topolnik's benefit.

"It's all true, Chief. I'm surrounded, totally surrounded. I'm surrounded by your love and care, Chief. I'll come out with my hands up. No tricks, Chief."

"Now he'll come out," predicted Kapustin-Iarkin, resting and leaning on the ski poles in front of him. Behind him the soldiers of the avant-garde, all ten of them, were already skiing up and gathering into a crowd.

Exactly according to Kapustin-Iarkin's prediction, the convict came out from behind the thick firs next to the track thirty meters from the waiting guard, his hands up and a big smile on his face. "That's all, Chief, I've surrendered. Before your eyes I throw away the shift key. I'm clean."

Br–n waved his raised hand, and in the dampish air some sort of metallic object flashed as it went flying into the bare twigs of the bushes, half covered with snow. A minute earlier he had thrown away the Finnish knife he had taken from the guard at the water tower, but now he was getting rid of the thing dearest to his heart, the shift key, an irreplaceable thing for a convict to have (it had passed unnoticed through an unbelievable number of searches and inspections).

Br–n moved unhurriedly, trying to guess the disposition of the "citizen-chief" so he could react immediately if something suspicious happened, but the main thing was to smile. He was convinced that they wouldn't shoot him if he smiled.

The soldiers, crowding behind the officers, also smiled involuntarily and looked at each other with satisfaction; the whole thing had ended easily and well, their participation in an armed expedition had not only added some variety to their monotonous life but also rejuvenated their nerves and awakened them from the torpor of service. Each felt that he was an essential witness to the capture of an exceptionally dangerous armed criminal, and each could actually consider himself a kind of hero.

But Kapustin-Iarkin definitely didn't feel like bringing that kind of "hero" back to the zone, he had to think of the others and keep in mind that breakouts are usually planned for the summer; ordinarily, in the winter and even in the spring before the snow melts, escapes aren't attempted. So this would be a good example for the coming season. You don't lose your stripes for this kind of thing.

When Br–n, taking tiny steps on his skis, had approached to within twenty steps, Kapustin-Iarkin grabbed the weapon on his back by the barrel, moved it quickly to the front, and clicked the lock without taking off his gloves.

"Chief! No need to be suspicious. I'm yours!" The runaway continued to smile, convinced that they wouldn't shoot him.

Topolnik also decided that he had to take his weapon from his back, but he didn't remove the catch.

"We've lots of men, they can tie the body to the skis and pull him," thought Kapustin-Iarkin, hearing his assistants breathing behind him, and he took the safety catch from the submachine gun.

"Station Berezay, Citizen Chief, we're there. I'm getting off."

Both Petya and Cheremichny were pitiful skiers, so if we were to say as one customarily does in a contemporary story from the arctic or in a good adventure novel with a chase, "They were about an hour apart" or, "they were only twenty minutes apart by skis," it would be totally untrue, because for Cheremichny it was like heavy combat to move on these heavy unwieldy skis, still covered with a thick layer of oil paint. And Petya's soft bindings, quickly pulled over his felt boots, came undone every so often and slid away. And so, if we add the fact that both skiers always fell going downhill, the action was unpredictable as to its duration. But the distance between them nevertheless decreased, if only because the track was more worn when Cheremichny came along, and he was inevitably approaching Petya.

After half an hour of gliding over the empty track, his fear of losing the cartridge clips was nudged aside by a new fear—of getting lost; the soldier started to suspect that he was trudging in the wrong direction. He stopped several times to listen, and there was silence up ahead. But when three startled white partridges fluttered out from under the fluffy paws of a fir tree—presumably Petya had disturbed them, so they were watching for a new danger—Cheremichny even forgot that he was armed and could defend himself. Fear would have gripped a braver man if the snow had exploded three meters away and some creatures had noisily flown by, rustling the air with their wings; Cheremichny could only get a good look at them and catch his breath as they flew away. After he had recovered from his fright, even horror, he had enough sense to realize that the track couldn't have been used very much if he was disturbing animals that had settled down for the night. The soldier wasn't actually trying to be heroic, and he wasn't thinking about victory—that is, he was the perfect representative of the positive hero, glorified by legend and held up for us to admire, who without thinking of honor finds himself in the right spot on the planet and does only, as he explains later, what anyone would have done in his place.

Ahead of him Petya was charging forward, deeply convinced that he was carrying out Kapustin-Iarkin's plan precisely and that as a result of his encircling maneuver the hardened criminal would be driven exactly to within firing range of the army proceeding below. With a thrill of morbid enjoyment, slightly mixed with fear, Petya was anticipating triumph and victory.

One of the numerous hills coming up from the fir forest had an arch on top, formed by the bent branch of a slim birch. The skier who had broken the trail before Petya had evidently knocked against this arch or touched it while diving under it; a tall crest of snow had fallen from the birch, leaving only small pieces of frozen, grainy snow on the tree, but the branch hadn't straightened out because its scraggly mane of naked twigs had frozen tight to some fir twigs. It's very important for the reader to picture all this as realistically as possible, since Petya, due to his exceptional height, allowed his Kuban cap, pushed back in the heat of the pursuit, to touch the birch trunk even though he bent down. The cap with the tarnished NKVD emblem rolled over the crust back down along the track. Petya stopped on the other side of the arch to look after his head gear, and he stood still while considering whether to turn back for it and then go uphill again; this would waste time and the desperate criminal might get away; on the other hand, Petya had no other marks of authority than the emblem on his cap and perhaps not even any right at all to pursue the criminal and drive him in the right direction.

Trampling the snow while deliberating, Petya began to turn clumsily. By then the soldier Cheremichny had recovered from his meeting with the partridges and was already approaching from the other end of the gently sloping open field.

Kapustin-Iarkin held his submachine gun by the handle and looked intently at the approaching Br–n. The latter was, of course, trying to smile with his face, but his eyes were dim and worried.

If one could at this moment have looked beneath Kapustin-Iarkin's Kuban cap into his skull and read his thoughts, one would find absolutely nothing to read. "It has to be done," this was approximately how his decision shaped up, and he had an enormous number of arguments to support it. Plus the fact that he hadn't managed to kill the other, that first one; this helped to confirm the only correct decision now. The voices of the soldiers behind him who had survived the meeting with the hardened criminal reenforced his conviction that his action would be correctly interpreted. "Yeah, I wouldn't want to meet him face to face," "Look how he walks," they whispered on all sides, convinced that Br–n would in a second throw himself at them and bite them, or maybe choke them, instead of collapsing on his shaking legs.

The blame for breakouts always falls on the shoulders of the guards, and to prevent further escape attempts it was necessary, as Kapustin-Iarkin liked to say, "to hit the nail on the head."

Kapustin-Iarkin hadn't decided yet on which particular step he would do it, but it was clear that the convict would get no closer than ten steps.

At this very moment, somewhere high up and farther along, the dull rattle of a machine-gun blast spilled out with a loud and booming sound.

Kapustin-Iarkin pricked up his ears, and at that same minute he forgot about his intention.

The shots sounded like a hammer knocking very, very rapidly on a board, but Topolnik's practiced ear interpreted it correctly. "Some fucking bastard's been hit. Which one of your soldiers is up there, Kukhovarenko?" he shouted to the commander of the submachine-gun unit.

"Cheremichny, he's probably lost, he hasn't been seen for a long time. I thought he was straggling."

A scream, a faint scream, came from the same distant place where the knocking sound of the gun had come from. Everyone fell silent and stood still, listening, and in the burned clearing you could distinctly hear the river below, the falling water thundering and splashing.

"... dee." Another scream.

"He's yelling, 'Ready,' Citizen Chief." The rescued Br–n was the first to figure it out; his hearing and sight had remained at their most alert.

"Who's ready?" roared Kapustin-larkin as though Br–n wasn't telling him about the scream that they had all heard but about a letter or telegram he had received.

"He's trying to tell you that he's brought down someone," explained Br–n.

Kapustin-larkin raised his submachine gun and fired a burst in the air to let the lost soldier know where he was.

Br–n didn't take his eyes off the fiery tongues on the quivering muzzle and followed with his eyes the cartridge cases sprayed out fanwise. "Those were for me," a thought flashed through his mind, and his heart smiled and calmed down, not completely, of course; it kept on beating hard inside him, near the left nipple, but it wasn't jumping around any more. It had recognized the actions of this idiot as both normal and appropriate.

The meeting between Cheremichny and Petya happened like this.

The soldier got a running start up the gentle rise, working his poles energetically and not taking his eyes off the crumbly track, and therefore he noticed Petya only when the latter had already started down toward him.

"Stop, stop, or I'll shoot!" promised Cheremichny while attempting to stop; then he threw down his poles and the thick three-fingered gloves, intended specifically for shooting but actually making it absolutely impossible to do so.

On the downhill run the freezing air burned Petya's sweaty head. He heard the cry from below and saw the soldier, but he couldn't catch his words.

Cheremichny saw him coming toward him waving his wooden ski poles, looking very sinister in a padded jacket, a gaping black mouth, and crazy-looking bulging eyes. The sparse hair, sticky with sweat and cut like a boxer's, made his head look like a zek's while the padded jacket and sword-belt made him look like a partisan.

Perhaps it was mostly the fault of the dusk when people change into ghosts.

There was no time to think, and the criminal didn't obey the order but came flying straight at Cheremichny. The soldier stuck his left foot forward, put the butt stock to his shoulder, and, stiff with fear, fired a burst.

Petya crumpled instantly as though he had been punched in the chest with a fist. His legs with the skis on them slipped out from under him but his body fell straight down. One foot came out of the binding and the ski slid with a light rustle over the crust along the track past Cheremichny and on down the slope; the second ski stopped straight across the track.

"Rea-dee, rea-dee," came the soldier's heartrending cry; he couldn't tear his eyes away from the inveterate scoundrel, ready to fire again if he budged or tried to reach his holster.

The snow, stirred up when he fell, melted on the dead Petya's flustered face; clear and transparent drops were collecting near his eyes and rolled down toward his ear without disturbing the silence of the forest. Petya seemed to be weeping, staring with his wide-open surprised eyes at the bottomless emptiness of the dusky sky where straight above him the first tiny little star just lit up and quivered, timidly announcing the approach of the night.

On March 26, 1953, all the papers in the huge country published the national government's profound gratitude for the condolences expressed regarding the departure of the great leader, expressed in more than two hundred thousand messages arriving from heads of foreign governments, Soviet and foreign politicians, Party workers and social organizations, specially called meetings, workers' collectives, and individual persons. Since the messages continued to arrive, gratitude was expressed also for those who would arrive today and later.

But it's noteworthy that already the following day, Friday, March 27, the great leader's name wasn't mentioned a single time in the editorial "The Worker's Great Responsibility," and this was also the case with the subsequent editorials "Urgent Tasks of Irrigation Agriculture," "Inexhaustible Fountains of Creative Energy," "Toward New Successes in Socialist Culture," and so forth day after day. In comparison, on February 3 the great leader had been mentioned fourteen times in the brief report, only a quarter column long, of the annual General Meeting of the Academy of Sciences, and on February 23, the reader could find his name thirty-nine times in just the first column of the paper.

Historians will undoubtedly also meditate on the announcement of the death of the International Stalin Peace Prize laureate, Yves Farge, as he was returning by car on the night of March 28 from the town of Gory,* where he had traveled "in order to acquaint himself with the economic and cultural construction of the Georgian SSR," as reported by the Telegraph Agency of the Soviet Union, TASS. There followed a brief but convincing description of serious skull and brain damage, "in consequence of which a comatose condition developed with the onset of right-side hemiplegia and a sharp decline in the function of the cardiovascular system." According to the report, no one else was injured in this serious nighttime crash, not even the victim's wife.

Nor was the leader's name included in the editorial of March 28, entitled "The Strength of the Soviet System," a commentary on the "Law on Amnesty" printed in the same column. That idiot, the one who escaped first and then whimpered, "Uncle, don't kill me," would according to this law get off completely, since everyone under the age of eighteen was amnestied, along with pregnant women and women with children under the age of ten. They cleared the camps of old men over fifty-five and old women over fifty, and further of those suffering from serious and incurable diseases. The thief Br–n was also included in the amnesty since he was in for seven years, and while the amnesty applied to those who had terms shorter than five years, other terms were cut by half; that means that for seven he got three-and-a-half, but he had completed precisely three-and-a-half years in that ill-fated February. Naturally, the terms were not reduced by a second for those imprisoned for major misappropriation of socialist property, hooliganism, premeditated murder, or counterrevolutionary activities, nor did they receive any kind of clemency. It was stated clearly, "Amnesty does not apply to persons convicted of counterrevolutionary activity." For the sake of justice we must add that, although nothing was mentioned about it in the law, they soon released those still in prison without a sentence, as it were by inertia, after their terms for

---

*Gory, a small village in Georgia, is the birthplace of Stalin; Yves Farge (1899–1953) was a French journalist and statesman, an international peace activist, and recipient of the Stalin Peace Prize in 1952.

counterrevolutionary activity had expired. It was precisely those imprisoned without a sentence who were to be let out. And they were.

Just imagine, both that juvenile delinquent, caught first, and Br–n, caught later on the other side of the Niva, survived until the "Law." The confusion and the need to explain what had happened to Petya distracted Kapustin-larkin from his firm intention, and two days later when the "Law" was proclaimed, the situation in the camp changed totally; it became so tense that all forces had to be mobilized just to maintain order.

Otherwise nothing special happened during those days.

Time passed, the greatest ruler of all times ceased being called great and then people started saying that there had been something odd about his death; but there you are, this is only one more piece of evidence that the love of power reaches beyond the boundaries of both public and personal advantage.

St. Petersburg, 1989

About the Author   Mikhail Kuraev has been a screenwriter in Russia for over twenty years. He was a scriptwriter for Lenfilm Studio from 1961–1988. He has produced six films and has received several awards for his work.

About the Translator   Margareta O. Thompson is Assistant Professor in the Department of Germanic and Slavic Languages at the University of Georgia. She is the translator of *My Life with Mikhail Bulgakov*, by Lyubov Belozerskaia-Bulgakova, and *By Right of Memory*, by Aleksander Tvardovsky.

Library of Congress Cataloging-in-Publication Data
Kuraev, Mikhail.
[Selections. English. 1994]
Night patrol and other stories / Mikhail Kuraev : translated from the Russian by Margareta O. Thompson.
Contents: Captain Dikshtein — Night patrol — Petya on his way to the Heavenly Kingdom.
ISBN 0-8223-1402-9. — ISBN 0-8223-1415-0 (paper)
1. Kuraev, Mikhail—Translations into English. I. Title.
PG3482.8.U665A28   1994
891.73′44—dc20   93-30236 CIP